get out of my mind

By
Sotero Navarro

Acknowledgements:

Model, and author photos - Meredith Wise Navarro

Model - Nikko Knight

Snow White - Walt Disney productions

Gone With The Wind – MGM - Selznick International Pictures

Prevent Child Abuse America

Photo Credits: Scarlett's picture (at the end of the book)- Meredith Wise Navarro

for Scarlett

Table of Contents

CHAPTER 1 1

CHAPTER 2 16

CHAPTER 3 27

CHAPTER 4 29

CHAPTER 5 33

CHAPTER 6 38

CHAPTER 7 45

CHAPTER 8 50

CHAPTER 9 61

CHAPTER 10 69

CHAPTER 11 83

CHAPTER 12 88

CHAPTER 13 95

CHAPTER 14 107

CHAPTER 15 109

CHAPTER 16 125

CHAPTER 17 129

CHAPTER 18 138

CHAPTER 19 153

CHAPTER 20 161

CHAPTER 21 163

CHAPTER 22 171

CHAPTER 23 177

CHAPTER 24 186

CHAPTER 25 196

CHAPTER 26 198

CHAPTER 27 203

CHAPTER 28 210

CHAPTER 29 213

CHAPTER 30 218

CHAPTER 31 228

CHAPTER 32 232

CHAPTER 33 237

CHAPTER 34 246

CHAPTER 35 264

CHAPTER 36 267

CHAPTER 37 274

CHAPTER 38 277

CHAPTER 39 288

THE AFTERMATH 295

THE RESOLUTION..308

In Memoriam 312

"Boys are like flowers; a flower in a dark space with no sunlight, with neither moisture nor air, will wither away, however, if it is given care, sunshine, and air, it will grow straight and strong a boy is the same."

Father Michael Campagna, Hoosier Boys Town

CHAPTER 1

"Believe nothing you hear and only one half that you see."

– Edgar Allan Poe -

Turbulence unexpectedly interrupted the comfortable quiet in the coach section of the jumbo jet. As violent lightning strikes encompassed the entire plane, the overhead cabin lights started to blink. Off and on, off and on, taking the terrified passengers between pitch black dark and daylight.

An unsettled murmur between the passengers grew to loud gasps of terror as the thin metal skin of the aircraft began to groan. The plane sounded as if it would twist apart at any moment. The once smooth, steady whirring of the engines was replaced by a metallic knocking, sounding very much like a garbage disposal full of flatware.

Finally, the pilot's calm voice broke through the cacophony. He spoke slowly, in a deep, comforting voice despite the severity of the message.

"Ahh this is your pilot," he began. "We are about to lose our engines prepare for impact. And while you are at it," he continued in a low–prepared statement, "please bend over, grab your ankles and kiss your ass goodbye. And, of course, thank you for flying with us today."

The announcement ended with a crackle, followed by a horrendous ear-popping whooshing sound. With the cabin now depressurized and totally dark, Samantha Cross felt the excruciating lack of oxygen and slipped towards unconsciousness as her hand reached futilely for an out-of-reach oxygen mask.

The engines were engulfed by white flames, while clouds flew by at super speed generated by the free-falling, dead-in-the-sky plane.

Passengers, realizing their fate, grabbed onto armrests in unison, bracing for what was coming next. Screaming, crying, and praying that once filled the cabin quieted to a spattering of gabble, then stopped completely as passengers quickly lost consciousness.

Alas, the plane reacted with a tremble, which swiftly erupted into a violent vibration. Useless oxygen masks swung back and forth like a line of party lights on a pier as a storm approached. Inexplicably, the drink cart remained steady in the blackened cabin. A cup of gin and tonic sat undelivered to an unresponsive passenger.

Within the failing plane only shrilling emergency alarms interrupted the dead silence, increasing to a maddening decibel.

Ordinarily, the clock's agitating alarm was met with much loathing. However, this morning, after the startling nightmare had left her feeling badly shaken, middle-aged Samantha "Sam" Cross allowed the demonic blaring of the clock to continue.

For once, her annoying alarm was music to hear as she slowly began unclenching stiff fingers from the tangled bed sheets. She managed a liberating blink and then was able to move her bloodshot eyes. She had been staring wildly at the bedroom ceiling, searching for any semblance of life.

Slowly, relief replaced the terror she had just endured during the absolute worst of nightmares. As if on cue, she felt the onset of another hot flash. Frustrated, Sam ripped off the satin sheets and rolled, exhausted, onto her side. Her pulse was still pounding faster than she cared to acknowledge.

"I hope my heart doesn't explode like that damn plane did in my damn dream," she swore emotionally, which was followed by a rush of warm tears. "Don't swear, goddammit," she sniffled angrily, "that is a sign of weakness. You are not weak because you're a woman; you are strong because you *are* a woman!" This was the new mantra she had introduced into her daily life to combat stress, the burden of work overload, and the torment of the change of life.

Sam instinctively rubbed her head gently with her fingertips, a minor remedy whenever the onset of another damn migraine approached.

Still suffering the after-effects of the pre-dawn nightmare, it left her feeling out of sorts. It felt like a wine hangover.

Thus began another dismal day for Sam. She pondered for a moment about writing down the still-fresh account of the dream, knowing from experience that it would soon be a faint memory, a story to share over a glass of wine with friends. "Friends?" she sighed, "I have a few acquaintances from work but no real friends."

Sipping a hot cup of espresso to help her function, Sam prepared for another day as a Magistrate in Family Court, a dream job that fulfilled her desire to help families with serious legal problems.

She looked over her daily agenda: a deluge of calls to return, working some active cases and distressing meetings with attorneys with hats-in-hand, seeking favors for their clients. "Another full day," she moaned with resignation. "Time to roll."

She stared at the list, especially angst-ridden was the first meeting of the day with a defense lawyer from out-of-state of whom she knew nothing about. He had contacted her with a troubling tale – claiming to have information to share concerning a client of his. Though she knew nothing about the attorney, she knew his client very well.

A sense of uneasiness wafted throughout Samantha's tidy office as she suffered another intense hot flash. They accompanied her to work like an undesired companion as she sat stiffly behind her spotless mahogany desk.

Now she had to deal with an annoying whoosh emanating from the cooling system of the ancient courthouse as it accompanied the intermittent crackled breathing from the obese elderly gent. He had introduced himself as the honorable Patrick Beauregard.

He was squeezed uncomfortably into a chair across from her and smelled of cheap cigars. Next to him sat a bored looking young man in his early twenties who was as short as his attorney was wide. His hair was cut in a buzz style, more conservative than the outrageous mohawk he wore the last time Sam saw him. The three individuals sat in collective silence, staring at a tattered green backpack.

It sat listing slightly to one side, its rough appearance in stark contrast to the shiny desktop. In the far corner of the office, an antique grandfather's clock struck the top of the hour chime too loudly for Sam's pounding migraine. The red-faced lawyer sat smugly, hands folded, resting on his ample stomach, his laborious breathing disturbing as it sliced through the silence of the spacious office. Finally, the smug lawyer stood up, adjusted his rumpled three-piece suit, and began his presentation. His mouth was barely visible, camouflaged by wild, grey facial hair that had overgrown his round red face. Without any words, he paced to within a few inches of Samantha's chair, creeping her out; Sam wished the slob would sit back down. Instead, the lawyer began a strange dissertation.

"I'm here to tell you, *My Lady*, before you are the writings of a mystical being, the chosen one, a man-boy among elder scholars of high intellect and great wisdom, plus all good things." After a lengthy pause for effect, or because his laborious breathing needed time to re-boot, the lawyer continued with his hyperbole-filled condescending dialogue.

"These writings are protection from demons and are illuminations of good-spirits. Sam sat astonished, turned off by where the old man's story was heading. She instead turned her attention to Beauregard's disinterested client with a look of disbelief.

"As I assume you know, *My Lady,* there are outlandish charges against my client here. What I have laid out before you are revelations that, I assure you, will exonerate him and show that he, rather than being a perpetrator, was an ally in one man's fight against evil!

"Our hope is that turning over the contents of these historical documents to you, *My Lady,* will add credibility to my client's defense. Since I do not have a license to practice here in this Commonwealth that perhaps you would be lead counsel."

Samantha's jaw dropped. She was trying hard to listen, to absorb what she had just heard through a still pulsating migraine. Listening is what she excelled at in her two decades in Family Court. Sam knew she had to end this wacky rant. Feeling light-headed, she quietly rose from her chair and, without saying a word, slowly made her way to her personal restroom. Nausea rushed through her body as she splashed cold water on her face. Patting her face dry, Sam stared dejectedly into the bathroom mirror at her rapidly aging face.

"Come on now, you can't let anyone see you like this. You are better than that, damn it. First, that damn nightmare this morning, now you must deal with this idiot." With a sudden surge of energy, Sam coughed up a gob, spit it into the toilet, and contently watched it swirl down the drain.

"There," she sneered, "how's that for one man's fight against evil?" A quick adjustment of her bra, followed by another glance in the mirror, revealed a composed, attractive, fifty-five-year-old woman. Wearing a confident grin, with her head held high and a bounce to her step, Sam returned to the whispering pair sitting uneasily at her desk awaiting her return volley. With restored poise

Sam popped onto her swivel chair and rolled uncomfortably close to the sweating attorney, who was taken back by her sudden vigor.

"Excuse me for the interruption," she smiled slyly as she nodded towards the restroom, "must have been last night's dinner." Looking at the business card that the obese man had given her, Sam milked the moment. "Mr. Patrick Beauregard?" she read out loud slowly for emphasis, "I want to tell you something."

The smugness previously exhibited was gone, replaced by a red and white-lined frown with beads of sweat on his forehead.

"From here on, if we are ever to meet up again, *Sir,* I would appreciate it if you would address me as Your Honor. I am not '*Your Lady*'. I will look at that bag of trash at my leisure, but for now, kindly wait for your client outside. I have a full docket today. But first, you need not refer to him as your client. He has a name, and I know it well. After all, I gave it to him."

With the arrogant codger out the door with his proverbial tail between his legs, Samantha turned her attention to twenty-four-year-old Ezequiel 'Zeke' Callahan. "Well, that was delightful; where did you find that clown?"

Amused by Sam's quick critique of his attorney, Zeke rose from his seat with a crooked smile on his youthful face. His slight frame and short stature gave the young man an adolescent appearance. Gone were the punkish mohawk haircut and oversized earrings he wore the last time she had laid eyes on him.

His life then appeared to be spiraling out of control. Sam now waited to hear what trouble he was involved in. Since 'the accident', Zeke sadly reminded Sam how her family had steadily deteriorated to the point they were today: non-existent.

Casually, Zeke strolled over to a closed window and opened it as he nodded towards the door through which his rotund lawyer had just exited.

"Whew, he has a scent about him. Hey, you have a kiss for your son?" Sam sat looking curiously at her son, who quickly added, "I mean, one of those chocolate kisses you always kept in your desk for good kids." Zeke smiled, obviously amused with himself.

Sam was just as quick to reply, "I don't see any good kids here. Plus, I gave up candy some time ago. You know sugar is bad for you." Sam immediately recalled a similar message she gave to a young Zeke many years and thousands of tears ago. Not in the mood for small talk, she moved on to the point at hand to avoid another emotional spectacle.

"So, Zeke, what trouble have you gotten yourself into now?" she asked brusquely. Her question brought painful memories of Zeke's lengthy list of youthful offenses that had begun as truancy and juvenile shoplifting. More recently, the crimes had escalated in seriousness to stealing cars for joyrides.

Before Zeke could answer his mother's question, in a serious tone she asked the obvious.

"What are you being charged with? Is Beauregard serious about using that cockamamie defense?"

"Hey, slow down, Your Honor. Don't underestimate that old coot or the evidence in that backpack. Beauregard comes highly recommended by a friend of mine in Florida. We think there is a good chance there is enough to clear me of all charges or at least get me probation. I'll have Ol' Blowhard send over a copy of the charges. But now, I need to go with him and get some other things straightened out.

"I hope you will do me a favor and read the stuff in there." he pleaded, trying hard to sound earnest as he pointed to the backpack. "I remember how good you were at reading things and explaining things. Just be open-minded; not everything is written with a sound mind. Plus, who knows the law better than you?"

"You mean, who knows better how to save your ass from being put away?" Sam quickly responded with a tone of anger. "Anyway, I told you then that I was done helping you after you stiffed me on bail money, and yet you continue to do stupid things. You are an adult now. You, and you alone, are responsible for your actions," she added, combining a fed-up retort with a stern lecture.

With head bowed Zeke looked pained by Sam's professional assertion, as well as her motherly lecture. Before turning toward the office door and displaying his familiar dramatic pose, he added one more plea.

"I'm sorry for the pain I've caused you in the past, but I'm prepared to turn things around and own up to what I've done."

Sam stared at her troubled son with a sense of pity and guilt as he left in the company of an individual who, she was sure from her experience, would worsen the ordeal that Zeke faced. Every time she previously said goodbye to Zeke, she always wondered whether it would be the last time. Privately, Sam admitted she had always allowed her motherly compassion to interfere with her dealings with Zeke.

Depending on how serious these charges are that he is facing, she was inclined to step aside and let the predicament he was in play out.

"Don't do it, Samantha," she sighed, "you're already on the verge of a nervous breakdown; you don't need this. He's playing you once more. Then again, he's right, you are a lawyer and a damned good one. If he goes into a court appearance with that two-bit shyster Beauregard, he will get eaten alive. Most importantly, he is my son, and it is my fault, to a large extent, that he's a troubled soul."

That evening, Samantha tried her best to ease a growing anxiety with a glass of her favorite wine in front of a soothing fire. Relaxation was difficult to realize, however, as the fire was whipped by gusty winds from a passing storm, pea-sized hail pinged on her balcony, and windows rattled. Sam muttered, "I hope this isn't one of those crazy dreams I've been having lately," while lighting an array of candles. "You never know with these crazy Central Kentucky storms," she added, relieved that it wasn't a dream but real-time.

She worried as she read and re-read the incoming fax containing the charges against her son, who was in a more critical predicament than even a nightmare could portray. The words on the fax jumped out at her startled eyes.

United State District Court

Criminal Complaint – Offense on this date before

The Eastern District of Kentucky

By the law of the United States of America

Court – Lexington KVS

Ezequiel Callahan

Interstate Auto Theft

Federal Kidnapping

"This can't be!" Sam let loose with an expletive-laden tirade. Sam's aging cat, Nellie, wobbled out of the room in search of some peace and quiet from the outside storm and her distraught owner. It suddenly felt prudent for Sam to dig into the mysterious backpack that had arrived earlier.

"OMG!" Out of a pile of messy notes, one water-stained paper stood out. It had landed in a peculiar way apart from the rest of the pile. Samantha, usually a person of logic, thought it was, as old Beauregard had suggested, a spiritual encounter. Sam managed a sickly smile at that absurd thought.

> *"I was doing just fine for once. Living with Grams and Gramps - it was the best thing that ever happened to me. I had space - room to run - to find a small taste of what it felt to be free. Gone was the constant fear of letting my guard down and*

> *having someone bully me or mentally abuse me. I always*
> *seemed to be the target of someone - a predator seeing an easy*
> *prey for their insatiable appetite of showing what they think is*
> *power, but it is their flaw as a human being, a weakness to*
> *pursue. Wild animal instincts that may serve creatures well, but*
> *had no place in a civil society."*

Sam's summary of the perplexing collection of peculiar notes in her possession, letters, and facts was not what she had hoped for as she tried to mask the contents together, a daunting task. Most urgent was to see if any of these writings had any relevance to where Atticus Carlisle was. When that was determined to be non-existent, a further examination established that there was indeed damning evidence against Zeke, just as the feds had disclosed in the warrant.

Declaring herself as a lead attorney was of utmost importance on Sam's checklist. The next would be a meeting with the Attorney General's office. It was not a pleasurable idea but a necessary course of action. It was essential to understand the particulars of the charges against her son, Zeke. Next, she would need to authenticate the charges, validate evidence, and seek a continuance to review said evidence and other pertinent information.

Bail would probably be excessive, if any, considering the seriousness of the charges and Zeke being a flight risk with a lengthy rap sheet.

With a deep sigh of angst, Sam reaffirmed the significance of her duty to proceed with what lay before her. "Remember, you chose this when you took on the struggles of law school, then laid to rest the words of doubters by passing the bar exam. More importantly, you chose this boy to be yours, a perilous endeavor that one must have the will to go forth with the understanding that you may go it alone. There was no guarantee of a village to raise this child. These are the very things you have lectured about to those before you in your Family Court."

In the wake of her broken marriage, Sam thought she could manage to raise her own son by making decisions like she had done countless times in Family Court, with a high degree of success. After her divorce and still reeling from 'the accident', Sam thought she could just apply the same logic to her dealings with Zeke, like recommending family or individual therapy. When that did not seem to be the answer for his high school years, Sam shifted gears and sent Zeke out of state, away to an acclaimed academy in Indiana, renowned for its academics and discipline.

Sadly, this expensive venture only seemed to exacerbate the problem, as evidenced by his expulsion before he could graduate. Still carrying the baggage of self-destruction at 18 years old, Zeke had coveted someone else's vehicle. This indiscretion landed him in serious trouble. Sam had to compromise some of her most valued professional standards, as well as her personal funds, to keep Zeke out of prison.

Since her early days as a law student, Sam Cross had been labeled as a fighter, as was evident in her pursuit of a law degree. Without family support she defiantly, and without a whimper, worked a couple of minimum-wage jobs while maintaining the rigors of challenging classes. When the pipedream of passing the bar exam and becoming an attorney came to fruition with little fanfare, she jumped into the male dominated field by making a name for herself in the prosecutor's office in her home county. Her experience there eventually led to another aspiration, that of aiding families, especially children, by ascending to the prestigious position of Magistrate in the Family Court.

This crossroad in her legal career was navigated with a precise approach. Nothing else was on her plate other than bettering the lives of neglected children and battered women, her two life-changing projects. All worthy efforts on her part, but at what price?

Of course, as the passage, which has been attributed to several luminaries, "no good deed goes unpunished," especially applies to a profession for resolving disputes. Despite her rate of success in helping families by going beyond the call of duty, she was content to carry mounting triumphs under the radar.

In the meantime, Zeke's life had a sketchy beginning. He was born to a woman known to be a drug and alcohol abuser. His mother was serving time for a parole violation for using drugs and alcohol after an earlier conviction. Then, she compounded the situation with a reckless pregnancy and now was being opposed by the then young prosecutor, Samantha Cross, in a family court hearing that was addressing her request to be released to give birth.

Arguing on behalf of the Family Court, Samantha adamantly opposed the request, based on the woman's re-offense along with the testimony of the woman's mother, who testified the unborn child would be at risk if her daughter was set free. She testified that she would be unable to care for the child because of health issues.

Because of that testimony, Samantha argued that after its birth, the baby should be made a ward of the state. Subsequently, the court denied the woman's request and ruled she would remain behind bars. When the time came, she would be taken to a hospital to give birth and then returned to jail to serve out her sentence.

Samantha Cross, the young attorney, was naturally passionate about her job as an advocate for children as young as toddlers. Now, she had successfully advocated for an unborn child.

After this favorable ruling, Sam once again faced an all-too-common occurrence – an anticlimactic feeling. Sure, she was quite satisfied to have had a hand in giving a defenseless newborn a chance, which was more than it had before. Now, as would happen frequently, Sam's mood shifted to dealing with the recurring dilemma of being childless.

Years prior, an excruciating pain had led to an exam where a ruptured cyst was discovered and treated. The outcome was anything but completely satisfying to Samantha, as her doctor informed her that the condition had rendered her most likely unable to conceive children. When in-vitro fertilization failed to give the young couple any hope of ever having children, things steadily deteriorated between the two.

After a short stay in hospital the young addict was returned to prison. The baby, a charmer of a tiny boy, was kept in the hospital nursery and monitored closely for withdrawal symptoms since his mother had used alcohol and drugs during her pregnancy.

The infant quickly captured the hearts of his attending nurses, who playfully squabbled over who would tend to the tiny one. By temporarily naming the baby Ezequiel, the staff gave the child a name meaning "for God's strength."

Those involved in the case knew from experience that the little boy would need all the divine intervention that can be bestowed on someone so young, so vulnerable. Samantha made a point to remain updated on the little one's progress, even visiting tiny Ezequiel on her own time, all in the name of being personally involved in his situation. Progressing well enough, Ezequiel showed remarkable resistance to any withdrawal symptoms, though it was soon evident that he would probably have slow physical growth as a child and be smallish his entire life. Negotiations with the birth mother resulted in preparing the baby for adoption; there was always a demand for infants to adopt. With internal resources, Sam seized the opportunity to monitor the baby closely. Using her position with the Family Court, Samantha risked a conflict of interest and maneuvered herself into the picture with the adorable baby. She eventually won approval to adopt the bundle of joy and eventually was appointed as the proud mother of a baby boy whose name officially became - Ezequiel Callahan.

As life sped on in an idyllic manner for the Callahan family, things were bright for the rambunctious little Zeke and his professional parents. Samantha returned to her work with the courts and quickly became a Magistrate with a future as a full-time Judge not that far off. While Mr. Callahan became a fixture as a public defender, he found time to dote on his son, whom he seemed to adore greatly.

Eventually, when young Zeke's rambunctious conduct escalated to a more troublesome behavior, Samantha took time away from her position to address her son's concerns. Not until reaching the age of six years old did Zeke begin showing signs of more than just normal child-like mischievous tendencies. It was then that specialists diagnosed young Ezequiel as having ADHD, which would impact his behavior throughout his childhood and eventually into early adulthood. From her experience on the bench, Sam knew cases like Zeke's were complicated to diagnose and, in some cases, treat, although the medical field was just about unanimous that this mental health condition, exhibited by difficulty maintaining attention, was treatable through medication.

Although Zeke had his ups and downs as a rambunctious little boy, early detection and the best of medications seemed to blend in well with his advancement. He was doing well enough in school and with a trusted nanny, and Sam was able to resume her old job as a fill-in judge.

This complicated period eventually coincided with a marvelous event. Miraculously, unexpected news arrived for an already busy family. They were expecting!

This event held truth to the phenomenon that sometimes, after adopting, some couples have surprisingly conceived. Once again, work would take a backseat to having a healthy baby, and she would have to wait for a delightful while for the birth of her son, Thomas.

Thomas Sr. happily pulled back the reins in pursuit of any advancement in the Public Defender's office. Zeke evidently benefitted from having a baby brother and a more visible father at home as his life took on an upward tick in behavior and aptitude. With growing kids, a husband who mentored his boys and picked up the slack for Samantha, she was able to keep her busy work schedule from becoming overwhelming. The only complaint from the happy parents was how time was flying by in the boys precious growing years.

As too often happens in a family with the best intentions, and try as one may, the Callahan family were victims of an unexplainable, catastrophic tragedy that hit with no rhyme or reason. It was a reality check, not planned or deserved; it was shameless bad luck. It was being undeserving victims of 'the accident'.

CHAPTER 2

"She is beauty, and she's the beast rolled into one".

– Gena Showalter

Vivien's mother, a devoted admirer of movies, especially the classics with *Gone with the Wind* as her all-time favorite, was grooming her daughter to be a Hollywood starlet. It was logical that she named her daughter *Vivien* after Vivien Leigh, who played Scarlett O'Hara in that classic. Ms. Leigh was also the wife of leading actor Laurence Olivier.

"If only I had a name like that," mused Vivien. "Accepting the Oscar *Vivien Olivier*! Now, that has a refined ring to it, unlike MacDonald." Vivien hated her last name. Pronounced and spelled differently, it was still associated with a fast-food giant, the one with a clown as its trademark.

Her dream was to find a young man with class, from a family with money, lots of money. He should be of Irish Catholic descent like her; if not, he could convert. In line with her strict Catholic beliefs, she would remain a virgin until married. The assumption was that she would attend college. She would make sure to resist the temptation of evil. It had long been assumed that she would attend nearby Northwestern University, where her father had obtained his law degree. He was counting on saving on living expenditures for his extravagant daughter.

Born and raised in the affluent Chicago suburb of Winnetka, Illinois, Vivien had it all. Blessed with a piercing beauty, she had bright green eyes that lit up her face. Intelligence, as indicated by all her awards, she ranked at the top of her class scholastically. Supportive parents, a wealthy father who, if he didn't make possible her whimsical desires, there would be hell to pay. And undeterred ambition.

Brushing her hair one hundred times to make it extra shiny was a myth, and eighteen-year-old Vivien MacDonald knew it, yet she continued with the process. The ritual began with her mother when Vivien was a toddler and her mother a beauty pageant mom-in-waiting. Years of trophies and ribbons followed, to collect dust on expensive display shelves. Now, sitting at a posh vanity dresser brushing her hair while admiring her reflection in the oval-shaped mirror, all that was missing was a "who's the fairest of them all."

As a high school senior, she seemed destined to follow in the footsteps of her movie star idol, Ann-Margret, who had attended the same high school in the Chicago suburb of Wilmette. Unlike the famous Ms. Margret, Vivien's hair was a beautiful natural Irish red.

She was soon to graduate as Valedictorian, number one in her class, with numerous scholarship offers from lesser-known public institutions. Like Ann-Margret, it was assumed that Vivien would also attend nearby Northwestern University and become another successful alumnus of the entertainment industry. This would also seem a no-brainer for her father, who, as an alumnus of the prestigious university, was privy to available scholastic scholarships.

He was nervously hoping that his valuable connections as a corporate lawyer and being a Northwestern alum would land his overindulged daughter a scholarship at the nearby university. He needed to avoid another substantial hit to his suffering portfolio.

Vivien, however, figured she could prosper better going to the most prestigious private school in the country, with a more personal environment, where her talents could be better appreciated. Enter Julliard, a famous, private performing arts conservatory, where she could graduate with a Bachelor of Arts degree.

The Julliard School is perhaps the most difficult private school to attend because admission there is highly competitive, with an overall acceptance rate between five and eight percent. When she failed to receive acceptance, she was literally floored while still clutching her rejection letter. After much agonizing, she was able to regain her composure with the help of sedatives. Vivien, though still dramatically weakened, had survived the undeserved rejection.

As for her mother, she remained incredulous and foaming with hateful thoughts of retaliation. She elected to defiantly distance herself from her attorney husband for not dropping everything and suing the pants off the critically acclaimed school in New York. Mrs. MacDonald tried easing her little girl's pain by composing a letter harboring disdain and veiled threats to The Julliard School. Once the apocalypse was averted and a prayer asking for strength was recited, Vivien and her mother resumed the search. Eventually, the right fit for Vivien was revealed - Saint Genesius College in picturesque Northern Kentucky. Picturesque for sure, if you are a country girl, but for a big-city debutante?

Research revealed that Genesius of Rome is a legendary Christian saint, considered the patron saint of actors. That fact was not only the highlight but also the overwhelming selling point for Vivien and her enabling mother. The submissive father could only go along with their strength of will or risk the wrath of the two persuasive women.

A slick brochure about the school described it as an institution of faith, offering a healthy, mind-cleansing environment with a unique range of degrees from engineering to the arts. Their sports programs had grown in recent years, according to the school's brochure, though the school's focus was on minor sports like Bowling, Volleyball, and Cross Country. Vivien had little interest in physical sports or the sweaty Neanderthals who participated in them. Her initial focus at this refined private college was something she should easily be able to check off her narcissistic list. She had a strong desire to find a refined, southern gentleman there.

For quite a while, Vivien found herself daydreaming of the man who could meet her needs: an intellect, someone with movie star looks, with financial potential - perhaps an heir to his family's fortune.

He must also possess a Southern charm, someone who would cater to her every need. Someone like Vivien Leigh's co-star in *Gone with the Wind*, a Clark Gable type. Most importantly, if she were to find such a man to be a future spouse, he must own a fashionable family name, a classy surname. Vivien felt that her last name, MacDonald, lacked class and distinctiveness. Thus, it was a detriment to her completeness as a starlet, making her eager to remove it from her celebrity name.

St. Genesius College, a private liberal arts school with a recognized drama department, offered her an application. The college refrained from offering scholastic scholarships, though there were entitlements for some select sports, like squash and cross-country, for both sexes. That was of no concern to Vivien as she knew her father would have no problem writing a check for his little girl. In fact, she later admitted, it was so he *had* to pay for her higher education.

Outside of Louisville, Kentucky, the school was described as 120 acres of *"Splendid Southern Sophistication."* Born and raised near Chicago, a school outside of Louisville seemed an odd fit for the vibrant young lady accustomed to the big city buzz. However, after researching the area, she was taken by a story about the bluebloods of the enormously rich racehorse industry and the surrounding stately Victorian homes of old Kentucky.

In the school's well-worded brochure, with pictures of fabulously groomed grounds, Vivien found the place to her fancy, to be a place of southern elegance and charm, a departure from the griminess and noise of Chicago and the hustle and bustle that came with it.

Key to her prestige, besides being accepted to a renowned college, would be to land an early invitation to the prestigious national sorority, Kappa Alpha Theta. The very one that was nationally famous, the same one her idol, Ann-Margret, had given prominence to while attending Northwestern. Everything considered, with acceptance to a prominent college in place and a game plan, Vivien MacDonald's ambitious future was one step closer to fruition.

It was now - pity the rat bastard who stood in her vindictive way.

School was off to a grand start with the pairing of her and a girl of Southern pedigree who appeared, to Vivien, to have neither the looks nor the brains that *she* possessed. As Vivien stormed into life on campus, it became apparent to her that she had no rival from any other female with *her* elegance.

If the attention she was receiving from the school's opposite sex was an indication, she should have her pick of an attendant soon. Weeks and the first trimester passed, and life on the historic looking campus was quickly becoming humdrum to the actress-in-waiting. Classes so far were not very challenging, and she was bothered that she was not standing out among her peers as much as she had in high school. Most disparaging was that her choice of sorority chapter had not invited her for an interview.

Then, there was the matter of finding Mr. Right. Sure, she made herself approachable around the campus, most regularly at the sizeable student hall, where the intellects tended to gather. Thus far, no one met her criteria or had deserved a second look.

It would not be long after Vivien's arrival at the tranquil, private school outside of Louisville that she succumbed to homesickness and boredom. Vivien was accustomed to her mother's pampering, but here she was reliant on her own care. It did not help that her dorm-mate was a diva herself, who also could not cook. In fact, her fellow freshman was gung-ho about the country atmosphere and was addicted to remaining skinny and trying to fit in with the class of beautiful people. While her willowy roommate soon received feelers from a couple of on-campus seniorities, Vivien had yet to hear from any.

Vivien, of course, blamed her mother for not coming to her rescue. The future movie star was sure that without her mother's care, she was resigned to eating junk food. A few unwanted pounds were already padding her otherwise perfect body.

"I know what the problem is I need you down here cooking for me. There is nothing but fried food and junk." Vivien begged her mother to come to her rescue on a desperate phone call home because she had gained three whole pounds.

Used to promptly winning her way, Vivien's patience was wearing thin. As usual, her reaction to these times of stress was a boiling rage of vengeance, and she was beginning to plan her wrath. Against whom? Who was responsible? Her father? Her mother? She felt fat and knew that was not her own doing. There seemed to be a lack of handsome, suave young men. Until she saw him. Appearing like Humphrey Bogart in Casablanca, sans the cigarette dangling from his slightly impaired mouth. Not as refined as old 'Bogie.' He was more John Wayne than Clark Gable. He had that distinguished dimpled square jaw, an attractive feature, especially when he smiled.

He looked a little too country, yet possibly more handsome than 'Bogie.' Vivien almost blushed as she imagined the young gent saying over a martini, "Here's looking at you, kid." Eventually she plotted an introduction to the young man. Once the prey gets trapped in the web, the black widow wraps up her victim tightly, then uses her fangs to inject her victim with venom and digestive enzymes that will first kill and then liquefy the body.

Appearing disinterested, Vivien strategically looked away for a second. Glancing back, their wandering eyes locked like targets on a radar screen. He resumed his conversation with a young man who could pass as a high schooler.

"Perhaps he's gay," pondered Vivien. Unalarmed, she added, "That's alright. I am sure I can change him with some charm. After all, I am a graduate of the *Swiss School of Charm.* Even if it is an online finishing school, it was rewarding. Now it is time to display my talent learned," she mused. It was time to twist silky fiber into a long, continuous thread.

> *"Oh, what a tangled web we weave.*
>
> *When first we practice to deceive."*
>
> *–Sir Walter Scott*

When Hank Carlisle met his new roommate at the start of the fall semester, he was initially taken aback by the skinny boy with an apparent speech disorder. It wasn't until the two freshmen became more acquainted that they realized the arrangement could work for both. One was a jock of sorts who grew up in nearby horse country, a popular high schooler whose achievements were impressive, not only for his feats as a distance runner but also for his work in the classroom.

Academics might have been even better if he could have increased his study time. Practices were punishing long only because they took time away from his studies and his work at home, which was now limited to weekends.

Phil Arnold, on the other hand, came from New York City, a bustling city hundreds of miles away in distance, light years away in lifestyle. Hank, who admitted never meeting someone gay before, asked if he was gay. Phil answered with a smile and nary a stutter, with a resounding "Yes."

"After I came out, I no longer felt accepted in my own home. So, I left and moved in with my older brother. I graduated high school with honors, and my stutter subsided. They say a nervous condition led to my developing a stutter in the first place. Once I came out, I found peace."

In the meantime, Hank excelled that first semester. Much like his cross-country races in high school, Hank's first semester grades were superb.

Even better, Phil Arnold and Hank, the diligent duo, were proving to be a formidable pair in the classroom. When Hank relayed the good news to Vivien, she seemed less than enthused.

"Well, congratulations," she offered solemnly, a strange reaction Hank thought. A peek at selfishness? Enough of a hint into this girl's personality to raise a red flag? "Maybe just a downer day for her," reflected Hank.

This moment of discovery was quickly erased by Hank's stirring hormones. As he tried to squeeze in more time with his newfound interest, he found himself more attracted to the vivacious Vivien MacDonald.

For the charming red-haired nineteen-year-old, her tactical pursuit of country-leaning Hank Carlisle was proceeding painfully slowly. Another fault – impatience. She cared little about sharing his time with the silly running practices and meets, or as she put it, circle jerks. Vivien felt she had to move more quickly with this handsome but unsophisticated country boy. His commitment to running would soon end with the season's approaching finale. Perhaps most alarming was Hank's continual commitment to Phil Arnold and the two's devotion to studying together.

Conversely, Vivien's grades were disappointing. She felt she had to do something, or daddy big bucks might pull the plug on her blank check. A new strategy emerged as she turned in a diabolical direction to justify her means. Her entry in her diary was simple "Get rid of Arnold."

Brilliant dancing flames lit up the darkening sky in a perfect glow from the balefire, called that rather than a bonfire due to its being made from bales of straw or wood. Regardless of the name, the late autumn fire was a perfect setting for Vivien's next move toward control of Hank Carlisle. Despite her distaste for chilled weather, Vivien felt lifted by the momentum of her pursuit, and she felt energized.

Vivien's demeanor had soured to a new low recently because of her hasty decision to enroll in the far-away, stuffy old college.

"It's all that damn Julliard's fault for not accepting me to their overrated school. One who would have been a credit to their program." Instead, she stood outside with a gross runny nose to watch a roaring fire while a crowd of students waved their hands all over the place as some did to demonstrate joy and praise in some churches back home. Vivien felt the act kind of weird or, as she thought privately, so gay. But she joined in for a moment so she could discretely brush a drip from her dainty nose.

Speaking of gay, she thought briefly of Ph-Ph-Ph-Phil Arnold, Hank's stuttering roommate. Thinking about how to rid Hank of his constant companion, she was willing to go to great lengths to coerce the nerdy lad to transfer from the dorm he shared with Hank.

"Hank as in *hick*, but that is acceptable for now," she slyly laughed. It was the surname that mattered most, and Carlisle had a formidable ring to it. With young Carlisle's arm firmly around her slight shoulders, Vivien felt smug, knowing she had sunk her hook into the buff, ambitious young man. He fit in with her immediate and devious long-term plans. Would these naughty plans evolve into more diabolic deeds? She was well on her way to falling into a life of trolling.

Hank Carlisle found himself increasingly turned on by the pretty redhead at his side. When he first met Vivien, he was taken by her beauty but quickly determined she was not his type. He had opportunities to become a 'thing' with girls like Vivien but avoided them for being too uppity and full of themselves. Being a farm boy from generations of farmers, Hank's idea of a female companion was someone with a similar background. "A farmer's daughter would suit me just fine," he wrote in a friend's yearbook.

It was futile to get serious with any girl in high school. Between running cross-country, his studies, and the ever-present chores around the farm, Hank had little time for a social life, let alone romance.

This girl was different, flirtatious, yet grounded by her faith. Their most recent date had ended with heavy petting and a promise that the upcoming weekend, with Phil gone home, they were going to take the next step in their relationship.

Preparing for the big night was more nerve-wracking than preparing for a big cross-country meet or helping a heifer deliver a calf on the farm. Hank wanted to make sure he was well prepared and did his due diligence online. Number one was safety, which meant purchasing condoms, a pressure-filled moment at an off-campus pharmacy.

For the ever-conniving Vivien, an online search was also in order, not for a "how to" on sex. No, she was looking for some pertinent answers. She typed in "How to get rid of a roommate?" "How do you get vengeance on someone who dissed you?" "What to expect after sex?" "How to get pregnant?"

None of these searches would produce the answers she sought in ridding Hank of his roommate, one Phil Arnold, an unlikely adversary for anyone. His wrongdoing towards Vivien? Nothing directly; her only criticism of the unassuming individual was his being a distraction to Hank. There were constant study sessions, making it more difficult to groom the handsome farm boy for bigger and better things. In her growing desire for control, how is a poor girl to get pregnant if there are any limitations on the number of encounters between her and Hank? Yes, her most recent, fiendish whim was to become pregnant. "Then I would have to leave school; I am tiring of this place already what a mistake coming here was.

"I will then need to convalesce, ideally at Hank's family ranch, as I nurture the little girl. Yes, I am sure I will have a tiny angel within me, one who I can begin to groom at an early age into being a movie star. I can envision living at the sprawling Carlisle family estate, like the ones I saw during my initial visit down here. I would have attendees at the ready around the clock, primarily one who would serve as my maid, just like in *Gone with the Wind*. I would have to perfect my Southern Belle accent; I already have red hair and beautiful green eyes. I would run the entire estate, eventually turning the place into a real-life movie set, perhaps for a re-make of *Gone with the Wind*."

Vivien's other guiltless target was the prestigious on-campus sorority which had the audacity to exclude her from their little cliquish group.

Neither internet search for a quick resolve came without significant risks; a clandestine smear campaign against Phil because of his sexuality? Torching the sorority's full of southern charm porch? Thoughts of hurling a Molotov cocktail at the elegant house gave her pause and a bit of a naughty rush. No, she would let the sorority house and poor Phil Arnold escape for now without being stung by her poisonous venom.

Instead, she found interest in another form of deceit from a site she stumbled upon in her search for deception. Vivien MacDonald was now ready, despite her devout faith, to forgo her vow to wait until marriage. Instead, she would incorporate a new form of warfare; it was time to use s-e-x for her personal advancement.

CHAPTER 3

"Till death do us part"

– Lenny Zitzke

Hank Carlisle was not a dreamer; in fact, he seldom slept much past daybreak, a routine since he was big enough to do regular chores on the farm. Then came cross-country running in high school, which meant even less sleep. Hank was now having trouble rising from his childhood bed upstairs in the old farmhouse with its noisy wood floors. Vivien was standing by an open window overlooking the old red barn, talking quietly into her ever-present phone. Without having to wonder, Hank knew the receptor of the one-way conversation had to be Vivien's mother from the Chicagoland area. The two were having another early talk about Vivien's horrible experience at the Carlisle's primitive estate.

"Mother, you must come down here and help me. There is no Victorian home or beautiful Spanish hacienda. Only an old, musty farmhouse with tight living quarters, badly in need of fresh paint. I feel claustrophobic and miserable without a/c; when you open a window, it smells of cow or pig poo."

Hank explained to his close friend at work, "I wrote a letter to Phil at school and advised him of my situation with the hope I could resume school next semester. He honestly told me I was the least likely guy to ever knock up someone and have a shotgun wedding. He added that he wished me luck. He also had me laughing by saying that Vivien always made him glad he was homosexual. She also made him s-t-t-t-u-tter.

"When Vivien told me that she was pregnant, it was like a punch to the gut. I'm on a comfortable roll at school. I am getting great grades, preparing for the fall, and running full-time. I haven't known Vivien all that long, and I thought she was on birth control; I don't know what to think.

"My parents were adamant that I needed to man up and provide for my child. So, I looked up an old friend of mine for a job in construction. Soon after, I married Vivien in a private ceremony at the courthouse in town.

"Vivien was becoming more agitated and told me we had to have a very large, very expensive wedding when we got back to her home. If she thinks I'm moving to a large city like Chicago, she has another think coming in that pretty little head of hers.

"She is smart and has been a bit of a help to me with my studies, especially when Phil suddenly moved to a different dorm. I did not understand that move, except he was not comfortable around Vivien. She would come to our room, and it wasn't long before she was making romantic advances. She was always plotting to have sex, forcing Phil to leave and head to the library. Phil eventually had enough; he told me he met someone in one of his classes with whom he shared some interests. Still, it was weird timing."

CHAPTER 4

"Accept the reality and move on."

– Hetal Manilal

"Mother, I need you to help me. I was deceived into thinking that this was a high-class set-up here, not a goddamn fruit stand." Vivien was once again putting the pressure on her frustrated mother to put some heat on Mr. MacDonald for additional items for the luxurious lakeside apartment that she and Hank occupied in Evanston, Illinois, an affluent suburb of Chicago, with their three-year-old daughter – Elizabeth, as in Elizabeth Taylor, "Lizzy" Carlisle.

Hank had succumbed to demands that Vivien had placed on him about moving back to her childhood home. By the time Lizzy was walking, she had adapted well to the wide-open spaces of the Carlisle farm. Fearing that little Lizzy would become attached to farm life, Vivien knew at what time to be proactive. When she and Lizzy flew home to Chicago, she pled her case to her parents that it was for her to come home to civilization, not only for her fragile mental health but for poor Lizzy, whose future was at stake. "You surely do not want your granddaughter to grow up at that horrible place. She will be mistreated down there. They will make her quit school and become a flipping farm hand. What about me? I am about to have a nervous breakdown; I need to come home please, I can get a job on T.V. here," sobbed the distraught young Mrs. Carlisle, or was that the helpless Lauren Bacall in her pleading husky voice.

Despite not being taken by his daughter's latest charade, Mr. MacDonald worked on a plan that should appease all, especially his bank account, which was taking a hit for every flight he provided for his homesick daughter and his enabling wife.

Now three years of age, Lizzy required more space - as did the ambitious Vivien. As much as Hank resisted perks from his grateful father-in-law, Vivien interceded with hands out. Mr. MacDonald was able to set young Hank up with an intern position in a huge engineering firm he did business with and schooling in Chicago's Loop.

"Vivien dear, do not use God's name in vain. How distressing it is to see you still taking those barbiturates and smoking those God-awful cigarettes."

"My God, Mother, you just got here, and already you're nagging me," Vivien snarled. "These are meds prescribed by my doctor, which are vital in dealing with my post-partum depression."

"You had Liz three years ago, Vivien." Mrs. MacDonald caught herself from further irritating her daughter, who was easily disturbed, to the point of throwing her out. "At least try another doctor; it doesn't hurt to get a second opinion. All I care about is your health," said Mrs. MacDonald, trying to sound sincere. It was her granddaughter, Elizabeth, whom Mrs. MacDonald suddenly cared most about. She worried that Vivien was using post-partum depression from Lizzy's birth three years prior as a ticket to her ever-on-hand supply of medicines.

Vivien Carlisle's life was spiraling out of control, and an unspoken but understood public warning was issued to all who dared cross her. People who once were social allies of Vivien and Hank distanced themselves from the tumultuous Vivien, who was quick to explode on her husband at the slightest provocation.

Things were reaching a desperation point for the increasingly despondent Hank. He began to look forward to work trips abroad for projects, but they were becoming increasingly scarce due to the worldwide downturn. He was, however, made privy to a potential assignment to China for a mega long-term endeavor. Hank disclosed to a co-worker friend his feelings on the state of his marriage.

"Boy, I would love to get away for a while - as you probably know, things at home have been increasingly stressful. Even Lizzy has been steered away from me. I try doing things with her when I am home, and it seems like her mother is poisoning her with lies about me," Hank shared his dilemma with his friend and project partner from work.

Running and its volunteer work opportunities brought Hank some much-needed relief from his increasingly suffering home life. A network of running trails in his new surroundings of Evanston, Illinois, provided Hank with ample and satisfying outlets for his long-time passion for running. Still, it was an uncomfortable distance away from the only home he ever knew. He terribly missed country life with its room to breathe. He missed his parents as well and felt they needed his presence around the farm because of growing financial difficulties.

Opportunities to feed his competitive cravings were plenty. There were organized 5K runs, which he still excelled at, in the run-friendly surrounding communities. Through contacts made within the running club he belonged to, Hank was an active volunteer coach and an aid at area urban schools in need of someone with his expertise. Vivien Carlisle, in the meantime, was perpetually seeking her own claim to fame in the world of cinema. Her latest quest was to groom her young daughter, Lizzy, for a life as an actress. However, this venture, like that of her own ill-fated acting pursuit, was terribly expensive.

With her and her father now estranged, cash was tight for Vivien. Hank was exercising his practical-minded handling of the money, a source of contention between the couple. "You damn well know Hank, ah "Kitty!" Vivien screamed, using the derogatory name "Kitty" as in Kitty Carlisle, the old television personality, a not very flattering utterance. "I need more money; Lizzy needs clothes, and there are pageants to enter."

Hank cut off his excited wife, "Hold it there, Viv. I do not want to hear that there is no more money for that stuff. From now on, we need to be smarter about what we spend on. From what I have seen, Viv, there doesn't seem to be any incentive to continue this acting folly. Lizzy might be better served to focus on academics or maybe sports. I have tried to get her to run with me, but she always refuses. She says, "Mommy doesn't want me to run with you. She says I will get hurt."

"Now, how am I supposed to introduce her to something different than acting if you are going to poison her with b.s.?" Hank angrily stated his case before marching out of the room with authority.

CHAPTER 5

"Being brushed aside is the easiest way to discard a child."

– Sherrie Campbell

"Four years old, going on 20!!" laughed Hank as he talked with his boss and friend Ted Knight about his son, Atticus. "Sometimes he looks a little off, but he quickly brightens up when I am with him."

Ted, like Hank, had climbed the ranks of the company to a senior position among project engineers. Both men carried reputations of reliable principals in the company's success as the firm grew worldwide. Both men were integral to the company's venture in China as head engineer of the prime position of Far East Coordinator and his assistant.

Ted admired a picture of the boy proudly shown by Hank.

"He looks like a chip off the old block, except he seems to have all the hair," he laughed. "A future runner?"

Hank laughed before answering Ted's questions proudly. "I am hoping that he will like to run. It's a great sport, and he's a great kid, which is why I am hesitant to leave him for such an extended period. Atticus is the name of an old movie character that Vivien chose while I pushed for my dad's name – Harold."

Ted chuckled, "I think Vivien got it right this time, buddy. Listen, I understand your predicament, as I told you at the office. We are offering you lifelong security, and this power plant job is going to be a huge goldmine. The Chinese government is ready to commit to our proposal, but one of the loose ends that we are trying to tie up is their request for you as the lead engineer, based on the job you so masterfully did in Beijing four years ago on their plant expansion there. We would supply you and your family with housing and have a school set up." Ted concluded his pitch to his old friend and co-worker. Hank stood wistfully, shaking his head, "Vivien will have none of it. She thinks China is a dark, depressing country, beneath her standards, not a place for her and Lizzy. She said I could take Atticus if I wanted. I would not be able to work and take care of him at the same time, and she knows it."

"Sorry about your troubles at home, pal," Ted consoled. "I am sure you will do what's right. Just keep in mind that we will eagerly work with you on some kind of rotation to come home at comfortable intervals. There is also an English community off-site that I hear is expanding with the coming project, with professional care for children of foreigners."

The last words from Ted significantly raised Hank's interest. They shook hands firmly, with assurances that Hank would give Ted a decision on the job offer soon.

With rare time off to relax and to enjoy precious time at home before a decision on the job offer, Hank used the opportunity to take stock of all he had and the future. Life had returned to pre-Atticus days after all hopes of another child being a marriage saver failed miserably. Hank and Vivien's relationship reverted to their pre-counseling animosity, giving credence to Hank's fear that he had fallen for another trap set by the hellish Vivien.

There was always the fear of something or someone setting her off. In his absence, while he was at the sanctuary of work, eleven-year-old Lizzy, and her little dynamite of a then four-year-old brother, Atticus, would take turns irritating their mother, who was busy with her latest venture of creating a beauty cosmetic line.

Lizzy was not thrilled with a four-year-old brother to deal with. In fact, there was not much about life that seemed to please the insecure, almost teen.

Enormous state-run projects such as China's bold venture, a massive coal-power facility in Fengcheng City, are ripe with red tape and the never-ending potential for corruption. No different was this huge undertaking, and ever since the deal was finalized, moving forth had become more of a crawl. Despite Hank's declining the offer as head project engineer, the power plant deal was made with much fanfare in China. Back in Chicago, Hank was promoted to a secondary role in the operation, overseeing the project electronically. With delays almost immediately caused by poor planning, Hank sat in his office feeling extremely helpless, knowing if he were only there, he could possibly do something, perhaps through one of his previous contacts in the government.

Ever since he rejected his company's generous offer to take the China position, Hank became his son's devoted playmate and companion. They had spent a couple of enjoyable weeks that summer down in Kentucky at Hank's parent's farm where he had grown up. There was even an occasion for Hank, with Atticus in tow, to volunteer at an organized track meet at the county school Hank had attended. An old classmate of Hank's had invited him to officiate and be a starter at the prestigious event. Atticus was awestruck by the huge, noisy event. He especially enjoyed the pop! of the starter's gun, and was an honorary starter when Hank held his son's tiny finger on the trigger and squeezed off a shot for him. The gun reminded Atticus of his toy cap pistol, a treasured gift from his father for his birthday. Hank's parents loved having their playful grandson on their scaled-down farm, while little Atticus loved the spacious grounds of the farm because of all the available room to explore and run!

Vivien was pleased that she had prevailed in her rebuff of Hank going to China for an extended stay. As she had shared with her therapist during the time the job offer was still up in the air, "Sure, it is four months today, then shit happens, and it's a year. Then he finds himself falling for some little China doll, hell no!"

Vivien's angry rant to her therapist produced fabricated tears before she rose defiantly and recited in her best drama dialog, "Quite frankly, *dahling*, I'm not one to mess with; I am in charge here."

Back in her up-scale Winnetka, Illinois home, which Vivien insisted be referred to as a mansion, her new project, an "ultimate" skin care product, failed to generate any interest from industry investors. Anti-aging cream should indicate positive results on the product's model. With Vivien as the illustrated model, the result was underwhelming.

Vivien's physical health was declining. Not one to take responsibility for her actions, the mid-thirty-year-old blamed the weight gain on the birth of her four-year-old son. Then there was a rare respiratory ailment which she said was causing a constant cough, never mind that she was puffing a pack a day. Her voice that once was soft and sexy, the voice her father had spent a small fortune on for specialized lessons during her ill-fated attempt at an acting career, now rasped like a much older person. Ironically, she started smoking to imitate the voices of old-time movie starlets, but her opportunities to portray any parts were floating away like an exhaled puff of smoke.

Her once luxurious red hair had been dyed, waved, frizzed, and straightened so often during weekly visits with her personal stylist that it suffered from any semblance of fresh-looking growth.

Her list of ailments was growing longer as her increasingly estranged husband's affection for her waned. Vivien had contracted a bacterial infection that rendered the young mother unable to walk without the aid of a walker, or occasionally a wheelchair. Doctors were unable to put a name to the affliction, describing it instead as a serious infection that attacked Vivien's nervous system.

Forced to provide his suffering wife with a daily visiting nurse, a suspicious Hank felt obligated to indulge Vivien. "I came home from a trip to Kentucky, and we had moved to her parents' huge house. Everything in the apartment, all mine, and Atticus' clothes, were piled on the floor of the old ballroom. She had convinced her father that, with her sickness, she needed more room. I believe the parents were glad to rid themselves of Vivien, so they bought a place in Florida and just left the house to their crazy daughter."

"We have reached an impasse with the Chinese government on the Fengcheng City deal," said the CEO of Hank's firm. Costs for the yet-to-be-finalized contract are soaring daily. The company, if it were a ship, would be taking on water in Titanic proportions.

"Our fifty-year-old business is in dire shape, with much hinging on next month's meeting. In hindsight, perhaps we should not have gone all in but chosen a collaborative approach instead. I am taking a step back from the final negotiations, asking Hank and Ted to close this mess so we can get on with what we do best, which is building a world-class power generation facility. They will leave in three weeks."

After the pep talk and cool-aid, people went about their business to make it happen.

CHAPTER 6

"Bullying is so common that it's viewed as almost 'normal' but it should never be."

– Choi Si-won

Lizzy was left readying herself for an unexciting first day of school. She applied a thin layer of her mother's latest skincare concoction, then proceeded with the latest fashion of make-up. She chose a pair of skin-tight jeans paired with a smart open jacket.

Atticus, on the other hand, was petrified, unable to concentrate on his *Lucky Charms* as Daddy fixed a lunch box full of goodies to eat. When? With who? Hank tried assuring young Atticus on all questions that edgy morning.

He muttered to himself while tending to a nick on his finger from skinning some apple slices for the kindergartener.

Mixed emotions engulfed Hank as he watched his boy, Atticus Carlisle, walk slowly into the ivy-covered school. The five-year-old, along with about 20 other kids of various sizes, loudly followed a young lady into the busy elementary school.

Hank had been proactive and reached out to associates for referrals for help with the kid's morning routine. Help arrived in the form of a middle-aged woman with great references and experience. Not trusting his wife to be a dependable provider in sending two children off to school each morning was a difficult pill to swallow. Vivien was resigned to the lower floor of the opulent house, becoming more and more isolated in the huge office that had been converted into her living quarters.

With or without a walker, her ample body would have trouble traversing the winding staircase. Of late, she was only visible outside her room for challenging trips to the kitchen.

Feeling so connected to Atticus was terrific for Hank. However, that made leaving him more difficult, even if only for a short time. Once more, Hank was dreading the upcoming separation, and his normal confident persona was shaken by an odd feeling of foreboding.

Ted's office in the downtown Prudential Building smelled of fresh disinfectant and stale coffee. Thirty floors below, a driver waited to take him and Hank to O'Hare Field for the all-important trip to China and the make-or-break meeting with the Chinese officials.

Much work had been put forth since the organizational shake-up at work, with Ted and Hank not missing a beat in sliding into the lead engineer chair and chief negotiator.

The Chinese official's ultimatum for a start-up time was the final sticking point. These kinds of concessions can make a project worthless if you run into delays, whether they be manmade or acts of God. On the other hand, a company stands to make tons of money if bonus dates are met or exceeded.

Champagne flowed freely among the team of lawyers and the rest of the company's weary team of field engineers and staffers. The 11th hour signing of the massive, billion-dollar-plus power plant development sent the whole team into a prolonged celebration after what had seemed like an eternity to finalize the ambitious agreement.

Halloween in Chicago is notorious for its unpredictable weather. Goblins of all ages are likely to see beautiful colored Indian summer days, early frost on freezing pumpkins, chilly, soaked-to-the-bone costumes, and even snow flurries were possible. It was during this time that a frustrated Lizzy decided to pull a prank on her innocent little brother, who she claimed was a source of irritation.

Ever since her father had left, Lizzy had inherited the position of caregiver. Hank had left household duties in what he thought to be capable hands. He had hired a nanny to prepare breakfast, make school lunches for both children, and, of course, dote on his increasingly suffering wife.

Vivien was livid when Hank deserted her and the children to go overseas to work, even if it was for a shortened period. Money was still of high importance to her, but why on earth couldn't he have made that same salary here in Chicago where he could help her with her latest project?

Vivien had begun a tell-all memoir, starting with her own angry, *One Woman's Rejection in a Man's World.* Before his departure, Hank had wisely denied Vivien access to any funds for her new venture.

"Write down your story, and we'll look it over when I get back and see what it looks like," was his answer to his demanding wife, who wanted to hire an editor even before she had written much more than the title of her book.

"You are so damn condescending," yelled Vivien. "You think I can't do this? You'll see. I won't need you anymore. I will decorate this mansion back to its intended beauty and throw lavish parties once more, and we will say, "Hank who?"

Hank's final reaction to Vivien's wants before he left was one of disinterest.

Two weeks into the new household arrangement, the hammer dropped in a vengeful moment on the professional and kind nanny Hank had hired. The woman was unceremoniously fired by Vivien on a fabricated charge of insubordination.

Vivien was quick to blame the absent father to Lizzy and the confused young Atticus. Lizzy bought into the blame game against her father and how this was indicative of how a ruthless man treats his family.

Lizzy was forced to take on added duties in the crumbling Carlisle family. Her most loathed job was getting a stubbornly slow five-year-old dressed and ready for school. All the while needing to put her best face on, which was working well, she thought. Though she lacked her mother's once stark beauty and charm, both in body and mind, Lizzy was a willing student of her mother.

"Do as I say, *dahling,* and everything will work out just delightfully for us," Vivien smiled. Though Vivien could still express herself in a flowing, rhythmical manner from her acting days, she had exchanged the sensual raspy voice she sought years ago with an irritable-sounding nagging cough. Years of smoking and a developing case of asthma had left her with a painful-sounding voice. Vivien continued her customary manipulative lecture to young Lizzy Carlisle.

"Honey, we need each other now more than ever. Your father left us in bad shape financially. Now that you are transitioning from childhood to young womanhood, you are going to want to spread your wings, so to speak." Vivien winked, smiling slyly at the confused girl. "If we work together well, you will see we'll have more money. That is why I had to let the nanny go. If we take care of the boy ourselves, we can then make better use of your father's money."

Lizzy bought into her mother's devious plan, convinced Vivien's enabling her to have free rein handling of her little brother sounded rewarding - in a devious way. The novelty of being the primary caretaker of Atticus quickly dissolved for the immature Lizzy, and it was beginning to interfere with her blossoming social life.

With an unusually warm spell in play with Halloween approaching, Lizzy came up with a nasty plan. Atticus was the bearer of a head full of light brown hair. While Hank was home, he attempted to show his son the finer things in life, like introducing him to running. With understanding the sport, long hair meant wind resistance. He was not a big fan of his son's overabundance of long hair, which he had inherited from his mother. In Hank's absence, neither Vivien nor Lizzy ever thought about having Atticus's locks cropped.

Halloween arrived peacefully for Atticus as he rose excitedly from his bed and bounded down the home's elegant staircase. Downstairs, Lizzy stopped her morning preparations and greeted her sibling with a rare smile. Not the usual complaining about his noisy run down the pristine staircase and instead of the usual scolding, "Quiet down, brat, you will wake up Mother, now hurry up and eat your breakfast." The five-year-old's eyes searched the vast kitchen area for a glimpse of his costume but did not see one, only a pink-laced little girl's dress. His gleeful mood, in anticipation of donning a promised hero costume, quickly turned to worry as he sensed something was not right.

Lizzy's new boyfriend was a distasteful-looking boy who found the little kindergartener a nuisance. Atticus also felt a dislike for the greasy-looking teen named Jimmy Lee Walker. He instantly nicknamed him Pecker Head.

The peculiar boy, in turn, found young Atticus a necessary evil if he wanted to establish good standing with the well-to-do girl. With Lizzy came the boy with a weird name and dropping the lad off each morning at a school near the high school he and Lizzy attended. He found the added duty increased his chance of being late for school, where he was a Senior. He enjoyed the fact that Lizzy lived close by, and her house was a great place to hang out. They had good food and the latest game system with an enormous television. Most appealing, there was minimal adult presence.

On this day, there was an amusing distraction - the boy was dressed as a girl. Sure, it was Halloween, and schools held costume parties, but cross-dressing at such an innocent age? He couldn't help but snicker even though Lizzy had asked him prior not to make anything of the prank. Something about his being a pest, and this was payback.

Meanwhile, Atticus was still sniffling in the back seat, wiping an occasional tear with the sleeve of the tiny dress that Lizzy said had been hers when she was his age.

"No way I'm going as a girl," he cried in protest. He had taken his argument to Vivien in her room, but she was too upset with something else to intervene or even listen to his plight. Still, Atticus was adamant. No way would he dress as a girl until Lizzy reasoned with him that the note sent home from school about the party was that girls were to dress as boys and boys as girls. And it was all for fun, and special treats would be handed out afterward. Despite all the pleading, threatening, and crying, Pecker Head pulled up to Atticus's school, the rear speakers of the car vibrating loudly, drawing unwanted attention to Atticus from surprised children and adults alike. Shortly after Lizzy practically pushed him out of the car, Atticus was surrounded by a group of classmates and some parents as well. Much pointing and giggling by the kids and anxious looks by the group sent Atticus into a near panic of despair. He did all he could to follow his teacher into the intimidating brick building rather than bolt for parts unknown. His teacher was alarmed that her normally cheerful student was having difficulty entering the school and that he was dressed as a girl!

"Atticus!" she exclaimed, "what is the matter dear? Why are you dressed up like that? Didn't your mother get the note that we are having a little party, but there would be no costumes? Who dressed you?" As the teacher shielded the now crying Atticus from the curious onlookers, the hall was cleared, and the embarrassed boy was led to the office, where he was met with even more astonished personnel.

Vivien did not take kindly to being disturbed by the school principal, who informed her that Atticus had been tricked into wearing a dress for a Halloween party where no costumes were required. She could hear through the phone his embarrassment, vocalized in an angry crescendo, the misery he was feeling over being tricked by

Lizzy. Yet, she felt no sympathy for the kindergartener, only fury for having to pick him up from school.

"Damn that girl, I'll fix her when she gets home. Now I must get dressed, call a ride, go down there and get an earful. His father should be here to handle this, but no, he is in China chasing after some China Doll," she yelled at her phone after hanging up with the school.

Atticus remained beside himself in his room for the remainder of the day until his sister came home with her creepy boyfriend, supposedly to answer her mother about the day's heartless prank on her defenseless little brother. Atticus strained to hear downstairs for the hammer to drop on the now hated Lizzy. He was praying for the maximum sentence – perhaps grounded for life! Or maybe sent off to live with a band of roving carneys. Atticus could hear Vivien's raspy voice in an angry-sounding crescendo, much to his satisfaction. An awful sound soon wafted up to the deflated feeling Atticus laughter!

"You shouldn't have Liz," began Vivien, trying to sound angry with her daughter. "What about you, young man? What part did you play in this shit?"

"Sorry Mrs. Carlisle, but I didn't know anything about this. I was just driving your beautiful children to school." 17-year-old Jimmy Lee Walker apologized, trying to sound sincere even with the juvenile-sounding suck-up thrown in for good measure. "It was all in fun, just a Halloween prank," he added, then paused for effect. "But he looked so cute!"

Vivien stared hard at the boy whom she detested at first. Now she saw someone in him that she once knew and admired, but who?

After Jimmy Lee's comment about how cute Atticus looked created visual flashes in their heads, the three could not suppress the spontaneous laughter. Upstairs, the crushed five-year-old sat on the floor, too devastated to cry.

CHAPTER 7

"Never feel guilty for starting again"

– Rupi Kaur

Having already put out a handful of fires, it felt as if Hank had taken on the role of arbiter instead of negotiator. The massive project in China was a frustrating series of false starts, supply chain delays, and negotiations for the safety of the two distinct labor forces. The American workers, an army of engineers, craftsmen, and general laborers, demanded the same worksite protections they were afforded in the U.S. An agreement with the Chinese government was reached for stringent safety protocols to be followed by all workers.

During the most recent of many meetings detailing the progress at the plant, Hank addressed an array of government and construction leaders and compared the progress to that of an infant learning how to crawl before learning how to walk.

"After a painfully slow crawl, the 'baby' is beginning to take substantial steps. We can anticipate the day when it will be running like an Olympic athlete. This plant, the world's largest facility of its kind, will be a model of the technology for years to come. We, here and in the United States, are proud to be part of such a grand undertaking to deliver a clean, affordable energy source for this growing region.

"Building materials are being delivered closer to the schedule, supply chain issues are mostly resolved, and the material storage facilities are ready for deliveries."

None of the advances would have been possible without the work of a dedicated team of interpreters. Hank had been observing a beautiful, petite thirty-something with the darkest and smoothest skin he had ever seen. Her name was Sonya, which brought no hint as to her ethnicity. Her command of English was better than most natives and without any hint of an accent. Sonya was also fluent in the complex Chinese language. Upon meeting, she had extended her hand to Hank in a Western greeting, then bowed deeply in respect to the custom of the Chinese.

Hank's eyes followed as Sonya moved confidently around the room. Her grace and poise in the testosterone-filled room of dignitaries and construction professionals was admirable. He quickly tried thinking of a reason to talk to her. As Sonya appeared to be heading towards a door, Hank took a deep breath and followed.

"Hey, what are you doing?" he said to himself. "Remember, this is a country where you must be extra careful not to offend a female stranger. Just be yourself and ask her what?"

"Excuse me," Hank uttered as he clumsily reached for the door handle. "Try to act normal," he firmly reminded himself. He did not want to offend or dishonor the young woman, so he was unsure if they should step back into the meeting room or continue through to the hallway. Sonya moved easily into the hall, away from the noisy gathering. Even though the pair had just greeted each other a few minutes before, Hank again offered his hand.

"I just wanted to thank you for all you did today; you speak English very well."

"Thank you." Sonya politely replied, "I should, I am of dual citizenship."

With that school-boy introduction and with dignitaries and wealthy businessmen in attendance, Hank Carlisle, part Native American, part Irish farm boy from Kentucky, and Sonya Lee Turner, an interpreter with an African American father and a Chinese mother, mingled innocently enough.

"I teach English at a Chinese-American co-op school outside of Fengcheng City. On occasion, I am hired to do some interpreting at special events. It helps pay the rent." Sonya won over Hank Carlisle's interest with the simplest of openings, honesty, and humility.

Hank, on the other hand, was at a loss for words. Not very sophisticated for someone who just helped broker a billion-dollar project between two superpowers!

"I want to bring my son to Fengcheng City soon. Your school sounds like an environment I would be very interested in for him."

It was a casual beginning for Sonya and Hank, and both hoped later they could share a laugh over the uneasy moments. Yes, this *had* to be a beginning.

Hank made a point to follow up with the lovely interpreter before his return to the States for the holidays. He learned that Sonya's father, an African American from Detroit, had served the U.S. government as a diplomat. He had wed a Chinese woman who worked at the embassy in a secretarial position. Sonya was their only child, and the couple resided in the Washington, D.C., area. Sonya chose to stay in China, much to her parent's displeasure. Marrying her childhood sweetheart was a given and satisfying to both until her ambitious nature interfered with the couple's relationship. Sonya's background created conflicts in her professional goals, as did her mixed race, in a nation of genuine pride and wariness.

After years of teaching, Sonya sought out new opportunities. Her fluency in both English and Chinese led to a position as an interpreter, a less restrictive opportunity in a restrictive country. The new job required travel outside of her spouse's arbitrary borders, revealing a controlling side of him she had not seen before. His attempts to stifle her growing independence led to the breakup of their marriage.

Childless and now without a husband, Sonya dug into her work and changed the direction of her future. She had decided to leave the Communist-run country and relocate to the United States to be near her aging parents. Meeting the handsome American stirred deep emotions in Sonya, none more so than when she received an e-mail from Mr. Carlisle on the pretense of discussing business. She would think of little else other than the handsome, athletic-looking Hank Carlisle until their meeting.

Any feelings of guilt were undeserved for Sonya and Hank. At the time of their first encounter, one was divorced, and the other legally and emotionally separated. His marriage to Vivien had been over for years, yet she had managed to stall any divorce proceedings by presenting Hank with the son he so wanted.

Considering the complicated situation Hank had back in the States, the two agreed to keep their meetings outwardly professional. Deception was not a part of Hank's make-up, either professionally or personally. With at least a month-long separation ahead for a trip to Chicago for the Christmas holiday, the future of this new relationship was intriguingly unclear. His conscience was eased by the outcome of the assignment at a local restaurant. There was some small talk, abundant laughter, and brief business discussions, but much of the evening turned out as hoped: a casual dinner for two people whose lives had become all work with no social life.

They found out about each other over a communal sit-down buffet where they shared traditional Chinese dishes. Laughter and pleasantry dominated the outstanding evening for two lonely people in search of connectivity.

In fact, Hank momentarily forgot about his troubles abroad and gave staying in China for the holidays a miniscule thought. But, recent communication from home reminded Hank that his priority had to be to return to address the chaos at home. The persistent complaints from Atticus were disturbing to Hank. Atticus claimed he was being bullied by his mother and sister at home and by his classmates and other students at school. Vivien was her usual obnoxious self, constantly complaining about her meager budget and appearing to be indifferent to her son's plight. Lizzy seemed undaunted by her brother's claims and was disinterested in having any discussions with her father about anything except wanting a car.

These conflicting reports from Winnetka, Illinois, made Hank feel he must make the trip home to mend some broken spirits. However, things were much worse than he could have imagined.

CHAPTER 8

"Life begins on the other side of despair"

– Jean-Paul Sartre

"Listen up, my sweet little *dahlings*." Vivien began her pep-talk with Lizzy and Atticus, her precious gifts from God, as she dramatically called them at that conniving moment. She was becoming a shell of her former self right before Atticus' weary eyes. Beginning with Vivien calling for a family meeting, Atticus watched his mother closely, fearing that she could go ballistic at any moment.

With the ever-present walker next to her, she plopped down at the once-marveled, expensive wood dining room table that was perpetually polished to extreme slickness. Dinner parties had been occasions to remember. When an inebriated guest mishandled their drink, a rent-a-server from the caterer would wipe up the exotic wood table. Now, young Atticus sat doodling new words from school on the dust-layered table top as his mother's gasping voice raised higher, a painful octave higher.

"Your father has been working his behind off for, ahem, for us. We must not burden him with any nonsense, like small stuff that he need not be bothered with. You must make sure we do not say anything that may upset him.

"We will fix things around here ourselves! As far as school, young man, come Monday morning, I will march down to school and demand they do something about the bullying, if that is what it really is, of course." Not lost on Atticus was how she smiled when talking about his being bullied and how she always avoided using his name when it was she, in fact, who gave him that stupid name.

Lizzy stared at her little brother for a long minute before echoing her mother's plea, but more bluntly.

"Mother's right, brat, you better not say anything to Father, or you will wish you were dead. Mother needs more money than the little bit he gives her now. If he gets pissed off, we will all suffer and have to move to the ghetto. If you think you're messed up now, in the ghetto, you may not even go to school! They will make you join a gang, and if you don't, they'll kill you!" Lizzy finished her threat-filled statement and stared down her petrified brother.

"Liz, honey, there is no reason to threaten or call names. We need your daddy to feel everything is wonderful here at home and that we are all getting along, and we want him home for good. We need him so we can have the things we need, that we are accustomed to." Vivien's message to the children left no question as to the desired impression she sought to make on Hank upon his return home.

"It's hard to explain, Ted," Hank related to his friend and former boss at the company. Ted was now retired and eager to hear about the grand strides that he heard were being made in China. After detailing the good news there, Ted listened with much interest to Hank's account of things back at the Carlisle household. "There is a weird sense that something is not right. Atticus seemed disengaged and not very forthcoming. I asked him what was wrong, and he just balled up and looks all sad. I visited his school and spoke to his teacher, and she did not paint a very pretty picture, though she said he was very smart and at the top of the class for learning his words. But it seems he was having a hard time with a couple of boys in his class who were teasing him, downplaying the incident. The worst reported incident yet, he was sent to school on Halloween dressed as a girl! Vivien was put on notice over that incident. Then, she showed up after ignoring earlier requests for her presence concerning the bullying. She preceded to go ballistic toward the principal, and the police were called to quell her threatening tirade."

Ted wore a look of shock. He remembered the young couple after their arrival: the young college intern with a bright future and his vivacious wife who aspired to be an actress. They looked the part of the new suburbanites: ambitious, educated, and nice-looking. Ted could only shake his head at the distressing direction Vivien's life had taken.

"I'm sorry Hank, she sounds so spiteful now. It is always the children that suffer in these situations."

"That's why I've decided to take a serious course of action."

"We are done, Viv." Thus began Hank's unrehearsed speech to his wife of close to twenty tumultuous years, a talk from the heart, given in his best solemn and distinct manner before, predictably, an outburst by Vivien interrupted him. This time Hank's not so gentle persuasion convinced her to listen up and let him speak.

Three chain-smoked cigarettes by Vivien later, Hank finished his demands for an irrevocable separation, the grand finale. Vivien listened intently to Hank's master plan, given in a voice she once found seductive. Her angry role was replaced with a disinterested pout that she had long ago perfected. "I want a quick divorce. I want to stay in China while this project is built, until its completion. I want custody of Atticus and want him to live with me over there."

There were other points he expressed, but Vivien's attention was diverted when the subjects of support for Lizzy and a buyout were mentioned. With the boy living here with her and Lizzy, she could count on steady payments for his wellbeing.

But the cash buyout was interesting and could be the coup de grace she deserved, she joyfully reasoned. As far as losing her man, she quickly reasoned she could return to her old self, reclaiming her beauty and grace and possibly latching onto some available aristocrat. She could once again rise to prominence in the local social scene. The boy was just a nuisance to her and Lizzy anyway, she surmised, and she would have the necessary funds to pump into her suffering beauty product line. She and Lizzy could travel the world, the next Judy Garland and Liza. Catching herself before her facial expression gave her dreamy reaction away, Vivien returned to a mournful scowl – she must play this act out for all its worth, as Betty Davis once did, for maximum returns.

Back in Fengcheng City, Hank's first contact was with a yearning Sonya, where he shared with her his version of his conversation with the volatile Vivien. It is now in the hands of lawyers to finalize the dissolution of the marriage.

"I wasn't too surprised that she agreed to my mandates in the divorce papers," he said with cautious relief.

Just in time for the Chinese New Year, the future looked bright for the newly connected couple. Chinese lore says how you feel and what you are doing on this day will be prominent all year. It boded well for the future if this dreamlike moment was an indication.

Two longing individuals finally found themselves in a long-awaited encircling embrace as fireworks welcoming in the Year of the Dragon shot off into the sky above the setting sun. An optimistic omen of things to come?

Later that day, after rockets and thundering booms ceased, a dog-tired Hank shared with an attentive Sonya the rest of his good news. "Once I offered to sweeten the pot, Vivien unconsciously lit up. I was able to read her bad acting and knew this was going to be all about the money.

"The divorce laws in my state say once all papers are signed and filed, the divorce will be final 30 days later. Most satisfying to me is that I am getting custody of Atticus. He will be joining me here, I mean us, after this school year ends."

A telling smile crossed his relieved face and remained intact as he slowly fell deeply asleep. His compelling voice remained fresh to a compassionate Sonya as she shut the light that had shone on her handsome company. She closed her happy eyes quickly, giving her soon-to-be wonderful time ahead a final thought.

Soon after Hank's divorce becomes final, they will be a couple, and then a long-desired child will be here for her, along with his father, to give her the love and care she had not received before. Now, this will be his home, and I will become his mother, a good mother! A-t-t-i-c-u-s, she pronounced in her head as she dozed off, content.

News of his father gaining sole custody of him was met with puzzlement by Atticus's 6-year-old brain. He was eavesdropping on a discussion between his mother and sister.

"I gave your father custody of Atticus," began Vivien before being interrupted by Lizzy.

"Why did you do that? You let him get over on you, what made you "

Vivien stopped Lizzy, and her misled negative critique with the wave of the hand that was not holding a cigarette. Labored laughter followed as Vivien caught her breath and proceeded to defend her decision to her daughter.

For a 6-year-old child, Atticus showed the ingenuity of an older person. Using the heating grate in his bedroom and an extended vacuum hose, he was able to listen in on conversations from the dining room downstairs.

"Do you really want that pesky boy around here? So why not let your father take him wherever and let us live our lives in prosperity? Bet your bottom dollar, I made sure I was compensated for giving up my dear boy," she slyly bared yellowing teeth. "Of course, there will be child support for my needy, *dahling* daughter, and he will pay for a live-in nanny of my choosing. Who needs anything or anyone else?"

"You mean there will be money for a car for me?" Suddenly excited, Lizzy was starry-eyed.

With an improved and happy outlook by everyone in the residence, Atticus playfully bounded around the house. His progress at school took an immediate turn for the better, especially reading, which had become more desirable a pastime than even video games.

Like a chameleon utilizing its ability to change colors, Vivien changed her desire to accommodate her husband in their pending dissolution of marriage. It had not taken long for Vivien to resume her assault on all things rational. What fueled her change of heart for a civil resolution was difficult to pinpoint. For one, Vivien was becoming increasingly irritated with life in general. Specifically, her rebellious daughter Lizzy was becoming more and more defiant – and difficult to control.

Lizzy knew once the divorce was final and Atticus was off to live with her father, she would be all that her mother had; thus, she could get away with murder.

It did not take long for Vivien to entertain the opinion that she might have been duped by Hank, even though her own lawyer insisted that she had received a more than fair settlement. In a grand move of defiance, Vivien hired a new lawyer who, by using an emergency defense, admitted on her behalf that Vivien's previous lawyer was incompetent. She had failed to admit into evidence that Vivien was, at that moment of judgment, not of sound mind. A delay in the proclamation was awarded Vivien, and so crumbled righteousness.

Her 6-year-old son was mysteriously bouncing off the walls like perhaps he knew his fate. Had Hank told him? In violation of the agreement? If these issues were not enough, her skincare line had yet to attract any interest for financial backing. Furious, she contemplated filing a class-action suit against the cosmetic industry for sexual discrimination.

"Why, you little ingrate!" Vivien barked at Atticus. She had confronted her son as to her suspicion about Hank telling him about moving in with him. "I heard you tell Lizzy that you were going to live with your dead-beat of a father. For sneaking around listening in on our conversations, you get no dinner, now up to your room. I'll tell the nanny you are not to have anything to eat tonight."

"But you fired Mrs. Rossi yesterday, she… "

"Never mind, boy, up to your room! You are just like your father, not to be trusted." Distraught, Atticus quietly grabbed some leftover ham from the fridge and ambled up the staircase to his lonely room to amuse himself with his books and fantasize about a life with his beloved father.

Life at the Carlisle home was decaying with crumbling spirit, and once again, low morale sucked the life out of the once proud, affluent house. Lizzy was showing her displeasure with whatever crossed her angry path, even if her on-again, off-again relationship with Jimmy Lee Walker was back on. She blamed her mother for delaying her demand for a car now that she had turned sixteen years of age. She began to tire from having to accommodate her boyfriend, for chauffeuring her around.

Atticus continued to feel the impact of Lizzy's discourse, which meant the juvenile pranks were becoming more serious. When he woke that cold April morning, his usual routine was slowed by a feeling of terror. It crept through his young body like a frosty caterpillar.

When the bullying at the mansion increased in intensity, Lizzy warned him they would continue unless he started getting up for school promptly and not delaying her day. Since his father returned to China early in the year, Lizzy had given her brother unsolicited, often vicious grief.

Because of his elation at living with his father, Atticus was able to handle anything thrown his way by his scheming sister. With every passing month and despite reassuring phone calls from his father, Atticus was becoming a bit uneasy.

"You are going to come live with me," Atticus replayed his father's words in his head. His father's strong, medium-deep voice continued to assure him it was real. "You will like the school here, and best of all, we will all be together. We will play, travel, and of course, we will run, and run, and heck, we might run the length of the Great Wall of China together."

Those encouraging words held things together momentarily for the eight-year-old boy who was excited about joining his father far away from the abuse he was experiencing at the mansion. Over 6,500 miles away, escaping the carnage was utmost in his suffering mind.

Settling back into the massive job that lay ahead was an enviable task for Hank. Now more familiar with the project's surroundings and potential, Hank was quick to resume his duties as one of the heads of this historic mission. Even though it was common wisdom to never let your guard down against wickedness, love is known to blind one's common sense.

Word of a change, not only of a new attorney for Vivien, an appeal to reopen the child custody agreement had also been granted, reduced Hank's morale to a serious low. Delaying the divorce under a far-fetched claim was unjustifiable and disgraceful.

In the meantime, Hank inherited a dedicated assistant to help ease his heavy workload. "Welcome aboard, Jeff, and I hope you'll like it here as much as I do." Hank welcomed the 30-yr.old Jeff Fisher to the elaborate trailer at the remote job sight. Jeff was a native of San Francisco and a highly respected Mechanical Engineer who had been hand-picked by Hank for the job. The two were destined to play huge controlling roles in a game-changing endeavor of the magnitude not seen in China since the construction of the Great Wall. They were the bosses and had on hand a team of very capable underlings, assuring a wide coordination of crafts to work as fingers in a glove. Yet Hank and Jeff spent a good part of their work day on-site, where the project was finally coming to fruition.

Bricklayers, carpenters, electricians, iron workers, and many more trades descended on the mammoth work city in mass. Even with a vast Chinese workforce from throughout the provinces and beyond, there were also a large contingent of Americans.

There were so many Americans that it looked like a small town in the States. In fact, it was, with a commissary, American food, and a school. Hank was proud and relieved he was able to win that point during negotiations. He caught himself daydreaming about Atticus living with him and Sonya when they married and going to school there and prospering from the experience. He became concerned a bit by Vivien's most recent inexplicable maneuvering. His lawyer informed him that she had hired another attorney, who had filed for a delay in the pending divorce so she could re-negotiate the settlement. His lawyer, however, assured him that it was a frivolous effort and would not interfere with plans except for a minor delay.

When he began to worry, there was always something that would bring him back to reality, like the latest check-off of a job that required someone with authority to physically sign the job-completed form. Rather than delay until the field supervisor assigned to the area could make it there, Hank, without any hesitation, headed out to the highly active and hazardous location.

With the expected annual flu warnings during the harsh Chicago area winter, Atticus was bit by the bug, sapping the active boy of his strength.

Vivien, as a last resort, took Atticus to the hospital filled with people suffering from the latest nasty influenza. She felt she couldn't risk the costly penalty for child endangerment if Atticus succumbed to the influenza that had furiously laid into the young lad. Plus, she gave thought to the handsome amount of child support from Hank. Vivien made a flamboyant entrance to the emergency room with the horribly sick boy in tow. On cue, Vivian created a scene at the hospital that was fit for Broadway as she descended on a registration associate to demand Atticus be admitted.

"I'm sorry, ma'am, but," the elderly lady began, only to be cut off by an impatient Vivien.

"I'll tell you what, you get him well, and I will have someone pick him up. I am not well myself and can't care for him in this condition. My husband has excellent insurance, and my family is well connected in the area."

Hospital staff were able to settle Vivien down long enough to explain that she would have to stay with her son until a doctor could see him, establish a diagnosis and a course of action. After an interminable wait for the doctor and hearing that Atticus was to be admitted for further care, an exhausted Vivien returned to the comforts of her stately home. She was too tired to remember the treatment plan, nor did she care. She only had enough strength to revel in another triumphal dispute against unfairness.

Meanwhile, abandoned to the care of the hospital staff, alone in a sterile room with weird sounds of medical machinery and an IV in his skinny arm, Atticus lay shivering, too ill to dwell much on his situation. The strong antibiotics brought down his fever, and a saline drip rehydrated his shriveled body. Caring doctors and nurses showered him with warm blankets and unfamiliar treats. Child services was notified about how his mother appeared unable or unwilling to care for him. Most disturbing was the dangerous degree of dehydration and fever.

Finally, arrangements were made to release him. Atticus had worried that he might be destined to be left there in the hospital, where who knows what might await him. At least at the mansion, he knew what awaited him. His own bed, Mrs. Mathews - the most recent of housekeepers, his precious writings, comforting books, and most importantly, his father. Better were the chances that his father would find him at home rather than in a hospital.

Hank's lawyer back in Winnetka was pleased to instruct his secretary to e-mail Hank in China the good news that Vivien's attempt to reopen the divorce settlement was denied, and the divorce would no longer be delayed. When he arrived home the following week, his signature would be all that was needed for his marriage to Vivien to be dissolved. He would also receive a text from Sonya on her lunch hour that read: "We'll do it all – as a family – I love you!!!"

CHAPTER 9

"Do not apologize for crying. Without this emotion, we are only robots."

–Elizabeth Gilbert

Vivien was too preoccupied with her new lawyer's call to acknowledge Atticus on their chauffeured ride home from the hospital. His release, however, came with a stern warning from the case worker that there appeared to be signs of potential neglect, borderline malnutrition, and a serious lack of hygiene. A licensed and qualified member of the Child Protective Services would be following up with a random visit to their home.

Vivien seemed more interested with a possible lawsuit against the hospital for libel rather than the news delivered by her attorney concerning the pending divorce. As if on cue, Vivien went off on her defenseless son, blaming the weakened boy for her deprived circumstances

"Well, another stressful situation you have caused me. What did I ever do to deserve you and your father? I'm glad you're going to live with him. If they think you're too skinny now, just wait until you have to eat rice with chopsticks every day."

With that, Vivien burst into a laughing fit. Her own medical problems caught up to her in her celebration of someone else's distress, reducing her to tears and choking on her own bile. Vivien's outburst had sent chills through Atticus's seriously thin body and up his protruding spine.

Long-time participants in the construction industry will tell anyone who asks there are two things that can kill a project once it begins: unusually bad weather and accidents. Better known as acts of God and human error.

Scattered throughout the center of the once pristine, barren landscape of the central province of Jiangxi rose a concrete city.

Dotted about the area, with a mountain-range-like appearance, were the countless ladders and scaffolds, temporary structures used to support work crews and materials during construction and repairs. To erect scaffolding on the scale required for this project was a critical safety concern. Jointly among the various key operatives, a thorough plan was developed for daily inspections of the complex linking miles of vertical ladders and platforms at bloodcurdling heights and with frightening overhangs. Unsafe scaffolding has the potential to result in serious injury or even death. Foremost of concern and subject to the highest degree of scrutiny are couplers, a fitting used to join components together, and scaffold ties, used to tie in the scaffolding to structures. Future investigation would examine which of these components were responsible for the sudden disconnect of the ladder, thus separating from the side of the concrete cooling tower being built.

With a steady invasion of tradesmen, laborers of various skill levels, engineers, planners, and bookkeepers, not to mention commissary workers and ever-present medical staff, the humongous work area took on a life of its own. In these early days of construction, there seems little method to the madness of territorial boundaries, job descriptions, and protocol.

Starting out as a design on paper to the implementation with hopes of becoming the masterpiece promised, the result would become an important part of these many people's legacy. At this point in the grind, the necessity for proper detailed checklists is of utmost importance. No one knew this better than Hank, a habit he learned from experience. To speed up an inspection of a finished vital instrument, Hank took it upon himself to do the sign-off rather than send the crew who would normally do so. Hank felt good about being out among the masses of the workforce, who came together as a unified group to execute a coordinated game plan. While he plodded through the vast numbers of different teams of workers, that would become one common theme. Traffic was halted as a crane executed a precarious lift, so he had a rare moment to appreciate the gorgeous weather.

"What a remarkable day!" he marveled while adjusting his hard hat and gazing skyward. "I cannot wait to get Atticus over here, to devote the time to him that he deserves. No more feeling guilty about placing my job over what is best for my son. To have him with *me, not his mother.*"

From feeling at fault for the pain Atticus had endured in his absence, he became optimistic for the near future. Atticus would come at last to live with him, and the two would become one. He would nurture his son to become a conscientious man, as his own father had for him while growing up on the family farm. They would actively run the fantastic countryside here, and he would benefit from an outstanding school system here as well. Perhaps he could learn his stepmother's first language – Chinese. Yes, his stepmother! In fact, he might grow into calling her mother!!

Hank and Sonya would marry soon after his arrival, and the pending divorce became final. He would learn from his new love her spirituality from her Buddhist upbringing, as well as compassion and love, the things he lacked in his current life. After a couple of years here in China, he would be financially set, and professionally, he would have accomplished something grand with the completion of this project. Retiring from traveling and job pressure, the three would return to Kentucky and the family farm, where he would take care of his parents in their golden years.

When he was cleared to proceed to the job site, he did so with a clear head and the feeling of fulfilling love and resolve in his heart. Hank took pride in his fine physical condition at the age of forty-two, which he attributed to growing up on a farm and continuing to be an active runner. His new assistant, Jeff, ten years his junior, marveled at how well-conditioned he was after playing racquetball with him. There were also futile attempts to keep up with him while walking the massive construction grounds. So, it was not out of the ordinary for Hank to take on physical opportunities like climbing scaffolding, a welcome departure from the daily deluge of paperwork, and fielding never-ending phone calls.

Taking the challenge of strength and stamina for the hand-over-hand climb was by now second nature to Hank as he began his lengthy ascent towards the dark clouds that had suddenly moved in, seeming to swallow the top of the tower. Feeling determined to move the inspection along and maybe still thinking about personal issues, Hank was a picture of fitness and coordination as he firmly scaled the scaffolding's steel ladder rungs, hand-over-hand-over-hand

With nothing to do while he convalesced in his room at home, Atticus became a fervent watcher of TV game shows. He daydreamed of winning tons of money, buying his own jet airplane, and flying to his dad, hoping never to see his mother and sister again. When he was well enough, he scaled the soaring library shelves to search the old encyclopedias to find out how many hours it takes to fly to China.

Atticus lived for phone calls from Hank, and waited with great anticipation. He also listened for the telephone to ring downstairs and hoped that Mrs. Mathews would interrupt her soap opera viewing to answer the phone. If in fact it was his father, then hopefully, she would give the phone to him and not to his bitter mother. He hoped this divorce thing would hurry up and happen so he could finally go live with his father.

Whenever Lizzy was home and mother and daughter were occupying the same space, it was guaranteed there would be constant yelling. Somehow these daily disputes would escalate to unwarranted consequences for Atticus, who casually observed the clashes between the two, leading to himself being the fall guy. The last phone call from his father found Atticus breaking down and whispering, *"Daddy, come and get me, please. They are so mean, I hate them."*

Hank was full of hope and had put Atticus at ease with his response. "Son, listen carefully," he began slowly in his deep, reassuring voice. "First of all, do not say hate; we do not hate. Now, the good news is my lawyer says he expects this mess to be over soon. Once it happens and arrangements can be made, you will be over here with me, so be patient a while longer. I will call you as soon as I hear the good news. Remember, I love you, and this will all be over soon." Those were indeed cruelly prophetic words.

Hearing the alarm of dispatched emergency equipment sent chills through the body of Hank's assistant, Jeff. Knowing his boss was in the affected area, Jeff tried reaching Hank via two-way radio with no luck. He rushed to the site in a company four-wheeler. Arriving at the base of the newly erected cooling tower, Jeff's heart sank seeing the chaos of emergency personnel working in vain on the body of Hank Carlisle.

Not receiving a Wednesday phone call from his father was a cause of concern for Atticus. He was an expert on time and schedule and was long aware of the thirteen-hour time difference. Any deviation from the schedule made the boy anxious, especially that fateful day when 9 a.m. local time meant 10 p.m. in China and time for his father to call. The day turned to night and Atticus disappointedly trudged to bed, knowing it was the next morning in China and his father would be working. *"Maybe tomorrow he'll call me,"* sadly lamented Atticus.

The phone rang loudly, like phones ring when one is about to receive bad news. Unable to beat the suddenly spry nanny to the phone, Atticus stood by, expecting to be handed the phone for the call from China. The call was from China, not from Hank for his son, but rather for Vivien from someone with the company.

Waking up Vivien was always risky business due to her rude temperament. Listening from outside the door, Atticus strained to hear the phone conversation but heard only his mother's sleepy, raspy voice muttering something in a rare, for her, quiet tone. After he heard the phone being hung up, all Atticus could hear was a cigarette lighter flicking. Retreating from his listening post, Atticus slowly made the climb up the dusty staircase to his room. Reaching his door, a despondent Atticus was properly shocked by a bloodcurdling scream from his mother's room.

A scream that sounded partially mortified, partially calm. When he awoke the next morning, Atticus realized he was in the same position from the previous night, with mouth agape as if he had fallen asleep in mid-cry, with his mother's odd delayed response to the late evening call from someone from his father's company.

When he heard his mother scream, he remembered how he wanted to run down to her room but opted not to, expecting the worst. And the news was ghastly. Atticus's young age was a benefit to him, for he couldn't understand the long-range ramifications of this disaster.

"Oh, my little boy, how can I tell you?" Atticus had not entered his mother's chamber in many months, nor did she spend much time in the rest of the house. He was equally shocked by Vivien's demand for his presence in her bedroom, the call which had wakened everyone from a deep slumber, and now, as she leaned precariously on her elaborate walker in front of her glorious custom-made bed, she was a sight to behold. Her once silky skin was rough and pale, and her nightgown did little to hide her excessive weight.

No longer did she flaunt beautiful strawberry-blonde hair that appeared to have been brushed already. She reached out to her stunned son, whose first reaction was to take a step back from this strange, apparent caring motion from his mother.

Vivien had not held him for as long as he could remember unless it was followed by an angry slap or yank of his hair. "I received a call from your father's boss, and, well, my dear, your father is dead. He was in a terrible accident in China. Evidently, he fell from a very high distance. I told him numerous times not to go over there." Vivien's rant continued for many blubbering minutes until Atticus was led from his mother's untidy room by a comforting Mrs. Mathews. She was weeping from the horrible news and close to dealing a precise backhand blow to her employer's face, knowing that she would be prosecuted by Vivien, worse yet, be fired. She would never see this poor boy that she had grown to pity and care for, thus protecting him from further harm than he had already endured from this evil person, his supposed mother.

"Liz, dear, how does this pendant go with my dress?" The cameo pendant, an early gift from Hank, contrasted stylishly with her flowing black dress. Lizzy was silent to her mother's question as she, too, prepared for the funeral of her father.

"This reminds me of when you were a little girl. We would play dress-up, and have tea and laugh. Then we would end up watching old movies, remember?"

"Yes, and you were a hundred pounds lighter then!" was Lizzy's disrespectful answer.

"Well, young lady, if you don't have something nice to say, don't say anything," huffed Vivien as she stood before the mirror. "I may have put on a few pounds, but that is what happens when you trust doctors, and they pump you full of drugs. Plus, raising two kids, practically by oneself, is hard. Then there is the female oppression handed down by the male-dominated society, and you have a very stressful environment. No wonder that a woman's health ends up suffering from the injustice of it all.

"I will tell you what else: your father never listened to me. I gave up a lot for that man. We were once a hot couple, like Bogie and Hepburn, Elizabeth Taylor and Richard Burton." Vivien stopped talking, allowing herself a moment to reflect on her and Hank in their early years. "He was such a hunk, so smart at building things," her voice trailing off to the point where a tear of emotion almost escaped her stone-cold eye. Lizzy had already slipped out of her mother's room halfway through Vivien's spiel of self-pity and unusually kind words for her dead husband. She was preparing for her part as the grieving widow, a role for which she was perfectly cast.

Ignored in this painful time, some 7,000 miles away in a Buddhist temple, a frail-looking Sonya recited a prayer for her lost love. When her last text to Hank remained unanswered, she had a feeling unlike any other. She raced to the gate of the worksite, arriving just as the ambulance was leaving for the closest hospital in the province. Too late to embrace the man whom she loved the way his wife would not.

Sonya's grief was excruciatingly difficult. She wanted to reach out to Hank's kids back in the States, but how? She begged an official for information on his final flight home and waited in sorrow back at her place. While Vivien had declined the company's offer to fly her to China to accompany the body back home, old friend and confidant Ted was a willing escort. Since he knew of Sonya and other details of his friend's life, he was a comforting ally to Sonya in the hours leading up to the plane's departure.

Vivien was a mere curiosity at her husband's funeral. Many of those in attendance had not seen Vivien in some time and were taken aback by her appearance. She was, nonetheless, lifted by the horrid stares given by onlookers as she assumed the role of Jackie Kennedy during the days after her husband's, President John F. Kennedy, assassination. She remembered intently watching with her mother the sad funeral coverage of the most beloved Catholic this side of the pope. Young Vivien had focused on the elegant Mrs. Kennedy in her sophisticated dress and pillbox hat, with the black veil being the focal point.

Desiring for the interment to be a production all would remember, she tried to direct Hank's children to emulate John's and Jackie's children, John-John and Caroline. Vivien's portrayal of the grieving widow was a master class in dramatic acting. The kids were having none of the charade.

CHAPTER 10

"Show me a hero, and I'll write you a tragedy"

– F. Scott Fitzgerald

"You will do as I say, you little brat!" With that demand, a serious yank of the young boy's abundant long hair left Atticus writhing, a painful emphasis of how serious the middle-aged woman was about dispensing capital punishment to combat her son's defiance. The boy's crime? Not complying with his mother's command that he greet each gentleman visitor of hers with a firm handshake and her scripted greeting: 'Hello, sir, my name is Atticus Carlisle. Welcome to our humble home.'

Atticus' greeting this day, however, lacked the quality of strength that she demanded from her disengaged son. Vivien's engaging with these men-of-means was an attempt to justify her means: to pursue her destiny of making a name for herself in Hollywood. She would put the movie industry on its heels, an industry of stuffy old men, much like these guests she was courting.

Eleven-year-old Atticus was instructed to gratefully accept any monetary donation from these visitors, then retreat upstairs to his room, where he waited for his mother to beckon him by way of a time-worn bell. Vivien would collect the bounty then reward Atticus with a muffin, if he was lucky. Mischievously, Atticus sometimes lingered near his mother's quarters, where he tried to make sense of the odd noises permeating from the room, a room he was barred from *ever* entering. The extravagant quarters made the humble home reference in the prepared greeting comical. Vivien Carlisle cared not about exaggeration because she knew she was destined to be an actress and or a director.

Never one to skip a good lawsuit, Vivien was also following newfound direction in her arsenal of personal causes to do battle for, always to her benefit. She kept busy preparing and filing suits against all who were associated with the death of her dear husband and father of her traumatized children.

First to be targeted was Hank's employer because of their proximity as well as being the sole U.S. entity. Also making the lineup of at-fault offenders was the multinational conglomerate of investors in the huge power plant project, which primarily meant the Chinese government. Various contractors and manufacturers and, of course, the scaffolding erectors rounded out the hit list of people to sue.

All the while, young Atticus sank deeper into the depths of depression. He became increasingly withdrawn at school and at home. If not for his part-time nanny, some-time teacher, and full-time cook, Mrs. Mathews, he would have had little communication with anyone. First, it was public school, then home school, and now parochial school. Confusion led to spending more of his time at home in his room playing, studying, and plotting. He was scheming in his lonely head how he would get revenge on his hateful sister and or her vicious boyfriend, Pecker Head.

He believed there would never be any revenge or running away. Mrs. Mathews slowly introduced her young ward to the outdoors and running, where a new mindset was born. Not that Atticus was unfamiliar with running. On the contrary, his father had exposed him to the sport at an early age. Valuable training time was denied to Atticus when his parents chose to battle over dominance, which eventually splintered the family into fragmented parts.

Atticus remembered his father constantly reassuring him that someday he would come home and take him away, and the two would be together and have fun forevermore. It was not to be as those promises were dashed when he became collateral damage in the war of the Carlisle's. Atticus was left to his imagination, feeling despair and confusion when his father left him to go to China. He felt loathing for his evil mother and his equally evil sister, Lizzy. Not having a mean fragment in his undeveloped body, Atticus could only embrace payback as the end that would justify the means.

He would scare them, and then they would know how he felt. First on his list would be Lizzy, who was everything he did not want to be. He would stand up to her and her boyfriend. He excitedly wrote page upon page of profound compositions to be filed, bulk-style, stuffed into his father's outdated but beloved backpack.

It had not taken long after the death of his father for Atticus to realize that he would need to write down the precious few memories he had of his father. Especially when the torrent of abuse, both physical and verbal, resumed. It triggered selective memory, the tendency to remember only what he wanted to remember. His solution for this phenomenon was to write down not just the good things he wanted to remember but also the bad things he had to remember, not just in the present but someday down an isolated road.

Down in the neat yet dusty basement, Atticus tiptoed around a maze of spider webs. His heart accelerated as he skirted around a dirty dog pen, left in the same location from when he had been deviously locked up one night by the nauseating Jimmy Lee Walker. The sight of the metal cage sent chills up his body. A new addition to the storage space was a pile of random articles, the only personal effects of his late father, Hank. Atticus wondered if the ghost of his father was possibly amongst the rubble. If so, and if he appeared, how would he react?

Virtually everything present in the basement was his fathers. His workshop was filled with quality tools. There was a treadmill, and heavy weights in another corner. Pictures and trophies from Hank as a young runner excited Atticus. He spent the rest of his time thumbing through photos that momentarily brought his father back to life.

One picture of a lovely Oriental woman stuck out. A large X defiled her face, most likely drawn by Vivien. She had picked over the collection and had left her mark on the picture of the other woman.

Looking about the dank basement, Atticus hit upon an idea, one wonderfully exciting impression. *"Spiders in Lizzy's bed would do the trick,"* he thought nervously, *but how would I catch them? Yuck!"* His father's tools could be a brutal resolve, a hammer blow to her head. A screwdriver in the eye? Either option would be a harsh choice as he hated the sight of blood. He scrounged further for a better answer, secretly hoping there would be none so he would forget this folly. At that moment an open drawer exposed a familiar item, the fake pistol. It appeared to be the same starter gun his father had shown him.

Atticus remembered being down here with his father after a track meet the two had attended. His father was devoted to volunteering for area track functions, and Atticus warmly remembered accompanying his father to a track meet.

Hank's job at the meet was as a starter for the races. He had explained to Atticus, "Now, son, ALWAYS handle a gun with respect and care. NEVER point a gun at someone, and NEVER investigate the barrel. This is a starter pistol, and it doesn't shoot bullets; it just makes the sound of a real gun, a loud one, which signals the runners to "go!"

Atticus thought for a moment, back to that day and seeing his father put the pistol in a drawer. Was it this one? It looked like it. As for pointing it at his sister, he would not. He would just shoot it into the air like his father did to start the runners.

The sharp POP the gun had produced that day would scare the bejesus out of Lizzy as she slept. Gently holding the small gun, his little hands shook slightly. His pursed lips turned to a forced grin as he wrapped the gun in a rag then ran up to his room to conceal his cache. There he would devise a plan where, after a dress rehearsal, he would scare his sister to tears. Then, she would leave him alone.

Never had Atticus possessed a toy gun in his short life. Now, a pistol, even one that only shot blanks, occupied a place in his bedroom, right under his mattress.

A good night's sleep was difficult enough to come by since his father's passing. But with his father's fake gun under his frail body, where it would be a prop in a harmless prank, he slept even less.

Three nights passed with the enticing metal bedfellow. Each night he snuck closer to his sister's bedroom only to get cold feet. Quietly retreating to his room, Atticus carefully returned the fake gun back to its place of safety.

Come Friday morning, Atticus thankfully concluded he was losing the desire to pursue his plan with the starter pistol, which should cure his acute case of sleep deprivation. That morning, Atticus uncharacteristically dozed off over his cereal bowl while Lizzy made final preparations to her make-up upstairs.

Seeing her little brother's state of swoon as she descended the staircase aggravated her morning mental attitude. Lizzy had already been put on notice by the school concerning her repeated tardiness. Passing behind the dozing boy, she picked his spoon up from the table and whacked him hard to the back of his head.

Startled and in embarrassing pain, Atticus jumped up from his chair in a retaliatory manner, inducing a taunting response from his angry sister. "Go ahead, you little brat! I'll kick your ass if you touch me. Get that stupid backpack, and let's go."

With that one-way exchange done, and near tears from the whack to his head, and with his feelings crushed, Atticus muttered, *"Just you wait, Lizzy, you're going to get it; tonight's the night, you'll see."*

If Atticus wanted to fall asleep quickly, having his father's discarded alarm clock with its noisy ticking under his pillow was not the answer. Growing louder, the clatter from the old-style clock was begging to overwhelm the quiet of the sleeping house. Atticus had learned to find comfort in silence from years of being screamed at. Unlike most kids his age, he looked forward to the darkness and tranquility of nighttime.

He was startled awake, surprised that he had dozed off so easily. He forced his eyes open. Atticus used his other prized possession, his father's old flashlight, to reveal the time to be slightly past the 3 o'clock mark. There seemed to be no controlling the moment. "It's time, now or never," thought Atticus, as the old clock produced louder and faster-sounding ticks, his heartbeat keeping up with the clock.

The pistol seemed heavier as he tiptoed toward his sister's bedroom. Not taking into consideration the closed door to Lizzy's room, Atticus fumbled with the flashlight in one hand and the gun in the other, reminding himself that he just wanted to scare Lizzy, and hopefully, that would encourage her to stop abusing him.

With clammy trembling hands, he managed to open the door and stick the gun into the room. Hearing his sister's light breathing, Atticus made a mental reminder that he would fire the starter pistol, run back to his room, where he would jump in his bed, pull the sheets over his head, and pretend to be in a deep sleep.

Atticus suddenly wished he had done a test-fire of the gun in the basement. Using only two bony fingers, he aimed at the ceiling; the trigger was surprisingly effortless to pull. Expecting a harmless POP, the loud, resounding blast heard and felt was not the sound that Atticus remembered. Plaster fell from the ceiling as Lizzy let out a blood-curdling scream. By reflex, a second shot discharged from the gun, striking Lizzy, though Vivien would forever swear it was murder.

Atticus saw Lizzy's strange bedfellow, Pecker Head, make a mad dash through the bedroom door, screaming as he flew stark naked past him down the stairs, where he encountered an equally startled Vivien.

Finally, there was maddening silence; Atticus was unable to move his youthful feet fast enough to return to his room, as was his infantile plan all along to feign sleep.

With a phone in her shaking hand, wearing a floor-length housecoat and with a head full of bulky curlers, stood a ghastly-looking Mrs. Mathews. She was screaming at the 9-1-1 operator about a shooting, and her hysteria caused her to repeat the word *shooting* three times. Vivien stood at the foot of the stairs, clutching her chest as if in cardiac arrest. She was wearing a robe adorned with an impressive number of feathers, looking like a fat ostrich about to feint. But she was standing - something Atticus had not seen for as long as he could remember. Filling out the odd trio was Pecker Head, shaking with fright and still nude, standing behind Vivien for cover, which was easily attainable.

There was mass confusion and hollering as the police and EMTs arrived at the scene. Panting under his blanket, Atticus tried unsuccessfully to hold his breath to control his breathing. His heart raced faster as he heard many shoes pounding up the staircase. Lizzy's room was deathly quiet by the time the police eventually reached Atticus' room. Through little tightly squinted eyes, Atticus saw the lights switch on as someone violently pulled back the blankets.

The police, with guns drawn, were shouting commands that Atticus didn't understand. By the time Atticus was finally able to open his fear-filled eyes, someone had already secured the smoking gun.

Besides the sight of blue uniforms on this mind-boggling night, the dazed boy noticed his mother screaming hysterically at him. Because he was in shock, Atticus did not hear what Vivien was yelling, partly because he was so stunned to see her on her feet. He had not seen his mother walk unassisted - in forever. Atticus flung his head back onto his pillow, forced open his eyes, and waited helplessly for his punishment to come.

At eleven years old, Atticus had lost his only ally and friend, his father. Now, he was to lose his freedom. His fragile sanity, which he had awkwardly tried to protect, would be in jeopardy next.

All the excruciating memories from this point in the seemingly endless, horror-filled night were banished from Atticus's troubled mind by using a skill set acquired from many lonely moments.

The quiet of the juvenile detention center was an eerie welcoming for the newest detainee. Until a switch was activated and all hell broke loose. Phones began to ring, and voices were raised. Much anger seemed to be directed at Atticus, though he was not sure. It seemed that there was annoyance at it being the middle of the night, and this kid single-handedly woke up the entire community. Arguments among staffers, police, and callers appeared to be escalating. Was this kid even in the right place? If he shot and killed someone, shouldn't he be in a more secure location? Where are his parents?

Life in the Juvenile Detention Home was somewhat of a luxury for Atticus, a break from always looking over his shoulder at the mansion, especially the last few years since his father's death. There was the constant screaming between Vivien and Lizzy, and then there was Pecker Head. Life had become a vicious cycle, and something had to give.

Here at the Juvey hall, things were different after his unexpected arrival and admission: no screaming, three meals a day, an exercise room with a running track!

Speaking of track, Atticus's trial seemed to be on a fast track to go before a judge. Known to everyone except Atticus, his lawyer was not to be trusted with a case of this magnitude.

One odd move by his attorney was requesting a speedy trial before a judge. Both the state and defense were going to base their case on mental capacity and premeditation. A total of four psychologists, two for the state and two for the defense, thoroughly examined Atticus and reported their findings to the Judge. Emergency personnel described the scene at the mansion the night of the shooting. A couple of notes Atticus had written were introduced as evidence. These notes indicated a desire to retaliate for some kind of abuse. Atticus showed the only semblance of interest when his notes of anger at how he was being treated at home were discussed.

Vivien was only too willing to share her account of that fateful night with a room full of sympathetic onlookers. She especially directed her sob story to the elderly man who would be judge and jury.

Testimony was limited to a stack of psychiatric reports full of various professional opinions. Their conclusion was that the accused, Atticus Carlisle, was of sound mind and intelligence and possessed the maturity to understand right from wrong.

Here was a widow whose testimony was portraying her son as a conniving killer. A boy who might be a danger to the community if allowed to walk free.

On the other hand, there was the mother's sense of duty that Vivien tearfully possessed to protect her son from harm. Then, there was the fact that he truly was responsible for her sweet daughter's horrible death.

"Ever since my dear husband's tragic death, my daughter has been my rock, my caretaker. I found a note that Atticus had written; in it were threats to Lizzy. He was going to stab her or poison her he obviously wanted her dead.

"To not reprimand this person," Vivien slowly pointed to Atticus, her eleven-year-old son, "means my dear daughter will have died in vain." Near emotional collapse, Vivien was helped down from the stand as people in the courtroom froze in place. She had performed her act to an *Oscar*-winning level.

Although Vivien's story was filled with inaccuracies, deceits, and falsehoods, she was oh-so believable because of her script. Even Atticus, who had been sitting stone-faced looking down solemnly, slowly raised his head as her performance ended. Despite being the main character in the actual scene, Atticus was so taken by Vivien's testimony he too believed her account he had murdered Lizzy, just as he had planned.

'Another glimpse into darkness' was how Atticus described his arrival at the jail facility across the state line in Wisconsin. Rising out of fields of corn was the juvenile prison, like a sphinx rising from a desert, its crumbling face giving off the look of decay. When the eleven-year-old Atticus impishly arrived at the prison, he was greeted by unimaginable smells and sounds.

Thus, it was a dreaded move to yet another unknown location, one that in reality, compared to relocating from a mansion to a dungeon.

This latest move was challenged by Atticus's court-appointed attorney, whose representation of Atticus Carlisle was criticized by some as lacking in adequate defense of the court's decision for one so young to be incarcerated. He wasn't set to be released from the facility until age eighteen. This decision showed little consideration for any medical findings on young Atticus, even though he was thoroughly examined by four psychologists who were split on the boy's culpability. Weighing heavily on the Judge's decision had been Vivien Carlisle's crucial testimony wrought with ghastly details. According to the judge's ruling, the ancient building would house Atticus for the next seven years until he reached the age of compensating.

He quickly fabricated the name, *the other place*, for the disgusting facility, never to refer to its real name. The other place that would be his home for a very long time.

If released, there would be countless reports, evaluations, and programs to complete. Either way, the severity of the sentence was a triumph for Vivien courtesy of her dramatic appearance at her son's trial. Rushing Hills Juvenile Jail was known for its tough rehabilitation for hardcore youthful offenders. Home for those assigned to the aging facility was an enduring group of teens who usually lacked any kind of family structure.

Fifty-one months, three weeks, and four arduous days later, Atticus was learning. He finally understood, though he may never thoroughly grasp, the art of deception. It was still only a word to him, not an actual act of trickery but rather a means of survival. For much of his stay at the other place, Atticus was subjected to threats, violence, and ever-ready seclusion. In the beginning, Atticus was like a wounded creature in the wild. Separated from the rest of the pack, Atticus was easy prey to other inmates because of this vulnerability.

At that early period of his tenure, Atticus' saving grace was he had little to be removed from. Older inmates with aggressive tendencies sought the weaker inmate's money for their own wants in the facility's commissary.

Drugs were always in high demand, primarily for their worth as a swapping entity. Word quickly spread that the young boy, nick-named "the kid," was not worth the bother trying to extort anything of value from. Gossip in the joint was that his mama threw him under the bus and washed her hands of the boy. In fact, it was common knowledge amongst the prison populace that the kid's mother was his biggest adversary, to the extent she extolled the police and the courts that her son was a danger to society and should be banished to a remote penal institute forever.

His crime? Killing her daughter, his sister. Coincidentally, when the news spread throughout the facility that the kid had murdered someone, a new sense of respect was rendered for Carlisle, a place on the prison's respected pedestal. Atticus cared little about how others portrayed him; he knew he was just a ghost in a sick hallucination.

Atticus was tested, evaluated, and diagnosed numerous times, seventy-one times, according to his calculations, for the duration of his stay at Rushing Hills.

As well as being labeled as bipolar, manic-depressive, anti-social, and with a psychotic disorder, Atticus was also considered borderline thought disorder.

Efforts to secure his release to his Grandparents had been futile; all efforts thus far proved costly and time-consuming. Atticus's estranged mother had blocked all attempts to hand over custody to her late husband's parents, a gesture that sounded like a righteous move, which probably would depict why she opposed their efforts.

Vivien always maintained the trauma she experienced the night of the murder had prevented her from visiting her son. She had become a patient in a renowned therapy group and secured a new high-level law firm to handle ever-present litigation.

She was able to pay for expensive privileges, among other extravagant necessities, because of Hank's life insurance settlement, lawsuits against Hank's employer, sub-contractors, and even the Chinese government. Her hope was that by maintaining custody of Atticus, even though she was now very well off, the sizable annuity she was aware of for Atticus would be sufficient to live the life of royalty on her new venture and reside the rest of her life somewhere more suitable for royalty - as in Fiji or Tahiti.

"Are you going to see your mother before you go?" asked Dr. Kelsey, the home's most recent head shrink. Atticus, who had learned to choose his words carefully when he did speak, could not decide on a response to the doctor's question and remained silent. He was adept at choosing to not speak. Talking always led to trouble, which was his mantra. Writing continued to be a serious outlet in lieu of speaking as he determinedly documented the dreadfulness that surrounded him much as it had at the home he grew up in: the mansion, as his mother had insisted he call it. Though his former residence was a relatively short distance away from the juvenile prison, it might as well have been across the country, for he had only one visitor, a friend of his late father, who would visit on holidays, days that were meaningless to the stoic teen. Ted continued to seek his release and was overcome when he eventually helped secure his emancipation to overjoyed grandparents.

Most extraordinary was the overturning of the previous misdiagnosis, whereas Doctor Kelsey quickly identified Atticus Carlisle with Asperger syndrome, part of the autism spectrum. He attributed his acute anxiety to years of child abuse compounded by his mental deficiency. With proper prescribed medication, his condition would be controlled. Working outside normal channels, the doctor had given this case a high priority. He aggressively advocated for Mr. and Mrs. Carlisle in Lexington, Kentucky, to be appointed as guardians of their grandson. For Atticus, the goal was to live in a loving and stable environment with a patient and caring family. The Carlisle's understood their grandson was not a danger to himself or anyone else. He saw the world differently from most, and he was always trying to put order to his chaotic life.

Putting an end to their grandson's miscarriage of justice, the elder Carlisle's felt they could put an end to this dreadful era and help young Atticus, their late son's boy, heal from this long and unwarranted ordeal.

After the diagnosis of this specific disorder, Atticus showed little reaction. Mostly, he expressed some relief for the good news because, he reasoned, it meant he would have no more tests and no more delving into the functioning of his broken brain.

When informed that he was being released to his grandparents, who lived on a farm almost 400 miles away, Atticus was overcome with bewilderment. The call into the superintendent's office had been brief, without any fanfare, devoid of any emotion. A form letter read somberly by a blank-looking clerk.

'Released to the custody of Harold and Madge Carlisle.'

> *"Should I be concerned? Of course, I should always be concerned about the unknown. Plus, the final court order indicated that I would still need to be analyzed and monitored until I turned twenty-one years of age. When I returned to my room, I immediately laid down and began a strenuous attempt to remember my trip to this very same place as a four-year-old child."*

Atticus appreciated Dr. Kelsey. In his almost five years in the boys home, he had seen and been diagnosed by a few psychiatrists, each with their own prognosis, but were unified in labeling his condition as mentally defective. If only the court had ruled that he was guilty but mentally ill, he might have been confined to a hospital for a while, prescribed the right therapy and medicine, and subsequently properly treated and then released. Dr. Kelsey, on the other hand, felt drawn to his patient and appeared to be sympathetic to the troubled young man with his tragic and abusive past. Reading his files, he felt the previous diagnosis and treatment extreme, as was being confined to this archaic facility. Dr. Kelsey was aware of the usual consequence when a boy of Atticus' age, with an obvious lack of maturity, was often easy prey to older, more experienced, and hardened fellow inmates.

CHAPTER 11

"You cannot friend a hawk unless you are a hawk yourself, alone and only a sojourner in the land, without friends or the need of them."

– Stephen King

Watching their grandson run through the crop-laden fields from their wrap-around porch was heartwarming to Hank's parents. Mr. and Mrs. Carlisle's modest farmhouse and flat fields were surrounded by low rolling hills which provided a quiet sanctuary for Atticus to decompress from the horrors of life. To build up strength and stamina. To let his mind concentrate on something other than survival.

They shared moments like these to marvel at how much Atticus reminded them of the skinny lad's father, their son, Hank.

Like his dad, Atticus appeared passionate about running. Early on at his new home, Mr. and Mrs. Carlisle expressed their hope he would follow in his father's footsteps and run competitively, an endeavor that seemed to have taught him discipline and focus. Thus far, it struck his grandparents that Atticus lacked much of his father's concentration. He seemed to have a short attention span and was easily distracted. Of course, he was still adjusting to life here after five years of confinement, under strict rules and with hardened older boys who took delight in harassing him. One other thing that was evident was young Atticus' fascination with hawks. He showed an alertness to the hawks as they circled above the trees.

Smiling stiffly at his wife, Mr. Carlisle tried reassuring her, hoping to keep her from to fretting. However, she was immersed in a cloud of worry. When they were contacted by someone from their son's company about the horrible accident in China and that their loving Hank had died at the construction site from a fall, their world came crashing down around them. Mrs. Carlisle kept the card; a joyful celebration card Hank had sent her and his father a month before his death.

"Dear Mom and Dad, this is to let you know that a decision has been made. Once my divorce is final, I will have custody of Atticus and will bring him here to China. Lizzy will remain with Vivien – God help her! When this job is done in a couple of years, I am done with working in this high-stress job and will return to the U.S. (Kentucky) for good. Who knows, I may try my hand at farming! I would love to keep the place going for another generation with me and Atticus. Oh, I have met a beautiful girl, a real lady! We will be married here, but we hope to renew our vows from your beautiful gazebo! Hopefully, you both will love her as I do. I believe Atticus will find her a loving stepmom as well.

"There is much more to tell you, but I wanted to share this wonderful news with you both.

"Your loving son, Hank"

Now, Atticus was theirs. Vivien had greedily fought to retain custody and, more accurately, control of the large trust fund set up for his care. Atticus, however, was old enough to have a say in his fate. He had not yet changed his name, as he indicated when his gramps asked him what he wanted to be called. *"I want to change my name to Hawk!"* he nearly shouted back as his answer. Gramps showed a genuine smile of approval at his grandson's request.

"You will probably have to wait until you are twenty-one to make that legal, but as of today, around here, your name is Hawk! I never cared for that name your mother gave you anyway."

He wanted nothing to do with his mother and was relieved to know his grandparents were there to fight for him. With some likenesses to their late son, also a troubled soul after his marriage to Vivien, Harold and Madge Carlisle were determined to provide Hawk with a warm, loving home. They hoped the sunshine, clean air, and abundant love would be the remedy to the abuse and devastation he had encountered living with his unstable mother while his father was in China. Then there was Hank dying in the accident, followed by being put away in a disgusting juvenile prison for years as the extreme punishment for the accidental death of their granddaughter. Atticus had been exposed to all these despicable events in his short life.

Prior to every teen's anxious ascent to high school, Atticus received notification of his class schedule for his first semester in a real high school. Much to his disappointment, he was enrolled in special-needs classes.

"I do not want to be in special needs classes with a bunch of slow kids. It will be the same thing as 'the other place.' The kids will tease me and pick on me like before." Atticus made clear his opposition to his grandparent's idea. He would rather not re-live the special-needs environment he recently experienced at the unbearable detention home he called the other place. His grandparents tried to reassure him it was a temporary situation, just until he caught up. All the while, they agonized for their grandson as his anxiousness rose, and they realized how his past would, at least in the beginning, shape his future.

> *"When I was informed that my grandfather had made a deal that upon me turning 16 years old, I would be allowed to live with him and my grandmother, and they would become my guardians - I did not believe it. I was told by a lawyer working as a child-rights advocate that I just had to go to monthly meetings - for what I did not know. People have been in my head regularly for the last five years; even as a battered child, I was the one being examined; there should be no mystery as to what they will find. I began to fear that my grandparents might tire of me after a while or that I may mess up and get returned to 'the other place.' I knew then I would have to really try hard to forget where I had been... I knew I could do it, though. It took me a while, but I forgot my mother and sister, both of whom were responsible for me being locked up for almost five years, or worse sounding - 1,815 days!"*

Vaguely, that was how Atticus remembered being at the farm as a kid, tucked neatly on a small tract of land that was currently in hay. Curiously, the Carlisle farm was swallowed up by the immaculate and enormous neighboring horse farms. This was the famous country home of first-class racehorses and breeding farms, with its rolling hills and Kentucky bluegrass. It is hard not to fall in love with the land and majestic thoroughbreds.

Atticus tried recalling his visit with his father when he was a mere four-year-old. He did remember that his father showed him where he had run in his youth, through fields, streams, and hills. Hank's experience of training on the Carlisle farm served him well in high school, where he became a star on the talented cross-country team. Atticus soon became relaxed enough to start running and displayed to his grandparents similar athleticism they had seen in their son. Considering his recent incarceration and subsequent lack of participation in outdoor activities, Atticus seemed like a natural. But while Hank had a natural gift for being intense and focused, his son appeared to have a short attention span and to be easily distracted. Of course, he was adjusting to life on the farm after five years of boundaries and under strict rules placed with hardened older boys who took delight in harassing and bullying him.

"He's like a foal getting his legs out from under him," observed Mr. Carlisle, trying to reassure his wife. Mrs. Carlisle had started to feel like her son had returned home to his roots, to her hugs; she wanted to believe his soul was in this special boy. Suffering from her own health problems, Mr. Carlisle hoped that Atticus would not be a burden to his wife; he hoped that he hadn't made a mistake taking his grandson in. "But, if not us, then who?" he questioned himself.

"First, my only son, Hank, chooses to become an engineer instead of operating the farm, pretty much sealing the deal that after six generations of our family farming this same soil, that I will be the last. My dear wife has spent her entire life on a farm, much of it as a farmer's wife and homemaker, a job just as hard, if not harder, than farming." Recent years had not been kind to Mr. Carlisle due to his wife's health and the farm's financial troubles. "The recession almost cost us the farm. We ended up selling off good land, leaving us with a manageable ten acres. Worst was Hank. You can always replace your land; you cannot replace a child. Or can you? Is she on to something by saying Atticus could be our son's spirit, returning through him? Shared native lore tells us that it is possible."

CHAPTER 12

"True friendship comes when the silence between two people is comfortable."

– David Tyson

"I have been here for two years, and I have changed, some for the good; I can write better and am learning at school how to use a computer. I have learned a lot at school; I even made the honor roll! That was neat. I was beginning to really accept school. I went half a day to special education classes and then the other half to regular classes; it's called 'mainstreaming'; it's placing special needs kids in a general education classroom during certain times. I have learned a lot of neat stuff in regular classes, but the kids kind of freak me out with their stares and stuff. I have an idea that I am not liked by the kids in regular classes because my hair is buzzed short all the time (Gramp's idea), and I do not say anything to anyone after I whisper "here" for roll call. They probably think I am the type to come to school with a rifle and shoot the place up. If they only knew that I am a peaceful guy. Ever since the disaster I would never pick up a gun, let alone shoot one. In special-ed classes, everyone is nice. There are kids like me with Autism, Down Syndrome, Cerebral Palsy, and other challenges. They all seem to look up to me. I have one friend – Sophia, she doesn't speak. We met on the school bus; she lives near me, and her family owns a small ranch next door with a track and a barn. We started seeing each other after school; sometimes, I would run over to her ranch (under 8 minutes.), and we would walk around her property. She likes to hold hands; it felt kind of weird at first to me, but I soon learned to like it. I kissed her in the barn one day, but only once; it was very cool. I am going to try and remember it - I just do not want to do anything wrong. I am always afraid of being sent back to 'the other place.' I am still afraid of saying the wrong thing and getting into trouble, although I have read up on some laws and realize I should not have been at that 'other place' in the first place and cannot see any reason why I would have to ever return there, but still... you never know."

Atticus Carlisle

It wasn't long before a passing acquaintance with Sophia meandered into a meaningful relationship. It was conveniently driven by the relative proximity of the Carlisle farm to little Sophia's family ranch. At approximately one mile, it was a mere jaunt for Atticus, the obsessed runner. Soon, the pair could be seen walking down the gravel road separating the two families, not holding hands but instead hooking pinkies.

Having been diagnosed as being on the spectrum explained why he bore many of this developmental disability's challenges. Most obvious were his problems with social interaction, shyness, and verbal communication. Characteristics that were overlooked by many at his trial. Things that should have affected his sentence.

With Sophia, Atticus momentarily lost his shyness and looked deep into his first friend's soul. Another awakening was staring into those chestnut-colored eyes, the beautiful color of the coat of many a statuesque racehorse in this region. Atticus was totally unaccustomed to looking into someone's eyes, which made the experience with Sophia more special.

With the increasing time Atticus spent at Sophia's home, the more her father became concerned about the tall, handsome *Gringo,* he with odd mannerisms. What were his intentions? The two teens were far from the typical 15 & 16-year-olds, with Atticus painfully shy and withdrawn and little Sophia outgoing despite her being unable to speak. Both were dealing with their own distinct challenges. However, the two communicated almost entirely silently, relying on written words and eye contact, which, in his late teens, was a unique experience for Atticus. Sophia called Atticus - Bud, as in "my Bud," in her notes to him. While Atticus would utter the only Spanish he knew, *Chica,* as in *"my little Chica."*

Atticus was thinking not of the future but of how the present was becoming hopeful and comfortable, like he was starting to belong. He was becoming more insightful, more inquisitive.

He still was spooked by the very idea of becoming comfortable, alarmed that it was too late to be relaxed. He remained convinced that he must always be on guard. The other place would be just that, another ember in his fiery life, something slowly, steadily, forgotten.

Unfazed by an early morning heat wave, Atticus ran, as he did most mornings of summer break, to Sophia's ranch. While checking his constant companion - a fitness watch – the silence was broken by the familiar screech of a hawk, which Atticus quickly surmised was alerting him to potential danger. Suddenly unnerved, he scanned the littered grounds as he felt a stir in his wondering mind. Something was missing. There was no sign of life anywhere on a ranch that was always abuzz with activity. No Sophia jogging her horse around the track. There was no adult movement around the faded red barn. No nothing except for a pickup truck with a large horse trailer attached to it. Thinking they were all eating in the farmhouse, Atticus strolled casually up the stairs leading to the wrap-around porch. The door opened suddenly as one of the familiar ranch hands exited hurriedly.

"Hola! Muchacho, nobody here; they go back home to Texas." The ranch hand smiled politely and then rushed past a stunned Atticus. Before he reached the truck, the ranch hand stopped, turned, and walked back to Atticus. "Sophia." He placed a letter in Atticus's hand. "Adios, Vaya con Dios."

Atticus watched the truck and trailer pull away, shocked by the Spanish words and broken English he just heard and what they meant. He walked slowly over to the barn where he and Sophia would sit and watch her pony and hold hands. Where he once leaned over and gave her a peck on her cheek. He opened the letter from her, which turned out to be a touching poem.

When you hold my hand,

I see beautiful butterflies

Circling around my head,

It makes me feel wonderfully silly.

I sometimes dream of the two of us being wed.

I guess I'm being a childish filly.

For now, I'm just happy that you're my Bud.

-Sophia

Atticus stared at the uneven note and tried to make sense of it all but could only feel emptiness; it seemed that he was all alone again. He felt the compulsion to do what he usually did when he felt down like he was now, run. One perfect summer day had melted away, while a wonderful relationship dissolved in the blink of an eye. Throughout his relatively short life, Atticus never possessed the insightfulness of why people leave people. Whether it be through death or a mutual arrangement, there was always the fear out there that the person you connected with most could vanish at any time. But why? Atticus once wrote about his thoughts on death.

> *"As far as death is concerned, it's full of theories. There are the interpretations by science, theologians, and religions, all of whom have their own opinions. Leaving, whether by death or voluntarily, meant the same: the person had left. It was complicated by the suddenness of a person disappearing in an instant, like my father had."*

Confused, Atticus ran, his head stationary as if absorbing every bump in the dirt road. Eventually, he pulled up and checked his watch. His sense of emptiness was leading to hunger, so he circled back toward the sanctuary of the Carlisle farm and his Gram's cooking.

Along the way back to the farm and focused on his run, Atticus encountered a group of runners spread out over many yards. Not wanting to jog behind them, he picked up his pace. Even though he had already run about three miles, he had much left in the tank as he smoothly and steadily passed this group of teens his age, cross-country runners doing summer conditioning work before the fall season.

Pacing his runners from the luxury of a golf cart, the team's coach caught sight of the runner, left his boys, and followed the new kid.

Raymond Riley, the school's veteran cross-country coach, watched the young, spindly-legged runner finish his run before driving up to the boy, who was stopped at the trail's end.

"Excuse me, can you tell me how far you just ran?" Coach Riley allowed Atticus to catch his breath before answering.

"I think it was about three miles," Atticus answered softly, avoiding any visual contact.

Coach Riley whistled in amazement. "Wow, that was quite the finish for running 5k."

"More like 4.8 K," Atticus corrected.

Smiling as he studied the boy's demeanor, the man extended a hand. "I'm Coach Riley of the school's cross-country team; what's your name? What grade are you in?" The brief one-way conversation was over as the team caught up to the pair.

"I'm Atticus Carlisle; I'm going to be a junior."

Coach Riley's eyes lit up. "I ran with a Hank Carlisle years ago."

"That was my father," Atticus responded.

The coach responded with much admiration. "Wow! I ran cross-country with your father; he was a great runner, had lots of desire, was a great teammate, and was a good friend. Are you thinking about coming out for the team?"

Atticus remained quiet at the Coach's inquiry, as always, he was hesitant to talk to anyone. He had evidently lost his first girlfriend, his only friend, that morning. He hadn't the will to talk about running, or for that matter, anything at that moment.

Nonetheless, Coach Riley left with an invite. "Why don't you come out for the team in the fall? We meet here for a run every morning. Bring your shoes and plenty of water."

That evening at the dinner table, Atticus mentioned the chance meeting to his grandparents. Both thought joining the team was a great idea. A wary Atticus was not so certain.

In the coming days, Atticus advanced his devotion to running; he began running longer and faster. He gave little thought to joining the school's cross-country team, but rather he ran to ease the sadness he felt from losing his friend Sophia. In fact, the thought of making any more acquaintances had vanished with Sophia. It promised to be a long hot summer.

One morning, he again encountered a group of boys running in unison on the road. Not wanting to appear willing to join in their training jaunt, Atticus instinctively picked up his pace. He knew he could certainly catch and pass the tiring group, which he did with not so much as the slightest glance or nod.

Surprising himself with his newfound running prowess, he wondered if he was as fast as his father. *"Probably not,"* Atticus figured. After all, he was a running legend from these parts. With his feet still gliding unforced over the hard, sunbaked ground, Atticus returned to the farm. Harold stood in the barn alongside a neighbor from a nearby farm, admiring the sweaty runner, like a lathered thoroughbred after a rigorous workout.

"Maybe Ma is right. That boy may be the reincarnation of our son, Hank," Harold stated matter-of-factly. Spitting out a piece of straw, the elder man and his neighbor stepped out of the barn to watch.

"He sure can run; he might be faster than his father was at that age, and his father was a stud. This kid is like *Secretariat;* the longer the distance, the better he gets."

As Atticus did a final cool-down trot around the property, Harold concluded his positive assessment. "He can run all day like a young stallion. He was born to run. I'm afraid that someday, like that character *Forest Gump,* he'll run until he can't run any more, and sadly never come back. Back to the society and the family that failed him."

CHAPTER 13

"Try and fail, but never fail to try!"

– Jared Leto

"When Grams and Gramps talked about me trying out for the boy's cross-country team, they said I should do it for me. I had doubts, but now I felt the need to do it for them. A couple of weeks ago, I said no to the coach's offer. Then, I had just lost Sophia and thought of nothing else but her. Since then, I have run maybe a hundred miles, and I feel much stronger and faster. But just as lonely."

Besides a renewed interest in serious running, Atticus, ever the thinker, was motivated to start up a horseshoeing/farrier business with his gramps as his tutor. Harold Carlisle was once adept at the blacksmith side of the trade. His old anvil and forge had laid dormant for years. It now pleased Mr. Carlisle that his grandson was eager to take up the skill.

With Sophia sadly gone, there would be no swing-by to her family's farm this summer for an afternoon spent mostly in captivating silence. His courage to try different things was commendable, a testament to how far he had come. His medication was now administered by his grandmother, leaving no room for forgetting or doubling up doses. Without question, adhering to a strict regimen of medication and a stable lifestyle was part of the reason he was becoming a responsible individual. His future was looking brighter if he could keep the past hidden in a secure location. Day by day, his focus became stronger on two ultimate goals: graduating from school the following year and seeing the end of his mandatory psychotherapy when he turns twenty-one.

Atticus' return to school for his junior year had arrived as an afterthought. Everything was met as a duty and performed admirably in the classroom and around the track. He was quietly satisfied with how he had fit in with the cross-country team. Of course, when it comes to running, what can go wrong? Unless success is met with distress.

His purpose on the team dealt with the practice runs. While the other boys had their individual strategy drills and conditioning runs, Atticus would only run in practice and serve as the rabbit for the team's top runners. This became problematic when Atticus would forget that he was also relied on to let his teammates win, especially the top runners. He was okay with how his season on the team had gone until disinterest eventually kicked in.

With a surge of apathy pushing Atticus towards cross-country extinction, the season came to a merciful end with a meaningless varsity letter. He hung up his running shoes in the dusty barn, thinking they would become part of the permanent décor.

Atticus was ready to concentrate on blacksmithing for the summer. He used his ability to focus to block out the distractions while forming the dangerously hot materials with the rather primitive tools of the trade. He had an empathy for why horses needed the shoes and how to measure and custom fit each hoof. His confidence grew as he mastered each step of the process. Atticus sold the fourth set of shoes he ever made to a nearby farmer. Gramps was a patient master, and he was proud to have his special grandson as his willing student.

Returning to school for his monumental senior year, there was little room for thoughts of competitive running. Only anxious notions of graduating were present in his focused mind.

Coach Riley had other ideas for his incoming senior. He hoped Atticus could build on his impressive junior year and run in real events this season. First, the antsy coach had to convince him to return to the team. So far Atticus had opted to pass on the offer. He remained steadfast in concentrating entirely on making good grades and finishing school forever. He cared not to be in the public eye as the special-ed kid who was following in his father's footsteps as a long-distance runner. One season was enough for him, and soon he would be able to run whenever he desired.

Coach Riley was prepared to approach Atticus and his grandfather about re-joining the team. "How am I going to sell this kid on running this season" pondered the desperate coach. "All my experienced kids graduated in June; this is going to be the most inexperienced team we have ever had here. We need help, and this Carlisle kid could be the answer."

As if handed down from the heavens, a couple of weeks before school resumed, good news was timely passed on to Coach Riley by Atticus's school counselor. Credits were favorably located in his records, making him eligible to graduate early after the first of the year, rather than spring. Because of his history with the Carlisle family, the coach was delegated to present the good news to the Carlisle's. Soon, Atticus was a member of the school's cross-country team.

Later, at the midway point of the season, Coach Riley was facing a dilemma: what to do about Atticus. Sitting alongside his assistant, the coach was in a reflective mood. His focal point was his senior runner, Atticus Carlisle.

"I love the kid, and I am still glad we reached out to him to run for us; however, it's frustrating. It's just not working out. Not just for us, of course, but also for him. I hope we did right by him, I mean, we got him to say a sentence or two, up from two words last season," chuckled the coach. "He is a better runner than his dad was, but of course, not the leader Hank was. With Hank, it was like having another coach on the team. At the same time, I wanted this boy to contribute to the team, not be a novelty. Atticus is a runner with a runner's body, long and lean. Whereas his dad was shorter and bulkier. I find it so frustrating that I can't do more for him, but I realize he's still dealing with demons from his past. What's a given is he is good, state-ranked capable when he is right. Sometimes, he lacks the fire, the competitive edge is just not there. It's not a bad thing, it happens all the time, but this guy is good, like that wild mustang; he just wants to run. Sometimes, he won't let anyone pass him; sometimes, he runs out and says, "Catch me if you can."

"We have worked hard not to put too much pressure on him and dealt with him respectfully. Now, the success could be his albatross. With his psychological challenges and his good looks combined, he makes a good story. These things will bring increased notoriety to him and the program, which might be good for us but overwhelming for someone as private as Carlisle. No matter how hard we try to shield him from the demands and commotion, there are going to be challenges being in the public eye. I'd like to just call him in here and tell him – look kid, you're really good, but you need your space. Perhaps you should just kick back at your grandparents. Run the hills and fields when you want; quit running from things and go forward. As we coaches like to say there's nothing between you and the finish line but air. Damn, I'd really love his legacy to be that he led his team to the state championship, that he finished in the top ten individually."

Coach Riley's assistant noticed the fiery coach pause a second as he momentarily choked up before finishing up his sentimental speech.

"I would like to tell him it's okay to pass on being the center of attention. You have fought the good fight; your daddy is proud of you. You are not a quitter; you are a survivor."

Thus far, one match he might dominate; the next he could be just mediocre. One mile in a race will be a trot, the next a 'burn' in elite time. Coach Riley's approach was determined, he would deal with the withdrawn Atticus Carlisle with kid gloves.

Coach Riley was resigned to the unpredictable nature of his team with or without Atticus. As coach Riley had warned, he would require seasoning in his first year of true competitive running and may struggle at first before showing any semblance of consistency.

"Here is a kid that gave us all he had going on two seasons. Now, he is hitting the proverbial wall; it would be wrong to push him. With much fanfare during sectionals week, Atticus began to feel increasingly uneasy. Up to now, his season had been an inconsistent venture. There had been a couple of wins as well as a couple of DNF's (did not finish). In a couple of meets, we were forced to just scratch him because of an injury; mostly, he's just going through the motions.

"Despite all the hoopla of the area sectionals, newspapers and the electronic media are covering the end of his career like he is a god-damn rock star. Sectionals are next week, and this circus will be over soon. I'm torn between helping Carlisle make it to state, which he's certainly capable of doing, or just sit him and get ready for next season. Or should we let him do his thing and try to win the sectional for our program's seventh straight year, may I add."

Coach sat back in his office chair pondering his strategy, while in another part of the vast school, Atticus sat passively in a boring third-period English class.

Gazing outside through a spotless window on a beautiful late fall day, he daydreamed not of any big upcoming race but of graduating early. Then he'd be free; Gramps had already promised him a horse of his own, a Palomino, his favorite, and then he would really be free. There would be no more fuss made by nosey reporters trying to get him to talk, making a big thing out of his running. Most of all, he relished the end of running on a hamster wheel.

Mr. Carlisle sat his disengaged grandson down for a talk the night before Sectionals. Atticus seemed to be receptive to his Gramps talk; now, it was a matter of recalling what he had heard.

Race day greeted Atticus with a surprising lack of nerves and feeling grateful for conditions to his liking: a low humidity, breezy day. He calmly closed his eyes and let his free spirit take over to deliver him 4 miles later as the first to hit the tape at the finish line in record time. Glancing over at the small gathering of onlookers as he tried to catch his breath, Atticus caught sight of his grandfather. *"Is this what winning something special feels like?"* Atticus wondered for a collective second.

Coach Riley, who had taken the reserved approach with his new star runner, stood near the finish line with tears in his eyes, awaiting Atticus. Also standing nearby in the gallery was Atticus' gramps in a wet parka. Mr. Carlisle proudly stood erect, a hand out to his side, as if his son Hank was there with him. The two watched their son, and now their grandson, triumph over not only this competition but some of life's cruel obstacles by which Atticus had been surrounded. There would hopefully be more victories; fewer challenges would also be appreciated.

As Atticus stood at the awards booth, a passing shower, unaware to Atticus, had subsided, and a gorgeous rainbow emerged. Nearby, a pair of hawks jockeyed silently for a shot at a busy rodent in the nearby woods. It appeared to finally come together for Atticus Carlisle, Sectional Champion!

Cross-country is a sport that ranks in the lower tier among high school sports in interest and, consequently, revenue. Regional week would not be the norm; along with 'Atticus Hysteria,' things were about to get crazy. In fact, more interest was suddenly shown in the sport than anyone could remember. Just qualifying for state was a big deal for any runner; to do that, one must finish in the top 10 in their regional. With four regionals scheduled for next weekend, that means the top 40 runners will meet next for the State Finals in Frankfort.

For Atticus Carlisle to make it to State would be a victory for the downtrodden and browbeaten, the challenged, and most importantly, for him. Atticus's amazing story of tragedy and misfortune remained unpublicized, almost a miracle in this age of social media and a lack of privacy. It wasn't long before a story broke about Atticus losing his father to a horrible accident. Hank Carlisle, the report said, a fellow alum of Central High School, was killed in a construction accident in

China when Atticus was eight years old. Expectations and now the intrusion into his privacy by the public, media, fellow students, and others were becoming overwhelming. *"I just want to be left alone,"* Atticus Carlisle would repeat softly to himself. Recently, with help from proper medicine usage and exercise, Atticus had been able to avoid pressure. Sure, it was a daily battle, but Atticus had earned the upper hand since his release from the other place and his relocation to his grandparent's central Kentucky farm.

His coaches and family had been preaching for two seasons now the importance of team mentality, a culture that had never been taught in his material world upbringing. Atticus had agreed to participate in the team venture, with the understanding he would be able to run long distances, as his father had done, in this same environment. Factually, there was more to it, which through no fault of his own, was lost on Atticus. Blame it on his lack of maturity.

Now, as Coach Riley had feared, though not to the extent he had feared would happen, would he have had enough? Would the hoopla incite him into a fearless runner who knew he was as good as anyone, and with newfound swagger, he could win state!

"Well, here it comes, the shit is going to hit the fan," Coach Riley sighed aloud after reading another newspaper article. This is not good, it's only goddamn Monday, and already we got this," he pointed to the discarded newspaper. "Is it possible we can isolate Carlisle until we leave Friday? I hope so, and this boy is running his ass off right now - nobody can beat him but himself."

Back at the Carlisle farm, Atticus and his Gramps finished their fruit-laden breakfast quickly. Atticus looked up at his grams with a look a puppy might give, seeking more food in his bowl. Mrs. Carlisle was beside herself for not having set before her grandson some of her blue-ribbon hotcakes. She was under a strict request from Coach Riley, who had secretly contacted her asking to please limit Atticus carb intake this week as his last weigh-in had shown a slight gain lately. Atticus felt the change in his diet and how Gramps, for once, had opted out of before school work on some horseshoe project. Like the pot of water that was on the gas stove, a growing sense of pressure was beginning to boil. Atticus had tried not to think about the upcoming regionals since sectionals had ended. Easier said than done, as his mind had developed a response of its own and refused to be denied a chance to rouse anxiousness. He just wanted to do his school work, his chores at the farm, and run its beautiful and peaceful countryside.

Drawing words out of Atticus was a major mission for anyone, let alone his coach of two seasons. With Atticus and his grandfather seated at his cluttered desk, Coach Riley listened to the elder Mr. Carlisle speak on Atticus's behalf.

"Coach, my grandson, and his family have been very appreciative of the opportunity to be part of the cross-country program. As you know, my son, Hank, was a big part of the program as well years ago. So, it pains me to say that Atticus wants to end his participation now due to the intense pressure he feels because of all the attention he's receiving. We've had cars driving by the farm, reporters coming to the house unannounced, and the phone rings constantly. He regrets having to do this to you and the team with regionals coming up on Saturday, but he's not up for it. He fears his grades are suffering because of it, and his chance to graduate on time will be affected."

Coach Riley seemed calmly prepared for this, but deep down, it was still a bombshell. The veteran coach had begun to think maybe, just maybe, this story would have a Hollywood ending. "Well, Mr. Carlisle, I appreciate you and Atticus coming down here and letting me know of this decision. We try to maintain a family environment in our program, and if someone in our family has a problem, we support that person as best we can. "Atticus." Coach Riley looked across at Atticus, who was obviously uneasy with this meeting. "I feel very close to you, son," Coach Riley continued. "Don't worry, we'll do whatever will make the end of your career here memorable. You've already proved you belong and will always be welcomed here as a family member. Now, we can take care of this in one of two ways. We can scratch you from the regionals on Saturday. Runners are always pulling their hamstrings; we can say that you tweaked your hammy in practice and won't be able to run Saturday. Thus, you won't be going to state either. Or, you can still run"

Coach Riley's last words to Atticus were very persuasive, with all present at the meeting hesitantly in agreement. "Listen, Atticus, if you just lay low until early Saturday, no practices, we'll drive you and your grandfather here up to Frankfort. No teammates, no press, no strange bed; you can eat whatever you want that morning. Most importantly, there will be no talk of State. When the race begins, just focus on what's ahead of you; don't look back. Just run! Pretend you're running back to your grandparent's farm. Run until they tell you to stop. No thinking; you're just out for a run".

A last-minute adjustment to soft earplugs brought Atticus to the zero hour, the point before runners line up and jockey for meaningless positions. Atticus stood casually, hands on knees, looking down. When the starter's gun went off Atticus, not hearing the pop, was left behind at the line, having already lost precious seconds to the rest of the field. Unlike a short sprint race, long races are won by the runners who have enough thrust at the race end, not necessarily being the first one out. Not hearing the all-too-familiar starter's gun fired could be a welcome departure for Atticus. However, his poor start did not bode well against quality competition. Among the runners was a strong quartet of cross-country runners, all of whom had already committed to colleges throughout the Southeast region.

Finally, Atticus showed some effort to pull up to an upper-pack third. There was no way to see the smaller packs of leaders up ahead. However, if there were ten runners per pack, that meant that nobody in this third group was probably going to make the top tier of eligible runners, that being the top ten. It was time for drastic measures.

Suddenly, it seemed he realized his predicament - he was losing position to the twenty-or-so runners in the groups in front of him. He would soon be too far back to make up any ground, let alone make it to the top ten. Plus, he would have to run with a group of fading runners, which he had never been comfortable doing.

"So what?" was his inner response, *"If I just pull up now, it's all over. I could go home with Gramps, and I would be done."*

Instinct is a runner's main attribute, and it kicked in the nick of time. *"If this is my last race, I want to finish it on my terms: no earplugs and running as fast as I can."*

With a sense of relief, Atticus took out the irritating earplugs. He was instantly overcome by the cheering crowd and the thunderous steps of runners traversing throughout the hilly course with him. Instinctively, Atticus pulled away from the trailing pack and the annoying noise. He now began, with authority, a powerful thrust of an early stretch run; probably too early. It was, he figured, his last chance as he powered past runners in desperation. The uptick in the wind flowing through his lengthy hair felt invigorating. Now, able to hear the wonderous chirping of birds and the sounds of freedom, natural speed kicked in.

Because of the noise-dulling earplugs, Atticus also had not heard the screeching overhead. Now he noticed four or five hawks circling effortlessly above him as if hovering in the same position in the sky. Nearing the finish line, Atticus threw both arms into the air, as a gesture of triumph, for he had finished in the top ten! Or perhaps his gesture was a salute to *two*, the Indian word for *the hawk*.

Surrounded by the merriment and exultation of tired runners and cheering onlookers stood an uncomfortable lad with steely blue eyes, long, curly blondish hair, and a kiss of a chocolate milk tan from the substantial amount of time spent outdoors. Atticus accepted a ribbon signifying a top-ten finish! He had qualified for state! Atticus would be one of the favorites to win the state championship the following week in the state Capitol.

A lazy afternoon was interrupted by the home's phone. Mr. Carlisle hurriedly answered the bothersome ringing that the ill Mrs. Carlisle fortunately slept through.

On the line was a newspaper reporter from Chicago laying out a plan for a story on his grandson. It would entail some highly personal questions concerning Atticus' past. Despite a court order to seal the records detailing his past, word had leaked out that as a child, Atticus had ended up incarcerated in a juvenile detention prison in a landmark case that helped change some children in prison laws.

During the coming week, the reporter would like access to Atticus in his preparation for the upcoming state championship and week. He would also like to monitor his current life as he assimilates back to being a private citizen.

"The story would be run on Sunday in conjunction with the Saturday meet results. Time is of the essence here," the reporter added. "The story is out there; all one must do is have the right sources, and you've got the whole story: dates, names, and addresses."

Finally, the reporter added promises of discretion and honesty with the possibility of a book deal. "These other guys, the paparazzi, they are all a bunch of leeches. They prey on your country values. I know money is an issue today with you small farmers. Who knows? There may be a book deal out of this story, something I can help you with. I talked with Coach Riley this morning. He seems to be on board with this and has promised me access to the school's facilities and all his runners."

Mr. Carlisle quietly hung up the phone so as not to disturb Madge. His anger level warranted a somewhat intense response, like a healthy slam of the phone or something more than "the frickin' nerve of him."

Seated before him in his office was Atticus, his star runner, and his terse-looking grandfather. Instantly, Coach Riley felt a sense of dread engulf the office.

"Coach, I am heading to the main office after I leave here to request that Atticus finish out his senior year at home. What do they call it? Virtual school? The next time you see my grandson is when he attends his graduation ceremony and receives his much-deserved diploma. And don't you worry about this poor farmer. I'll keep my frickin' integrity."

CHAPTER 14

"To be a man is to suffer for others.

God help us to be men!"

– Cesar Chavez

Approaching his 21st birthday, Atticus Carlisle found he was in an increasingly comfortable place. Gone was the pain of losing his neighbor and friend, his first and only girlfriend, Sophia. Also behind him was the awkward way his high school cross-country career came crashing down around him. Turning twenty-one held little significance. It was not the status symbol to him that it was to mere mortals.

"It's not a big deal," he told his latest psychiatrist after the doctor mentioned his upcoming birthday. *"It doesn't mean that much to me, other than I won't have to do this anymore,"* Atticus deadpanned, looking around the typically sterile office. *"What's important to me now is helping my grandparents keep the farm. I'm trying to help out more around the farm."*

Long-gone recollections of childhood abuse, misdiagnoses, death, and deceit were replaced by thoughts of lost love and hope. Though he still imagines a moment, especially when he laces up for a run. He transforms himself into eighteen-year-old Atticus at the starting line of the Kentucky state cross-country championship. He begins the race without the benefit of a starter gun being shot. After a smooth start, he makes a move at the 2-mile mark and smokes the opposition with a flying finish.

The doctor noted the tone of Atticus's voice and how he still avoided direct eye contact when he spoke, which was consistent for people with Asperger's. Despite his extremely high intelligence he lacked the understanding of finances, appearing to be in denial of his gloomy financial future as support would, inevitably, fade away.

These were things the doctor would detail through a court-ordered concluding report. The conclusion was that, from worry to paranoia, his anti-anxiety medication would deal with these neurological bouts. How effective the drugs were would be determined by how severe the feeling of distress was. His stay with his grandparents over the last five years had limited many of these moments. Now, with increased pressure, real or imagined, there was always a cause for dispirited feelings.

If it were not for Grams keeping the meds in her possession, Atticus would certainly double up on his dose as he did many times at the other place, which would hopefully relieve the mood. Sometimes it would, other times it would make matters worse. One constant was the notion that it was always worth the risk when moments seemed out of control. Or so he thought.

Atticus revealed that he dared not discuss this with anyone, for they surely would not understand and would likely have him locked up in the looney bin as Vivien often threatened. Despite Atticus's desire to aid his grandparents, he was truthfully a drain on them as well.

In fact, while his grandson was attending his last session in Lexington, Harold Carlisle was figuring out what his budget would look like without the monthly trip to Lexington: it was insignificant. Still, Mr. Carlisle was proud of Atticus for getting to this point in his life. He was a free man, except for the challenges from which he would never be free.

CHAPTER 15

"When people show you who they are, believe them the first time."

– Maya Angelou

Another court ordered group session for youthful offenders was concluding. Two hours of vanishing words spoken by professionals to people with obvious social deficiencies. Some with proven mental disorders, such as Atticus Carlisle, and those playing the system, like one Ezequiel "Zeke" Callahan. All with common motivation - they had to be there.

This was, mercifully, Atticus's final meeting, fulfilling the questionable judgement handed down by a juvenile court five years earlier. Atticus's reaction was his typical disconnected self. Bothered by the same old babble, he offered an occasional sheepish glance around the room.

There was the usual assortment of wayward souls for his final gathering, with varying stories of misfortune. Capturing the newly turned 21year-old's attention was never easy, but this time there was an exception: in a corner, on a metal chair, sat a jittery young man of bizarre appearance. His red mohawk stood out against his pasty complexion. He sported a pierced eyebrow and tattooed arms, which only served to draw attention to himself.

Atticus seemed only mildly interested in the completion of years of therapy and counseling. Inwardly, he struggled with how he should feel as he exited the ancient facility, supposedly for the last time. Too good to be true?

Outside the painted brick building, dirtied by years of neglect, Atticus waited stoically, as he had dozens of times before, for his grandfather to take him back home. He was suddenly roused from his serene trance by an approaching figure.

"Hey, man! Hey, excuse me, can I bum a cigarette?" Atticus turned to face the red-mohawked, pasty-faced, weird looking young man from the group session.

"No," replied Atticus meekly.

"That's ok, man," replied the smiling punk-looking young man, who also appeared to be in his early 20s, as he, in turn, sized up the thinly built and handsome Atticus. "I need to quit that nasty habit anyway." This last exchange with the odd stranger reminded Atticus of his own mother, who disgustingly smoked for as long as he could remember. The young man stuck out his hand and introduced himself. "I'm Zeke," followed by a barrage of questions. "Where you headed, man?"

After a long pause, Atticus answered quietly, *"I'm waiting for my Gramps; we live in Newtown, we…"*

"Weird." Zeke interrupted, "Hey, think you can give me a ride? I'm staying with a friend in Centerville. My car is in the shop. You work out? You look really fit, man. Tell me, what do you do? What did you say your name was?"

Not trying very hard to keep up with the rapid-fire grilling from this strange young guy, Atticus finally mumbled, *"My name is Atticus Carlisle, I've…"* Just then, Atticus' grandfather pulled up in his old farm pickup truck. Before Atticus could speak, Zeke was introducing himself and bombarding a startled Mr. Carlisle with questions.

"Hello, sir," Zeke announced, smiling broadly while holding out a greasy, small hand. "Excuse the dirty hands, sir. I'm a mechanic by trade. I came here straight from a job at the shop. I see by the smoke coming out of the tailpipe that your fine truck might be burning some oil. I can check it out for you sometime if you like. I do good work and can give you a break in exchange for a ride home."

Being caught off-guard, Mr. Carlisle thought for a second. He was taken aback by Zeke's boldness and outlandish appearance. He also noticed the young man appeared to have a slight drag to a leg. Sympathetic, Mr. Carlisle agreed to give the freaky-looking fella a ride since it was on the way to his farm. Perhaps he would take him up on looking at his pickup truck, his prized possession. Riding past the attractive sedan parked in front of the building, Zeke gave a peek to admire the vehicle he had 'borrowed' so he could attend his court-ordered meeting. "Too bad I can't keep that ride; it sure is sweet."

By the time the elderly man pulled off the highway into a neat looking subdivision, Zeke had the elderly farmer laughing and warming up to him with tales that were so obviously absurd that Mr. Carlisle cared not about their truthfulness. Zeke was pushing his seldom-used affable button. In his country-boy life, Mr. Carlisle had seen his share of snake oil salesmen and con artists. He was taught early on to identify these mind-hustlers and their sales pitch and adhere to the 'if they sound too good to be true, they probably are.' By the time Zeke exited the truck in front of a nice-looking home, all in the truck were in a cheerful mood, and the location of the Carlisle farm was given to the grinning Zeke. Mr. Carlisle was certain that he probably would not be seeing the punk-looking young man again. He got what he was after, a ride and a pack of smokes.

Zeke stood watching with amusement as the pickup belched a small cloud of blueish smoke and headed back to the highway.

He smiled faintly at the about-face the elder man exhibited in regards to him working on the older truck, obviously skeptical about Zeke passing himself off as a mechanic. A deep drag of the unfiltered cigarette produced a cloud of smoke in the still air that obscured the vanishing pickup except for its red oblong taillights. With a glance skyward, Zeke detected some rain on the way and chose to move quickly. It was a lengthy walk to his friend's trailer park on the other side of the tracks, which served as the barrier between two distinct parts of town. Flicking the harsh cigarette away, Zeke's high-strung manner turned as gloomy as the chilled darkness had become. He set out on his trek with a solitary dog barking in the distance of the quiet sub-division he had just departed.

Atticus's eyes drooped to a closed position after his belated 21st birthday celebration, delayed because Madge was too ill to prepare something special for the occasion. Now Grams, returned to good health with a vengeance, had whipped up a special treat for her grandson, her famous double-chocolate cake with butter crème icing.

It had been a couple of weeks since Atticus' chance meeting with the punk-looking fellow with weird mannerisms named Zeke. His promise to come by and tune up the old pickup truck was a fading memory since that night.

Atticus was comfortably settling into life as a free man. No more therapeutic programs, psychologists, psychiatrists, or any obligations to the courts. That was of little comfort to Mr. Carlisle. Though pleased his adult grandson had reached this level of freedom, he still had concerns over long term plans for Atticus, how to keep the farm afloat, and most urgent, Mrs. Carlisle's health. His wife now required thrice weekly dialysis. The nearest facility was in Lexington, adding unbearable costs to the already stretched family finances. It had been a couple of weeks since his chance meeting with Zeke.

"Didn't that fellow from Centerville say he could work on the truck?" Mr. Carlisle pensively recalled. The Carlisle's depended on that old pickup now more than ever with the extra miles for the trips for his wife's dialysis.

There was always the option of selling the farm as property in the area was always in demand. But selling the farm that had in the family for generations was a last resort.

As if on cue, the serenity of the farm was interrupted by a vehicle traveling up the long gravel driveway, kicking up an impressive cloud of dust. Harold reckoned it was a visitor with serious intentions. When the car slid to a gravel-crunching stop, the driver made a dramatic exit by jumping out of the roof of a once hot-looking Camaro convertible. Mr. Carlisle took off his straw hat, scratched his gray hair, and mumbled a cautious cliché. "Be careful what you wish for." The driver with a somewhat familiar face approached him with a giant smile and outstretched hand.

Zeke's appearance had taken on a dramatic change since the last meeting between him and Atticus and his grandfather. Gone was the hideous-looking red mohawk haircut, replaced by a more conventual buzz style. Outside of an inconspicuous cross earring, no piercing was evident, and a neat plaid shirt covered much of his tattoos. Too stunned to speak at the sight of the eccentric young man from their earlier encounter, Mr. Carlisle was joined by his apprehensive and equally shocked grandson in a less than welcoming greeting.

"What's buzzing, Cuz?" Zeke, smiling broadly, offered up as he provided a tense Atticus with a gregarious handshake and bro hug.

"What the… how did he know where we live? I've got great memory skills, but I barely remember anything from that night. I think he said he was in a band; we gave him a ride home from the clinic, and that was it." Atticus thought to himself, confused by the reckless arrival.

"Nice place here, dude," began Zeke, "love it out here in the country, man, ah so um, quiet, peaceful. One could get lost out here." Zeke explained to the elder Carlisle the reason for his arrival. "Sir, you were kind enough to give me a much-appreciated ride home to my friend's, and I indicated to you that in return, I would be happy to look at your pickup truck and see what ails it. I'm a man of my word, sir," added Zeke, brimming with pride.

After the awkward introduction, Zeke was able to get himself a tour of the farm, conducted by a still suspicious Mr. Carlisle and an equally stunned Atticus. A quick review of the pickup truck resulted in an optimistic assessment by Zeke, the self-proclaimed car mechanic. Further appraisal of the surroundings bared a covered-up automobile in a rather large outbuilding. The 1973 Ford Galaxy was protected by a tattered cover and tons of dust. Zeke was informed the vehicle had been driven by Mr. Carlisle's son, and Atticus's father, throughout high school. Taking special interest in the old car, Zeke made a mental note of the middle-of-the-road classic, hoping to use it as a negotiable tool. He made a great effort to win Atticus's trust during the time spent with the grandfather and leery grandson, who was not eager to disconnect from his grandfather's side. Zeke knew that connecting with the troubled young man was paramount in achieving good relations with the older man. Mr. Carlisle excused himself to help his wife prepare dinner for the family and the surprise guest, who took that opportunity to break the ice with the uncomfortable Atticus.

Inner thoughts can be so telling. While sipping his coffee and half listening to more stories from Zeke, Mr. Carlisle's thoughts were all over the place. Throughout his many years he had listened to some of God's finest story-telling creations. The young man currently speaking was certainly holding his own with the best of them. From the pulpit, to car salesmen, to politicians, to the absolute best - fellow farmers, the good old boys network, this lad has some gift. But of greater important to him was what Zeke wanted.

He could sound sincere and compassionate, but Mr. Carlisle could detect an edge to him as well. What he could offer as a mechanic and possible farm hand could be beneficial to the farm operation. The potential to be a good arrangement outweighed the red flag.

Getting both the pickup and Hank's old car tuned up was expensive but done to Mr. Carlisle's satisfaction. Zeek had met the agreed upon conditions to remain at the farm, which meant room and board.

Zeke was hopeful that staying in the country home would soothe the beast in his troubled psyche. But, as he had found throughout his young life, great spikes of excitement were a bitch. Periods of comfortable near-normalcy were followed by inevitable thrill-rides, which a counselor once described as self-sabotage

"Something inside you triggers these desires of self-destruction, of the need to punish yourself. It is not the end result that spurs you to commit these acts; it's the chase; it's a game to you." It was all babble-rabble to Zeke, like every other discourse he had to listen to.

As he had done to some degree of success, Zeke tried increasing the intensity of his activity, an attempt at self-treatment at the onset of an episode, to decrease the symptoms of his behavioral lapses. Occasionally overwhelming anxiety or sinking into an extended bout of depression, was the unfortunate outcome of his wasted efforts. It was sometimes just better to go with it.

Teaching one to drive was challenging enough, especially one 21-year-old who has never driven and is on the Autism Spectrum. Still, with Mr. Carlisle's approval (only on local roads), the idea was hatched to teach the unsteady Atticus to drive using his father's dilapidated 1973 Ford Galaxy. Soon, the two twenty-somethings, alike in age but in other ways very different, became road brothers in the bluegrass countryside. Once Atticus, surprising even to the cocky Zeke, got the hang of driving around the neighboring soft roads, Zeke was anxious to press the issue. Utilizing the thrice-a-week schedule that corresponded with Mr. and Mrs. Carlisle's travel to dialysis in Lexington, the driving lessons expanded at Zeke's direction to nearby paved roads and eventually highways. Atticus had become used to the routine of their more frequent trips around the county and was only slightly concerned by the latest deception that Zeke had connived.

Atticus was in no hurry to get an official driver's license, believing his movements would be monitored by increased surveillance; an example of his ever-present mistrust and paranoia.

The fact that these road trips in and about the Lexington metro area to random locations were increasing was not lost on Atticus, who, nevertheless, found being the designated driver a bit of a charge in his mundane life. Only constant reminders of "you're going too slow" and "speed up or the cops will pull you over for holding up traffic," bothered him.

The moment was not lost on Atticus, "Going too slow?" he laughed. "Never have I been in trouble for doing anything too slowly."

As this odd co-op between Atticus and Zeke blossomed, Mr. Carlisle developed suspicions concerning the farm's new boarder and mentor for their grandson.

Atticus, in his familiar paranoid state, was beginning to have concerns about the frequency of short stops at various convenience stores. Zeke would always return from these stops with chocolate donuts (Atticus's favorite) or cigarettes and countless other novelties. Atticus would hurriedly drive away at Zeke's direction, and neither would say anything further.

The minute Zeke observed the unforgettable sight of a police car's light flashing in the side-view mirror, he calmly directed Atticus to "stop the car, dude."

"Now? Here? Why?" Atticus asked, as he too, noticed the police car behind them. "Just stop, man, it'll be alright. You probably forgot to use your turn signal back there, or maybe there's a taillight out," an increasingly hyper Zeke added.

Finally, Atticus was able to make his leg work and pressed the brake a bit harshly. The car, his father's prized vehicle, screeched to a halt. Without thinking, Atticus nervously wiped chocolate covered fingers off on the front of his t-shirt while Zeke nonchalantly lit a cigarette, producing screams from the first on-scene police.

"Raise your hands, NOW!"

In the time it took for the police to run a plate check, a backup squad car arrived. Zeke knew this would be more than a burned-out light bulb, that the gig was up. Reacting based on his experience, Zeke knew he needed to do something quickly. Exiting the older Ford, he immediately raised his hands skyward with a lit cigarette dangling down from his smirking mouth until the officer in the squad car squawked out instructions.

"Stop right there, spit that cigarette out, and get down on the ground." Then it was the other officer's turn. "Driver, turn off the car and slowly raise your hands out the window." Atticus shuddered at the command, trying to comprehend what was transpiring as the angry officer continued to shout too loudly.

Atticus froze at the squawk coming from the menacing radio as he mourned the thought of being incarcerated – again! He caught sight of Zeke out of the corner of his eye; from his knees, Zeke was holding his arms up in the air and shouting, "Don't shoot, don't shoot, we're both crazy, we're just a little crazy!" Zeke yelled the absurd plea, which the police took as an attempt to incite them. They proceeded to rush the pair and roughly handcuff each of them, stun guns at the ready.

Harold Carlisle always prided himself in being from a hard-working farming family in neighboring Kentucky horse country. Early pioneers had pressed into the rich land near where the Carlisle farm now sat. Nearby self-sufficient native tribes were soon displaced by waves of incomers. Some pioneers eventually co-existed with the peaceful natives and began families of their own. This was how the Carlisle family tree was rooted.

Harold Carlisle and his siblings were brought up to appreciate a good day's work and education, which he and his wife of 50 years, Madge, had passed on to their son, Hank, and accounted for his success in the classroom, athletically, and in his professional life. Now, the elder Carlisle's health was becoming of concern as both were facing issues that were limiting their ability to work their dream property. They had begun selling off parcels of the once huge body of fertile Kentucky land. Animals that were once a staple of their livelihood were sadly sold off as well.

Initially, Harold Carlisle was reluctant to give up their prized farm with the hope they could live out their lives there, and hoping their son would take over the operations, thus keeping the farm in the family. Then tragedy struck when their loving son was killed in a horrible accident in China. Now, Mr. Carlisle was beside himself since receiving a call from the county Sheriff's Department that their grandson, of a tragic upbringing with both a mental disorder and cognitive impairments, had been arrested for his involvement in a string of convenience store robberies, driving without a license and being in the company of a habitual petty thief.

When the detective told him that the apparent culprit who manipulated his grandson in the perpetration of these crimes was the person that he had trusted to stay at his home, to be a companion to Atticus, Mr. Carlisle was devastated.

"How could I have been so stupid to have trusted such a low life?" Mr. Carlisle disclosed this to his wife, who shared in his grief. They traveled to pick up their grandson from the county jail, where he was being held with twenty-four-year-old and repeat petty criminal - Ezequiel "Zeke" Callahan.

Fortunately, Atticus was released to the Carlisle's on O.R. (own recognizance.) The detective on the case explained to the greatly pained grandparents that Atticus was apparently duped by Callahan for some sick yet unknown reason.

"There had been at least five other robberies like this one in recent weeks that could be tied to Callahan and your grandson. He was an unknowing accomplice who always drove and never actually went into any of the locations, and it appears that Zeke Callahan has no regard for the justice system. He comes from a well-to-do family who continue to cater to him and will probably bail him out in the morning. Hopefully, there will be a court order for him to not have any contact with your grandson or be anywhere near your home. If he tries to contact you or Atticus, give us a call, and we will pick him up. He usually gets off with house arrest or some kind of therapy, but this time I believe we can charge him for being a habitual offender, and he will finally have to serve some hard time. One more thing: Atticus will have to make a certified statement, maybe even testify in court. You might want to talk with a doctor about how to handle that."

Spring brought with it the smell of freshness, new beginnings, and hope. It had been six weeks since that fateful day when all that Atticus could think of was that he was going to be locked up again, becoming prey for despicable, meaner, and stronger prisoners.

Since the humiliating incident with Zeke Callahan, time had been kinder to Atticus. Though he had grown cautiously fond of and had prospered under Zeke's tutelage, he was glad to be rid of him.

Updates from the detectives working the case against Zeke were becoming rarer. However, the threat of Atticus having to testify was still out there. Zeke had made bail and was released from jail with the conciliatory requirement that he wear an ankle monitor, and with instructions that under no circumstances should he have any contact with Atticus.

The last requirement made Atticus feel little relief as he was still having nightmares of Zeke sneaking into the farmhouse and slitting his throat. Unfortunately for Mr. and Mrs. Carlisle, things were moving too slowly for their liking. According to the prosecutor's office, Zeke's lawyer had successfully delayed all proceedings.

Atticus lost track of time and moved on quickly from the incident. He still felt hurt by what Zeke had done to him. *"I thought we were friends,"* he had confided to his grandpa upon returning home from his short detention at the county jail.

As time flew by and early birds returned to feed and roost, Atticus gave little thought to what happened and what ramifications he still faced. With letting one's guard down comes the increased chance of being hit with a life-altering haymaker.

It was early April and hope sprung eternal for Atticus as he finished up another morning run over the family's coming-to-life property and the surrounding tranquil countryside. The sizeable pasture of Kentucky's renowned blue grass was showing off its high-quality lushness. Bluegrass is green most of the year, but in the spring, bluegrass produces bluish-purple buds that give a rich blue cast to the grass when seen in large fields.

Atticus recalled the long-ago words of his father. "This is God's country, son; admire it, protect it, enjoy it." Which is what he was doing as he finished up his thought-provoking run. Moments like this inspired thoughts of his father and his strong calmness.

Abruptly, tranquility was interrupted by a noisy cast of hawks sounding an alarm; not usually observed in flocks, these birds are only seen on their own or in a pair.

With his grandparents off to another dialysis appointment in Lexington for much of the day, Atticus had his day precisely planned. He was determined to work on some blacksmithing; he would make more horseshoes and add them to an already growing inventory of unsold shoes. He prepared the forge using the natural gas line that Zeke had assembled during his stay. He had taught Atticus that the color of the flame indicates the temperature for the workability of the metal. The ideal heat for most metal working is the bright yellow-orange color that indicates forging heat.

Sitting on the shop stool, also something that Zeke had made, the sounds of a dragging chain snapped Atticus out of his deep thoughts, causing him to jump up and stumble over the stool. Standing before him, barely five feet seven inches high, was Zeke himself, looking like someone out of the scene of a prison break with a contraption on one ankle. Shuffling towards him, Atticus instinctively rushed to gather his hammer as the two pairs of eyes met. Atticus was convinced he was staring at Lucifer himself.

"What are you doing here?" Atticus asked. Zeke's head was now shaved, and a red, overgrown goatee made for an evil-looking grin on his pale face.

"Howdy partner, you don't need that," Zeke scoffed, pointing to the hammer in Atticus's hand. "That is unless you are planning on using that on some hot steel, not my chrome dome," he laughed as he rubbed his head. "You like?" Zeke quickly asked, stroking his chin hair, his smile returning.

"My grandfather will be back soon," Atticus lied quietly.

"Well then, we better hurry up," Zeke replied, turning toward the road. As he turned, Atticus was horrified to see what appeared to be a rubber club in Zeke's waistband.

"Listen, man, I need you to help me; I like your grandparents and appreciate their hospitality and generosity. With this little personal problem of ours, we need to do something for their safety."

"This must be a dream," Atticus pondered as he stood amazed at what he was hearing from Zeke and his foolproof, well-devised plan.

"I need you to cut off this damn ankle monitor first, and then we'll weld it back together and place it on a train, which will lead the authorities to look for us in the wrong direction. After a while, when this blows over, and they stop looking for us, you can come back."

"What the? What the?" interrupted a shaking Atticus, *"you want me to…"*

"Wait for a minute, man," interrupted an increasingly anxious Zeke while constantly checking the desolate road for any sight of trouble. "We need to act fast; there is no time for argument. You'll see this is necessary, and everything will be fine. If you stay here, they'll make you go to court, and they will make you testify against me and then make you confess, and we'll both go to prison for a very long time." Pretending to catch his breath, Zeke paused for dramatic effect.

Standing in stunned silence, Atticus felt locked in time. He carried the pressure, a constant unwanted companion that was only constrained, he reasoned, with the help of his meds. He was unable to make a move for his meds, let alone run, due to being frozen with fear.

Straining to comprehend all or even some of what he heard coming from Zeke's mouth was becoming more worrisome. Words were words, but the sinister-sounding Lucifer was frightening. What should he do? He couldn't deal with the thought of being locked up again.

Zeke's agenda was greatly simpler: run or perhaps spend some serious time in prison. With his GPS ankle bracelet precariously cut off by a trembling Atticus, relief washed over a sweating Zeke as he began to believe that this plan might work.

Zeke nodded approvingly at Atticus, who looked increasingly distressed and ready to bolt. Zeke had seen the young man run, had seen the ribbons in the Carlisle household where he heard some tales of Atticus's feats on his feet, and didn't want to have to try and chase a bona-fide, long-distance runner. He had felt forced to resort to some sort of scare tactic to ensure that Atticus would not run before reaching the nearby railroad tracks. "Remember, if you don't come with me, you will get locked up, and they'll throw away the key. Then your grandparents will have to sell everything just to try and get you out."

Through Zeke's pre-scheme reconnaissance, he had observed a steady run of 100+ car trains that often-times slowed at this point, a perfect place to attach the GPS ankle bracelet to a car. He would toss it on a train headed north and hope the authorities would assume they were heading north and to search for them there.

Zeke felt a rush of accomplishment with how things were progressing with the escape. He figured the major obstacle would be how to convince Atticus to go on the lamb with him.

Zeke knew he was delusional about pulling off this plan. He was not out of the woods with this scheme to flee with the one person who could punch his ticket to hard time in a state correctional facility.

His lawyer, a Public Defender, had done a good job in winning a delay and in beginning talks on a plea deal offered by the DA's office.

Ultimately, the state's case would rely on the testimony of Atticus Carlisle, who is on the autism spectrum. While the prosecution was confident that the case against Ezekiel Callahan was airtight, they also knew Atticus had to testify against his former mentor. Authorities thought they were diligent in preventing any contact between Zeke and the prosecution's star, yet vulnerable, witness. Thus far, no violations of the no-contact order had occurred. On this day, through a mutual agreement, Zeke was granted a pass for the privilege of visiting his psychiatrist in Lexington for a pre-trial exam. There was a firm designated time to report and a procedure to follow upon his arrival at his destination. His understanding was that he had precious little time before anyone would be alerted to his ridiculously desperate scheme.

"Come on, slow-poke, we've places to go," Zeke half-smiled, trying an ill-fated attempt at humor in hopes of putting the stone-faced Atticus in better spirits. After successfully securing the compromised ankle bracelet to an accommodating box car, Zeke led the pair of runaways to a concealed car he had stolen that day from a nearby shopping mall and tagged with a license plate lifted from a business complex.

"Here we come, Rey," Zeke exclaimed looking skyward. "I hope you come through for me. You know I can't stand being locked up."

"Who is Rey? Why are we going there? Where are we going?"

It would be a stretch to call Rey Jindal Zeke's associate. More accurate would be to label their relationship as mentor and apprentice. As the stolen sedan pulled onto the highway, with clear skies beginning to share space with threatening clouds, Zeke understood the future could be bright; if not, it could get horribly dark.

CHAPTER 16

"Misery acquaints a man with strange bedfellows."

– William Shakespeare

While another affluent parent sat outside his impressive office, Mr. Reyansh "Rey" Jindal would not rush to welcome her into his near-lush surroundings. Driven by a powerful combination of ambition and retaliation, he had just about reached the pinnacle of his career in Educational Administration - his position with the school. His job was to serve in the planning, coordinating, and administration of school activities and programs. In other words, he already ran the whole show but was not being compensated financially yet.

Reyansh would not rest until his name meant something to those in the private education sector. Why not someday have a school named after him? It would be a better choice than many. Hell, Yale was named after a slave trader.

Glancing through a stack of enrollment applications to the academy, Rey could only smile at the impressive size. It was a far cry from when he was first hired as an assistant to the Chancellor at the J.T. Boe Academy. Back then, the boarding and prep school for grades 9 through 12 was struggling financially. Needing a shot in the arm and afraid to remove the ancient Chancellor, Arthur Kennedy, a new position was created, and who better to bring in than a vibrant alumnus, one Reyansh Jindal. He had outstanding credentials as a student at the academy before his remarkable ascension to the Ivy League. Rey realized that accepting the offer to return to his former school was overlooking more impressive offers from notable corporations. Nonetheless, the big picture at J.T. Boe was clear: the Chancellor would soon have to go. Rey's goal was to be Chancellor, where perks would be bountiful. Like that office with the killer view and that imposing leather chair. Not to mention the administration's deep pockets, leading to his managing an enormous budget.

Concluding another typical visit with the parents of an underwhelming child, Rey pledged that their son would leave J.T. Boe as a fine young man ready for college, ready to succeed in a dog-eat-dog world. Any shortcomings their student had in behavior or scholastics would be left behind, as here they would be dealt with in a respectful but firm way.

Self-consciously, Reyansh Jindal took a rare moment for reflection and leaned back in his black vinyl chair. "Old habits are hard to break," grinned Reyansh, as he caught himself once again patting down the hair on the top of his head, recalling that as a young male Sikh he wore a patka on his head; a sign of humbleness. His father and other elders in his family wore a pagri, as do millions of elder male members of the Sikh community.

As he stared passively at the rest of his bargain-basement décor, a grin grew on his olive-skinned face. "Someday, Papa, I'll have real leather furniture and plush carpeting, with expensive paintings on rich paneled walls." His present office looked out at a busy highway, while at the other side of the building, his boss and school chancellor, Mr. Kennedy, had a grand office which overlooked a pristine freshwater lake lined intermittently with giant, graceful willow trees. For a moment, one would think they were in an exclusive resort area in upper New England. Instead, this place was surrounded by acres upon acres of corn fields in Southern Indiana. All was not that bad. In fact, Rey Jindal was doing very well for himself after a rocky beginning in America.

The role that he enjoyed most was classifying applicants by potential to do enough to keep elitist parents interested in their son's future, to control one's purse strings. An example lay exclusively off to the side, indicating a unique (wealthy parents) individual. He fits the need for Rey Jindal in his search for his next protégé. He seemed to be a real challenge for a job requiring one to be focused, teachable, and flexible. What this boy has going for him is having lawyers as parents. Usually, this means money and being too busy to get too involved.

Picking up the intriguing file from the side of his desk, the name of the applicant caught his attention. This unsettled boy, Ezequiel, which means *God strengthens*, could be the chosen one, a recruiter's dream. He appeared to be slick, hopefully loyal, a hurried, smart kid, lacking in direction. The kind of boy who might have a hidden talent that is being wasted on petty recklessness. He has faced tragedy with, understandably, no clue of how to deal with it. "Hmmm, sounds all too familiar."

Reyansh's tone defied his eagerness to impress his next candidate. He asserted an air of authority over the young man who had cockily emphasized that his name was Zeke. "I'm the chief administrator of admissions, and I determine who stays and who goes," while pacing around his desk towards his latest recruit. Zeke sat disinterestedly looking at the ceiling, but worse, with his feet propped on Rey's desk. With a quick swipe from Rey's powerful hand, Ezequiel's feet hit the floor with a loud thud. The fourteen-year-old jumped up and defiantly faced the school administrator. Rey reacted with a defensive stance; one he had used when he wrestled for the school years ago. Ezequiel was taken aback by Rey's reaction to his own threatening move and froze until Rey broke out in a quick smirk.

"I could have put you in a front chin lock and rendered you helpless, just as I did while wrestling here at J.T. Boe, where I won a state championship. Rey motioned at a picture hanging on his wall.

"First of all, you'll answer to me, no one else. No teachers, no coaches. Only me. You will be my eyes and ears out there," Rey pointed out to the imposing school grounds. You will be the connection to the recruits for whatever they need; just come to me. You will work for me; you will address me as Mr. Jindal; you will go to classes and maintain a high grade-point average and take your meds. You are Ezequiel; it sounds more professional. Zeke was that punk who was headed for a future making license plates in prison. You will be given three squares a day and a room all to yourself. Listen to me, Ezequiel, and you will leave here a made man. You will be able to be independent and be someone, got it?"

"Yes sir, ahh Rey," using a shortened version of the administrator's name. "The name is Zeke, and I smoke Marlboros, and I'll come here, anything to get away from that shithole life with my idiot parents."

Rey drew back and took a deep breath, trying hard not to show anger and show young Mr. Callahan the door. Instead, he exhaled a hearty laugh that almost brought tears to his eyes.

This decisive encounter would affect a spattering of individuals, linking out to form a massive chain, forcing more people to face life-changing options, both good and bad. Isn't that the way of the world, the way it has always been?

CHAPTER 17

"And here I go again on my own, going down the only road I've ever known"

– Lynn Hall, Whitesnake

Waylon Jennings's rough-edged voice sang out on the radio as squeaky wipers kept the beat to a lively country song. Zeke kept his focus on the drive through Chattanooga, Tennessee, and the tricky mountain roads. His mind was moving back and forth, from watching the road to watching the speed. He was used to driving his borrowed vehicles fast before disposing of them unharmed.

"We need to go back; I forgot my meds. It's time for my meds. I need my meds." Atticus's voice, sounding irritable, rose to an almost audible tone. *"I need to go to the bathroom; I need some paper to write on. How far are we going?"*

"Easy partner, not so fast. We cannot go back. I can pick up something for you in Miami."

"Miami? That's about 12 hours away. I can't wait that long for my meds. I can't wait that long to pee."

Zeke sat in a stolen car with its third set of stolen license plates, staring at a bright red pharmacy sign promoting 24-hour service. Noticing that there were cameras along the store's perimeter, Zeke prayed that he was parked far enough away from view. This was the time to throw caution to the wind, as Reyansh, at the academy, had taught him. Zeke turned to face a shivering Atticus, who was either cold or trembling from withdrawal from his meds, as Zeke had seen before in a drug and alcohol facility.

"I will, be right back; you stay under the blankets and don't move. I'll get your meds and some munchies. You'll be alright, but if something does happen, just blame me. Hang tight, and do not make any noise; I'll be right out," Zeke instructed before exiting the unfamiliar auto.

Atticus remained still, allowing himself to peek out over the blankets, his eyes frozen on the front doors of the store except for a quick glance at the nearby rear seat door handle. Voices in his head whispered, *"Get out! Get out! RUN!!"* His trembling body said differently.

Zeke cautiously shuffled into the pharmacy, preparing for the worst, and praying for the best. He had lost all tolerance for fear after his brother's accident until now. This, on the other hand, was beyond doing crazy things for thrills; this could be *bad.*

Without any prior plan for how to get some anxiety medication for his passenger, who was on the verge of a meltdown, he was trying to devise a plan on the fly. Remembering another thing Rey had taught him, always have an exit plan. It was obvious he had none.

"I could rush the counter, scream 'this is a holdup,' snatch the meds and leave quickly." Glancing about, Zeke concluded that the plan was no good with so many customers in the store. He sighed to himself with some sense of relief.

"I could speak to the pharmacist. 'Please sir or ma'am, my friend is freaking-out in the car, and he's in need of some *Ritalin,* and I'll… nah, that won't work either."

Zeke was in a sticky situation for sure; all his options were coming up as too dicey. Walking further towards the back, he became more edgy. His brain wasn't working fast enough, which he was not accustomed to, especially not with his hijacked victim out in a stolen vehicle in the middle of Georgia with another day of driving to South Florida ahead. Ready to abandon his current dilemma, Zeke nervously walked down an aisle and acted interested in an item on the shelf, taking a minute to compose himself, when he did a double take. There, on a fully stocked shelf, sat abundant packages of sleep aides.

"Whoa," he excitedly mumbled, "this might work, and I have enough money to buy this and munchies. This straight life is not all bad, less stressful for sure," he grinned.

Nearby to the pharmacy, tucked away in a half-populated strip mall, he found a Mexican eatery with part of the word *Restaur te* burnt out. One lonely vehicle sat parked outside, and it seemed like a good place to chill, and to work on making Atticus comfortable for the final push to Miami Beach and freedom.

It seemed at first that Atticus was going to resume his pissing-n-moaning from earlier. *"It smells bad in here,"* he whispered, trying to sound stern, before chugging a glass of water after tasting a chip with the hot salsa that came pre-meal.

Zeke ordered for the two while trying to explain to Atticus about Mexican cuisine. He then proceeded to open his purchase from the pharmacy and hand over a couple of the sleep aid tablets. Atticus hesitantly downed the pills with a glass of water followed by a few sips of an unfamiliar-sounding beverage. It was served in an oddly shaped, heavy glass, and was called a Margarita. After a stout drink for the greenhorn Atticus, and a substantial amount of Mexican food, the two were set to depart on the next leg of the trip. Zeke planned to drive all night to arrive in Miami by mid-afternoon. Or so he hoped. Armed with a bounty of cigarettes and coffee and hoping that his passenger would sleep as long as possible, at least through the night, a steady rain fell.

Zeke took a precautionary peek at his passenger, who was buried in the backseat under a horde of blankets, clothing, and food wrappers. It looked to Zeke that the sleep aids, washed down by a margarita, had worked.

Taking a glance at Atticus with his look of innocence, Zeke was reminded of his little brother, Thomas. However, Atticus was breathing softly, unlike the last time he saw Thomas, his sweet four-year-old brother, lying so peacefully with his hands folded prayer-like across his chest, not breathing in his casket.

To this day, Zeke would experience an emotional reaction when thinking back to the most horrible of days. Most times, he would tear up as he just did, one more grain of sand in an ocean of pain. Other times, his grief turned to anger, and he would smash something. Once, he broke his hand punching a car door.

It struck Zeke that his mission may be to accept Atticus as a foster brother, finish the work he had started with Thomas, and convey that dedication to Atticus.

"Who knows what all this means," he shrugged, shuddering from the cold, steady rain. Perhaps taking care of Atticus could be his salvation from the torment he had lived with for the past dozen years.

Certainly, Zeke knew that midnight was upon them and they still had four hundred miles to go to Miami. He could not trust Atticus to help drive on the interstate with all the meds in his system. Zeke just prayed he would sleep until they arrived in Miami, then not wake up and start to cry for Gram's pancakes.

With wipers operating wildly, Zeke tried to keep his mind active, to focus on the task at hand. It occurred to him that he was a pull-over by a curious cop away from ending this journey and his freedom. "Never mind that crap, it's time to bisect the long-ass state of Florida. My man, Rey, awaits us with free passes to bliss and obscurity." Rain would bring with it the same harsh memories, whether he chose them to or not. He was uneasily resigned to living through 'the accident' for the infinitude of time. He knew he must; it was his destiny to bear that cross. Having Atticus wake up worked in his favor as he would at least be some companionship for the last three hours, even if he was still not talking much, still angry from his being carried away from the security of home and, of course, Gram's cooking.

Taken from the quiet hills of Kentucky to the cacophonous streets of Miami, Atticus was overcome by the honking taxis and pleading pan handlers. His stomach was burning from the unfamiliar food and drink from the late-night stop at the Mexican restaurant. Besides all the racket, Atticus was suffering emotionally from the lack of anxiety meds and the excessively long trip, in a stolen car, no less. There were many brown-skinned people, speaking different dialects of Spanish. Atticus faced the robust surge of the crowds, terrible smells, and stifling heat by concentrating on keeping up with the only person within 1,047 miles whom he knew.

Atticus had little recall of his life in the Chicagoland area. Most of his childhood was spent alone in his bedroom in the mansion. One faint memory was a trip to Chicago on a bitterly cold day, with the only warmth being his father's hand, to which he held tightly among the crowds on the busy streets.

Two pale and very young-looking boys, sadly haggard and oddly dressed for such a trendy location, stood at the entrance of a posh café searching the crowd for Zeke's contact. With much relief, he spotted Rey Jindal at an isolated beachfront table working an expensive looking phone. Zeke's tense demeanor changed dramatically as the former student and school administrator turned compadres embraced warmly.

"Hola, amigo!" The greeting in smooth Spanish came from the familiar deeply-tanned face. Rey returned to his seat, comfortably dressed, and sporting impressive-looking bling and designer shades.

"So, this is the young man you told me of?" Rey questioned Zeke while examining Atticus, who looked overwhelmed as he compiled a list in his head of things he had found appalling thus far.

When a carafe of Cuban coffee arrived at the table, Atticus greeted the aroma with a multitude of grimaces; he acted like he was going to die from the pungent smell. Trays of Cuban delicacies arrived, eliciting a nauseating moan from Atticus. He refused to eat the foreign food before him. Rey, fearing he might be on the verge of witnessing a hunger strike, ordered up some American-style hot wings, which Atticus ferociously devoured.

"He will be alright, Rey," Zeke read correctly Rey's observation of Atticus and his distinct mannerisms. Not sounding all that convincing, Zeke added, "I will be there every step of the way with him and guarantee you that he will be fine."

"Hey man, remember I spent three years around you and know that you are not always right," Rey smiled nervously.

Zeke was impressed at what his former mentor had accomplished. "Tell me, Rey, how did you do all this in such a short time?"

"After leaving the boring confines of nowhere Indiana, I lucked out by getting hooked up back here in sunny Florida. I sort of fell into this opportunity in South Beach. My father always wanted to live on the beach, and now I'm doing it, and I am loving it. I recruit internationally for workers for the cruise lines and other entities here and off-shore. The pay is very good, and the perks are incredible, as you can see."

Rey looked around laughing, arms spread, using the café and the young ladies parading around in scant clothing over fit-tanned bodies as an illustration of his unique work environment.

While Atticus was finishing his plateful of wings, Rey pulled Zeke away from the table to explain more in private. "You know you mean a lot to me, especially with what we accomplished at J.T. Boe."

As he was prone to do, Zeke countered quickly, "Yeah, maybe so, but I made you a lot of money, and I saved your ass by taking the hit for you for that, ahh, little controversy the school tried to tie you to."

"I know you did, man, and I do appreciate it. That's why I did what I did for you and for your friend here," Rey added with a sincere bow.

"You will work together on cruise liners for as long as you need, make some money, keep a low profile; just keep your nose clean."

Rey handed over a binder filled with false documents for Zeke and his strange companion, who looked like a deer in headlights, tagging along closely with Zeke but never looking up. As promised, false ID cards were provided, and menial employment was procured by greasing the right person's palm on a soon to depart cruise liner for the two young men.

Rey explained that these jobs are customarily secure for one season of continuous excursions, up to a year. "You'll start out helping to prepare the ship for the next cruise, which requires a lot of long hours and plenty of elbow grease. You will be assigned a job. Maybe as a dishwasher or in housekeeping. If you're lucky, maybe a job as a concierge, where one's job is dedicated to catering to a select few overindulged passengers. I have you set up in a nice room near here for a couple of days, and some cash for necessities. Get some rest, get some clothes." Rey looked at the young men with disgust at their apparel, and tweaked his nose at their questionable hygiene. "Keep an eye on your boy there, and since I get a portion of your salaries, stay out of trouble. You can be rewarded for satisfactory reviews with an upgrade, like having your own quarters and not having to sleep in a galley full of indigent workers."

The flight to freedom concluded with a dramatic finale as Atticus unexpectedly stood at the end of the world, or so it seemed to the stunned twenty-one-year-old as he stared at the endless indigo-colored body of water. He realized he was beholding the mighty Atlantic Ocean!

Atticus remembered another visit near his home with his father to the shore of Lake Michigan, the Indian word for Big Lake. Recalling that moment of many years earlier surprised him for a chilling moment. He remembered it being a painfully cold day as the north east wind, called the hawk by the locals, nearly froze his small body; but his father's large, warm hand erased the bitter feeling.

Now, with calculations skipping about his head as he stared across the vastness of the ocean, Atticus understood how people once thought the world was flat. Reality was that beyond the horizon, thousands of miles away, around 6,400 miles Atticus quickly calculated, lay Africa.

If staring in awe at the ocean for a few minutes was not spectacular enough, the next encounter blew away the two young men from Kentucky. Steps around the corner of the pier from the marvelous view, Zeke and Atticus were now beholding a behemoth sight!

Sitting silently in the warm water, stretching out to one thousand feet, and weighing over 200,000 gross tons, was a very large cruise ship. Atticus was quick to look up at the ship and count 14 decks high and strongly whispered to Zeke, *"I can't work on no ship. I hate heights, I don't like crowds, I hate water."*

Fortunately for the buoyant Zeke, he was able to secure some anti-anxiety meds from Rey for his traveling companion, and hopefully, Atticus would soon be up for the challenge of becoming a member of the ship's crew.

This was not how Zeke had envisioned Rey to hook him up. He coveted Rey to have put him up in Miami Beach, where it would be sun and sand, fast women, and fast cars to fulfill his stay, while things cooled off back home. However, hiding out on a cruise ship for a couple of months could be even sweeter.

"How hard can this be?" Zeke wondered to himself, "This is a floating hotel, all the food and drink one can handle, gorgeous young women in bikinis, and there is money to be made. I sure can use some money. Maybe I'll be able to afford to lay up on one of these exotic islands we're going to anchor at during scheduled ports.

"Sure, that will mean staying on after this week of preparing the ship to venture out into the pristine waters of the Caribbean Seas. Yeah, I will have to break the news to the boy that we are signed up to turn in our work clothes for shiny, clean, pressed uniforms. By the looks of it, he will agree to anything. At this point, he has no choice, it's either sink or swim."

Zeke had to forcibly take the sluggish boy wonder by the arm, lead him up a waiting plank, then to the dark bowels of the ship where neither American knew what awaited them down below in the chilling darkness.

Meanwhile, Atticus was becoming testy again, and his irritability was rising with the scorching Miami heat. Pulling Zeke aside, Atticus started rattling off a list of important requests. *"I need to call my grandparents; I need to get out of this heat; it's making me sick. And I need to run. I haven't run in 72 hours."*

"Listen man," Zeke implored. "You can't call home just yet; they might be tracing all calls. Don't worry, and we'll soon be cruising on this hotel on water. I just read the brochure. There is plenty of a/c and food, man, there will be all you want There is even a running track on the ship, so you will be able to get your runs in. You can't run now because I'm in no condition to go chasing after your ass. So, sit tight, we will soon be living the life of kings." Zeke smiled, trying to ease Atticus's concerns.

"Zeke," Atticus whispered before Zeke returned to his contact. *"I can't go on no ship or be on no frickin' ocean. I'm afraid of water."*

Climbing the gangway, the runaways boarded the ship. Once inside, the foul-smelling lower deck swallowed the two new employees of the ocean liner *Adventures of the World*. Atticus staggered through the traffic of forklifts, workers, and security of apparently every nationality. Ugly sounds of chaos only added to the intimidating atmosphere. Foreign languages intermingled with the stench of bleach, chlorine, and stale garbage.

Atticus, fearing being grabbed out of line to work around the cause of the disgusting smell, stuck closely to Zeke for his own safety. Ironically, Zeke was the one responsible for him being in this mess.

CHAPTER 18

"People destined to meet will do so, apparently by chance, at precisely the right moment."

– Ralph Waldo Emerson

Zeke was the spokesman for the duo as they checked in at the designated table set up to verify identification, work, and living quarters assignments. Additionally, they queued up at the medical room where the physicals were done fast track style.

This last process brought a level of concern for Zeke as Atticus would be separated from him for a while. Hopefully, he would not freak out and disclose to the medical staff that he was there against his own will; then, all this maneuvering would be for naught.

Both men were given quantities of *Dramamine* for dreaded seasickness since they were new to the high seas. Descending further below the water line, steep steel stairs led the pair to the crew area, where they would eat, sleep, and live.

How the hard-to-please Atticus would react to the astonishing conditions, which were far removed from the comforts of his home in Kentucky, was to be seen.

With the ship docked at its assigned pier for a three-day turnaround, the layover was considered a good-news vs. bad-news blessing for new hires like Atticus and Zeke. The good news being that, with the ship temporarily docked, it allowed those personnel that were just returning from a cruise on sometimes rough seas to recapture their equilibrium and their land legs. For new employees like Zeke and Atticus, it was an important opportunity to learn the ship and its intimidating enormity.

The meds helped make Atticus into a more comfortable, less self-indulgent, more seaworthy shipmate. Zeke managed to acquire access to the ship-top running track for Atticus. Getting the longtime runner to utilize this procurement was a challenge. The long trek to the top deck of the ship, the wind speed at this elevation and the view of the dangerous water below made Atticus balk at first glance. As he studied the proportions and layout of the track, his curiosity and excitement grew. After the first hundred yards he was off and running.

Preparing the ship and crew for its next voyage into the pristine blue waters of the Caribbean Sea was a daunting task. Drills were repeated until the basic maneuvers became second nature. Key for most employees was to laboriously get the ship ready for departure and learn their assigned jobs amongst the noise and sweltering heat with the ship's A/C down for repair. Work was grueling for the new pair from the more laid-back and tranquil back country of Kentucky. Hours were long and food was sparse.

With the skill of a spokesman for a sure thing, Zeke, after bunking with a group of men from the Philippines, was able to say the right things to the crew's labor leader. He and Atticus were noticeably more comfortable in the tight quarters of their own tiny cabin. He had been unsettled by the others' constant chatter on their phones and to each other in their strange languages.

How could the mass confusion of overhauling the cruise ship evolve into the finely-tuned, immaculate, seaworthy floating resort? With a combination of exhaustion after a string of grueling twelve-hour work days and excitement over the impending departure date for the revamped ship's maiden voyage.

Reggae music playing at a volume near blaring level annoyed Atticus. He was trying to keep his focus as he stood before the buffet's abundance of piping hot pickings. The young man's ravenous appetite had not waned since boarding the ship.

"Better load up with the carbs, mate," a young Filipino man with long hair and an oddly heavy Australian accent, politely yelled to Atticus behind him in line over the loud music. "Heard that once we load and head out, the food is lacking as they concentrate, understandably, on catering to the passengers."

With loaded plates, the two found themselves at the same table to eat their bounty. "I'm Arthur," said the slight man as he extended his hand. "I play in one of the ship's two resident bands. Unlike the other band that plays the locally popular Reggae music, we play rock-and-roll. We cover the band, Journey; perhaps you have heard of them?" Not waiting for Atticus to put his fork down for a moment to reply, the Filipino continued as he speared another piece of fried shrimp from his plate. "I'm the lead singer; I'm our Steve Perry. I do pretty well if I do say so myself."

Talking was not Atticus's preference, especially when he was concentrating on his meal. While he paused from shoveling food into his mouth, he peered about for Zeke, who would hopefully take the cue and return the conversation with the stranger sitting across from him, and probably relish it.

After the more than plentiful meal, finished without Zeke's annoying company, Atticus left for a quieter area as Arthur, the singer, found a more receptive audience.

He found a remote, shaded spot, thankfully with no one around, while on the level below the open deck was filling up with countless workers ready to revel in the party. Having enjoyed a lengthy run on the deserted and sparkling clean track on the upper level, Atticus recalled the decadent feast that would be available throughout the evening. He parked his tired, thin body on a chaise lounge and quickly succumbed to his first nap in an utterly long time. Sleep came to Atticus before he could again dwell on the unreal turn of events that had landed him on this farfetched expedition, a trip that would test his continued existence. His faraway sleep was aided by the calm sea, while the muffled, rhythmic beat soothed Atticus into submission.

Despite the shade covering his still-pale body, his skin was quite warm in the mid-day heat. Unnerving droplets of cold water turned the peacefully content Atticus into an awakened beast. Jumping up from his sanctuary of the last hour into an inferno of rage, with arms flailing and fists clenched, he swung at the culprit and just missed the ducking Zeke.

"Hey man, easy now," Zeke shouted, startled at this outburst by his normally meek companion. Young Atticus shook his head to clear a flashback from a childhood experience of abuse. With head down, he slowly walked away, embarrassed by his outburst. The cold water had awakened him from a needed nap and roused a bad dream from a distant past. Zeke was quick to stop him, "Hey man, don't worry about it, my bad. I shouldn't have startled you like that, sorry. Hey I know what. Let's go back to the cabin and chill, then we'll clean up. Tonight's going to be a p-a-r-t-y!"

The more Zeke indulged in alcohol, mixing with his ADHD meds and boredom, and the more his impulsive tendencies kicked in, the more he was prone to irrational and stupid conduct. He had been forced to give his charge, Atticus, more rope since they joined the ship, but he always strained to keep himself focused and to know where Atticus was at all times.

Their jobs had been assigned so they would work together initially. Now Zeke, thanks to his quirky negotiating skills, had maneuvered his way into a larger cabin for the two because of his new position. With the tricks he picked up being on the streets at such an early age and the exclusive lessons passed on by his mentor, Rey Jindal, at the private boy's school, Zeke was already a polished hustler.

Before taking his turn in the shower, Zeke left Atticus some homework, breaking out the new employee manual, an array of complimentary toiletries, and the all-encompassing handbook.

Engrossed with his assignment, Atticus studied the basics of seafaring and the ship's vital information. He especially was pleased with the challenge of memorizing all the ship's levels and other important particulars of the giant vessel.

When Zeke reappeared, he noticed Atticus fumbling with a pack of complimentary prophylactics. "You know what those are?" With no reply from Atticus forthcoming, Zeke volunteered, "They're condoms, you know, rubbers, dude."

Atticus didn't waste any time countering with an *"I know, I've read about them, they stop you from getting sick from sex."*

Getting back to the welcome bag, Zeke continued with a dissertation on sex education. "Just as important as this being a health aid, when used properly, these can prevent one from making unwanted babies. Have you ever been with a girl?"

"Sure, I have. I had a girlfriend named Sophia, we kissed once, and it was okay."

With a sly grin, Zeke offered up, "Let me show you another use for them, as he headed back into the very small bathroom. Returning to Atticus with a hand behind his back, Zeke produced one of the condoms filled with water. He tossed it to Atticus, which burst tsunami-like upon contact with his hands, causing Zeke to laugh with gusto at the drenched recipient. His laugh was contagious, and before long, Atticus joined in the fun. Wearing their party clothes, they were both soaked to the skin. They made a stop at the huge staff laundry, stripped to their skivvies, and threw their outerwear into a dryer. A few minutes later, they donned their warm tropical shirts and stylish black cargo shorts to make their grand entrance to the already in progress festivities.

Atticus was tall and erect, with his hair becoming longer and straighter and his good looks causing heads to turn. Zeke, once again, was going through a change in appearance. His thinning hair was more prevalent, and there were the erratic beginnings of a beard and a youthful mustache. Their heights and builds were noticeably different. Atticus carried his lean, six-foot-plus frame stiffly, unlike the lithe, fluid motion he exhibited on the track. He ran with the graceful strides of a long-distance runner. Zeke was quite a bit shorter, though he seemed even shorter because of his much thicker frame and tough guy gait.

Atticus carried his head tilted down as if he was intentionally trying to go incognito. Zeke, on the other hand, despite his walk, held his head confidently, his shuffle becoming more of a swagger. Feeling comfortable in his fresh skin, Zeke circled the throngs of revelers for a little diversity in conversation and cheer.

With the last hour of the day's sunlight vanishing and feeling good about the success of the getaway, Zeke felt cocky enough to let his guard down and indulge. He rationalized that Atticus would harmlessly stay put in their cabin and watch some Spanish station on the room's cheap TV. As for his pledge to himself, his days as a petty thief were over. His newfound sobriety could wait another day.

Darkness had not clouded the party's exuberance nor reduced the number of those in attendance. In fact, the number of partygoers was on the rise, as if the open deck was letting more people in as walk-up patrons, which would be understandable if not for the fact that the hotel was a mile out to sea.

A refreshing sea breeze rose in intensity, sending a pinch of a cool feeling through the young American, the kind he felt when a thought of his father would surface. Atticus wandered back into the party in search of more food. After he ate his fill, he began a search for Zeke, who had the key to the cabin; it promised to be a challenge. He carefully snaked his way through the multinational crowd of people spewing a loud mixture of foreign languages along with the background sound of Caribbean music. Finally, a well-lubricated Zeke was located playing blackjack at a portable gaming table set up on the jam-packed crew deck.

Securing the room key from Zeke would prove to be a challenging chore for Atticus, as he timidly tried to get Zeke's attention. He stood at the table where even his slurring speech was rapid. Zeke's disjointed appearance was that of a preacher addressing the small, disinterested congregation from his pulpit while fidgeting with his voluminous stack of chips.

In this case, the other four players were equally fast-speaking young men of Filipino descent. All players appeared to be having a grand time, even if there was a language difference. Finally, after waving off Atticus a few times, Zeke embraced his partner in crime, lent him the room key, and gave him a twenty-five-dollar chip.

"Here, man, why don't you have a good time? Gamble a little, dance a little – go talk to a girl or two – and dude don't wait up for me." Zeke winked, nodding at the pretty Oriental girl holding onto his arm, his eyes shadowed by an abundance of alcohol. "One more thing, kiddo," Zeke clumsily whispered close to Atticus' ear. "Watch what you say, Buddy, okay?"

Wearily, Atticus walked away and trudged over to a secluded area along the ship's edge overlooking the ocean's beauty. A shimmer of moonlight served as a picturesque beacon on the black water. Atticus could see a far-off flash of lightning light up a couple of hidden clouds in the amazing sky.

Behind the ship, late-night lights still shone brightly, illuminating where they had launched for this one-mile trial run, out from and back into, the port of Miami. Atticus did an about-face towards the cabin, but decided he would first re-visit the lure of fresh pizza, now the primary attraction in the food line.

"What are these, sir?" Atticus barely heard the question over the loud music. Instinctively, he slowly turned around but failed to look at whoever asked the question, and as usual, ignored talking to strangers. When the question was uttered once more, this time Atticus turned around to peek at where the question, spoken in a foreign accent, was coming from. He came eye to eye with a light-skinned girl. He didn't notice her short brown hair but was instantly mesmerized by an attractive pair of smoky grey eyes. "I ah, sorry," she politely apologized before pointing at some peppers next to the pepperoni. After that brief introduction, and unfamiliar with the peppers in question, Atticus dashed to an empty stool at a trash-filled table. Before he could bite into a slice of pizza, he noticed the girl who had spoken to him circling the deck, obviously looking for a place to sit and eat. Seeing the kind American from the pizza bar, she meekly approached Atticus, which instantly sent his heartbeat into a gallop.

"Someone sit here?" she softly asked in broken English. After an awkward delay while he tried not to choke, he replied a shaky *"No."*

Standing up, Atticus offered his stool as he stole a glance at the pretty, lanky young lady while she quietly ate. Simultaneously, he recognized the performer taking the stage, singing about being faithful. He remembered something about what the bragging singer had said to him, "If you're trying to get lucky with a girl, ask her to dance when I sing a ballad." Atticus reminded himself that he had never danced with a girl, and right now was not the time to start. Before long, Atticus and the girl were quietly in irregular conversation. At least the young lady was speaking, while the uncomfortable twenty-one-year-old was concentrating on the mispronounced words coming from her mouth.

Nervously, Atticus walked over to a secluded area along the ship's edge overlooking the ocean's splendor, where Nina, the Ukrainian beauty, stood in silhouette beneath a shimmering moonlight. Serving as a picturesque beacon on the black water, Atticus caught sight of another dainty flash of lightning. Before long, as if by the hand of fate, two isolated individuals, one gregarious, one subdued, started to connect emotionally.

Sunrise emerged as an early wake-up call for countless stragglers from the previous night's revelry. There would be some personnel waking up to a stranger next to them or, better yet, a former stranger;

they now shared intimacy as did Atticus and his companion of the previous night – Nina.

The next thing Atticus remembers is waking up with a female, not any female, but Nina, the effervescent young lady from Ukraine. There would be no rush to wake up from this dream, nor would there be any desire to erase this dream from his mind.

Standing menacingly over him, Zeke was shaking Atticus to life with the zest of one who could not believe what he was seeing.

"Hey man," hollered Zeke, "Hey man, I've been looking all over for you. I had to get someone from housekeeping to let me in the cabin. Lo-and-behold, you weren't there and who the hell is this?" His attention was directed at the pretty girl pulling a sheet up over her face.

Zeke was speechless for once, reacting like a parent, discovering their teenager in a compromising position with a boyfriend or girlfriend. After a couple of minutes to compose himself, Zeke was ready to continue. But it was Atticus, the silent one, who commandeered the discussion.

"We talked most of the night, then she wanted to have sex, and so did I, I guess. I forgot about the water balloons. I hope she doesn't get too sick. It started when she kissed me, and I kissed her back."

"Okay, okay. T.M.I! That's more information than I need to know," Zeke stated firmly through a sick grimace.

"Say goodnight, I mean good morning, to your friend here, and come on, we have a busy day. There is a lot to clean up and supplies to store before the first passengers come aboard in a couple of days," Zeke mumbled, motioning towards scattered trash along the deck. Partygoers were still strewn around the deck, passed out on chaise lounges.

After a short goodbye to Nina and an awkward kiss on her cheek, Atticus Carlisle, with a spring to his walk and a hung-over Ezequiel

"Zeke" Callahan, headed from their cabin into the next chapter in the unlikely voyage. For the two who, despite their chaotic beginning and seemingly huge practical differences, were entering into a fused relationship.

Finishing up early on the second day meant another free day. Zeke, with some hesitation, left Atticus aboard the vessel with the ever-present Nina. Unable to spend his last time off with his own newfound friend, Zeke was doubly crabby, having to keep watch on his charge – Atticus. However, he did find a bit of comedic entertainment watching Nina try to teach Atticus how to swim, "That boy will never learn to swim; he has no buoyancy, cracked up Zeke to himself behind dark glasses.

After a rocky first day at sea, the ship docked at the busy port of Costa Maya, Mexico. Zeke was able to make a run into town to pick up supplies for himself and Atticus, who had Zeke acting like a worried parent. They were going to spend their few hours off while the tourists oohed-and-aahed, exploring some beautiful sights on the island. Zeke was growing wary of the pretty Ukrainian girl with grey eyes that would cause any mortal's heart to flutter.

Funds were at a minimum until their first paychecks were received. There was enough for, besides the essentials, a couple of cheap bottles of rum for Zeke to use to barter in exchange for some warm beer. For Atticus, it was some hair gel for his increasingly long hair and prophylactics. For what? Zeke didn't want to think about it. "Maybe he wants to throw water balloons with the Ukrainian girl," Zeke grumbled.

"Man, I can't believe we're having this discussion," Zeke said to Atticus with exasperation. "First of all, you just met her. You don't know her. Maybe she wants to get married to get into the States, to become a citizen. Ever think of that? Plus, you can't get married, you can't use your real name. You can't get married as Carlos or whatever your phony ID says.

"But we want to get married when we finish this next trip – besides, the captain can marry us. Nina asked and…"

"Okay. Look out over here." Zeke led Atticus to the crew deck railing and pointed out into the ocean, "See there? This big-ass ocean? There's more fish in that sea; you don't have to marry the first girl that comes along and gives you a little."

Atticus defiantly walked away and headed up for a run before stopping to yell back at Zeke, *"Then I want to go home and take Nina with me, and we'll get married there at the farm."*

Zeke watched as Atticus accelerated up the stairway, frustrated by the whole babysitting scene, having to watch his fellow fugitive as if he were a child. Now that Atticus had become much more vocal, Zeke felt he had to be more careful of who Atticus spoke to. "I liked him better when he didn't talk." Zeke shook his head and stared out onto the green water of the port area.

"Water, water everywhere; I'm tired of the same shit. I want to see some land, for Christ's sake. I'm tired of being anyone's keeper, let alone this guy who has so many issues. Now he wants to get married? I need to do something and do it fast."

The voice on the other end of the phone was calming to Zeke's flustered tone. After Zeke gave his friend Rey the low-down on his predicament with Atticus and his Ukrainian girlfriend, a resolve appeared to be forthcoming.

Rey would send word back in a couple of days. "Well, you're in luck, my friend. I made some calls, and I was able to get the young lady flipped to another ship when you guys get to Cozumel tomorrow. She will be united with other Ukrainians and will get a healthy raise for her troubles, so she'll be alright. Now, about your boy. I've received good reports on the two of you. I hope this doesn't interfere with you guys keeping up the good work; it means a lot to me and my services."

With some reservations, Zeke mentally prepared for the maneuvering to happen and then dealt with the expected pained reaction from the love-struck Atticus.

"If I see one more pair of dirty undies or another unflushed toilet, I'm going to puke," Zeke shouted out to Atticus, who either could not hear over the vacuum cleaner or chose to ignore him as usual.

"I'm tired of this crap, literally!" continued Zeke as he hesitantly started to wash the mini cabin commode. After the tiny room had been cleaned to the pair's required timed completion, Zeke spotted a shiny gold ring on a corner table. The ring was an immediate enticement, the likes of which he had not been tempted before on this job. Unfortunately, he could find no reason to resist the overwhelming urge. Zeke knew from experience it was futile to resist the impulse.

"Seven minutes and forty seconds, close door," announced Atticus without emotion. This was his role when the two worked together in housekeeping. Atticus seemed to feed off the standard allotted time; it fed into his OCD, and it consumed much of his time now that he and Zeke were paired in their new work detail. This assignment was fine with Zeke, for he relished the quiet as he readied himself for some side action.

When the home office of the cruise line was notified via radio reports of multiple complaints from passengers upon the conclusion of their cruise about missing expensive pieces of jewelry, an immediate investigation was launched. Thefts from passenger cabins lead to horrible consequences for the company.

Usually, these incidents were isolated and explained away when the reported missing item turned up. Revealing to the lead investigator, however, was how the names of a duo cleaning team seemed to raise a red flag. Accompanying photos showed two young men, neither of whom looked Hispanic as their names would suggest.

In fact, the two seemed to resemble each other despite one appearing wild-eyed and nervous and the other almost unresponsive. Possibly medicated? But they were almost as white as the towels they delivered to the cabin, not like men of color. Unfortunately, this was not surprising as many foreign, or, in this case, American workers in the cruise liner business carried falsified identification. Having worked in security for various ocean liners, the investigator knew what steps needed to be taken to expedite a resolution to this case.

Good police work? Or a stroke of good luck? Either way, normal surveillance of Zeke and Atticus on the following cruise produced almost immediate results.

With the first port-of-call came the rush of oily human flesh to various excursions for the day at port. Among the throngs of departures from the ship was Zeke, who bypassed all taxis and sight-seeing opportunities. Instead of hitting the beach or visiting one of the many historical sights, he headed by foot to the less attractive nearby downtown section and its array of shops, bars, and pawn brokers. Zeke picked a bad time to leave Atticus aboard the ship, unlike the last time he left him with Nina, the departed. This time, he was alone in his running. His swim lessons with Nina were over, so there was no reason to go to the pool. Zeke had reminded Atticus that there was to be no mingling with anyone he didn't recognize, no more falling in love. After pawning the two rings he appropriated on the last cruise, Zeke found the nearest tavern to the port area and proudly rewarded himself for his first theft since swearing off such indiscretions. His growing thirst for disobedience was served, and he could return to the ship with much-needed cash and, once again, for the lost count of time, a vow to abstain from this lifestyle.

Human Resources review of the findings of the question of theft on their cruise liner showed that a theft occurred on at least two cruises and that the parties culpable for the crimes were Zeke and Atticus, aka Jose Hernandez and Carlos Fernandez, respectively, as both men claimed on their obviously fake identification cards.

Having been interviewed separately, it was decided that the liner would indeed charge the one who talked a lot of nonsense, and claimed to be crazy, with theft after finding his toiletry bag contained, among multi-packs of condoms, a diamond ring, like the one on file as reported missing from a passenger. With evidence in hand, he admitted to picking up the jewelry off the carpeted area so as not to accidentally vacuum up the gem.

His partner seemed oblivious to any theft from any of the rooms that were cleaned by the pair. *"I was only worried that we did a room in seven minutes and forty seconds from the time that we got into a room to when we closed the door."*

In fact, Atticus swore to not knowing much about the pair's personal activities and seemed mentally challenged. With agreements detailed to the authorities at the port of Belize, the pair would be discharged at that time, and Zeke would be held so the American authorities could check to see if he was wanted in the States.

Atticus would be sent on his way with his backpack, little money, no job, and now no Zeke. Being escorted from the ship was traumatic as the two were led in separate directions to different twists of fates. The only words spoken by Zeke or Atticus was a strange statement from Zeke, turning to Atticus with an intense, almost-convincing stare. "Stay strong, man; I will find you; I will get you home." The four heavily armed policemen, with their rifles held high, walked Zeke to his next fate while Atticus sat on a bench waiting as instructed for someone to pick him up and return him home. With one last harrowing glance, Atticus caught a painful glimpse of Zeke being loaded into a yellow police van, and confused, he wondered if he'd ever see that wicked person again.

He was also relieved that it wasn't him in handcuffs to be locked up at the other place.

"Where am I? This has to be a dream! I am sitting under a coconut tree where I slept fitfully last night between munching on unripe fruit. I am over 2,500 miles from home. All I have is the clothes that I'm wearing, plus a work uniform. I have a few dollars in my backpack, with lots of notes and a pencil that is nothing more than a point. I am also out of paper and writing this on a piece of cardboard that I pulled out of the street trash can.

"I am staring out across a huge amount of water; my calculations tell me I'm looking at the Caribbean Sea. I hate water! The idiot who got me here sits in jail across the bay. I do not know where to go. The police who released me said I should go to the U.S. embassy, then they locked the gates behind me. What a concept: getting locked out of jail. My very first impression of Belize was it is an old port city full of activity. Street vendors and panhandlers were at the ready for tourists tendered from the magnificent ship "Adventures of the World." Though no white beaches were evident, it still carried some old colony attractions. I was more concerned with why I was being taken off the ship along with Zeke. It must be something bad he did; if so, they will just send him to prison because he's dangerous and send me home because I am innocent.

"I am tired of being scared, of being in a strange place where people look and speak differently than I am used to. I tried calculating how far I am from home and came up with a figure of approximately (I hate not having an exact total) 2,500 miles, give or take a hundred. There is a huge body of water - the Gulf of Mexico - between here and the United States. If I run fifty miles a day, the equivalent of two marathons a day, it would take me a couple of months to get home. Plus, I would have to run through Mexico, where I would probably meet up with bandits who would cut me up alive for my money. A crazy couple of weeks ago (336 hours ago), I was working peacefully on a pair of horseshoes, and suddenly Lucifer showed up and took me away from the calmness of the central United States to the confusion of Central America!"

CHAPTER 19

*"Belize draws the eccentric, the madcap, and the
downright mad."*

— Unknown

ourists and careless vendors with a disregard for cleanliness somehow helped Atticus find a job. Their poor manners led to ever-present trash and were partly responsible for Atticus being offered a cleanup job by an odd-looking stranger who was standing out front of a sleazy-looking bar. His luck seemed to turn when he was subsequently offered the position of dishwasher, which soon grew to include janitor and busboy, for the couple of weeks left before the tourist season slowed. Included with the pay would be a room in a neighboring village. Atticus found out that a substantial portion of his pay was taken out for rent.

Still, having stumbled onto a job hours after being unceremoniously removed from the still-docked ship offshore, seemed fortunate. He figured he better make some money. Enough to get home, in case Zeke didn't come back for him as promised, which seemed likely considering his predicament. The room, in the meantime, was a ten-minute run away, ideal for the American running enthusiast. Plus, how hard can washing a few dishes, wiping off some tables, and cleaning floors be? It had to be easier than working on the cruise ship.

Then there was the coup de grace; he could eat to his heart's content of the bar's delicious-smelling food. Yes, things might be looking up. Even an overhead group of playful-looking hawks seemed to be circling in a friendly manner, another good sign or so thought young Atticus Carlisle. He was well aware his paranoia always lurked nearby, waiting impatiently to surface its ugliness at a moment's notice.

He reasoned that this temporary arrangement was necessary, seeing that the only other option, asking for help at the U.S. Embassy, was risky. What if they turned him over to the local police, who had roughly escorted both him and Zeke from the dock to the nearby jail? He wondered what would happen to him if he was locked up in this faraway, dangerous place. Forever? Unfortunately, the Sunset Bar and Grill was in as sketchy a place as possible.

Sounding every bit like a drill instructor on steroids, the bizarre-looking man barked out his instructions. "The first thing you do is fasten the chicken's neck onto this special cutting board." The jovial man instantly turned evil-looking as his hand came down with a swift chop from a hatchet that looked quite small in his large hand. And the head of another unsuspecting chicken rolled into a bloodied barrel. With a hint of evil and indifference in his booming voice, the lesson to his new co-worker continued.

"We then scald it for five minutes." A wicked grin formed on the large man's red face as he continued. "Then we place what's left into this wonderful contraption." The man proudly pointed to the apparatus, which resembled a large bingo drum, its overused crank hanging by a thread. "It will pluck most of the feathers off the chicken's carcass like this." A few minutes later, he proudly held up the featherless figure, which resembled a gag rubber chicken. "Then booya! Clean as a whistle and ready to fry."

Atticus Carlisle had met the anti-Christ, and his name was Mutha, a behemoth of a man. His white hair was tied back, and he wore what looked like a once-white tarp as an apron. It was covered with blood splatters and looked as though he had gotten the worst in a paintball fight.

"It is named after yours truly: Mutha. It's a Mutha Plucker. Get it?" Practically hollering, Mutha had made his point to his trembling assistant. Turning serious, he readied the hatchet for another strike, thus, the disgusting introduction for the young American to his foul assignment. Sickening as the brutal operation was, there were more disgusting jobs to be done, like cleaning out the gross septic tank at the Sunset Bar and Grill in the heart of Belize City, Belize. He had been assigned that morning to work with the freak called Mutha, a huge departure from his daily job of busboy, dishwasher, and general cleanup, which he had been hired to do almost three weeks prior. Meanwhile… swat! Another unfortunate chicken lost its head for the sake of someone's desire for a fine meal. Atticus quickly turned away from the carnage with disgust when he heard the large man squeal like a child. He turned in time to see a headless chicken dance around in panic. Mutha's laugh returned as he pointed at the frantic escapee. He seemed to amuse himself as he pressed on wickedly; at the same moment, a green tint appeared across the horrified face of his new punk assistant as the mound of chicken heads grew, their dead eyes appearing wider and wider.

"There will be no dancing around in their future. I've been at this job for a long time, and I've seen my share of chickens run around after chopping off their head. There was one that ran into the bar while the bar was full of tourists. They have nerves throughout their bodies which keep their muscles moving even without their heads. Hell, there have been reports of chickens living days, weeks, even months afterward." Mutha gave a sly grin as he paused a minute before continuing his irksome dialogue. "Whew, it's hot," he said, looking up at the sky, "this how it was when we got hit with the big one.

"Yes, it was ten years - almost to the day. A front had stalled over the nearby Caribbean Sea, sending a damaging hurricane here, a direct hit! That's pretty much right where you're standing. It was awesome, man.

"There is danger here; people think this is paradise; well, it can be hell, too. Not long ago, there was a major earthquake in Haiti. Now Haiti's a thousand miles out to sea. The earthquake triggered a massive tsunami. I remember the wave as high as that large tree outside. You can't outrun a tsunami. You have to get to high ground before it hits. We also were affected by a volcano eruption a few years ago that was on St. Vincent, TWO thousand miles away, and we still got hit by tons of ash. Now that was crazy. Hundreds of chickens could be seen in outlying areas covered with ash – choking to death."

With these disturbing tales said, a soothing melody rang out from the bells at the old courthouse nearby, announcing the welcoming midday break. Craving for the arrival of high noon with urgency, Atticus fought a boiling case of nausea. As an avid long-distance runner, the young American knew about pace when he ran competitively or for pleasure. This situation called for an all-out dash, much to the delight of veteran employees of the bar, who were beginning their break as well. Their game of dominoes was suspended at the sight of the American who had exited the back area in an extreme hurry. This could only mean one bloody thing to the bar's staff, who had seen this display before. The skinny American had been exposed to *El Loco,* better known as Mutha, and his crazy chicken-plucking machine and his stories of impending doom.

In fact, at barely over three hours, this young man had lasted longer than most after venturing into the assassin's den. The locals had seen it all, even once seeing a busboy chased through the bar by a headless chicken, spewing blood as it ran before succumbing to the loss of its body's lifeline. A couple of side bets were made by the veterans watching Atticus's sickly scramble, even wagering on whether the American would return after the lengthy lunch break. They continued watching with amusement and lightly muffled laughter as the American sprinted out the open end of the three-walled Adobe building.

It felt to Atticus that he was beating the reggae music coming from the jukebox out the door as the familiar, happy beat faded from his ears. In desperation mode, Atticus was forced to do something that was highly unusual of him - he had run past Max, his only ally at the bar and, for that matter, in all of Belize City. The dark-skinned teen with an expansive midriff was happily manning the grease-stained gas grill, which would be discharging intense sounds and smells throughout the busy weekend. Looking like the person who had spent too much time at the buffet line, Max left mounds of cooking bacon, performing its irresistible and seductive wiggling on the grill, to mistrustful co-workers to mind as he hurried after Atticus with his hands full of sizzling bacon, straight from the jaws of the red-hot grill. Max left a trail of hot bacon grease until he caught up to Atticus, who looked like he was executing a prayer service to the crumbling asphalt in the alley while making terrible sounds, trying hard to vomit away the foul intestinal pain. Atticus appeared well beyond help anytime soon. Max walked away feeling bad for his new friend as he wolfed down perfectly done greasy bacon.

Sitting squarely at the wrong end of the well-being range, Atticus painfully kneeled, head-in-hands, after suffering through a nasty case of dry heaves which had produced little in the way of any physical relief; he felt hopeless and lost. With his backpack under his pounding head, Atticus succumbed to the darkness of forced slumber. Just as he had done so many times in his life growing up in anguished surroundings with a horribly cruel mother and an equally evil sister. Then there was the other place and its parade of terrifying residents. Sleep was a last resort, a true but too brief of a reprieve. As he dozed off, he mumbled a promise to himself that he would not return to the swamp known as the *Sunset Bar and Grill.*

> *"There I was, swaying gently on a heavenly hammock under two giant oak trees on the farm. It was a breezy day with clear blue skies, a perfect setting for a comfortable nap. Gramps was clearing some overgrown brush around his old blacksmith shop; he was going to teach me how to make horseshoes. I was excited about that. Grams was making to-die-for blueberry pancakes. After breakfast, I would be picking more blueberries from the vines growing along the fence line. Hey, what is that wonderful smell? It had to be Gram's apple pie, for which she was famous around these parts, won her a blue ribbon at the county fair one year. And there was the wonderful aroma of bacon. Wonderful bacon.*

> *"I was rudely awakened from this delicious dream, immediately resuming the disgusting feeling in my stomach. I was back to reality, and I did not like it one bit."*

His eyes opened wide; his thin body was drenched in sweat. Atticus shook out the cobwebs from his defensive doze. Unlike the deception his nap had produced, he really was smelling something wafting from the bar. What he wasn't expecting was to find Max's smooth, round face greeting him, inches away from his own face.

"G'day, mon, I was just checking to see if ye was still alive." Max seemed amused by the circumstance at hand, while Atticus instantly recalled that he was in the alley to throw up that morning's experience with the bloodthirsty Mutha. His wonderful daydream was not real but a reprieve from this morning's horrible episode. The nap had not erased the earlier events from his erratic memory but had hit pause on the real-time phenomena.

"Come on, mon, ye got to get back to work soon, get ye some food first. Get yourself together, mon; we got a busy time ahead, ye hear?" Max smiled widely, showing off an impressive set of pearly whites and speaking his hard-to-understand-lingo, which he described as a combination of Haitian and Jamaican Creole, Spanish and the national language of English.

"I'm not going back, I frickin' quit!" Atticus stated defiantly, with his voice rising to almost a normal level. He rose, wobbly gathered his meager belongings, and began to walk away

"Hold on, mon, ye can't quit. We need ye! Ye are the best worker we got. We got big ships coming in, anyway; how ye gonna make 'nuff money to get home if ye quit? I told the Boss Man ye need time to recover, and he agreed!

"He says ye take another hour to recuperate. Here are some bacon sandwiches; eat up and go for a run. I've made sure ye don't have to work with that *pendejo* anymore; ye will just work with *moi*."

Max seemed proud of his gesture of kindness as well as his ability to throw both a French and a Spanish word into his speech. Atticus was puzzled by the young local with dreads and a gift for gab with whatever language he spoke.

Max had come through for him before, which led Atticus to trust him enough recently to take him up on a questionable offer of room and board if Atticus would get him a job at the popular *Sunset Bar and Grill.* That arrangement had worked out for Atticus financially compared to the deplorable room that had come with the present menial job at the seedy bar. That room had proved costly, with the bar's Boss Man keeping half of his pay for the revolting lodging. Now, he once again had some money built up; it was a small amount, but if anyone else tried to take it from him, they'd have to kill him for it!

The perplexing quandary facing the immature American was whether to trust Max further. Though it was just as appalling as the Boss Man's place, at least it didn't cost him anything. Despite Max's plea for him to return to work, Atticus remained steadfast. Still, there were things to consider. How was he going to get out of paradise and get home without money? Which meant he still needed employment.

Reevaluating his choices for the immediate future, whether to return to work inside the house of horror or not, it became clearer that he was not in a very good position to resist. Nevertheless, he mulled over his final sensible option of throwing himself to the mercy of the American embassy.

"Hey, I'm an American. I'm a little bit crazy and need help getting home to my Gramps and Grams." He figured he would need to plead his case clearly and with conviction.

However, he knew, or thought he knew, that he would sound stupid. He didn't know what it was like to speak publicly, or with conviction. Seeking help at the embassy had a downside. What would happen if he was sent to a prison here in Belize? Atticus knew he could not risk that. He would not or could not endure being locked up again, especially in a foreign land where the dreadful unknown awaited him.

No, he had to try the conventional manner. He would continue working at the notorious *Sunset Bar and Grill.*

CHAPTER 20

"I have so much information stored up inside my brain that to add more, I need to clean out my mind's cache once in a while."

– James Hauenstein

"My mind is like a busy highway, traffic darting in and out, horns blaring, motors accelerating, stop and go. It is often very difficult to comprehend or concentrate. When I can settle the congestion down, it is manageable.

"But when there is too much going on in my head, that is when I get confused. That is why I write things down and hope I can find my notes later. That is why I worry that I will…I fear that I will forget my way home to my grandparents; that would be my end."

With a declining show of contempt, Atticus was consumed with scratching irritably at some flecks of dried chicken blood on his tattered trousers and off-white t-shirt from his chicken-plucking duties as he resumed his whining.

"I'm not a frickin' feather plucker," he bemoaned out loud but as usual, so quietly that no one could hear him anyway. His yearning to return home to the farm was escalating toward panic with every dreadful minute. Two thousand seven hundred miles from home, or as the numbers wiz would instantly calculate 2,679 miles.

The quiet American continued muttering to himself, *"It's all that frickin' Lucifer's fault that I'm still here. I should be home in Kentucky before I forget all about Gramp's and his farm, my horseshoe business, and, of course, Gram's pancakes."*

He whispered continuously, just as he always had, in a manner that had begun as a troubled child in a period of solitary development. As time went on, he developed his monotone voice in a barely discernable manner. One of Atticus's first life lessons was that his freely spoken words were usually taken out of context and used against him. This paved the way for excessive bullying combined with a heartless amount of punishment and abuse. Self-help also meant practically teaching himself how to speak, read and write.

Under the security of musty blankets on a rigid bed by the light of his flashlight, the only gift he had ever received from his callous mother, a filthy flashlight, he taught himself to write and speak quietly, very quietly.

His sister, who was their mother's apprentice in evilness, had a bedroom next to Atticus. Lizzy would immediately report any sound emitting from the small boy's room in violation of a strict decree by the *Evil Queen,* a name that Atticus stuck on his mother at an earlier time.

These early torments paved the way to his developing the ability to expunge matters of great anguish to a place in his mind where it would lie dormant, never to be remembered, unless by some cruel happenstance. Then, it would intermittently rear its ugly head in the form of an unwelcome flashback.

CHAPTER 21

"To anyone suffering from MENTAL ILLNESS, you are one badass mother fucker because nothing is more terrifying than battling with your own mind every single day."

– Unknown

This example of short-term memory loss was once incorrectly described in a doctor's testimony as a ruse – an attempt to be deceitful, especially when he showed such skillful ability to recall calculations, dates, and facts that contain figures.

Episodic memory requires noting important facts, locations, and events. This procedure began at an early age for the isolated lad, leading him to begin keeping random memos, first in his head, then to compensate for memory lapses, on paper.

Ordinary napkins, many of the soiled variety, were his favorite stationery – easy to find and free. But he had developed a habit of jotting down daily happenings to remember them for more than a few minutes. His filing system was to stuff these notes chaotically in his ever-present backpack.

These valuable notes, about half of which were found under his mattress, were cruelly confiscated and destroyed as he was forced to watch. Undeterred, Atticus always resumed his writings, mostly for future reference, yet seldom remembered their context or sometimes their location.

Like his memory, which alternated from an uncanny episodic memory to a more commonplace short-term memory deficiency, Atticus struggled with the perplexity of a wide range of peculiarities in certain aspects of his special life.

He could impressively remember incidents that happened years ago, especially numerical data, but was fuzzy on the details of things that happened a few minutes prior. He possessed the gift of being able to recite facts and figures that he had briefly browsed. Or he could calculate a difficult problem. Or he could go a whole semester without once speaking to anyone, including his class teacher.

He wrote down the horror of his morning with Mutha, the Goliath of a man with a blood-dripping hatchet. Atticus was adept at wiping events from his explicit memory by concentrating incidents away. For the present, he wolfed down his bounty of bacon piled high on stale bread, a hopeful cure for his irritable stomach. An extended belch produced some internal relief despite its less-than-stellar quality. *"At least it was not a chicken sandwich,* Atticus whispered gratefully. *I will never eat chicken again!"*

"Take it easy with those; that's all there'll be until we get back to Miami," Atticus remembered Zeke's warning a while back. Now, with his decision to re-enter the shady establishment, Atticus ignored Zeke's final words to him and chose to self-medicate as a way to cool his burning anxiety. *"I have no choice but to take these final two pills, hopefully, it'll get me back on track."*

For as long as Atticus could remember, he was prescribed some type of wonder drug, which he nicknamed happy pills, or as it was described to him, as necessary psychiatric medications to curb a lengthy list of mental deficiencies. Among the list of specific, sketchily identified disorders were manic depression, schizophrenia, and bipolar disorder, along with a list of lesser-known conditions. It wasn't until right before his dreadful stay at the other place had mercifully ended that he received the most accurate psychological diagnosis of high-functioning autism.

As a lad, Atticus remembered little of his only trip to the farm. He had traveled with his father, Hank, to where he had grown up on his parents' farm. He did recall it was where his father introduced him to running. In fact, Atticus had jogged around the same track his father had run on as a boy. Atticus also recalled the farm was vastly different from his childhood home. The mansion in Wilmette was part of

Chicago's topography of concrete and steel. While the farm was ubiquitous to the lush, dark green landscape of Kentucky.

Try as he might, Atticus could not recall much else, and rather than take that as a good sign, he thought perhaps it meant there might be something bad there on the tranquil-sounding farm.

Later, Atticus's dark mood brightened to the extent that he began counting minutes, not weeks, days, nor even hours; no, he kept a running count of minutes away from his release, more than a dozen years later, back to his grandparents' farm, with an implausible promise of a real school, good food, and a place to run outside. That would really be awesome, he thought, allowing himself a rare optimistic thought for the sprouting almost sixteen-year-old.

Atticus had rarely left the confines of Rushing Hills Juvenile Detention Center as an isolated and confused pre-teen boy. He only had, a handful of times, been volunteered by underpaid personnel to attend a local mega-church. There he was introduced to a program for troubled youth that espoused to deliver them to redemption. The church's prominent theme appeared to be exposing the Devil for his evil deeds and his influence on unsuspecting youth.

> *"This is how I came up with the nickname for Zeke – Lucifer. I thought he reminded me of the stories I had heard of the Devil. I knew there was something evil about that guy. I also know that without him, I am stuck here in paradise, where I need him to find me more meds."*

"Great strides have been made," the doctor put in his report, "since his release from the facility that was his home for part of his youth. After becoming a dependent of his grandparents, he thrived academically and athletically in high school and then graduated on time. His imprudent opinion that his entering into adulthood was no big deal is of concern to the state. His source of income for independence has minimal hope for any impact. His financial future is a conundrum. Atticus's grandparents, sooner or later, will probably be outlived by their grandson, who will likely be unable to keep their farm as a viable entity. How will the young man who, due to, or because of his affliction, most likely remembers his early abuse, his anti-social behavior, thrive?"

> *"When the shriek of a circling hawk resounded in the quiet of another steamy tropical day, I had a moment. I was having second thoughts about not returning to work. Despite the sweltering heat and having recovered from my earlier attack of awful queasiness, chills emerged in every part of my tense body. This had happened before on the occasions when my path had crossed with spiritual encounters. Such was the case with the graceful bird overhead who suddenly swooped down, leaving a trail of unrecognizable cackle in his wake. He smoothly landed on a tree and gave me a sideways glance that I hoped meant he was with me and everything was going to be okay."*

"If only I could fly like a hawk," murmured Atticus, *"one who utilizes thermal energy to soar, and gravity to descend."* Atticus could see himself as a hawk, a solitaire figure, a bird that doesn't venture too far away but has been documented to have flown up to a thousand miles in a day. By then, he could very well have forgotten where the farm was. This possibility sent a shudder through his delirious soul, giving him an additional sense of desperation.

Atticus surmised that this hawk could very well be a guide of sorts, perhaps from a previous encounter.

Just then, a scream rang down from above. Atticus need not scan the skies for long as he quickly located the source of the distinct sound. It had to be a messenger with much-needed news of hope, not of more despair.

His father had shared stories of the life of the Plains Indians, which Hank Carlisle claimed was their native heritage, "as are all things living."

Atticus had been mesmerized by his father's tales of Indian lore. His favorite stories were those of the red-tailed hawk who, as legend has it, was a symbol of power. He had taught them to be aware of omens, visions, or messages from the Spirit. Ever since this revelation from his father, Atticus had been mindful and respectful of this magnificent bird. Currently, with his mind still reeling from its earlier negative mode, perhaps the hawk was delivering a message of hope. Or was it a warning of impending danger?

Atticus impatiently dumped the belongings from the backpack, looking for his remaining stash of meds. After consuming the final two "happy pills," he was ready to resume his menial job. It would be a long couple of days with the onslaught of travelers and revelers. It hit the still-gloomy twenty-one-year-old that this was the ugly truth, it was his destiny. Inexplicably, the hawk gracefully lifted off from his perch, once more elegantly flying away to a fresh destination.

Simultaneously, Atticus crept across the familiar cobblestone street, unlike his usual quickstep pace. His fate is obvious; he must follow the money and return to his job at the *Sunset Bar and Grill*. With little trepidation, he returned to his former position as a chief dishwasher, busboy extraordinaire, and, most importantly, bar stocker. After all, the drinks must flow if you are to make any money. The one thing his job description did not include was frickin' assistant chicken plucker.

In front of the bar, the rickety gate squeaked shut behind him while a distant screech signaled a satisfied hawk about to feed on a fresh kill.

> *"The crazy idea of flying was just that, crazy. But running? If I start running now, and if I can run a full marathon a day, it will take a couple of months, and…aww, what is the use? I do not have running shoes, clothes, or food; all I have is this old backpack. What am I thinking? If I stay working here with the small amount I'm making, it will take forever. I would probably end up like that monster in there, alias Mutha, and still be here when I am, an old guy showing some young, scared soul how to use the Mutha Plucker."*

At least running was something he was adept at, as were many in a long line of his family lineage. Atticus's father was an extension of a line of long-distance runners in the same Kentucky area where Atticus currently resided with his Gramps and Grams. The family's history was said to encompass time back to the Civil War as early Carlisle men covered long distances as infantrymen running throughout the rolling hills of Kentucky.

After most Native Americans were forced to leave Kentucky during the "Indian removals" of the 1800s, a few escaped from removal, and some intermarried with whites.

Legend has it that moonshining was prominent in that area at that time. The swift runners prospered. When the Carlisle family turned to a more traditional way of living, farming and blacksmithing, the fixation on running continued.

Despite not having run on this typically tropical day, Atticus was drenched in sweat. At least he hadn't thrown up on his good shirt, his only shirt. His bare chest exposed a frightening sight. He felt around protruding ribs and realized he was becoming alarmingly thinner than even his usual skinny self.

If there was anything that Atticus needed now, it was a return to normalcy. Sameness, like he had settled into since he had been released as a sixteen-year-old from the other place as he insolently called it. To call it by its man-given name was giving that dreadful location undeserved status. *"It would be like calling her (Vivien) Mother, that would be giving her identity credibility."*

In the five years since being sent to live with his grandparents, whom he had only seen once as a little boy, life had taken on the feel of a Mark Twain book. There was a scaled-down family farm, a white, always in need of painting wood framed house, encircled by white picket fencing, also in need of a fresh coat of paint. There was wonderful freedom to move about the nearby hills, to explore and run up and down, near the luxurious horse farms of Lexington, Kentucky.

Atticus thought the family farm and its surroundings were a thing of beauty because of all its greenery. After splitting time growing up in a stone-cold mansion and then the large, gray metal encased the other place, the small farmhouse burst with compassion and warmth, not the coldness and emptiness of the other two dwellings, at which he worked hard to erase from his scarred mind.

The move to the farm allowed Atticus to settle into a routine. He was fed genuine food, not the slop he had been fed for far too many disgusting meals. He had attended a real school and received a real high school diploma! Atticus was also learning a trade as an apprentice blacksmith under Gramp's tutelage, to make useful items from metal using his worn tools, most notably crafting horseshoes in an area where that was big business. And with Gramp's encouragement, Atticus also worked towards becoming a farrier.

He had, startling in itself, excelled at cross country running while in school, difficult for someone on the spectrum, what with its discipline and interaction among many other individuals. A ten-minute run in any direction from his rural surroundings rose magnificent horse farms where the finest of thoroughbreds are products of expert breeding. Like these majestic animals, Atticus appeared to have been born to run, like a promising yearling on one of those fancy farms.

He remained slow to blend in with society. Being born into lasting reluctance, acceptance into the community would always be lacking. That was just fine with Atticus; a private, somewhat independent lifestyle was fine with him, as he seemed destined to forever prefer the solitude of life on the small family farm. Sadly, like a crop damaged by a string of violent storms, Atticus required special nurturing to return to normal potential, something that was showing promise until, as he grimly recounted, *"I fell prey to meeting up with the diabolical Lucifer."*

Religion created more questions than answers for a spiritually confused Atticus. As a child, he lacked any religious training or conviction. Nor did he grasp the meaning of adoration except for brief interactions with his distanced father. By the time he entered his late teens and was introduced to some mainstream classes at his new school, his reading list and curiosity grew, especially his preference for reading non-fiction, historical accounts, and biographies. He marveled at reliable facts, primarily those of dates and times and, of course, calculations, like those of ancient Mayans, a group who continued to exist in an indigent manner in this very same part of the world.

Atticus's question was could love or prayers, cure his fear, his clinical paranoia, which at that precise moment, was poisoning his soul? If only he understood the power of prayer or felt the perfect love, one that promises to cast away dreaded fear. He had no choice but to ride out another surge of anxiety and face the fact that the cherished meds to which he was wedded were gone, leaving open the proverbial rusty gate for this psychotic disorder to enter his soul.

CHAPTER 22

"Someday, all you will have to light your way will be a single ray of hope, and that will be enough."

– Kobi Yamada

"I have a break before we need to clean up. I am sitting outside amid the stench of spilled alcohol and smoke, dissecting a day I hope to soon forget. I had a bad start with 'Mutha,' the chicken killer, and then the severe anxiety attack that prompted me to take the last two of my pills. After that, I quit work, only to return after much prodding from Max. I went back to my familiar duties, cleaning tables and washing dishes. I got lost in my duties tending to a large crowd of locals who were out on a Friday night before two large ships of tourists docked for the weekend. They are in no hurry to leave. I think about this weekend with crazy crowds looking for some action, bringing with it confrontations, which I hate, for it makes me nervous. I allow myself to gaze at the cloudless sky and welcome the cool sea breeze under twinkling stars. I think about the wild animals in nearby jungles and wonder what their nights are like. I wish I could run the dark like them – FREELY."

Atticus and the rest of the crew were previously warned by the Boss Man that preparing for the busiest weekend of the year could be an all-night affair. His message came with stern orders that no one leave before the restaurant was completely clean, the bar was stocked, and all other essential measures are taken for a profitable two days. Armed guards stood by the ready, which made Atticus nervous because it symbolized dreaded hostility. Feeling robotic, Atticus tried to lose himself in his work.

Loud voices in the bar area shook Atticus from his duties and his wandering mind. Max had progressed from laboring with Atticus to multi-lingual greeter, an ideal position for the local seventeen-year-old, who was suddenly "the guy." He was engaged in an animated conversation with a short person wearing a beat-up floppy hat who, like Max, appeared amicable. Loud, but friendly. Blood rushed from

Atticus's face as Max turned to point in his direction. The stranger, who spun around quickly to seek out Atticus, was none other than Zeke, frickin' Lucifer himself.

> *"When I saw him in the bar that night, my first reaction was to turn and run. I felt my heart race like a jackrabbit's; I was in a panic. Was it my first ever prayer being answered? Or was the earlier hawk sighting delivering a warning of impending danger? Though his appearance at that moment was weird, in the brief time since I last saw him, he had aged. His clothing was mismatched and full of holes. Suddenly, I realized that the guy out there talking to Max, the person I blamed for being here, the one I wished was dead, was my only chance of getting out of there and going home. I knew if I were to get out of this foreign land, I would have to sell my soul to the devil and make peace with Lucifer."*

Atticus watched with mixed emotions as the gregarious Max led Zeke to his station. Zeke grinned, feeling relieved he had found his friend.

"What's up, my man? Long time no see, you miss me?" Zeke managed to put a smile on his strained face. Atticus surprised him with an instant response.

"I've been wishing you were dead or locked up somewhere far away and dangerous, like in Guatemala, 355 miles away. You said you were going to get me home."

Zeke, who was eager to move on with his news, first felt the need to describe the trials and tribulations of his past few weeks in paradise.

"Ok! I'm here to make good on that promise of getting you out of this *fucking* country. First, I will tell you what I went through to find you, so I think I deserve some respect."

Atticus was quick to interject with his own reply.

"Ok, but I hope you remember our deal...no "F" words, I told you I cannot stand that. Second, I am out of meds, and I need a refill, and I'm sleeping on the floor at Max's house, and my back hurts, and I haven't been able to run much..."

"Hold up with the sob story, dude, I really don't give a fuck that you don't dig the "F" word, but I'll do my best not to use it around you. When I got locked up and found out that you were released, I quickly made plans to escape.

"When an opportunity came while on a road work detail along a rural highway, I managed to slip away. It was brilliant! Walking through dense forests and wildly inhabited jungles, I injured my leg while climbing a tree to escape a wildcat.

"Then, like a weird action movie, I came upon a camp occupied by a ragtag group of acid freaks. Their niche, in their spaced-out minds, was to create their own kingdom in the jungle where there would be no lawman. Where crystal meth is their cash cow. One morning, while chilling with a couple of hopped-up Americans, this dude comes running out of the jungle on fire!

"He was lit up like a Christmas tree! He's screaming like something you never want to hear in this life. I tried to offer the waning victim first aid, but there was no helping the young man." Fortunately, Zeke was able to rid the poor soul of his cell phone, allowing him to contact his protector back in Miami, who owed him considerably for once saving his skin. Thus, he was able to procure safe passage back to Florida.

"I started walking all night, nonstop, like an animal. Roaming, eating off the land, crawling into some hole to sleep during the day, until I got here two weeks later.

"I don't want to hear anything about how bad you've had it; I've been scared straight; I want to get back home and pay my debt to society. I'll never do anything illegal again – I'm a changed person."

All this was said in one drawn-out breath. If Atticus didn't know better, he would have believed his fellow American's rambling; actually, he had stopped listening to Zeke's story mid-way through because of his prior deceitful ways.

Max, on the other hand, was hanging on Zeke's every word, mouth open, a rare moment when he was speechless. Zeke added more drama, real or not, and he was convincing.

"We have to get out of here now, so say goodbye to your friend here; I will tell you about the rest on the way."

Atticus was quick to resist Zeke's directive; he had already fallen for his dishonesty and ended up more than 2,650 miles from home.

"I can't leave now; we got two ships coming in this weekend. I need to be paid first."

Zeke looked at Atticus with amazement and added sternly, "No time, man, we have three days to get to a meeting area down south. It is called Punta Gorda. We need to hook up with some people who will take us to Miami, where you will find all the pills you need, then it's on to Kentucky and your Gramma's pancakes. First thing, we need to find some wheels. I'm not sure how far away it is, but we'll walk if we have to, right?"

"I got me a car," Max said excitedly in his Creole-Queen's English accent.

The young man with an impressive head of dreads which hung colorfully down to his shoulders, was becoming an irritant to Zeke. He nonetheless paused his conversation to a disconnected Atticus to ask Max, "You have a car? What kind of car? Where is it?"

"It's back at me crib," Max answered proudly. "If I go too, ye may use it. I know where Punta Gorda is. I have family near there."

"Ok," Zeke replied, suddenly interested in what Max had to say. "How far is that from here?"

"About 270 kilometers," Max replied.

Zeke's patience was running thin. "What's that in miles, man?" he sternly asked Max.

"One hundred seventy miles, probably 4 hours drive" Atticus, suddenly interested, interjected. Before Zeke could press Max any further, a baldish, middle-aged giant of a man rushed into the kitchen, stopping all further discussions of the proposed getaway. Appearing enraged by the gathering, the Boss Man yelled at the odd-ball looking trio, two of whom were being paid for what appeared to be an animated meeting.

"What have we here? We are busy out there with locals. We have tables to be cleaned, and you are both standing around talking? And who is this guy?" The Boss Man spewed spittle as he got in Zeke's face. "Unless you are wearing a goddamn apron, you have no business being back here." Turning his attention to Max and especially Atticus, the owner raised his voice even louder. "Now, let's move! Clean off those tables, and we are getting low on glasses!"

Atticus cowered a bit from the angry reproach by the Boss Man. Zeke made a sudden move forward but stopped cold in his tracks, sensibly for once, especially seeing as the boss was almost a foot and a half taller than he.

"Excuse me, sir, this is all my fault, you see. I was sent here to deliver tragic news to my friend here. His dear grandmother suddenly passed away, and we need to return to the States to tend to her affairs and this young man is our guide. So, if you can make these young men whole with what they have coming in wages, we'll be on our way."

After delivering the grief-riddled news, Zeke gave the sign of the cross while the Boss Man stood with arms folded across his ample chest, incredulous at what he had just heard from this fast-talking bum. The mean-looking security detail was standing nearby.

Zeke realized the need for a different tactic. "Sir, if I might have a minute alone with you, I believe we can resolve this dire situation to all's satisfaction."

Atticus stood out of earshot, feeling overcome by another wave of anxiety with nary a happy pill to be had, as his boss and Lucifer, his only source for meds, talked animatedly nearby.

> *"This can't be good,"* he moaned silently, *"the more he talks, the more he lies. We are liable to all get thrown in the sea for this, and no way is he getting us out of this one. But he is Lucifer, he has no soul to sell, but he seems able to worm himself out of anything."*

CHAPTER 23

"We feel free when we escape – even if it be but from the frying pan to the fire."

– Eric Hoffe

It was Zeke's negotiations with the Boss Man the previous night at the *Sunset Bar and Grill* that had led to an early morning fiasco.

For Atticus, there was evidence of tears of disgust despite his commitment to never allow himself to cry. Like drops of morning dew on the grass, tears rolled stubbornly down Atticus's grimy face as he dragged himself out of the nasty bar before some thug employee of the crooked Boss Man did.

Atticus wanted very badly to just return to a life as an ordinary, very private person. Instead, he felt like a pebble rolling slowly downhill, picking up more pebbles, racing down in avalanche proportions, blocking his getaway from coming to fruition.

For Maxwell "Max" Duvalier, leaving his current home in a village outside Belize City meant going back to his other home, the place of his mother's birth. It was he and his mother's sanctuary home ever since his father, Jacque "Black Jack," Duvalier, had gone berserk. His rage and destructive acts were fueled by lengthy bouts of alcohol abuse, fed by his own concealed distillery of lethal corn rum.

That brush with the law was a terrible period for Black Jack Duvalier as he feared he may have lost his family forever. Max and his mother sought refuge at the family's farm in Southern Belize, where the surrounding fertile land prospered near the spiritual and majestic Mayan Mountains.

After a period of solace and learning the peaceful Mayan ways, an allegedly cured Jacques Duvalier proposed an unpopular return to the valley. Since his prison term had expired, the remorseful convict sought to reunite with his wife and son. This pursuit of reconciliation took the former wanderer back to where his life had taken on a new delightful direction twenty years ago. Back then, he was a poor drifter who crossed paths with Max's mother. She was a brown, fourteen-year-old peasant Mayan girl, he a black Haitian age twenty-something, depending on which story he told.

Black Jack claimed to be a descendant of a famous black pirate leader, an offshoot of slaves brought over from Africa in the 1600's. According to legend, these loosely formed bands of pirates sailed in and about the inlets of the nearby Caribbean Sea. There, they wreaked havoc on the very same nations that had abducted and enslaved these native people of Africa.

Reunited and with promises of reform, Black Jack won back Rosetta but not so with Max, his grudge-bearing son. Cutting ties with his father was still difficult for Max but not as heartbreaking as his mother's departure. He would not be there to protect her if Black Jack were to backslide. Max's parents had left him behind in the southernmost part of Belize as they returned to the Belize City area and their deteriorating home. Not that long afterward, a restless Black Jack Duvalier expressed the desire to make a fresh start. He and his wife Rosetta would migrate to Mexico. He proposed that they could make some money and eventually join a caravan of peasants planning a mass exodus to the United States of America. Max, who never established a true father-son relationship with Black Jack, declined the offer and, at the very young age of seventeen years, returned north in solitude.

Max's return to the Belize City area was fueled by his need for funds to fulfill his mandatory checklist. The hope was that he would fix up and sell the house and Black Jack's classic automobile. This would hopefully help establish much-needed working capital. Then, he would return to Southern Belize to his then-new home, where he could marry his childhood girlfriend. He would then use the rest of his money on health care. They had already been told by a legitimate doctor that his kidney function was deteriorating and he would need extensive treatment soon.

Tho he was the owner of a clapboard shack and a German-made car, the car would be integral for him and his new American acquaintances to escape with.

Max's desire for his own quick departure was further heightened by recent, threatening developments with one of the local gangs in a neighboring village. Max was given a dire warning that he was now an intended target in retaliation for a recent intervention on his part when he interfered with their plan to do a "lick" on a foolish American. This brazen punk was provoking them by running daily through their turf back and forth from Belize City. He was obviously working at a business in the city and most likely carried cash. Max happened to be nearby when a trio of teens, gang bangers, had jumped out of the forest and tripped up Atticus during a run. Standing over the American with a raised bat, the group demanded money.

There was no way Atticus was going to give up any cash. His intention was to save enough money to get home. Max unexpectedly and immediately intervened. After conversing with the robbers, Max took Atticus aside. "Listen, mon. Ye listen to me. Ye better give these punks any money ye got. If ye do not, then ye find a bat to ye head." After the three punks ran off with Atticus's stash, Max explained to Atticus the reason for his strategy. After exchanging pleasantries and understanding Atticus's predicament, Max offered his new acquaintance a room rent-free if he could get him a job at the *Sunset Bar and Grill.*

Max's dealings with the young gang bangers were not over. They had sent a message that they knew his intimidating father was gone, and since Max now resided alone, he was an easy target for retaliation. This threat increased Max's desire to return to a peaceful place with extended family and a teenage Mayan girl who was waiting for him.

Zeke, on the other hand, needed no further incentive to be scared-straight and exit this perplexing Central American country where he had already visited the nasty accommodations in the notorious local prison. While their security may have seemed lax, their punishment was known to be extreme, especially to foreigners. This dangerous penal complex was widely known to be avoided at all costs.

With joyous thoughts of asylum within reach, the three young men had put their all into a night of intense manual labor, scouring and polishing every inch of the dirty establishment. They even de-soiled the area of Mutha's massacres, a job better suited for hazmat-certified personnel rather than three young men with neither experience nor desire to linger in the killer's den.

After a satisfactory job that would accommodate a weekend of hungry and thirsty cruise patrons was completed as agreed by the Boss Man to Zeke, the trio could sleep in the closed bar area, and then, come daybreak, they would be paid for their efforts with added bonuses. Atticus would receive his increased share that included all hours he had already worked.

Once drowsy heads and aching bodies lay down on straw mats on top of hard ground, sleep was slow to come for the three while thoughts of freedom and happier travels awaited them.

The nudge from one of the Boss Man's henchman's feet was as rude as the rooster's early alert that the sun was about to appear. Zeke rubbed confusion from sunken eyes, and he instantly remembered the deal he had made with the bar's owner. Daybreak was time to get paid, money well-earned, and the three wayward souls would be able to move on. They would be free to take the young American to his poor grandmother's funeral.

"Here's your money," the man grinned, a couple of gold teeth glistening in the fresh sunrise. When Zeke was handed the $50.00, he waited clumsily for the rest.

"What the *fuck?* We were promised $50.00 each, we need the rest of the money," demanded Zeke with fury. With the henchmen's smile fading away, he nodded over to the now disturbed security guard. "The boss said this is all you boys get. There was a quitting without proper notice fee to pay. I suggest you take this, and the three of you move on." Zeke's failure to secure compensation for himself as well as wages due for Atticus and Max made him furious. Without the anticipated funds for an immediate escape, there was great cause for concern. However, Zeke remained optimistic that an escape plan could be formulated. The key would be to pool whatever money the trio could muster up for gas and hope that Max's car was operable. The latter shouldn't be much of a problem as Zeke had proven in his capacity as an auto mechanic and part-time car thief that he could make any vehicle operable. He could also steal a car, but that risk could prove deadly, for as a recent escapee from the local jail, he would immediately be sent to the notorious state prison where conditions were legendarily awful. He was over-confident to a fault, but who could blame him? Sure, there was a slight blip to the getaway when the Boss Man had outfoxed Zeke. But as Atticus so eloquently put it,

> *"Lucifer is the master of squirming his way out of trouble -*
> *like the snake he is."*

Without a word to his housemate, Max or to the evil Zeke, Atticus rushed out of the seedy bar. He wished not that his two companions notice his misery, so Atticus broke into a swift trot down Belize City's main cobblestone street before shifting to an all-out run. He would not stop until reaching Max's house in the remote village of Victoria, a place best described as a slum. With a collapse worthy of a runner who had just run a marathon, Atticus lay spread eagle, an outline of skin and bones, mentally and physically exhausted after his brisk run from the bar in Belize City. Looking skyward through barely opened eyes, Atticus spotted a trio of hawks flying high up, scanning for food. They were taking advantage of rising warm air to soar overhead. *"Come down and peck my bones clean, I don't care anymore,"* mumbled a delirious Atticus, showing resignation. Through clouded eyes, Atticus observed the familiar pair approaching.

> *"When I saw Zeke and Max trudging up the gravel road of the dusty village, my heart sank. I saw they appeared to be struggling to make the final stretch of their march to Max's shack. Is that what I look like? I realized I had to pull myself together if I was to get out of here."*

Max's words came out in a high-pitched, melodic manner, something of a reggae sound. In the week that Atticus had lived and worked with the noisy local, he had picked up on his vernacular, which was a combination of Spanish from his mother's Mayan side and French from his father's Haitian side. Then there were his prominent dialects of Creole and the country's main language, English.

Seeing the peculiar pair of wanderers trudging toward him was painful for Atticus to watch. Both young men showed signs of exhaustion, giving Atticus some cause for concern. *"How are we supposed to get out of here if we don't even have the energy to walk?"*

Hiking through monster-sized trees and thorny sticker bushes had left the pair with hellacious scratches on their bare skin and burrs stuck to their thin clothing. "When I get out of here, I'll never go near another forest," Zeke grumbled, noticing that the scabbed-up abrasions from his recent flight through a forest from unjust incarceration had reopened.

To Max, the local seventeen-year-old, this was all an adventure. He was pleased to be leading Zeke toward his shack in the secluded village of Victoria, a poverty-plagued community. Almost an hour had passed since the two had been banished from the bar, and the once brash Zeke and his new partner, Max, were finally home from the disreputable *Sunset Bar and Grill*. Their leaving without full pay had left Zeke angry and with a bruised ego, unaccustomed to being on the raw end of a scam.

In his short life, twenty-four-year-old Zeke had gotten into more than his share of trouble and prided himself on being able to get out of jams. The more serious the offense, the more he took pride in avoiding major repercussions.

Max had developed a taking to the two Americans in the short time since he had encountered them. Atticus looked like an athlete from ancient Athens with his long locks and his gift for running smoothly and silently, like the nearby jungle cats. While Zeke was a mysterious sort to be sure, to Max he was a 'bad boy,' one that bragged about how he could talk his way out of trouble. Max, however, saw a bit of a spiritual mate in Zeke. Like himself, he was quick-tongued, a good talker, and short.

Max attempted to lift his American companion's mood with what he does best, by dispersing the fog of gloom washing over Zeke by being upbeat. Earlier that morning, as the three had dejectedly left the bar, Atticus had taken off in a frantic run. Zeke was not quick enough to stop his companion, nor did he care.

"Don't worry about him, amigo," Max told Zeke. "He knows the way to my village, he runs there and back from the city, and he is fast too; people are already calling him 'white Jaguar.'

"Me ancient Mayan people called the jaguar 'king.' The jaguar still rules the jungles of Belize. Like me boy, these large cats are best known for their shy, solitary nature and exquisitely spotted pelt," referring to Atticus lengthy brown curls for hair.

Zeke looked at Max with a combination of amazement and annoyance at his incessant chatter. Max proudly pointed to a partial clearing before them on the forest edge.

"Right there, me mon, I saw it as I was walking up to me house. It was a skinny, white boy on the ground, about to get his head bashed in by some boys I had seeing 'round the village.

"It turned out to be Atticus, who I only knew then by talk in the village of this crazy American, who was running alone near local gangbangers. The white boy was too naïve to give these dangerous marauders their due, to stay clear of the local lawless in search of easy prey. It was only a matter of time before a confrontation would occur between good and evil.

"I see the white boy sprawled out on this road, surrounded by hoodlums in their early teens. They are standing over Atticus; one *pachuco* is holding a cricket bat with nails sticking out the end, getting ready to come down on poor Atticus's head."

Max gave the story some added drama by raising his already high-pitched voice even higher. "I run toward the scene and scream for the gang to stop just before the cricket bat meets his skull. After reasoning with the wannabes, the boys backed off. First, I had to convince Atticus I was there to help him, but he had to give up any money he had. I knew that if these boys returned to their village empty-handed not only would it be bad for them, but next time, it might be the gang's seasoned veterans who would strike first and ask questions later.

"It could have been worse, though Atticus was beside himself about the money he gave up. I find out later that he still had some cash stashed away in his socks. Smart boy, your homey is."

Zeke perked up at the final part of Max's story. He barely shuddered at the idea that Atticus could have been killed in a mugging in his absence. But the part about Atticus having some money stashed away piqued his interest. Still, he itched and limped his way on until he and Max came upon the windowless, bowing clapboard house that Max called home.

"I hope the German car is in better shape than the house," thought Zeke to himself. Seeing Atticus resting in the yard up ahead gave the pair some much-needed relief and cautious optimism. They would need more than just wishing things would get better instead of worse. They would need a *frickin'* miracle.

"Just when I thought that Zeke, aka Lucifer, was crazy, he came up with his plan, which he swore was going to take us to the promised land. I am desperate for this madness to end. Madness? I must have been born into madness. It seems that I've had to deal with insanity my whole life because of the craziness of others. While at the same time, I am the one labeled with living with a mental disorder."

CHAPTER 24

"Beauty is in the eye of the beholder."

Margaret Wolfe Hungerford

Zeke's mind worked overtime as he circled the rubble of a once functioning automobile, now a pile of corroded metal. The salty ocean air had not been kind to the old car despite having been covered with tarps for protection.

He recalled happier times, when as a young boy riding in a car with joyful parents. Whenever a VW Beetle was spotted, whoever shouted "slug bug" first would win a point. However, that was then; now he could only gasp, "Well, Max was right; it is German-made," he said before spitting on the ground in utter disgust.

"It's not a *fucking* BMW," he swore loudly. He began the arduous task of exhuming the corpse to see what would be needed for a miraculous resuscitation.

Only after removing the tattered tarps and scraping off several years accumulation of iguana feces did the full body appear before the three sets of fatigued eyes riveted on their mode of transportation. Max, ever the optimist, said the car was once a means for his father's travels that sometimes supported the family and should be easily restored for the scheduled trip.

"Forget it!" Zeke was quick to yell. Turning to Max and Atticus, he added sternly, "I'll just have to steal a car back in Belize City, something with A/C," he added defiantly. It wasn't long before Zeke did an about-face. Zeke admitted to his delusional self that the risk would probably be too great. He was a fugitive facing a lengthy stay in a foreign country with a notorious prison system.

Returning to the skeleton of a car, Zeke cautiously and with a few persuasive yanks on the stubborn front latch, noisily raised the hood and swiftly jumped back in horror. Instead of an engine, there was a reptile the size of a small dog.

"Don't worry, mon," laughed Max, "He be dead, he not hurt you, he ees just another iguana, there's hundreds around here" he smiled.

Atticus meekly added, *"That's the trunk area. The engine is in the rear, and my father had one. It's rotting away on the farm; these cars are air-cooled. That's an early 1970's model. It's hard to tell with all the poop on it."*

"Alright, alright," yelled Zeke, perturbed by both Max and Atticus and their condescending comments. His face, already red from the sweltering heat, was turning to a glowing crimson and appeared to be melting with sweat. "I know where the fucking engine is."

Peering angrily at Atticus, who was looking away, Zeke continued his tirade. "You know what? I liked you better when you didn't say anything. Now you two remember - I'm the fucking mechanic here. I'm the one who is going to get us the fuck out of here. *Comprende*?" he added while peering harshly at Max; his steady onslaught of f-bombs was a breach of the deal he had made earlier with Atticus.

Continuing the inspection of the decomposed slug-bug, Zeke stood over the normal trunk area with a hand cradling his chin, like a vexed doctor with a critically ill patient. Though he could not do anything for the dead Iguana, Zeke, the self-proclaimed automotive genius, knew there was a way to get this bucket of bolts running. After all, he was the one who had boasted that he could get anything with four wheels running, with or without a key. Simple auto theft, taking a random vehicle for a joy ride, was his resume. Although now he may be facing grand theft auto.

The difference between joyriding and grand theft auto is that in the case of joyriding, the person who takes a car does so without intending to keep it. Each charge that Zeke had thus far faced had been reduced to a lesser charge, with a minimal fine the only punishment. "It pays to have a mother who is a magistrate judge," he often boasted.

This fixation began before he was old enough to drive and was mostly done just to prove he could. He stole from closed car lots, usually for joyrides, until he realized there was money to be made from this venture. Despite a couple of busts, Zeke possessed the gift to talk his way out of jams. Plus, in the beginning, it didn't hurt that his parents were up-and-coming lawyers.

By the time it took Zeke to do an extensive inspection of the old Beetle, Atticus and Max were beside themselves with anxiety, though only Max showed it. Atticus had retreated into his shell after being forced to give Zeke his remaining savings, which had remained stuffed securely in his wretched socks.

After much crude writing and calculating in the dirt, scratching his head, kicking at the dirt, and, of course, cursing, Zeke was ready to share his findings.

"We have pooled our money and valuables," began Zeke, with his voice once more commanding. "Still, we have limited money, so we must improvise. I am returning to Belize City for some supplies: rope, wire, and, of course, duct tape.

"You two need to go into the forest and get wood, lots of branches, anything you can haul. I'll be back later, but if I don't come back… " Zeke stopped himself, not wanting to sound too negative, but finished his thought nonetheless. "If I don't come back, you guys are on your own."

With the somewhat compassionate speech over, Max and Atticus moved away, but their thoughts were interlocked. They realized in unison they needed the brash, fearless one, or they would be up a river without a paddle or, in this case, drinking water, with little chance of surviving without it.

By the looks of his ragtag team, Zeke had very little confidence in the two wayward souls who depended on his plan. But then, what choice did he have other than the exuberant Max and the despondent

Atticus. Zeke was certain that they both lacked the street smarts to survive on their own. More importantly, could they be serviceable and contribute to the getaway? That would be the million-dollar question.

In Atticus, Zeke was counting on an autistic young man who, with or without his meds, could meltdown at any moment, yet he also knew his fellow American possessed some valuable skills working with metal. Max, on the other hand, was a local, but that night, he showed signs of having some strange health issues. Still, Max might be of some importance, especially, Zeke figured, if he could revive the slug-bug.

With all the group's money and hope, Zeke returned to Belize City. Allegedly, his goal for making the trip was for supplies, lifesaving water, and food, enough for two days of around-the-clock labor. Then, there would be the lifeline of parts to infuse the VW with to get it back up and running for the escape from paradise. Atticus tried hard not to think of the consequence of Zeke absconding with the group's funds and never to be seen again. His and Max's assignment of gathering many limbs and brush from the neighboring forest helped avoid too much worrying about Lucifer's return. Near the end of the detail that extended well into darkness, the duo of Max and Zeke were about to haul back to Max's house the last pile of dry timber. First, there would be a pause to catch their breath.

> *"I heard bizarre sounds coming from Max; as a runner,*
> *I've heard other runners gasping for air after a rugged race to*
> *the point of distress. This sounded really gross."*

Atticus glanced over at Max, who appeared dangerously close to dying. The young man's breathing was labored, his sizable belly slowly rising with each delayed, raspy breath.

"Max, are you dying?" Atticus nervously whispered, his voice sounding unusually loud in the stagnant forest. Both weary men remained propped against giant trees at the forest edge, trying to re-establish the energy to move.

Atticus was disturbed when he did not receive an answer from Max. With his tired body frozen in fear, he lacked the energy to crawl over to his strange companion and offer any assistance. He didn't know what he could do to help.

Earlier, the two had gagged down an array of roots and wild berries, the only food consumed by the pair since Zeke's earlier departure for Belize City. This was meant to be a brief break for Max and Atticus before dragging one more hefty pile of brush back to Max's shack. Eventually, Atticus shimmied his weakened body up the tree to get his feet under him while Max remained unresponsive.

Atticus stumbled back to the shack with the night's blackened darkness adding to the feeling of impending horror.

Zeke had still not returned when Atticus arrived at the dark house. Soon, the old cast iron stove would provide the only light on an otherwise pitch-black night. Unfamiliar noise then approached quickly, *"Now what?"* he thought, on the verge of another panic attack. Before he could answer his own question, the sounds of wheels rolling up the gravel road elevated Atticus's shaky awareness.

"Hey, where's Fat Boy?" were Zeke's first words as he labored with a deteriorating wooden cart. No answer from Atticus was instead followed by *"Where have you been? We have trouble, and Max is dying back there."*

After a brief pause, Zeke replied testily, "Well, if he's dead, then we don't need his ass. Now help me unload this wagon," pointing to the contents of the cart, consisting of wire, rope, firewood, duct tape, and glorious water.

Atticus detected the smell of alcohol on Zeke's breath, a horrible scent that Atticus detested from an earlier lifetime, forgotten until this moment.

"Quit saying bad things about Max. We need him, and we owe it to him to go and help him and quit using swear words, or else I'll just walk home."

Zeke stared at Atticus with amazement, "Well, looks like you might have grown a pair while I was gone. Sure, I'll quit swearing around you. You're right, and we need the human bowling ball to lead the way to freedom."

At Atticus's urging, the pair took the rope, the rickety cart, and some water Zeke had secured on his shopping expedition to find Max. Zeke was displeased with the unplanned rescue mission adding to an already full schedule. No higher than a two-wheeler, the wooden cart had two rear wheels along with a lone front wheel, making it somewhat stable. Stability was needed; the load consisting of one Maxwell Duvalier would be tested in taking his cumbersome body back to the house.

Thanks to forced-fed water and chocolate bars, Max regained consciousness but was still unable to walk back to the cabin. He was laid on the cart delicately for the precarious yet short trip. Rescuing Max had proven to be another laborious ordeal for the crew, already dealing with exhaustion and suffering from a lack of food, leaving the normally unflappable Zeke feeling increasingly uptight. After some lifesaving munchies were dispensed, Zeke finally was the bearer of promising news. He had been able, through his expertise in haggling, to make a deal for some nourishing, real food to be delivered at sunrise, and they would now re-energize until the rooster crowed.

Unable to sleep, Zeke eagerly laid out the entire inventory of supplies before him and somberly took stock of the meager array of parts and materials for the colossal job at hand. "What am I doing?" Zeke lamented, "Who the fuck am I kidding?" He glanced over at the innocent-looking Atticus, hoping he hadn't heard his early morning profanity. All would be for naught if the old couple he had encountered the previous night along an obscure crossroad not far from this village failed to show up as promised. Having lost their desolate property to the state in the name of progress and land grabbing, the old couple were on the move. Both had possession of a wooden cart upon which they carried their life's belongings, including chickens and fresh eggs for sale and an old goat. They would sell off what they still owned and, with the meager amount they received from the state, set off with dozens of other displaced citizens and immigrate to the north if they were lucky enough to make it safely, if at all.

Zeke, ever the good Samaritan and generous barterer, worked out a painstaking and lengthy arrangement. He would receive one cart, which had been more than adequate to carry supplies back to Max's place. The arrangement called for the old couple to receive Max's home and 20 US dollars. Zeke, perhaps due to the cost he paid out for someone else's home and someone else's money, felt the deal was a good one. However, it left their finances desperately low, especially when they still needed the trip's lifeblood, gasoline. He figured he could always siphon gas from a vehicle. He had once, as a last resort, done that distasteful undertaking. "Hell, I might as well steal the whole damn car."

There would be enough to feed them all for the couple of days it would take to complete repairs to the VW. The late-night deal was sealed with a couple of belts of some moonshine liquor that gave meaning to the word firewater!

'Sun-up' was the agreed upon time for the old man and his wife to be at the house. The wife's arrival, which was an hour past due, left Zeke to fear that the agreement was perhaps erased from the old man's memory by an overindulgence of his high-octane moonshine. Anxious about the late arrival, Zeke knew the success of the getaway was in the hands of the weathered couple living up to their end of the dubious deal.

With the new day's sun already at a scorching point, Zeke felt a ferocious hit to his will, a strong urge to just close his eyes and surrender.

From a deep slumber, Atticus awoke with intense hunger pains. He thought for a split-second he had caught a whiff of Gram's hotcakes, at this point, even a mirage would do.

"I immediately dismissed the aromatic whiff circling my aching head, trying to be suggestive and awaken my dying sense of smell. Ever since my release from the other place, and, before that, the dungeon (my name for my early childhood home), I seemed to have always been shut-in except for infrequent jaunts outdoors in secured areas. Once released and sent to live in Kentucky on my grandparent's farm, I finally came alive and soon found the joys of amazing smells all around me, while running through farms and over hills. Then there was Gram's cooking. No, not this time; I will not fall for that again. I won't be cruelly teased by any more falsehoods. I suddenly sensed the spirit of a hawk circling lazily overhead, and he seemed to be saying, "It's ok, you can open your eyes... you can smell... this time, it's genuine."

With the out-of-place squeaking of wooden wheels, life took on a new direction; that of prayers answered. Resembling a mini-circus parade, in the lead with a goat wearing a cowbell, an old peasant man was followed by his wife, with a stubborn burro pulling up the rear. Most importantly, in the rickety cart were cages of chickens.

"Hello, Mr. Zeke, pardon our lateness; these stubborn chickens kept us waiting for fresh eggs. We want to keep our end of the deal and prepare a meal for your group and assist your amazing venture." The old man's voice trailed off as he spotted the VW Beetle or what was left of it.

Max was unusually quiet except for, or because of, the smacking and slurping of the meal before him. He was unable to stop chewing through dry-parched lips and the lingering taste, hours later, of his own vomit.

Atticus was his usual soundless self, a trait of his since it was pounded into him as a child in the massive dining area of his mother's mansion. He marveled at Max's rebound from his apparent near-death experience a few hours earlier. He even ended his own pledge of never to consume eggs or chicken again after his unpleasant experience at the *Sunset Bar and Grill* and the butcher named *Mutha*. *"If I can eat roots and dirt, I can eat anything,"* he reasoned as his irritable queasiness slowly diminished.

Zeke sat cross-legged on the deck, eating moderately, leaving more for his ragtag crew whom he was depending on for the upcoming laborious marathon. The clock was ticking, and little had been accomplished. After breakfast was voraciously devoured, Zeke boasted to the somewhat revitalized pair how such a wonder of sustenance had arrived at their dilapidated doorstep.

"I knew I had to do something drastic if I were to get any work out of you two slugs. I headed out last night and literally stumbled upon this old couple." Zeke paused to point at the pair who were surveying their new digs. "They were selling eggs from a crude-looking wagon, and I found out that they were soon to be homeless and were looking to make a few bucks to move north. Right away I put on my best bargaining face."

Max and Atticus gave each other a curious look, both remembering Zeke's last ill-fated negotiations with the Boss Man. It turned out this deal included much of the trio's already meager cash and Max's property. Max started to object but was cut off by the determined voice of Zeke.

"We're done talking if we're to get out of here the day after tomorrow, end of story." Without any discussion as to whether Zeke's idea had any merit, the plan was outlined to the amazement of the other four people.

Atticus words showed rare confidence for something coming out of Zeke's mouth.

> *"After the most welcome of meals (real food) that I ever*
> *had (I even managed to get a run in) we began the arduous task*
> *of getting the VW Beetle put together and running all in a day*
> *and a half. I had already learned not to trust Lucifer, but in this*
> *case, I had no choice but to have some faith in him. When he*
> *gave us a not-so-convincing pep-talk and lined us up with our*

tasks, I would have to put my skill as a blacksmith to use. Still, I sensed some misgivings in Zeke's voice. I hope I am wrong, and we can get the heck out of here. "I saw the method to Zeke's madness in putting the car in the house, but I really had my doubts about us being able to physically do it in one piece."

Like a scene from a slapstick comedy, the remains of the car's front end protruded through the wall of the clapboard shack as though it was trying to break out of the decaying building. The rotten condition of the small building made it easy to create a crude entranceway through the outside wall. Placing half of the slug-bug inside was the first real test in the plan, which required physically lifting the car up onto a small stoop and then another lift into the house. Long abandoned, the house did not have electrical power, so the goal was to position the rear-engine vehicle's back end first in relatively safe proximity to the glowing fire provided by the huge woodburning stove. Hopefully, the antique wood stove would provide enough illumination for the anticipated all-night repairs on the forsaken vehicle.

Previously, while on personal terms with Atticus, Zeke had witnessed the peculiar guy make a pair of horseshoes on a solid anvil at his grandparent's farm. This fact was not lost on Zeke when devising a plan to repair the car. As the day progressed, there was a marked increase in stifling heat and humidity. Sharp, rusted edges on the car's shell added more danger to the hazardous job.

With crude ramps and pulleys in place, courtesy of Zeke's experience in moving automobiles, the move still needed some brute strength. Fortunately, more muscle came from a surprising source.

CHAPTER 25

"For all the things my hands have held, the best by far is you."

-Author unknown

Maxwell Duvalier was not only unusually short but obese as well. His appearance indicated some obvious health issues. Yet it was he, the man-child, who almost single-handedly saved the project by nearly lifting the heavy junk car all by himself.

With that quote, Rosetta-Lopez-Duvalier bid her seventeen-year-old son, Maxwell "Max" Duvalier, adieu. Max's reward for returning to his childhood home near Belize City was a clapboard house that was one tropical storm away from becoming a pile of rubble.

In the whisper of a baby's first shallow breath, life almost ended; there would be no burst of a newborn's cry, just a tiny gasp. Rosetta heard nothing as her world was also slipping away; she, too, was close to the inevitable.

Technically, still a child of fifteen, Rosetta knew enough about childbirth from her experience in her village in Southern Belize, where there was neither a hospital nor a certified doctor, just the village *medicine man* and teams of midwives.

Back then, Rosetta realized immediately that she and her baby were in a critical situation. She knew that this was much too early for her baby to be born, trying to figure out in her fragile condition whether she was much more or less six months along, and if the excessive bleeding from somewhere on her body could be fatal for both her and her unborn child. With his wife and baby in dire need of medical attention, Jacques drove as fast as he could to the hospital in Belize City while Rosetta, in semi-consciousness, prayed softly that her baby lived. Once Jacques was allowed at his wife's bedside, the couple prepared for the worst.

"Let's name him now," Rosetta whispered painfully.

"Me old man, he's named Maxwell. Can we name him that?" a frantic Jacques Duvalier, a twenty-something dark Haitian who spoke mostly French, replied nervously. Soon, a chaotic rush of lifesaving measures was administered to both mother and child with a large degree of pessimism.

When looking back at Max's perilous entry into the world, one can only wonder what led to his survival. Jacques admitted he had little hope for his son's survival but still whispered a wish to his son while holding him gently in his palms and urging him to "don't give up *mon petit garcon.*" It would be many days, flowing into weeks of weeping and depression, for things to improve enough for baby Max to travel to his new home.

Selfishly, Jacques began to resent his son. The baby was too noisy, he needed too much attention, bills were mounting, and Rosetta herself was recovering and would not be able to work for a long while.

Max was oblivious to all the turmoil around him. He was happy and content to be doted upon. But Max's premature birth led to many complications. He had a serious condition, blocked kidneys, that usually means these babies generally do not survive much beyond birth. In Max's case, his kidney obstruction was removed, but he would probably need dialysis early in life and eventually a kidney transplant. His result was he would face many challenges in his life, the least of them being of short size, the possibility of obesity and a shortened life.

CHAPTER 26

"Love is composed of a single soul inhabiting two bodies"

– Aristotle

Well into their seventies, the two thought they had seen everything until now, as they observed the entertaining yet serious event unfolding before them. Eva and Fernando Martinez already spent some head-scratching time staring in wonderment at the broken-down VW Beetle sitting partially inside the house.

The house was soon to be theirs, causing Zeke to worry about how the damage to the shack could be a potential last-minute deal breaker. Inside the shack, the antique wood-burning stove had just been the scene of mastery as the couple had whipped together a vast meal for the strange trio of young, desperate men. The cast iron would be a windfall as scrap, thought the old man. Right away the couple took to the plight of the three boys for obvious reasons.

Over fifty years ago, the Martinez's had fled El Salvador during its civil war for Belize. Both had come from well-to-do families. Back then, a young Fernando's family owned a widely popular brewery featuring the country's most popular craft beer. Eva Martinez also had a more lavish start to her adulthood in El Salvador. Her father owned a mega junkyard early on, making lots of money with the help of his government connections. He then parlayed his assets into Grand Prix race cars, which was a very popular sport in El Salvador and throughout South America. With his son as his primary driver, the family was seeing a windfall in the sport. Eva was a fixture at the tracks, with her father pushing his daughter to become established in the business side of the sport. Not wanting to go that boring route, she opted to drive cars at 200 miles per hour. Due to the circuit's unwritten rule against women drivers, Eva was limited to being a test driver for her father's cars. As tensions rose in the country, leading to a coup, the beginning of a lengthy civil war broke out in El Salvador. It seldom mattered which side your political affiliations were, and you were probably going to suffer if you had wealth. While her father and his business headed for a more stable political climate in Argentina, Eva and her industrious husband headed for Belize where entrepreneurs were known to prosper in the growing, peaceful country.

As it turns out, the timing turned against them, as any business venture came with trepidation with growing economic unrest. Trying to do things the right way, they heard the calling for people who could assist the growing suffering population in these difficult times. Their escape from oppression had been a risky adventure requiring, in the words of Fernando, luck, faith, and the help of others. Although they fell on hard times after a devastating recession a few years ago, their time in Belize had been blissful.

"As a form of paying it forward, we devoted our happy lives to helping others. Criss-crossing the country, we would set up places to establish ourselves long enough to help others. For poor families, we grew nutritious food and provided help with rearing kids and other social assistance. Then we met Ezekiel on the road and here we are. We believe things do happen for a reason. We only wish that we could do more."

As dusk approached, the fire was stoked to a higher degree of light and heat. Zeke, who had been working around the outside of the vehicle, had made great inroads mechanically. Atticus was performing his metal work talent slowly but steadily, working on restoring the car's wheels back to a functional condition.

Fernando and Max used a cart and manpower to haul enough wood for a two-day fire. All this done despite it being unbearably hot.

It was especially charming when he scrawled the transfer of ownership for the old shack on a wall, one of the three remaining intact walls. Besides humoring the pair, the couple seemed to be satisfied to no end, which came as a relief to Zeke, as it meant game on.

Atticus tackled his assigned, dangerously hot job, which Zeke had witnessed in Kentucky. "Ahh, Kentucky," Zeke sighed, never a particular fan of his home. "Too much open area, too rural, too backward," he often complained, setting his sights on his future life to be in the fast lane of a large city. As for his current intention, he felt closer to fulfilling his longing to leave Belize in the rear-view mirror and journey home quickly.

Zeke was pleased with the solitude of his situation, and he always preferred to work alone. He had a knack for putting his mechanical work on automatic, allowing his mind to wander. Not that he had any choice; his mental condition triggers attention deficiency.

Early intervention on his mother Samantha's part required she took some time away from work. Zeke's parents were given an early diagnosis of ADHD, a neurodevelopment disorder, often diagnosed in childhood and lasting into adulthood, as it now appeared was the case with an adult Zeke. It was apparent that with the proactiveness of his mother Samantha, the support of his father, and conventional medication, Zeke had turned the corner and could enter the customary era of K-12 schooling without issues, if he continued to take the prescribed medication.

Euphoria over early progress turned slowly sour. With the job of restoring the decrepit wheels suddenly going too slow, Zeke irritably placed Max to aid Atticus. This move sent Atticus into a foul mood, which was the first indication that the pressure and the heat were having a negative effect on the project.

"I'm a farrier, not a frickin' blacksmith," Atticus angrily but softly snapped back. This was followed by Atticus persistently adding the need for meds and more food.

With Zeke's temperature rising with the air temperature, he lashed out once more at his fellow American. "You need to settle down and concentrate on getting those wheels done! As far as meds, you'll soon have all you want when we get back to Miami. Food? You want more food, first finish these wheels, then we eat. Mrs. Martinez is preparing dinner as we speak." Atticus glanced over to the elderly lady, and jumped back in shock. He intercepted a flashback he hoped to never see again; Mrs. Martinez was plucking a dead chicken of its feathers. At least it was dead, and there was no sign of the terrible contraption, 'the Mutha Plucker.'

If the sight of a chicken being plucked was not bad enough, another attack on one of Atticus's sensitive senses was occurring. The odor of rotted eggs filled the air in and about the well-ventilated shack. Even the smoke billowing out of the old wood-burning stove failed to overcome the odor. Zeke began to think that perhaps the open engine compartment was the culprit. Zeke had the foresight to remove the empty gas tank prior to moving the car into the home. He had recently seen someone burned to a crisp, and with the stove so close to the engine, he did not want a repeat performance of that horror. Eventually, the terrible smell was traced back to smelly farts, as could be expected considering the volume of eggs being consumed by the crew, especially Atticus and Max.

Zeke had more to worry about than food and where it came from or the stench from a cloud of smelly flatulence. With fragments of a once operational engine spread out on the ground outside and with the correct tools in short supply, Zeke was nearing another defeatist interlude. "What am I doing? Who the fuck am I kidding?" Zeke uttered to himself after a painstakingly slow first day of the project. Hot-wiring a car was one thing. Overhauling a motor he had never worked on or stolen was another thing.

Once a deep black, the car was now a pockmarked grey color, and the once stylish ragtop was now more rag and not much top.

Zeke knew that if the approaching deadline were to be met, all hands had to be composed and united in getting everything done in a quick and orderly fashion. Nothing could be done about the heat; however, the cast iron stove had to be kept kiln hot. That meant Max and the old man had to make many time-consuming trips into the forest for more tinder. Some relief would be arriving in the coming weeks, but neither Zeke nor Atticus wanted to be here for the height of the ominous hurricane season.

CHAPTER 27

"United we stand, divided we fall."

– Aesop

"Go around the village and use your gift for talking to get us some help. We need to borrow some tools to put this car back together today! Get us anything else we can use too, and pronto!" Zeke pleaded with Max.

Relishing the opportunity to contribute to the cause, the local seventeen-year-old preferred talking to his remote neighbors over manual labor any day of the week.

Max was also eager to please Zeke, who, for some unknown reason, he was drawn to. As a youngster, Max had tried hard to win his rogue father's approval. He hoped to do the same with his new American acquaintance, who, like his memories of his distant father, had something of a rough edge to him.

When Max finally earned a chance to win his father's adulation, he felt he had failed miserably with disastrous results, which led to the incident that shaped his family's lives forever.

With the crew now introduced to new assignments, Zeke hoped that Max would be able to find some help and that Atticus could forge the wheels into a functional shape. Zeke was a big fan of the TV character "MacGyver" and would have to utilize some of his tricks to address the tire situation. Another example of how the passage of time had not been kind to the bug was that the old rubber was useless from rot.

In the past, Zeke felt a sense of pride when he was forced to use ingenuity in order to MacGyver a car. "One time, I even used a pair of nail clippers along with a generous quantity of duct tape to fix something mechanical," he recalled. However, much was riding on this venture, and it was also time to address the obvious need for tires if they were to travel two blocks, let alone two hundred miles. Incredibly, Zeke hit upon a mind-blowing alternative to rubber tires. Rotting rubber could be restored with animal skins, a remarkable solution if it works. Zeke remembered seeing it work on a MacGyver episode, but would it work? "Of course, it'll work," thought a suddenly optimistic young American, "after all, I'm MacGyver."

Creating an alternative battery for the ruined one in the car that seemed to have taken an iguana with it to its resting place was to be a tenuous project. One of the carts was sacrificed to provide wheel bearings, and the hand brake was rigged to serve as the car's brakes. Rigging the clutch required all the duct tape left on hand.

Zeke started early in life as a mischievous thief, a master at hot-wiring cars at a way-too-early age. By his thirteenth birthday, Zeke had already graduated to a delinquent status. Now, still without gasoline for the bug, there would be no test start or test run for the vehicle. Gratefully, gas was finally arranged via siphoning from another former acquaintance of the notorious Black Jack Duvalier.

Due to the still raging fires at the shack, Zeke wisely had the car rolled to a nearby hill, a fete that equaled in effort, the placing of the bug in the shack. But, with a growing team of citizens with little in worth, they rallied generously to get the project to the point of no return. While a large can of gasoline was tipped into the hilarious-looking automobile, most likely for the first time in a decade, the mood was taking a more positive aura. Feeling like the Wright brothers must have felt, the small crew of amateurs felt a combination of trepidation, then exhilaration. All that was missing was for Zeke, the test pilot, to climb aboard for the momentous launch. This exhibition was a warm 100 years later and a far cry from Kitty Hawk, where Wilbur and Orville Wright tested their aeronautic skills.

Back then, builders of the world's first successful motor-operated airplane, with much practice developing their skills as pilots, had already done extensive glider tests. During their first attempt at a powered flight, the engine stalled during take-off, and the plane was damaged. They spent three days repairing it. Then, three days later, in front of five witnesses, the modern age of aviation was born as the heavier-than-air gasoline-powered aircraft stayed aloft for 12 seconds.

Now, at the side village of Victoria in northern Belize, a dozen residents watched in various degrees of interest; final tweaking was taking place prior to a launch far less significant than the one at Kitty Hawk. That is, unless you were one of the three voyagers destined to be in the silly turtle, the name given to the revived auto by a neighborhood child who had come, along with her parents, to witness the sunrise resurrection. The hope was that it would travel much swifter than a turtle, fast enough to cover the 200 miles for a much-anticipated rendezvous.

> *"I never held a camera in my life; things I wanted to remember I would just write down on paper. This was the first time I wished I had a picture of something. I had no words to describe the finished product. I was especially satisfied with the wheels. They may look weird, but we just need them to work."*

Before Zeke lowered his five-foot-seven body into the driver's seat, he took one final walk around the amazing, first of its kind motor vehicle. The front hood, the trunk, which once held iguana carcasses, was welded shut since it wouldn't close on its own.

Yes, welded! Max did a marvelous job rounding up a small group of volunteers. One man had a temperamental portable welding machine, which Zeke used on a couple of delinquent areas, such as welding shut the two unusable doors. Another gentleman donated a tankful of gas from his truck if Zeke would do the distasteful job of siphoning the gasoline.

Suppose it takes a village to raise a child. The village of Victoria helped raise the old VW Beetle to new heights.

Zeke quietly surveyed the area of the clapboard house as a sly grin grew on his smug face at the sight of half a wall missing from the shack. "Brilliant; fucking brilliant," he snickered. He watched the forlorn Atticus pace in a pitiful circle with his hands in pockets filled with notes. His ever-present backpack was filled with more notes and letters, nothing else, no money and no meds. Zeke approached him warily. Meanwhile, the small crowd was getting impatient, some thinking that the short American was losing his will to attempt his take-off.

"Hey man, how you doing? You look like shit," Zeke coolly offered up. Atticus, lacking patience and showing a hint of desperation replied, *"I need my meds."*

"I know, dude," Zeke sympathetically replied. "If all goes well, we will be in Miami soon, and you'll get enough meds to last until you get back home. By the way, you did a great job on those wheels, and everything else."

Appreciation aside, Atticus was torn between wiping his mind clean and documenting everything he could remember.

> *"I needed to remind myself before I forgot it all, forgot how in the world I ended up here in Central America. One thousand five hundred ninety-three frickin' miles, as the hawk flies, from the farm? It was like I climbed aboard a magic carpet. One minute, I was on the farm making a pair of horseshoes, and the next thing I know I'm on a frickin' luxury ocean liner, setting sail for Belize City with Lucifer himself."*

Zeke took one final look from the top of a nearby rugged hill where a path had been worn, probably by poachers or rumrunners, two illegal enterprises in these parts.

Atticus took a sad look at Max's pitiful former shack. It was where he had slept intermittently the last ten days, and now it revealed a desolate hole in a fragile wall large enough to drive a, well, a VW Beetle through. Its lone remaining item of worth, the giant cast iron woodburning stove remained, with the black smoke that had emitted continuously the last couple of days now a pale grey and diminishing in volume. The antique had proved invaluable to the enterprise in several equally important ways. Mrs. Martinez was able to cook fresh and abundant meals, it had served as a forge, and had provided a necessary source of light. The intrepid couple's remaining cart sat outside, while the goat scavenged for anything edible, and the chickens pecked away at garbage.

Gazing over at Zeke, he suddenly appeared hesitant. He had checked the extensive repair list a handful of times already. Finally Eva, the project's unsung hero, whispered something to the pale-looking Zeke. Conspicuous by his absence was Fernando, who was also greatly instrumental in pulling this venture to this critical point.

The gathered crowd, now up to a good twenty people, was becoming restless. Small bets were overwhelmingly in favor of the car not starting up, let alone making it down the hill. People who had generously contributed to the old car stood by impatiently.

Finally sitting at the wheel, Zeke could not recall ever doubting himself before, a consequence of his ADHD. But now, he was trying very hard to convince himself to believe. "Now I know how Fred Flintstone felt at the wheel of the prehistoric family car," he nervously chuckled.

The idea was to give the bug a hefty push down the hill, pop the clutch at the appropriate speed and hope the overhauled engine kicked in. The clutch linkage was tenuously secured with some scrap wire and, of course, duct tape. Zeke's expertise had always been to hot-wire a car but this project required some engine-uity to make the motor start. The battery was bypassed by a new unproven prototype without the strength to start the car or be jumped, but enough to keep the vehicle running. Brakes were almost non-existent, rigged to be used in emergency only via the parking brake. "If the wheels don't fall off and the car doesn't blow up before this sucker starts, it will mean that MacGyver lives!"

With abundant calls and hollers, an all-out assault by the army of onlookers and volunteers, and with Atticus and Max as the front liners, the old car let loose with some anemic creaks and groans. Shortly, the vehicle was rolling downhill, but would it pick up enough speed to turn over the engine? After a few painful paces, some momentum was gained from the two-man charge who were encouraged by cheers from the growing crowd of spectators.

Zeke waited tolerantly for more speed before suddenly letting out a battle cry – "Pop the clutch!" A violent lurch occurred, trailed by a belch of black smoke, then silence, except for the heavy gasping of Atticus and Max, who had set the VW in motion. Zeke angrily pounded the steering wheel, swearing and already arguing to no one in particular, for one more chance! By the time Zeke climbed out of the cockpit, he had faced reality. The locals, who had offered much in support, sharing and labor, were now strolling back to their modest homes and some relief from the heat. Max and Atticus were visions of despair, still sitting where the fruits of their labor had left them exhausted.

Zeke shouted out to the pair, "Hey, that was close; let's give it another try; go bring the people back, Max. I'll make an adjustment on the carburetor, and then it should fire. Look, the dry animal skin for tires was a stroke of genius and held up."

"No way, *Jose,* that's it, mon, these people are not coming back, too hot, mon, we here do not it like too hot. Americans like the hot; we like the cooler night-time, mon."

With growing despair, Zeke was prepared to plead his case further when he was drowned out by the rumbling of a loud motor. Turning off the road was none other than Fernando behind the wheel of a farm tractor. His wife Eva was first to greet him, and the two exchanged a brief conversation. Then it was her and Zeke's turn to talk while the old man ran a chain around the precious chassis of the Beetle.

Eva had a plan for Zeke. Fernando would pull the old car back up the hill, and he would give Zeke something for the petrol. "Hopefully, it will help make it start." Zeke was grateful for pulling the car back to position but had misgivings about putting anything in the gas. "Here, take a mouthful of this and swallow it quickly then get another mouthful and slowly chuck it down the carburetor."

If the bottle of lucky potion looked familiar to Zeke, it was because it was the same homebrew that the old man had offered him at their first encounter. Now it tasted like rocket fuel; maybe the old man was on to something. At this point, everything was worth a try.

With a bit of struggle, the car was mechanically dragged up the hill, certainly faster than it would have been pushed by the dwindling number of hands available. If the project did not already have the looks of a circus, it now took on a "believe it or not" atmosphere as the elderly lady took over as pilot after convincing Zeke that she could start the car. In her youth, she was the only girl in a family of stock car racers in El Salvador. Zeke would better serve to help the already tired crew push the VW downhill at a more desired speed.

CHAPTER 28

"I am on the road again, goin' places that I may never see again; I can't wait to get on the road again."

– Willie Nelson

Spontaneous joy erupted amongst the remaining observers and the three fleeing young men. With precision, the elderly lady was carefully lifted out of the vehicle as Zeke deftly took over the precarious controls. Max, the excitable local who was leaving to begin a new life, looked back at the crowd, waving wildly as tears rolled freely down his chubby cheeks. He was able to see Fernando pass a jug of his potent brew to the adults in the fading crowd.

"Yo, Zeke, we movin' good, yes?" Max shouted, trying hard to be heard. Zeke was seated only inches away in the driver's seat but was unable to hear anything because the remainder of the rag top had been lost in the stiff wind. Regardless, the mood in the car remained hopeful amongst the three since that miraculous moment when Eva expertly popped the clutch, the old VW coughed, sputtered, then started! And continued to run! Pandemonium erupted among the few to witness the "miracle in Victoria" as it will forever be remembered.

Atticus, the weathered and stunned twenty-one-year-old American who was duped, perhaps even kidnapped, into this woeful situation, happily announced his latest calculation. *"If we get twenty miles to a gallon, then we should have enough to get there and on time."* All seemed well inside the crowded car, while overhead, four hawks attracted to the vibrant scene below them, broke off formation, and disappeared with a screech.

With hidden concern, Zeke was beginning to see some reason for doubt to enter his mind as he felt the speed fall off a few miles per hour despite running the car at full throttle. Atticus, from the back seat, caught the sudden bad vibe in the wind tunnel of the cramped auto, his long legs sticking up in the air, adding to the most unusual sight any traveler could see in these parts. He, too, could sense some change in the acceleration.

After two and a half hours they neared Dangria, a town halfway to their destination under normal speed. The mood in the car, as well as the turning to dusk sky, went gloomy.

Zeke didn't know whether to curse the VW Beetle or kiss the hood on the rear engine for getting them this far. Still, he carefully opened the latch and pretended to tweak the sizzling engine for the benefit of his fellow travelers. He knew it was futile to hope that anything he could do would help. The patient was dying a slow death.

Decreasing compression of the engine was obviously due to the main gasket deteriorating from the intense heat in the engine compartment. Zeke had been fearful of this, but without a new gasket, it was just a matter of time before it gave out completely.

Off to the south, the Mayan Mountains rose mightily, their outline appearing very far off.

"Okay, we have to take some side roads for a while; we can't stay on a highway going this slow, it will draw too much attention, and we would probably get pulled over." Silence in the vehicle was deafening except for the steady hiccup of the engine as it idled unevenly, much like the breathing of a dying person.

"We will keep heading south and pray for a miracle; as long as we don't turn the car off, maybe we can still make it to Punta Gorda. We will not make it for today's meet-up, but maybe we can hitch a ride with a fishing vessel; hell, I might swim across the damn Caribbean Sea to Miami," Zeke said, trying his best to rouse his fellow travelers and himself.

"You can't swim the Caribbean Sea to Miami; you'd have to go through Cuba, they'd shoot you," Atticus interjected sarcastically, and in a whisper.

The merciful end came before darkness over-ran dusk on a frontage road near another forest. "Can you go anywhere in this country without a damn forest around?" Zeke yelled cynically.

Max eagerly replied, "Not really, mon; over half the country is forest and jungle. Once, me ol' man took me hunting here, illegally, of course. It was the beginning of the end of our relationship as father and son."

Instead of a night of amazing personal revelations, some of which would evoke tears, in separate comfortable beds in Max's Mayan village, two weary Americans suffered bruised bodies and minds in a VW Beetle. Atticus's long legs stretched from his rear-seat perch practically to the windshield.

Zeke, though much shorter than Atticus, was also painfully cramped thanks to the rearrangement of various features in the little vehicle and the bulkiness of his front passenger, Max.

As dusk changed to darkness swarms of blood sucking insects found the exposed occupants of the car. The boys scrambled to cover as much flesh as possible with the few pieces of clothing each traveler carried. The itching bites tested their wills to survive the night. With real fear that some large predator would gobble up the three for a late-night meal, it was beginning to sound like a reasonable alternative to being eaten alive by mosquitoes.

Despite the trio's weariness, Max suggested a story-time to cast away the terror. Max urged the sharing of real-life experiences that helped shape their lives. With him first, of course.

CHAPTER 29

"Into the forest I go, to lose my mind and find my soul."

– John Muir

Born prematurely, Maxwell Duvalier was hailed as a miracle baby, whose dangerously early birth had rendered him critically underdeveloped, but with an amazing will to live. His destiny was to be forever small in stature when defined by height but live large in perseverance. Because of the family's meager financial situation, hours would be spent at the old wood-burning stove making Max's favorite meal of beans and rice. A cocoa-skinned Mayan girl from southern Belize, Rosetta doted on her less-than-healthy son to a fault, according to her husband. Occasionally, Black Jack would try and get his son interested in manly activities.

"It was to this very same jungle area that me *ol mon* brought me to hunt *Gibnut*. It is an ugly member of the rodent family and is considered a delicacy here in Belize. We are talking about hunting out of season without a hunting license and defying a court order against possession of a firearm. Ol' Black Jack was one crazy dude.

"On this day, he's using a borrowed ATV instead of his trusty Volkswagen; this vehicle.

"In case an ambitious conservation officer was to interrupt his poaching, the ATV would be better for a quick getaway through this familiar wild terrain.

"Besides the elusive ATV, Black Jack was liberally indulging in some of his personal supply of homemade rum, which ultimately led to a case of testiness in the Haitian man.

"After another healthy chug of the bootleg rum, I noticed it was starting to get dark. He slurred, "Listen up, boy, ye hold that damn flashlight real steady and shine it right in the little rat's eyes. Those little rats come out at night and make a lot of noise digging on the ground for food. The light will blind them for a second, and I will pop heem one. Een a couple of days, we will be eating like kings – filet of Gibnut, the royal rodent."

"Well, me first chance arrived, and I held the flashlight real steady, but when I heard a loud pop in me ear, I jumped. It was no wonder the shot missed, considering me ol' man's condition. He didn't see it that way, though, and scolded me. When the next attempt also went array, he really flipped out. 'Boy, you need to grow a pair,' he said forcefully and proceeded to grab me junk. So, I screamed. To this day, I've never felt such pain.

"When I finished wiping tears away, I turned around, and the ol' man and the ATV were gone. Here I am, eight years old, in the dark, like tonight's blackness, with various jungle noises emerging as the ATV's light quickly vanished, and I'm standing in the middle of nowhere.

"Now, I'm really freaked out, about to pass out from fear, when he suddenly reappears, laughing. When I return home, I'm still bawling like a baby and can't wait to tell me mother what Black Jack has done. He immediately collapsed in bed before me mother could confront him. She quickly took a more drastic approach.

"I stood in shock as me mother calmly boiled a pot of water. I'll always remember the look on her beautiful face. She did not speak, didn't have to; it was clear what her intentions were. Mother was going to pour the boiling water on her husband, Black Jack, most likely on his crotch. I pleaded with her - please, Mother, don't do it. You'll get sent to prison. I'll be all alone.

"Early the next morning, Rosetta Duvalier gathered up young Maxwell and her secret reserve of running money. Literally running to the bus depot, my mother stopped at the police station to report that her husband was once again running bootleg rum and poaching various game from the nearby jungles. Mother and child then boarded a bus for a Mayan village three hours to the south and didn't look back."

Almost on command, the still night in the jungle came to life with a buzz, as if reacting to Max's chilling story. "Okay, it's your turn, Atticus," who, evident by his silence, was not interested in sharing or was asleep. It was unlikely he was sleeping, considering the present predicament. It was then up to Zeke, who was still reeling from defeat because of the failure of the VW Beetle. Zeke felt empty and remained silent.

However, with the onset of hundreds of cicada males beginning courtship calls and unable to sleep, Zeke rethought his silence. With a blank stare that pierced through the darkening forest, Zeke was ready to detail an appalling story of his own. A confession, a farewell admission?

Lacking emotion, Zeke recited the tale of 'the accident' in a monotone voice, a departure from his usual animated self.

"I was eight years old, and all I remember is the persistent rain and then the flooding, which meant no school. My baby brother Thomas was four years old, and we were both bouncing off the walls. I had been diagnosed with ADHD, and was taking Ritalin. I was doing better at school and home. Having a little brother also helped greatly and made me feel important, but those couple of weeks were brutal. I was thankful I had Thomas as a little playmate and boy, we played; I know it probably drove my parents nuts, but we all survived. When the rains finally stopped, and after the intense cleanup ended and the nearby Kentucky River began to recede, we were free."

Zeke paused before continuing with his saga, hearing rustling outside in the near pitch-black night. He clutched the tire iron, which he moved to rest at his feet near the now useless pedals.

Peering over at Max, whose face was partially lit by a rising half-moon, he appeared to be focused on Zeke's story. Both men turned to glance at Atticus, who was apparently asleep. In the ominous stillness, Zeke, in a rare melancholy mood, proceeded with his attention-grabbing story.

"Brutally hot weather had set in as if to bake the ground dry in the aftermath of the record rain, but who cared? Thomas and I were not interested in the talk of a 100-year rain. The only thing we cared about was that the monsoon of Madison County was over, and we had exploring to do.

"Our big oak tree, with a swing hanging from a limb by long thick ropes, had survived, unlike other trees and fencing about our property.

"Dad told me before he let us out to watch Thomas while he dressed to accompany us for a day of fun. We were all ecstatic; we were going to unleash our pent-up energy and forget how we were on each other's nerves in the house. I let Thomas go first on the swing, and I happily pushed him to new heights as Dad came out and began walking over to join us. I laughed with enjoyment as I gave one more big guy push to impress Dad as I backed off to wave at him.

"Implanted in my head is the sound, the sound that seemed like all the sky was crashing down. Not the tree, but a sturdy limb, itself the size of a small tree, fell aimlessly onto my brother.

"I froze while Dad ran over and quickly attended to Thomas. He frantically screamed for me to call 9-1-1, but I couldn't move. All I could do was stare at my motionless brother under a limb that looked like it exploded, leaving a pile of shrapnel covering Thomas's entire small body."

With his feelings exposed, Zeke blinked once, back into obscurity. No peace was to come from his disclosure. His mind said, "Not so fast, boy, you have to figure out this mystery. Someone has to bear the blame for 'the accident'."

Zeke remained silent yet his mind would not quit. He was sapped by telling his story, a story he had never recited to anyone, never to any well-meaning psychiatrist or court-appointed psychologist. He had something to take away from his disclosure.

"No one, I've never spilled my inner feelings to anyone, let alone to myself. But now I have, to someone I barely know. I guess I probably always wanted to be liked, to be wanted and close to people. So, I just acted crazy to get over 'the accident'. The harder I tried, the more fucked-up my life became. I tried to distract myself from the guilt by stealing. I treated others like shit to alter the deep-seated fear that, eventually, they would treat me like crap too. I just wanted to do anything to keep that damn demon at bay."

Four-year-old Thomas Callahan was laid to rest not far from the swollen Kentucky River where he had once gone fishing with his father and brother Zeke. Little Thomas' death was counted among the dozen deaths attributed to the freak line of powerful storms that ripped through Northern Kentucky that spring. High winds, heavy rains, and even three tornadoes touched down in isolated areas. It was determined that, most likely, the limb fell on the innocent child because the tree was damaged, as many in the area had been during the recent storms.

Still guilt, blame and sorrow had combined to be the perfect personal storm. It could not have been just an accident. Someone had to be responsible.

Max, meanwhile, had calmed his emotions and wanted to hear more – Atticus must have a past. Of the three, considering his obvious impairment, Atticus had to have a story. When no response from him followed, Max succumbed to becoming part of the jungle's stillness.

Understandably, Atticus was not sleeping, nor would he indulge anyone with horror stories from his childhood, which he had long ago erased from his mind. To awaken buried memories of his mother and sister would be a dangerous resurrection. As it had been in his conflicting youth, the darkness was his soul mate; he would relish the peace.

CHAPTER 30

"Don't give up before the miracle happens."

– Fannie Flagg

Nothing stimulated one's senses as a trek through a magnificent forest at daybreak, when life changes shifts. Nocturnal creatures seek out the solitude of sleep after an active night, while diurnal animals begin their daytime routine of existence. For conservation officer Oscar Herrera, he could not ask for a better time to start his day than to be one with the moment. His government parks job dealt with areas of wilderness that encompass more than half of the country of Belize.

It was rather unusual for an indigenous Mayan, such as Oscar, to hold any government position. As an indigent citizen in a country where it was difficult to raise a family while trying to keep one's head above the poverty line, early mornings were a great time to explore and clear his mind

His sense of tranquility was disturbed by the presence of a bizarre medium in the secluded area of the forest, giving Oscar Herrera pause and then extreme excitement. His imagination took over as he gave himself the sign of the cross. *"Dios Mio*, this has to be a space vehicle."

During his tenure as a conservation officer in Belize, Herrera had run across many illegal activities. Mostly trespassing or poaching, even a meth lab, but never an extraterrestrial encounter. But why not here? It wasn't that far away from where the big one hit. Oscar was a student of the ancient phenomenon and knew that further north, on Mexico's Yucatan Peninsula, a six-mile-wide asteroid hit, causing the dinosaur extinction. This vehicle could be a prelude to further visitors to follow. If true, Oscar knew he was looking at financial security for life; he could be looking at millions.

Walking closer, he noticed what a crude job of camouflaging the craft was given and how close it looked to an old VW Beetle.

It may have kept four-legged predators away overnight, but it was an easy spot for the lone uniformed man who took his job seriously. He was adept at finding illegal activities in the expansive, protected forests and rainforests.

Perhaps the craft had crashed into this remote area of Central America, possibly killing the passengers, or maybe they walked away and attempted to infiltrate Earth's society.

"Ay, maldito," Herrera swore as he noticed some human movement in the rear seat of the car. He reached for his pistol, pulled it from the holster and crept closer to the vehicle. He reminded himself that the pistol was useless except as a perceived threat since he had no ammunition in the weapon, a cost-cutting casualty. He carried a bulky, antique rifle in the old government truck but had no time to retrieve it. Meanwhile, two young white men and a young black man were visible. They had either overdosed or were intoxicated from some poisonous mushrooms. Regardless, it was a huge let-down to find out he had run across some low-life earthlings, not aliens.

Officer Herrera thought of calling in a report but figured there would be no signal anyway. He could use the radio as a ploy if needed. He was still embarrassed that the VW wasn't a spacecraft, nor were the passengers, aliens. Oscar crept closer to the foul-smelling vehicle. These three punks should be easy to at least ticket for vagrancy. However, if needed because drugs, guns, or theft were involved, Herrera could arrest and haul them away in his aging Chevy Suburban. The reality was if the vagrants wanted to, they could charge him and easily overcome him, but he was hoping it would turn out to be three *marijuano*s hiding out, and hopefully, he would have them turn over their stash, and he would let them go. As a ranger with the national interior office, outside that one time stumbling upon a mini meth lab,

Oscar had not encountered anyone who was a hardcore drug supplier or maker, just your everyday poacher or hunters without licenses.

His career with the Belize national parks division began as a guide at one of 12 recognized Mayan ruins in the county. Up until Herrera's subsequent hiring in his present position, he was the exception, as Mayans in Belize are considered indigenous people and second-class citizens. Oscar was educated and wanted to help the country maintain a safe environment for animals in the precious rainforest and jungles. He was handed the roving position that had him traveling extensively between forests in central Belize and to the south; most of the time, he worked solo. Basically, Oscar also was assigned to monitor illegal activities and report these actions to a regional station. There, more experienced rangers would follow up and reap the rewards, usually in the form of good reviews or healthy payoffs by the offenders.

Tapping the side of the clunker, Oscar loudly announced his position to the stunned men. "Raise your hands and get out, slowly" he commanded. Seeing the motley crew of three exit the small vehicle with hands raised brought immediate comical relief to a tense moment.

"Now! I need everything out of the car, and I hope I don't find anything, drugs, guns or animal trophies."

Rags passing as clothing, old iguana feces, chicken bones, and, of course, Atticus's ever-present battered bag, left Officer Herrera dumbfounded as to what he had uncovered.

Herrera took Max, the obvious local citizen, aside for further information while the devastated pair of Americans with similar fears of lengthy jail sentences or worse, stood by on stiff legs.

While Zeke stood alongside a struggling Atticus without exchanging words, both men were contemplating a run for it; nobody would find them. True that, however, survival in the dense wilderness would be more than a challenge, each quickly realized. Zeke wished it was he who had gone with the conservation officer for a confab; perhaps he could have negotiated a deal. Maybe, just maybe, the affable Max could get the officer to let this encounter pass. Unlikely, he worried.

> *"To say things looked bleak was a frickin' understatement. An armed officer had found us out here in the middle of nowhere, farther away from home than we were a day ago, in a frickin' jungle, with no identification on Zeke or me. He could shoot us on the spot, and animals would devour us in a matter of hours; who would ever know?"*

"Grab your stuff. We're going for a little ride. Maximillian here told me all about your troubles." Oscar Herrera, looking and sounding like a trooper in one of those spoof movies, removed his Hollywood shades and instructed the two Americans in a menacing tone to "sit in the back seat." In the background, Max puzzlingly hollered, *"Vaminos amigos."*

Upfront, Max and conservation officer Herrera amicably talked in various forms of Belizean/Mayan languages. National topics, most notably those affecting the Mayan populace, were discussed by the two Belizean natives, adding to the puzzlement of the two men in the roomy back seat.

Zeke sat motionless, unable to hear much over the squawking radio, desperate to learn information as to their destination.

Finally, Herrera spoke to the two backseat passengers. "In case you are wondering where we are heading, let me explain to you both."

Zeke and Atticus could not believe their good fortune when Herrera finally explained their destination. They were headed an hour away to a poor village in the district of Toledo, which was next to the home of Max's Mayan family.

From there, Punta Gorda was a short thirty miles away. However, it was too late for yesterday's proposed rendezvous. Once the exhilaration from the startling news sunk in, Zeke figured out another exit plan. If he could again link up with Rey in Miami, he hopefully could re-schedule a quick pick-up for himself and Atticus. He and Atticus would only need to secure transportation to Punta Gorda.

All the while Oscar Herrera detailed their destination, Max sat facing his compadres in the rear seat with a huge grin. "Max told me that he needs a kidney transplant and how you both were generously helping him get there. He also told me about your poor grandmama. God bless her; I hope you can make it home in time for the ceremony. You, Senor Zeke, are to be commended for protecting these two hombres and for being their divine leader in this immense journey, *Vaya con Dios todos.*"

Zeke didn't know what to believe. Was the officer being sarcastic or serious? A sideways glance at the smiling Max answered Zeke's self-query. He, in turn, felt a sense of pride for his protégé for his quick thinking.

Atticus, in the meantime, was confused as he did the calculations in his head relevant to another attempt to flee Belize. For such a small country, it sure was difficult to leave.

Best described as a dusty community, the farm was a co-op among a handful of families, each maintaining some semblance of ancient customs, which was a dying yet sacred world.

Max eagerly introduced Zeke and Atticus to his extended family, from its patriarch to its newest arrival and, of course, the petite girlfriend in waiting. A hot meal of beans and rice was eagerly shared with the *Gringos,* as was clean clothing, though it was very difficult to find something for the lanky Atticus. Resourceful seamstresses found some older clothing and then quickly made some alterations to properly outfit the *simpatico Americano.*

The trio's old clothes, with the scars of their travels from Belize City to the present, were sacrificed to a celebratory bonfire held in honor of the road warriors.

The biggest contribution from the community was the offer of the use of a mobile phone. Zeke gratefully made the all-important call to Rey Jindal in Miami.

When they were finally connected, Zeke learned that the initial meeting would not have taken place anyway, even if the Americans had made it to the scheduled meeting point. Thunderstorms had moved into the southern Florida Keys and Miami before moving into the gulf stream off the southeastern US coastline.

With pickup time coordinated for the following day and with transportation secured, the fugitive and his hostage were able to prepare for their getaway. It would be wise to get minds and bodies prepared for the long-awaited exodus.

Atticus never completed his note about Max. Even with his immeasurable vocabulary, he could not come up with a simple adjective to describe the jovial and caring one.

Unlike Atticus, the community's patriarch had many poignant things to say to two young American men.

"Thank you for returning our son, our brother, to us. We are indebted to you both. We wish you safe travels. If, for some reason things go wrong, you are welcome to stay here for as long as you want. People here have taken a liking to you both, especially the young single girls."

In private, Zeke spoke for the two Americans with words of gratitude to Max for his help. "That was a brilliant line of shit you fed that conservation officer. What was it again? Oh yeah, you need a transplant – a kidney transplant? Brilliant."

Max was quick to reply to Zeke's misguided gratitude.

"No, mon, eet's not a lie. I was born with under-developed kidneys, and I knew the day would come when I would need a new one. I am working with our resident medicine person. If that doesn't work, I might have to go to the U.S. for a new kidney. You guys have the best of everything, they say."

Zeke was taken aback by Max's admission and wished him well, as did Atticus with just a meaningful, compassionate stare. Zeke whispered a personal request to Max, "Hey man, forget that voodoo *bull-shit*, get your ass to the States, and get a damn kidney if that's what you need. Good luck, and I hope to see you again."

> *"Saying goodbye to Max was a new experience for me. I had parted ways with people who were close to me: my father left me without a goodbye, the same way with Sophia, and beautiful Nina from the cruise ship. Max was different; he was standing before me. I did not know what to say."*

A relentless foul-smelling stench slapped Atticus in the face as he and Zeke reached the pier where they would meet their destiny of leaving Belize. Zeke explained to Atticus that fishy smell was something one had to be around for a while to grow accustomed to. Atticus, ever susceptible to out-of-the-ordinary conditions to his sense of smell, disputed that possibility.

"Welcome to Punta Gorda," declared the wooden sign on the pier overlooking the Caribbean coast of southern Belize. Any delight from finally arriving at the port for their long-awaited departure from Central America, to begin their trip to Florida, was quickly dissolved when Atticus calculated that the distance home was now a couple hundred miles farther than from Belize City. Atticus had another immediate concern. How would they cross the vast, churning sea? All along the huge pier were fishing boats of various sizes, from small to not-as-small. That was troublesome for the worried American. Sighed Atticus. *"At least the cruise ship was large enough that you felt little movement most of the time."*

Zeke walked back to Atticus after making final arrangements with the designated contact. He seemed to be concerned but quickly turned a troubling frown to a rigid smile, a tell-tale sign that something may be amiss. "Okay, we're on." Zeke let the words hang for encouragement, but it was obvious there was more. "We will be going on a speed boat; they tell me it's a little choppy out there, so we'll need to hang on." Atticus could only sweat.

With a direct sea route, the small yacht jumped across the waves at consistent intervals, which seemed to delight Zeke, ever the thrill seeker. Atticus, on the other hand, was fighting through a raging case of sea sickness, something he had avoided on the cruise ship.

> *"The souped-up yacht was fast and bumpy, which was bad enough. When I had the nerve to open my eyes, I noticed hundreds of silvery fish. Obviously, there had to be sharks around to feed on them."*

The crew of two Cuban expatriates carefully guided the speedy yacht around their previous home island, into the Gulf of Mexico, to an islet where the *Americanos* disembarked. The yacht continued with its crew and hidden cargo to parts unknown.

What awaited Zeke and Atticus on the sparse strip of land was little more than a single runway, an abandoned hangar, and a boarded-up building. A lone amphibious aircraft sat idle on the runway. "I hope we don't have to fly this ourselves," quipped Zeke as he surveyed the plane. Atticus was too drained, suffering from mal de embarquement, to appreciate any joking around from Zeke. Other than the airstrip, the island seemed deserted.

Uneasiness rose when the pair caught sight of two figures approaching from behind the boarded-up building. As the pair walked slowly closer, it became evident that both men were armed, with hands resting on holstered guns. A scribbled writing indicated the frantic feeling Atticus felt.

"Here I am in the middle of nowhere. A distant shadow of an island could be seen, it must be Cuba. We better not be going there."

Both men looked to be middle-aged Latins, serious and unfriendly, when finally, the larger of the two spoke up and directed a stern question to a nervous Zeke. "What's the password?" he growled. Zeke seemed to be choking up, speechless for once. "It's a great day to fly, Si?" One of the stern hombres asked Zeke, what's the word? Zeke appeared confused. Atticus, however, was shut-eyed, and wishing hard for once to hear Zeke speak. Finally, he answered smoothly and distinctly "Johannesburg."

Laughter broke out between the two Latin men, joined in a delayed fashion by Zeke. "Alright, alright then, let's get out of here. There is some day-old fried chicken in the back, and I have something for the quiet one." Reaching into his jacket, he pulled out a pill bottle and tossed it to Atticus, "Here is some candy for you, muchacho," he grinned. Do not eat them all at once, and don't puke inside the plane, or we will throw you into the Gulf. Do you comprehend?"

"One more thing, new plans: We will land offshore near the Keys. A fishing boat will take you ashore, where a pink taxicab will be waiting for you."

For Atticus, this was certainly an eyes-shut-tight voyage with a seat belt stretched tightly across his lap. He concentrated on holding down any reverse flow of the cold fried chicken. Yes, chicken. The food he had sworn off from in Belize.

Comparing the runway landing of a commercial airplane to the water landing of a seaplane is like comparing the placid roll of a cruise ship to the ride of a wave jumping jet ski. Airliners are smoother and louder, and the reverse thrust during braking is a feeling of, "I hope this thing stops." With the smaller seaplane landing in choppy water comes a sudden, decelerating splash and the feeling the plane is going to disintegrate. The most immediate concern is that the plane is going to sink and all aboard are going to drown.

Still recuperating from the aforementioned mind-boggling transport, another test of his mettle awaited Atticus. In what had by then become a game of absurd adventures would continue with a middle-of-the-night ride in a pink taxi. The problem with this leg of the trip was there were dozens of pink taxis cruising the area.

Zeke bared a wide grin while Atticus exhibited little in the form of emotion, at least outwardly. Inside, he was feeling a chemically induced confusion. His short-term memory was dulled as well, probably credited to the new meds. Atticus was, however, clear on one thing: he was done with the Belize misadventure.

CHAPTER 31

"It always seems impossible until It's done."

– Nelson Mandela

Another revealing letter that Atticus Carlisle had authored had Samantha Cross shaking her head; "It is unbelievable that this young man is self-taught; I liken it to having taught myself the rules of law. I could have saved myself thousands of dollars in law school tuition," she mocked.

"This may be the most incredible achievement ever to cross my professional eyes, from a pup attorney to a Magistrate Judge spanning over 20 years. Any harm coming to this guy will justifiably scream out for extreme punishment by the feds. This would spell doom for my client, my son Ezequiel. After all, it was he who perpetrated a crime against this presumably innocent young man."

Samantha and her investigators had learned much about Atticus Carlisle. To the point they were aware of his dismal upbringing and his questionable defense and subsequent conviction in an obvious accidental death.

It would take a clear head and some deep thought to cerebrally scan for the person named R. Jindal. In her public profession, names had come and gone, but she knew she had the dogged patience to eventually putting a face or place to a name. Like most of the writings she had pulled out of the foul-smelling bag belonging to the mystifying Atticus Carlisle, the young man's transcripts were very damning to her son Zeke. Had Zeke truly kidnapped this boy with a developmental disorder? What were the two doing in Belize, a country she knew little about? Who is this R. Jindal, a name Sam thought sounded familiar to her? What was his connection to this mystery and Atticus Carlisle? "Good heavens, where are you, boy?" Without finding Mr. Carlisle, this case is heading down a dark path of no return. With Atticus whole and considering his mental capacity, there might be something to work with. He must be quickly located before the government ups the pending charges against Zeke.

Sitting on crucial evidence, the book-bag and its contents, could put Sam in a real legal bind. Sam chose to intentionally withhold evidence relevant to her son Zeke's legal proceedings, an offense that could land "Your Honor" with a lengthy jail term and disbarment. Most imperative, R. Jindal must be found, providing authorities hadn't found him already.

Sam anticipated Zeke would have answers to these burning questions, and that he would give up this mysterious Jindal person. Hopefully, this would happen at their meeting the following day at the Federal Detention Center, where Zeke sat painfully awaiting his fate.

Zeke's constant fear was that Atticus would be found dead somewhere, which meant his life would be over as well. Since sending him off to return home alone, Zeke worried Atticus could have fallen prey to someone worse than himself. Someone who might take advantage of him. Oh, the irony!

With dogged investigative work and a timely break through on the Jindal clue, the mounting case against her son took its first positive turn. It happened when Sam's sleeping brain awakened. Sure she was on the right path, Samantha hurriedly scoured her personal files for a man she had met outside of court, but who was clearly influential to Zeke's development. It was a vital memory.

She discovered the name that had been eluding her well-crafted legal mind among other evidence of a difficult period in her personal life. Filed near tear-stained divorce papers from the same era, the papers were an attestation of when Zeke was sent off to J.T. Boe, a boy's academy in Indiana. A place that had promised to make respectful men out of all its students.

With continuous after-shocks from 'the accident' contributing to the growing abandonment of their family values, desperate times were upon the Callahan family. Many times, Samantha had led people in her courtroom to counseling; at that point it was she and her husband who were uneasy participants.

Exacerbating her guilt at that time was the difficult decision to send their troubled son to boarding school. Ever since the tragic death of their younger son, Thomas, the Callahan couple desperately attempted to get Ezequiel back on track from his self-destructive misdirection, an obvious fall-out of his brother's untimely death. Ezequiel was convinced that had he not put Thomas on the swing, he would still be alive; that he was responsible for Thomas's death.

Much research for professional help had put the desperate couple in touch with a private all-male school in Indiana. Their bio indicated teaching discipline and high values. Academically, a bevy of statistics and testimonies just about guaranteed a successful high grade point average for one's four years of attendance. A frustrated Mr. Callahan had whispered to his unresponsive wife, "Sounds like a damn military school. I don't much care for these all-male institutions; the kids come out, after four years of mind-fuck; like robots."

Samantha could only roll her eyes at her soon-to-be ex-husband's take on the boys-only school.

In desperation, Sam's thoughts were of hope that this was the place to put her son on the straight and narrow. Despite their status as budding attorneys, the Callahan's were just another couple sitting in the outer office of Reyansh Jindal.

As time flew by, there was steady assurances by Mr. Jindal that her son was doing outstanding work and should be graduating on time with high accreditation. However, the administrator failed to mention that little Zeke had a couple of infractions in the small town, one being a joy ride in a borrowed car. Reyansh Jindal was able to have any word of this incident expunged from any report. The school, after all, was an important entity in the town.

Sam remembered being surprised at Zeke's turnaround and his adjustment to the strict environment, to the point that he desired to stay on campus all year long.

Now, her focus was on pursuing whether Reyansh and Rey Jindal were one and the same and what his involvement was in this somber, unlawful activity.

To understand Rey Jindal was to understand his arrival in the U.S. from India as an intense twelve-year-old.

CHAPTER 32

"Time doesn't heal emotional pain; you need to learn how to let go."

– Roy T. Bennett

Traffic that Monday morning on the Beachline Expressway was ultra-congested, a morbid parting shot courtesy of *karma,* he thought solemnly. A bit of irony, he presumed, after departing the obscenely congested streets of Punjab, India. Back then, it was "Let us move to sunny Florida – in the wide-open spaces of the mighty U.S.A." Now, in the last minutes of his life, he sat mired in an early morning traffic jam, a quick moving downpour significantly responsible.

After pulling off the highway, he kept to his pre-meditated rendezvous with destiny. Facing easterly, overlooking miles and miles of blue water on the far-off horizon, he felt contentment and at peace. He recalled how enchanted he was by the view during his first visit to the area a few years ago. With no second-guessing now, he prepared for his final prayer of atonement for the sin he was about to commit.

With a workman-like pace, Inderpal Jindal proceeded to carefully remove his precious turban and place it on the seat next to him, on top of a letter he was leaving for his son, Reyansh. With that done, he removed a pistol from the center console of the car, then calmly put the gun to his head. Staring blankly into the rearview mirror, he hoped he would see the damage as the bullet blew through his skull, liquifying the soft tissue as it pierced his brain. Only then would there be a fitting penance for the horrendous sin he was committing. Alas, the end ensued almost instantaneously.

As an Aerospace Engineer for India's space program in the country's Punjab state, Inderpal Jindal felt he had hit the wall in his career. Inter-agency messages being leaked to the engineering sector were worrisome. Most of the agency's directors were shifting directions and were seeking newer ideas from fresh-out-of-college engineering graduates. It became clear that India's Space Agency was not the place for a real future.

Inderpal realized that at 45 years old he needed to make a move and make it quick if he were to reach the heights in his career that he needed to accomplish. He was used to making important decisions as per tradition in his conservative way of life; his Sikh religion impressed upon him that the family's existence was, as head of household, squarely on his shoulders.

Inderpal Jindal was remembered as a righteous man who had made a sinful decision, and his faith would absolve him of his unbearable actions. Reyansh's father, an Indian emigrant, was attempting to fit into a new country that was dealing with its own identity through divisiveness.

This period, unfortunately, coincided with the Jindal family migrating to Florida, to an environment which saw a movement that fomented anti-Muslim sentiment. Fall-out from this bias carried over to other groups being persecuted because they looked the part. Any people similar in appearance were categorized and labeled as untrusting and even potentially a terrorist. Indian emigrants, for example, had long proved to be valuable citizens in this country with many outstanding contributions in the fields of medicine and science, yet then were looked upon wrongly with mistrust.

On the other hand, the Jindal family had been quite content with their present lifestyle. Mrs. Jindal had a well-established pediatric practice in India, and three pre-teen children. Two girls and the oldest, a proud young man who was bestowed as a future person in charge, a leading light.

America and its world-renowned space program immediately became a place of interest for Mr. Jindal to pursue. Who in that field would not find working for the top-rung of the space exploration ladder appealing? Along with positive input from other expats who had found that the U.S. was rich in people from all parts of the world, and all religions were represented and welcome.

Mr. Jindal was initially ecstatic with the move to the upper-middle-class area outside of Orlando, Florida, a mere one-hour drive to the coast. Initially, the Jindal family was adjusting well to the enormous transition. However, trouble was soon brewing like a hurricane looming out over the Atlantic. Trying to remain undeterred by the internal impetus being fanned by the frenzied backlash toward those who were Muslim, or who were mistaken as being of a certain sect, was becoming difficult to overcome. This bias, sparked by unrelated disturbances, affected the Jindal family, even though they were not Muslim or from a rogue country responsible for terrorist activity. Each member of the family had been subjected to some form of provocation, from discreetly to blatantly.

Within the peace-seeking family, there was a growing desire to resettle to a more upscale community nearer to the Atlantic Ocean, closer to Mr. Jindal's future employment at the John F. Kennedy Space Center at Cape Canaveral. Trouble was brewing for Inderpal Jindal; he felt that perhaps he did not fit into the agency's plans, nor was he feeling welcomed in this country's suspicious eyes.

Inderpal's direction faced another detour when his wife insolently indicated that she was returning to India with the couple's two daughters. She was leaving their son with him so that he may devote his time to raising Reyansh as he entered manhood.

Her desire was to return to her familiar life back in Punjab with her family and her medical practice, thus providing the teenage daughters with a more traditional upbringing. This news seemed to be the final nail, further devastating an already depressed Inderpal. He was a man who always leaned on his faith, primarily the teachings of his Sikh religion, which gave him some hope. Sikhism preaches that people of different religions or sexes are all equals in the eyes of God, a creed he practiced in his daily life. He could not see how this country, a melting pot of so many diverse societies, could mirror the class divisiveness he had witnessed his whole life back home.

He saw how it affected him and his family, and mourned that he could not do anything about it, Now, it had split the most important aspect of his life. Meanwhile, Mr. Jindal's 16-year-old son, Reyansh, was having difficulties at school as well, which led to Inderpal being called in for consultations.

Mr. Jindal became resigned to swallowing his pride and having to return home to India. His son, when informed of his father's plan, objected, and defiantly indicated that despite his troubles at school, he wanted to stay in the U.S. In fact, he would be willing to stay with his uncle, who was a doctor, in Miami.

Mr. Jindal came away feeling further desperate and wished he could do more for his son to secure a successful future for him. So, he sold his home. It wasn't the oceanfront dream house the family thought they desired, but it was a real home for the Jindal's for a short while. Afterward, he ventured toward the coast on a route he had maneuvered many times in his happier day when he was still employed by NASA.

"When my father took his life, I was incensed; what a cowardly act, I thought. Not to mention, this was a major sin. This went contrary to all he taught me. I was devastated, and it took a long time to deal with. It changed me, and I began to act crazy. I even quit practicing Sikhism. Finally, my uncle threatened to send me back to India, which ultimately made me try to change. I did not want to go back there and face all that ridicule and humiliation because my father had committed the biggest sin."

Reyansh's life with his uncle came at a price and, predictably, some initial adjustment for both uncle and nephew. However, when Reyansh grew increasingly combative and disinterested in his schoolwork, the uncle threatened to send his nephew back to India. When that threat didn't seem to encourage Reyansh to apply himself fully, the uncle felt he had no choice but to send his nephew to a very disciplined high school academy that stressed conduct and academics.

When he pleaded to stay with his uncle and his friends at school, his uncle shook his head emphatically at his increasingly Americanized nephew. "I also felt betrayed by your father's blasphemous act, but still, I must not go against my brother's last wishes, even if what he did was a major contradiction to our religious beliefs."

While sitting erect in the admission office at the prep school, his feet flat on the carpeted floor, Reyansh was trying hard to look receptive to the elderly man's orientation talk. "Here, you will forget your fears, you will be awarded the tools to succeed, and you will walk into this puzzling world with your head held high, brimming with confidence, and feeling prepared. Sir, this is your new beginning; make the most of it. You can become a credit to yourself, your family, and society. In what capacity you become a success is your call. We will provide you with the necessary tools to excel in whatever field you choose."

Reyansh immediately bought into the smooth motivational oration from the aged man and his classical voice. After being plunked down at the academy by his disappointed uncle, he diligently worked towards fulfilling his uncle's demands. A dedicated work ethic geared entirely to strengthening his mind and body ensued without wavering. He would graduate from his J.T. Boe secondary school commitment at the top of his class and become a state wrestling champion. Rey Jindal was ready to take on his next challenge, that of conquering the capitalist society and their unethical cliques; he would use their own problematic tactics to justify his revenge.

He would make his father worthy again.

CHAPTER 33

"You have to get lost before you can be found"

– Jeff Rasley

ey West Florida, the southernmost point in the U.S., is as tropical as Belize, meaning hot and surrounded by water, lending to occasional soothing breezes. In Atticus Carlisle's mind, he had not really left the Central American country. Disturbingly, Atticus realized through his calculations that he was still closer to Cuba than Miami. Like being served a hot dog when you ordered a steak, it may momentarily cure your hunger, but it was a horribly poor substitute. Miami was where Atticus really wanted to be right then. Suddenly, one pink taxi squealed to a stop beside the pair. Could this possibly be the beginning of the end of a harrowing journey?

By the time Atticus, along with his hopefully soon-to-be ex-traveling companion Zeke, sat down in the unconventional taxicab, Atticus figured the trip to Miami overall to be 165 miles. Forever a thinker, Zeke thought, "How cool if I could have lifted a car and raced to Miami."

Understandably, the new meds he had taken prior to the plane ride that brought him and Zeke to the Keys made the plane trip less traumatic than the small yacht that had scared the living bejesus out of him. Just as Atticus was recuperating from that ordeal, he, along with Zeke, was facing another torment.

As it worked out, the taxi ride was short lived. Rey had arranged for the least expensive option for the final leg of their overseas travels. The returning duo was awarded a bus ride to Miami via the scenic Overseas Highway, which includes the famous Seven Mile Bridge, a breathtaking sixty feet high. The weary runaways were dropped at the bus station for the five-hour trip. There were many stops to exchange passengers and for traffic on the islands.

Zeke had relished the exciting small plane flight. The deranged looking pilot had included some thrill-seeking maneuvers to his short flight plan. Zeke, however, was not a fan of buses. They were too confining and too slow. He especially did not like the idea of a five-hour, 165-mile trip, including crossing 42 different bridges. Atticus, on the other hand, was practically giddy that the awful ordeal was almost over. He was in the U.S. again, and that meant a lot, as well as having Lucifer to accompany him. As weird as that sounded, he understood that having never traveled alone, it was essential that he would be accompanied on this final leg of the trip from *hell*.

Being back in the U.S. came with serious consequences. Zeke, who a couple of days ago would have cut off his right arm to leave Belize for home, had new concerns. There could be a nationwide search for him and Atticus. He envisioned reports being aired on television and possibly wanted posters being plastered at rail and bus stations. Most definitely, there were serious concerns about the pair being spotted together or Atticus saying something to someone. Nevertheless, Zeke was certain that his best chance at survival was to get back to Miami and Rey Jindal, despite the risks.

Rolling along in the crowded bus was just another surreal experience, except Rey would meet them at the bus station in Miami. At least this excursion meant that they were in the U.S. - land of the free, home of the brave, one step closer to home.

Arriving in Miami was best described as grumpiness vs. crankiness. Both Zeke and Atticus had suffered through another disturbing road trip. Zeke complained, "I think I have had more bull-shit trips in one month with you than I have had in my whole life."

"I cannot believe he wants to blame me for this when, after all, it was him who kidnapped me," countered Atticus, too quietly to hear.

Five hours of shifting gears, exhaust fumes, crying babies and being crammed into filthy seats, was enough for anyone to bear, especially two highly emotional individuals. That the pair had to deal with discomfort was cause for volatility. Almost criminal was the loss of A/C on the bus, on one of South Florida's hottest days to date.

Finally back on the American mainland, where Rey Jindal had once again come through, Atticus wondered why he was so obliging to Zeke. Atticus privately hung the nickname "Enforcer" on him, in part due to his stylish wardrobe and how he carried himself so confidently.

Straight away. Zeke prepared to face his former mentor, Rey Jindal, as soon as they stepped off the bus. Rey was seated behind the wheel of his classy Cadillac Escalade at the pick-up location. Zeke quickly picked up on the odd scene. "Damn, if he's driving himself, he must be pissed."

Motioning Zeke to the passenger seat and Atticus to the rear door, the reaming began. "You gave me your word, man, that you would behave if I got you a job on a cruise ship. So, what do you do? You end up getting thrown off the ship! "I may lose my contract because of you; that would be devastating."

Rey turned up the volume of his surround sound, drowning out the rest of the discussion from Atticus, who sat nervously in the back seat. It was apparent that the clandestine front-seat meeting that Zeke had just had with Rey Jindal had resulted in an adjustment in travel plans.

"We need to take some precautions with your friend and send him on his way. Take this bag."

"Sorry, man," Zeke began, in his familiar tone of his that said there was more. Atticus sensed he was about to be slammed by another invisible club, wielded by Lucifer himself.

"I can't go back with you. I know I said I would go back with you, but after talking with Rey, I've decided to stay here to get my act together first. If I go back and turn myself in, well, you know that old stallion of yours back home? Imagine him locked up; that would be me. I cannot stand the idea of being locked up. You understand, right?"

As was customary, Atticus listened to what Zeke had to say without looking at him until he had finished, then he spoke up. *"You lied to me. You knew you were not going to take me back home."*

With what amounted to an outburst by Atticus, Zeke felt an unusual bout of humiliation at his co-traveler's stern words. He had been shamed by a wealthy entrepreneur, and now a person on the spectrum, within a matter of minutes. If the twenty-four-year-old felt any remorse, it did not manifest in his stance to force Atticus to make the trip on his own.

Disgrace aside, Zeke and Rey had it all figured out. To protect their own interests, Atticus must travel alone. He would receive a one-way bus ticket to Lexington, a pittance in spending money, and weak well-wishes. Also, an important exchange was necessary. Zeke insisted he hold Atticus's book bag with its contents in exchange for a nicer bag.

"No way, this is mine, I..." Atticus was cut off by the low growl of the Cadillac engine, obviously a signal by Mr. Jindal that time was up. Zeke stood with an angry Atticus at the bus station gate in silence.

When the line to board the bus began moving steadily, the apprehensive passenger and his escort were soon at the door. Zeke, a little unsteady about the moment, slipped cash into Atticus's sweaty palm and murmured, "Here, for the trip, money to buy some eats." Zeke held up Atticus's old bookbag with promises of returning it to him soon.

Atticus tried committing himself to survival first and foremost. *"I will get through this, I will get through this, I will FRICKING get through this!"* he repeated robotically until he began to believe it.

Believe? He had believed Zeke once too often, he concluded, when he said he would be traveling home with him. Unfortunately,

Atticus faced the grueling 24-hour bus ride back to Kentucky ALONE!

With time, Atticus avoided any threat of a meltdown with a rare feeling of calm. He surveyed the available seats, eventually picking a window seat near the rear of the stuffy bus. As he settled into it, he looked about and relished, for the moment, the sight of a sparsely occupied bus, unlike the tightly packed bus he had occupied with Zeke earlier in the day. Atticus took a deep breath; he was sure he would make it. He kept telling himself that after one more day, he would arrive in Lexington and finally sleep in his own bed. Gram's hotcakes for breakfast would put the finishing touch on a wonderful return home. Atticus was, in fact, enjoying the first portion of the bus ride, until they made the first stop. After loading more passengers, another stop ensued only a few miles away, with more vocal passengers boarding. Without much ground covered, the bus took on the atmosphere of a carnival on wheels.

As they hit the open road with the Florida countryside whisking by, Atticus tried distracting mind games along with a pill from his bottle of new meds. With comfort settling in, he gazed through the hazy window.

He quickly decided to indulge in another happy pill when Atticus realized he would be subjected to an unruly family who were horsing around on the bench seat behind him. He had overheard a talk between the woman and the man, and understood they were also headed to Lexington. He realized they could aid him in reaching his destination. All he would have to do was to follow the family behind him.

Thus far, this portion of his month-long travel had been successful. Atticus was able to easily follow the schedule of all stops and times, aided by the driver's convenient, no-nonsense announcements over the intercom. He confidently scratched off the continuance of stops and locations on the schedule. Soon came a much-desired stop, an opportunity to stretch stiffened legs.

When he re-boarded the bus, an alarm went off in his mind as he noticed an influx of new passengers joining the journey north, including a large man who chose to sit in the back next to Atticus. He instinctually reached for his bookbag to write; sadly, he remembered it had been confiscated by Lucifer, who had not provided any writing material with the new backpack. Instead, he took another dose of the strong barbiturate.

Atticus squinted through tired eyes. The sound from the new bus driver was undistinguishable garble. He looked groggily outside for a sign of where they were at that moment. He was pleased at the sight of a *Welcome to Tennessee* sign.

"Yes sir," he nearly exclaimed, *"Tennessee! Kentucky is next – then I am home."* He woke his neighbor passenger when he happily gasped loudly.

An interstate highway sign revealed to the slowly awakening passengers that they were on I-24. Atticus scanned his map for what stop would be next when he made the heart-rending discovery that the bus was on the wrong highway – I-24 instead of the expected I-75!

Reality struck Atticus regarding the error of his ways. Because he had taken an excess amount of medication, he was responsible for this god-awful predicament. Obviously, he had slept through a change of buses and any announcements given over the intercom. Feeling the onset of a panic attack, Atticus slowly exited the bus at the next stop. He walked into a wooden shack that served as the remote terminal. He observed a sign indicating he was in Signal Mountain, Tenn.

"At least I am in Tennessee, pretty soon, Kentucky?" he sighed.

He found the station was unmanned at that time of day, and the disinterested driver was not much help either, except to tell him that he could stay on the bus to Nashville and then transfer to Lexington at a high cost. This was taking on the feeling of a horror movie where someone is abducted by zombies or aliens.

Farther down the street, he came upon a trinket shop where he found a pad of paper and a novelty pencil. He fittingly saw a rack of postcards with different versions of the same theme, "Tennessee River." Back outside, he noticed an arrow pointing to a huge body of water below.

"Water! More frickin' water, everywhere. Where should I go now?" pondered Atticus as he ran his fingers through his long, unkempt hair.

He followed the signs to the park and found a bench near the tentacles of trails for hiking. Trying to write a detailed account of recent days was a test of his questionable memory, exacerbated by his chemical hangover. Atticus rose from the bench, circled the enclave of trailheads and picnic areas and encouraged himself to take a risk and join the array of serious joggers. Until he realized that he must do something with the cumbersome bag that held his life's meager belongings.

Counting out the small amount of cash Zeke had given him back in Miami, Atticus did not feel the need to stash the precious little cash he possessed in his sock, unlike in Belize City. When in fact, he would have been better off putting what money he had into his sock. Instead, he carelessly tossed the bills into the near-empty bag, among random clothing and his ticket stub to Lexington.

Also thrown into the bag was the bottle of pills that he smartly decided against using again, for it probably was the reason why he felt so anxiously confused still. Running a trail was certain to clear his head and stretch out cramped legs. After the painfully long trip on a bus from the waterlogged state of Florida to this point, it promised to be a very therapeutic run.

He methodically stretched the muscles in his back and legs when he found a track that was geared to runners. His new backpack was left near the trailhead, hung discreetly from an oak tree, safe hopefully from killer bears or rabid raccoons.

After an hour of blissfully heavy breathing and with a good sweat going, Atticus felt rejuvenated and semi-back to his *"I can fricking make it"* attitude. He headed for his backpack to find a change of clothes for a wash-up in the spacious public restroom, which was larger than some places he had stayed in recently. The feeling of exultation from the run and renewed resolve quickly shifted to terror as he discovered his bag was gone.

For a tropical minute, Atticus feared he was back in Belize, with the stifling heat and constant peril. Passing sightseers, tourists, serious hikers, and those who were just pleased to be on the road to nowhere, were oblivious to the troubled young man with dark hair who sat scowling at his latest, self-inflicted predicament. Sitting on the hard log bench, with his head cradled in his clammy hands, he thought over his misfortune at being stranded with no immediate plan for resolve. He realized, for the umpteenth time, he needed Zeke to get him home.

With shielded eyes, he glanced up the steep hill he had just clambered down, bemoaning the loss of his trusty writings-filled backpack to Zeke in Miami, and his replacement bag, with the last few articles he owned, in it. A figure of an old woman appeared. as if she was passing through a sheer curtain. Curiously, her walk, which was erect and swift, didn't match the gait of one who appeared to be well into her eighties. Atticus was quick to look away from the old woman and ignore her presence.

"Probably looking for a handout; well, she's coming to the wrong place," thought the annoyed Atticus. However, one in Atticus's predicament could not be too fussy about speaking to a stranger. After all, misery loves company; perhaps she could show him where to dumpster dive for a meal.

> *"The closer I got to the old lady, the more I tried telling myself it was not worth speaking with her about my lost backpack. Or the fact that I am lost because I over-slept on the bus. I just need a little assistance, then I will be alright...maybe. Why not talk to her? She seems harmless. I got this far on my*

own. I can do this...maybe. I have proven that I can fend for myself...maybe."

"I really wish I was back at the farm, running up that old dirt road behind the property where, when you get to the end of the road, there is an incline taking you up to tree top height. It may be the highest elevation in all Kentucky. Here it would be a dwarf hill."

CHAPTER 34

"Getting old is like climbing a mountain; you get a little out of breath, but the view is much better."

– Ingrid Bergman

From a lifetime of experience, Laura Rawlings was schooled in how to identify living creatures in distress. It was a skill developed by an old lady with long, scraggly white hair tied in identical, tightly woven braids. She and her late husband, Reggie, who began his career as a veterinarian, had spent many years devoted to humanitarian work that took them to faraway places. Work that involved crossing paths with organizations from the *Humane Society* to the *World Wildlife Fund.*

There was a time when she and Reggie had set out to save the planet with their various causes associated with the environment and all things living. Deeds and sacrifices were done for righteous reasons, not for any awards or recognition. Only because they felt it was their duty.

In later years, the pair became involved with more local projects as conservationists, establishing a local wildlife rescue center. There, they mended sick and injured birds and small mammals up until Reggie's death a few years earlier.

Throughout her years working with wildlife, Laura also studied the habits and behaviors of the most complex of creatures, as well as the most compassionate and most dangerous. Humans.

"Sure is a hot one today, eh?" The raspy voice caused Atticus to snap back to the present from where his mind had wandered. Creating a welcome shadow for Atticus was the old lady he had just noticed.

Obviously, she had come over to hit him up for some money, he presumed. *"I'll just ignore her. Maybe she'll leave me alone; I have to go but where?"*

"Here, young man, have a swig; it's from my eighty-foot deep well, good stuff. Here, it's good for you." Atticus could smell the foul liquid from his seat on the rock. At first, he refused the old lady's offer and too quickly tried standing up. When his knees buckled, the old lady grabbed Atticus's arm in a firm, steadying manner.

"Whoa there, we have to stop meeting like this, dear," Laura joked, smiling widely, revealing a toothless grin.

Atticus was shocked at the strength that the old lady had just displayed in stabilizing him. His recent run through the forest and the high altitude, or the lack of food in his stomach, had probably been the culprits for his wobbly moment. He realized he had no choice but to take a drink, while holding his nose with one hand.

The woman had his backpack!

"Oh my, is this yours?" she exclaimed, reading Atticus's reaction to the bag. "I was about to turn it in to the Welcome Center out on Court Street." She didn't need to hear the young man's answer to realize it was his. Atticus clutched the bag tightly and breathed a huge sigh of relief that money and meds were intact.

"I saw it laying on the ground. An animal, possibly the two-legged variety, probably pulled it down from its perch and was then unimpressed by the smelly contents," Laura laughed. "I figured it belonged to a transient, someone living on the run or something. Are you a writer? Where did you study writing? I saw a couple of letters inside, pretty good writing, whoever was the author."

Atticus clutched the backpack, not happy with the line of questioning by the old lady. *"I just write stuff, I taught myself."*

It was obvious the young man was reluctant to converse, so she decided to use the universal language for young explorers, which is what he appeared to be.

"Come with me, please, let me treat you at this place back down the hill; they have the best blueberry hotcakes in all Tennessee, and Kentucky, too." She smiled once more; the mention of food, especially pancakes, had caused Atticus to look up at the toothless woman. "I used to bake bread and sell it to them. It helped pay the bills. Now, I'm retired, or should I say just plain old tired."

What a strange sight, thought Atticus, before he quickly resumed his normal downward stare. She noticed Atticus's attention to her mouth and shamelessly smiled even wider.

"If I knew before I came out for a walk that I would be having lunch with such a handsome young man, I would have put the chompers in. Here they are," she added as she proudly pulled them out of her shirt pocket. The teeth looked fake to Atticus, like the kind of gag teeth you wind up causing them to clatter.

"Fine set they are, too," she proudly displayed for Atticus to see. He chose not to look while his belly gurgled with hunger. "Come on, you like hotcakes?"

"Yes, I do," Atticus mumbled without hesitation, *"but I bet they're not as good as my gram's pancakes,"* Atticus added, surprising himself with his boldness with the stranger. Instinctively, he held his backpack tighter, not eager to let the bag out of his sight or clutches again.

"You'll have to speak up, though," Laura pleaded. "I left my hearing aids back in my cabin. I put them on Bear, my old dog, so he can hear me when I return."

It seemed like a joke, but to Atticus, she probably was an old woman who was suffering from age-related hearing loss.

Over the special of all-you-can-eat pancakes, the odd duo of 21-year-old Atticus Carlisle and his octogenarian brunch companion shared niceties. Actually, it was the elderly woman who did the talking while the errant traveler did the devouring of hot cake after hot cake.

"In case you were wondering, my name is Laura. Laura Rawlings. I have a small place on the river about a mile down from here. Bought it with my husband Reggie. He passed a few years ago, and I have been waiting to join him, but my dog needs me."

Laura studied the silent young man sitting across from her in the tiny hillside restaurant. In turn, Atticus's reaction to the elderly lady was quizzical; he didn't know what to make of her either. She looked like she was on her last leg, yet she possessed a certain wit about her that indicated a high degree of astuteness. She had already proved that she could hike impressively for an old lady.

On the other hand, Laura recognized that Atticus was not looking at her. His barely audible voice was an obvious clue that he may have an intellectual disability of some sort. Probably *autism,* she assumed correctly. So, what was he doing here?

Laura's natural curiosity remained active in her later years, her compassion for the drifters and mutts of the land remained strong, and she had encountered many during her own long life. This guy here is a troubled soul, she assumed. Was he dealing with a serious health matter, or had his challenge put him in peril out here in the wild?

"Honey, you look like you could use a few pounds on that skinny frame of yours, but are you going to put them on in one sitting?" the waitress asked. She and Laura had a good laugh at that jab while Atticus continued to eat.

Laura added, "How does he 'stack up' with most of your customers?" Once more, the two women laughed, this time at the elderly one's pun. Atticus took a rare pause in his consumption of the almost-like-home pancakes, but after not grasping the quips of the ladies, he resumed making short work of his delicious extended meal.

When he finally felt full, the odd couple left the restaurant a dozen pancakes lighter. Laura offered to lead Atticus back to the unmanned bus station for information on when he might be able to resume his journey home. Much deciphering of a complicated pamphlet at the bus station revealed that Atticus was out of luck to leave anytime soon. The next bus to stop locally for a direct trip to Lexington was five days away. Laura tried to console Atticus with a gracious offer of assistance. "I can put you up for a few days; you can help me with a couple of minor tasks for room and board."

Walking to her shack in the woods, as Laura called it, she followed a mystical course, straight out of a children's book like *Snow White*. Atticus had secretly included the book among his few possessions in the detention center back in Wisconsin, until it grew legs and walked away, as many of his possessions eventually did over the five years of his confinement.

After walking about a mile through the enchanting forest filled with the calls from birds hidden in the canopy, they came upon a delightful-looking cabin, which rose out of an equally mystical glen.

Looking feeble after the long walk, Laura Rawlings donned a sweater despite the warm afternoon. The two sat on a deck covered in acorn shells and other yard waste. Her mutt, Bear, lay by her side, disinterested in the latest guest. The first thing Atticus did was to search his backpack for his new meds to make sure they were still there. Laura requested a peek at his street version of meds before searching for its medical name.

Laura sternly proclaimed, "These are strong anti-anxiety pills. These are for sleeping; no wonder you slept through your stop on the bus. Luckily, you didn't overdo it, or you might have never made it here. Whoever gave you these was not doing you a favor. In fact, they were possibly trying to kill you."

Atticus gave long pause to what Laura had just said, theorizing in his mind that just maybe she was right. He decided to jot down his suspicions, then stuffed the note into his new bookbag.

"I'm here because Lucifer took me away from the farm. I called him Lucifer because he was capable of trying to kill me so I couldn't testify against him. Then, there was Rey, the Enforcer Hmmm."

After his unflattering comment about his former captor, Atticus found himself with a pair of stronger vocal cords. Perhaps it was because of Laura's disclosure about his meds and how dangerous she said they were. Laura Rawlings could not believe what she heard and was about to ask Atticus to slow down and speak up. Atticus suddenly was experiencing an uncontrollable swell of words, like a bright light turned on by the flip of a switch.

"My name is Atticus. Vivien gave me that name after some movie character from the 60s. I'm from near Lexington. I live with Gramps and Grams on their farm. I have Asperger's, which is some kind of autism. I make horseshoes, I love to run, I was a runner in high school, I qualified for the state finals at Frankfort, but I did not go. I met this guy named Zeke who forced me to Miami, where we got jobs on a cruise ship. I do not like water, though I tried to learn to swim. I could not swim because I cannot float.

"I had sex – it was ok. I fell in love with her, she was another crew member. She had to go back home to Ukraine. At least that was what I was told. I think Zeke was behind her leaving the ship. He and I got fired from the ship because of him and got left in Belize. I did not like it there; it was too hot, and I got robbed. I met some bad individuals. We came back to Miami in a small plane and a fast boat; it was very scary.

"Zeke put me on a bus to return home, but I missed my change of bus and ended up here, and now I have to find a way home. I do not know if I have enough money; the next bus will be coming here next Tuesday; that's five days. I just want to go home. I left a note for Gramps that I was going away for a few days. I hope they are not worried. It has been 46 days, three hours and a few minutes since I left."

Laura could only sit in shock at the blow-by-blow given by the previously quiet Atticus. While she was pleased to have drawn out of her guest a great deal of the account of his experiences, she was amazed at the degree of adventure he had supposedly faced in the last few weeks. She was curious to hear more from the interesting but obviously cursed young man. She was certain he had more amazing accounts to share of his young life, an accurate understatement, to say the least.

"I'm in the process of cleaning up the old place," Laura interjected, side-tracking her guest from continuing his amazing story. "I want to leave the cabin presentable to the Park Service before I leave." Atticus was more than just curious at Laura's statement.

Laura promptly arrived upon a plan that would hopefully appease her and her guest. She didn't want to derail Atticus's obvious desire to chat, but she sensed the coming of a grand plan that could be the end-all for everyone present in the cabin. Now was the time for Laura to formulate and act upon a plan that had come to her in a passing thought while Atticus talked of being taken advantage of. She had to make sure that this would not turn into another case of him being exploited, of Atticus being used for someone's own ends. Without further delay, she ventured into another room where she created a checklist, convinced that she was on to a way out. Like Atticus she was passing through. For Laura Rawlings, the end of her life's trail was near.

She returned to Atticus aware that she had lost much of her short-term concentration, plus her special guest, the lost boy from Lexington, seemed ready to talk again. Before Atticus could continue speaking, Laura presented a tease of her proposal.

"Since your bus will not be here for a few days, what if I put you up with a soft bed and hot food until then? I promise at that time, I will help you with a ticket home."

Laura felt a surge of ingenuity; she had forgotten how good that felt. Back in the day, Reggie would constantly compliment his young wife on her quick wit and how she was able to respond to changing circumstances on the fly. Could she do that now?

The usually skeptical and unusually talkative Atticus quickly accepted the generous offer from the insightful elderly woman, enthused by her offer of help without having to ask for it. Before he had literally stumbled into Laura's life, Atticus was loath to ask anyone for assistance.

He sensed his new hostess and her old dog needed a break, while Atticus craved a short run through the quiet forest. The wind at his back was a wasted boost; he needed no aid as he was floating with contentment right then. Convinced he was going to make it home, he felt he could trust her offer of help. Laura, without a doubt, was the first person he met on this crazy trip who seemed sane. He was eager to get back to the cabin and tell Laura of his recollections of more reprehensible moments of his life.

It was weirdly revitalizing to remember hidden moments of his troubled life, and Atticus was eager now to disclose more. Unfortunately for him, Laura and her dog, Bear, were fast asleep. Day one at Laura's was over as far as interaction with his hostess. He would write the night away, notating valuable information on past and present events.

When Atticus turned in for the night, the soft bed was like none other. He had sorely missed the comfort of his bed at the farm during his recent travels. Sleeping comfortably for the first time since he left Kentucky, Atticus was awakened by an early morning symphony of birds from the natural aviary outside of his window. He had settled easily in at the log cabin despite being nearby to the swollen river's bank. *"For goodness sakes, more water,"* he sighed. *"I know the earth is 71% water, but does it have to be every frickin place I go? This place and Laura are great, but I cannot wait to get back home where the land is only a wonderful .3% water."*

In his mind, he had been exploited his whole life by those who should have been protecting him. Even his father, his closest influence, had failed him by going off to a faraway land to die. Two close female acquaintances had also abruptly left him just as he was beginning to feel comfortable in a typical couple's relationship.

For Laura, her aged memory, and the fact that she was dealing with an intelligent human with a form of autism, the tired old lady quickly established that the two people and the old mutt needed each other, and they had one shot at a fateful connection before it was too late for any, or all of them.

After a delicious breakfast of French toast and fruit, Atticus was ready to repay the old lady. He was prepared to work off the debt he felt he owed for his good fortune of having Laura take him in. His top priority was to detail more of his horrid life while it was present in his mind. Laura seemed eager as she curled up on her stuffed chair with teeth in hand.

"I never talked much as a kid; the more I spoke, the more trouble I got into. My earliest memories were of my father taking me to track meets as a kid. I was fascinated with what the athletes would do in various running and field events. I really liked the running events because of the starter pistol and the sound the starter gun made, the sudden clap. "And then, well then, there was the blackout, and the price to pay for what happened that dreadful night."

Atticus's voice trailed off while his expression momentarily darkened, as if he recalled something unpleasant. Laura knew not to force the issue, though she noticed an obvious increase in Atticus's overall confidence. She would hate to see the young man revert to his voiceless self.

"Tell me about your mother, hon," Laura whispered, gently trying to pull more information from him.

"Ah, Vivien, I don't think I ever called her mother; she always insisted that I call her by her name." Atticus stopped again, appearing to reassess his reason for being there. He slowly turned back to Laura, who was petting an equally attentive Bear, both anticipating more narrative from their restless guest.

"Vivien was evil, but it didn't bother me; we disengaged early on. I think my father took a job in China so he could get away from Vivien. He was going to take me to China to live with him and his new wife, but that never happened because he had an accident at work and died."

Atticus's matter of fact account of his mother and father seemed to illicit a tear from Laura. Perhaps her young guest had moved on from that period, or more likely, he was socially disconnected. Most anyone with that baggage to carry would have trouble reliving such trauma. He spoke matter of factly of horrible circumstances.

"My bedroom at the mansion was always cold. Day and night. Spring, summer, fall, and winter, always cold. Nevertheless, I spent a lot of time there. Vivien once scolded me when I called the place where we lived a house. It was a very large house, but she insisted that I call it a mansion. I dreamt there a lot but remembered little of my dreams. All I remember is that they were good dreams. Mostly, I just learned, studied, and taught myself upstairs in my cold room. And I forgot the humiliation that happened down below in the main part of the mansion, the house of horrors, as I would call it.

"I remember early in life I was told no one remembers anything from their first three years of life. I'm an exception because if I try hard, I can remember things from when I was about one! Conversely, if I try really hard, I can make myself forget something that just happened a minute ago."

Laura warily accepted Atticus's belief that he could, in fact, remember things back to infancy. She recalled that people with his disorder could have unusual memory abilities and accepted this declaration as his high-functioning autism speaking.

"I don't know if I want to revisit that day. I've done a good job of keeping the outcome buried in my mind whenever it surfaces. I think I'd like to try, but first, I think I have to take my meds". Atticus stopped, remembering he had no meds, just the dangerous long-acting drug that Lucifer had given him.

Laura suggested, "This could be your chance to permanently put that moment to rest and find peace; just wait to get home to take your prescribed medicine."

Atticus seriously pondered the old lady's advice before clearing his throat and allowing his inner self to rule.

"My sister, Lizzy, was becoming as cruel and evil as our mother. Lizzy was as different from me as possible, and she was eight years, three weeks, and four days older than me. She was not very happy when I entered the family picture. She was used to having everything she, or Vivien, wanted her to have, which included, as a fourteen-year-old freshman, an eighteen-year-old senior – a thug named Jimmy Lee Walker."

Atticus paused from his mostly emotionless but distinct story, seemingly on the verge of displaying some impenetrable reaction to this dreadful memory.

"I remembered from early on that she would do bad things to me, especially if she had to babysit me. There were innocent tricks played on me at first. Eventually, they became more serious episodes, which were becoming more criminal in nature. I guess Lizzy and Jimmy Lee, whom I called Pecker Head, thought I would not say anything to anyone. I never did, basically, because I never talked much.

"He would hit me on the side of my head and call me a retard. I cried and cried before finally telling Vivien, who pretended to be angry at Lizzy and her boyfriend. It was the last time I ever cried, until I was stranded in Belize."

Atticus recounted the incident in his usual unemotional way, sipping on some smelly water as he continued. *"I got grief from the two of them; for a long time, they called me a squealer. In fact, days later, Pecker Head got in my face with a cigarette dangling from his mouth. He took it between his fingers and held it real close to my arm, then it touched me. A terrible pain that I cannot forget - ever! I was frickin scared of him from then on, even more than I was when that frickin' gun went off."*

"Care to tell me about that?" Laura calmly asked, hoping that Atticus would already have the trust in her to be open about that incident. Also, she wondered if it was true that he had never cried again. It's hard to believe that one could live without expressing one of life's most essential emotions.

"I still can't talk about that yet, except to say that because of the shooting, I was sent to a youth prison; I was only eleven years old then. Supposedly, they changed the minimum age law because of me. I don't know; I can only say it was an accident that only happened because Lizzy and her boyfriend were constantly bullying me, and no one was stopping them. It got worse after the accident that killed my father. I was becoming more isolated – I was turning everything off.

"I was supposedly being homeschooled, but all that meant was I had access to some old encyclopedias, and Mrs. Mathews was occasionally helping me when she wasn't waiting on Vivien. I was all set to go live in China with my father; I had my things packed. Vivien, of course, who, after denying my father visits and contact, was now eager to see me go. I guess she was paid off. Anyway, I became silent; I did my talking in my head when I read in bed, which was often. I pronounced the words in my mind. I spoke to no one in particular, under the sheets or pillow until I fell asleep while my flashlight dimmed away to darkness. I was forced to steal batteries from Vivien so I could read in bed and roam the huge creepy house in the early hours. Atticus's voice then trailed off to his previous whisper-like voice.

"Yes, I was little, but I was fed up with Lizzy and her creepy boyfriend and their bullying. When my father died, I had no one I could talk to; I knew I had to fight back for myself, and I foolishly thought that I could scare them into leaving me alone. I came up with the idea of how I could scare Lizzy since her room was so close to mine. I would, on occasion, in the middle of the night, walk the quiet house; the only noise was the old wooden floors creaking. I would sometimes pause at Lizzy's room; her door was always left cracked open. I remember thinking how easy it would be to plunge a stake into her heart like one would do to an evil vampire."

After a long pause, in which Laura thought that Atticus was done with his story, he calmly and confidently resumed.

"Vivien, practically an invalid by then, was confined to a wheelchair. She usually stayed in her majestic bed chamber. About this time, I had overheard accounts about how Vivien, who was becoming a portly woman,

had received a large amount of money because of a suspicious fall on the sidewalk in front of an upscale restaurant after a convenient dusting of snow.

"Yes, I was little, but I was understanding more about Vivien and was becoming more fed-up with Lizzy and her creepy boyfriend and their bullying. After my father died, I had no one I could talk to. I knew then I had to fend for myself.

"Eventually, this led to more abuse by Lizzy and her senior boyfriend, Pecker Head, a person with an attitude as bad as his complexion.

"In my childhood, various forms of brutality were inflicted upon me, becoming more severe after my father's death. Pecker Head assumed the role of enforcer; it got to the point that if I looked at him the wrong way or other made-up infractions, he would berate me horribly, calling me the 'r' word, and worse. He eventually started to force me to take ice cold baths. The first time was allegedly for using up the hot water, leaving only lukewarm water for Lizzy and him to shower. When I resisted after stepping into the freezing tub, Pecker Head held me under the water. I struggled mightily, but the now twenty-year-old man held me down until I nearly drowned. Pecker Head had an evil laugh while I gasped for air, coughing uncontrollably from the choking. Then he lit a cigarette and told me if I didn't comply and take a bath next time without resistance for the time it took for him to smoke a cigarette, he would "finish the job." He finished his smoke by snuffing out the hot butt in the cold bath water, flicking the filter at me with a look of pure evil. From then on, I succumbed to his ghastly threats. I developed a real hatred of water from that. It is scary now as I relive it."

Atticus paused from his emotional tale and looked out at the angry-looking Ocoee River. He felt as if it was showing a reaction of disdain to the abuse Atticus had endured.

"There also was the time Lizzy and Pecker Head planned a party at the mansion while Vivien was gone for the weekend. The pair had big plans that included friends of questionable character. The only hindrance to having a legendary party was the presence of me, Lizzy's challenged eleven-year-old kid brother. Pecker Head came up with a solution; he had noticed a large, abandoned dog kennel in the basement. He tricked me into going to the

basement and then forced me, with the threat of bodily harm, to crawl into the cage. He gave me a couple of slices of baloney and a bowl of water, then secured the door with a huge Master lock.

"I spent much of the weekend starving and with no place to go to the bathroom other than in the corner of the cold cage. I rattled the cage for a very long time until the evil Pecker Head returned, screaming at me, threatening to burn me with the cigarette dangling from his foul mouth if I did not stop making a racket. His final threat before returning to the noisy party upstairs was, "Listen, you little shit. There's a big fella upstairs named Bubba. If you don't behave yourself, I'll send him down here to have his way with you."

"Of course, I literally bit my tongue for the rest of my time in the cage. Minutes turned into hours, hours into pitch blackness. I did not even have my flashlight. Blackness turned into peeks of an obstructed sunrise. I was quite surprised to be alive; I sensed, perhaps I didn't want to be alive."

Atticus and Laura needed another lengthy break after the account of the despicable abuse suffered at the hands of his sister and her dreadful boyfriend, ostensibly enabled by his ruthless mother.

Disturbed, Laura could not believe what she had just heard from Atticus: a sober narrative, a child lamenting his rotten luck, his vulnerability leading to being victimized.

Laura was grateful to have aided her young guest, to have prodded some of his buried past to the surface. She felt her time was running short and began the inevitable task of cutting off Atticus and his suppressed stories. It took a melancholy glance at old Bear to remind her it was time she asked Atticus for a gigantic favor, one she had cooked up the previous day in her tired mind.

Laura expected some push-back for her newly created plan. However, she had to try to convince the young man that perhaps it would be a privilege for him to help an old lady who had helped many a living creature. How tactless, she thought, after almost two whole days of tidying up the old cabin and sharing events in each other's lives, the time felt right for Laura to go beyond normal conversation.

"My dear," she began with weakening breath. I have a request for you, perhaps a selfish one, but if one can't be selfish on your deathbed, when can one be? I know I'm asking a lot from someone who has his own issues to deal with. I wish I could help you as well, but as you can see, I'm in no condition now. I believe you were sent by a spiritual entity as an answer to recent prayers.

"I have seen many creatures reach their end gracefully; they just lay down and go to eternal sleep. Others instinctively cannot let go and struggle until they finally succumb to a horrible death. Some suffering creatures are, as a last resort, mercifully euthanized. Lawmakers have ignored this delicate issue for citizens and their families; they call it assisted suicide, an ugly phrase. I prefer to think of it as an act of mercy."

Laura tried to reboot her mind by taking a heavy breath, which touched off a lengthy bout of coughing instead.

Atticus welcomed the drawn-out break, giving him an opportunity to try and swallow the story that Laura was struggling to serve up. He found her story disturbing so far; it sounded to him that Laura Rawlings, the old lady who mysteriously appeared after his ill-fated bus trip, wanted him to mercy kill her and her dog.

After her apology for the interruption to her story, Laura was ready to resume the rest of her final desires.

"As you can see my good boy, Bear, is not doing well either." Laura tried forcing a sympathetic smile. When she did, Atticus could see she was wearing her false teeth, making her more understandable. "I feel the end is near. If you would be so kind, I was wondering if you would bury us together with Reggie. He is buried up on a ledge by the large willow tree; I have drawn a map of the place I buried him years ago when I was more fit.

"Could you please make sure that my teeth are in? I am wearing them now, but you never know. A girl wants to look her best when reuniting with her true love."

Feeling another bout of anxiety, Atticus pondered taking one of the pills from the supply he had received from Zeke, but realized he needed to wait until Laura had the opportunity to finish her request. If that didn't work, he would delve into the unprescribed meds that Laura had deemed alarming. No matter, this was a desperate moment, and as they say, desperate times call for desperate measures. Unfortunately, he wasn't going anywhere; he still had three days to get through, and then he'd take Laura's advice and resume his prescribed meds when he returned home.

Practically running out of the cabin, Atticus was after much-needed separation from the sudden aura of doom emanating from inside the cabin. Certainly, Atticus would not let himself wipe the slate clean of what this time here at the cabin had meant to him in two short days. Laura had reached out to Atticus at a desperate moment for the confused traveler. While at her home, Atticus was able to, for the first time in his life, have the fortitude to relieve himself of dormant demons. Throughout his life, he had been probed, examined, doubted, cast out, suspected, and questioned by professionals and laymen alike. This wise old woman, a comforter to animals and a human, listened to Atticus without being judgmental.

Then she drops a bombshell that she and Bear were near death, and it sounded like they both were ready to die, and she wanted Atticus to bury her and Bear. Or did she want more? Laura spoke of being in favor of mercy killing; did she mean she wanted Atticus's help in dying alongside her dog?

"Why does everything have to be so frickin' hard?
Can I help someone die? I saw one person die before and
was locked up for a very long time for it. I do not ever want
to return to that frickin' other place ever again. Even if

she just wants me to bury her and her dog, I can't do that either.

"Running on shaky legs, I quickly turned the jog to a more energetic run without any unprescribed meds in my system. It felt good – fresh. I felt I could run a marathon, which still would be well short of the 252 miles to the farm. No, I was stuck here for three more days, then I was gone, no questions asked.

"In my short stay at Laura's, I have changed more than I had before getting kidnapped, getting hired on a luxury cruise liner, and getting stranded in Belize, a distressingly poor country in Central America.

"I overslept on a bus heading back to my grandparent's farm near Lexington. That, my goodness, is 40 days plus of pure insanity. It was Zeke's fault those people gave me bad medicine, and did not accompany me for the final leg of this dangerous trip that he was guilty of arranging. I should be home already; I should have never left in the first place.

"I hope Laura does not want me to kill her and her dog. Burying them both sounds just as gruesome. I am talking about dead bodies. I cannot touch them, let alone carry them to a grave and cover them up. I could probably get in just as much trouble for that as for shooting them; I would get locked up again; probably for the rest of my life."

These letters reflected how far Atticus had progressed in such a short time at Laura's hideaway, just steps from a national forest. The twenty-one-year-old's development in two days was mindboggling. Mastering a language in which one never had a formal education is a lesson in purpose.

When he spoke now, his voice was stronger, and he looked at Laura, not down at the floor. He began to take control of his feelings with a noticeably sharper memory, and he was at ease for the first time since leaving the farm far behind. In a roundabout way, Laura's bizarre appeal threatened to send Atticus's mental health in reverse, back to a high anxiety nature. He hoped for a good night's rest and that tomorrow would be a better day. He would happily throw himself into earning his keep for three more days.

Atticus awoke to the new day. Giving himself a convincing pep talk, he prepared for a cleansing run in the beauty of the forest near the Ocoee River. Songbirds were the only disruption to the stillness of the forest.

Unfazed by any troubles that may be accompanying him, Atticus ran with no purpose. Just the slightest of wind sent his long hair streaming behind him. It suddenly dawned on him that he had failed to look in on his hostess, Laura Rawlings, and her decrepit dog, Bear.

In fact, just an hour earlier, old Bear was conspicuous by not alerting to any noise that Atticus had made. Atticus was quite apprehensive about the prospect that Bear may have passed, but what about Laura? He had already convinced himself that Laura and her dog would definitely not perish before his departure in seventy-two hours.

He would be going home Tuesday morning, come hell or the dreaded high water.

Abruptly, Atticus felt a tinge of concern caused when an ample-sized hawk with a remarkable wingspan was being buzzed by a small bird a fraction of the hawk's size, setting off a raucous sound from the unfriendly feathered foe.

It was time to face the music back at Laura's cabin.

CHAPTER 35

"The only option to survive is to be brave."

– Noorena Shams

"*I* pulled back the window curtain to let a peek of glorious morning light in so I could see. There was no sound except for my heart beating through my chest. Passing Bear in the still cabin was strange; the old dog had not even lifted his huge head. When I touched old Bear, it was instantly telling; the dog was stiff, obviously dead. I double-checked before reaching for Laura to tell her that her dog was dead and she did not need to worry about him anymore. With the dentures in her hand on her lap, Laura sat with her glassy, blue-rimmed eyes partially open. I touched her forehead and immediately jumped back - she was cold despite the warm room. I had felt grief on the cruise ship in Belize, but this was different. I sat down and stared at an old lady who looked different from the way she had looked the last couple of days, in apparent pain and worry. I wondered if there was anything more I should have done for her. Now what? Do I really have to bury her and Bear? No way, worse yet, I would have to force her jaw open and slide her dentures in. I had not done anything this gross since picking up disembodied chicken heads in Belize. I had already decided I must go home, but there were still many hours before the bus would be in town, before leaving for Lexington and home.*

*There was an old barn cat at the farm who looked dead half the time. I swore she was dead, all stretched out, lying motionless in the sun. The other half of the time, she vanished and I asked Gramps what happened to the cat. He replied that she probably crawled in a hole and died."
Later, she would show up looking as good as ever.*

Atticus felt this was absolutely the time to take a pill. He knew it could not undo the uncanny prophecy or surreal circumstances of

Laura's and Bear's deaths. After a thorough search for meds of any sort, especially his, they were nowhere to be found; perhaps Laura had hidden them or thrown them out.

"Without Laura there, except in spirit, it became apparent to me that I could sneak a pill in, but I could not find them. Perhaps Laura had hidden them or thrown them out? What else was there to do?

"I chose a run; surely, I would find answers during another long run. Laura and old Bear would wait for their final resting place…but who would take them there?

"When I finally realized that I had not yet eaten, I felt alive. The old woman and old dog I stood before would never realize that sensation again. I did not feel any remorse for feeling hungry. It meant that I was still alive. The sun directly overhead indicated that it was midday. I usually had eaten twice by now, but then I realized the idea of eating in the cabin with two corpses.

"Standing over the fresh graves of Laura and her dog was so weird, and I have seen a lot of weirdness during this trip from hell. I felt no sadness for the departed; they both got what they needed - to pass on together. I noticed a hawk flying lazily overhead, a better send-off for Laura and Bear than I could have done. Sorry I could not bury you together, I said. I did not know what else to say except thank you for everything, though, especially the pancakes and the money to get me home from here. These writings detail "The day." That is what I decided to call this date that saw Laura and old Bear pass away."

A horrible physical ordeal was the best way to describe the planned burial, where Atticus thought the prearranged plot was overgrown and unprepared for the intensity of the project.

Land as hard as concrete due to a lack of precipitation or any groundwater, presented an immediate problem. Preparation required much picking and digging until there were graves large enough for the corpses. Thankfully for him and the dearly departed, his time at Laura's had physically rejuvenated the lean young man after his time in Belize. Laura proved difficult to move even though she weighed only 90 pounds. She was horribly bloated; it was extremely awkward to carry the fully bloated corpse up the embankment and place her next to Reggie's dusty gravesite.

> *"This part was not nearly as bad as forcing the dead woman's mouth open and cramming her dentures in. I am going to try hard to forget this part, especially the icky sounds."*

Transporting old Bear turned out to be a major task as well, with sweat trickling into Atticus's burning eyes. As with Laura's body, Bear's hardened corpse was quite a task to move. Using an old two-wheeler and secured with rope, Atticus was exhaustingly able to move the dog, albeit well short of the desired location, and finally dragged nearer the river.

With concern for Laura being disturbed in the 'hereafter' if Atticus ignored her wishes to bury her, Atticus had relented and correctly figured this would not delay his departure. Taking the better part of two days, the arduous task of grave digger had left Atticus unimaginably weakened once again. After a hot bath in the cabin's small tub, Atticus would set an old alarm clock and rise early for his welcome trip home.

CHAPTER 36

"Heroism often results as a response to extreme events."

– James Geary

A shift of the wind direction signaled a change in the weather. Storms were moving through the area and the threat of violent weather worried Atticus. He was not familiar with the area drainage capacity, so being on a hill next to a flowing river did not give him comfort. What did was knowing the cabin obviously had survived through decades of storms.

For the avid runner, pacing the confining cabin with the creaking floors wore on his nerves. Outdoors, the churning clouds brought a line of torrential looking downpours over the nearby mountain range; it was too wet to attempt a run outdoors. Atticus, also aware of the danger that lightning presented in any outdoor activity, knew this was no time for taking chances. *"What was one more day? 24-hours? What's another rotation of the Earth's axis."*

On hand in the sound cabin were plenty of supplies like pancake mix, goat milk, and brown eggs. As promised, Laura had left Atticus some money, and with the meager cash he had on hand from his trip, he figured he had plenty for his bus ride home. Still, the issue of no meds to be found in the cabin was perhaps not so peculiar after all, raising more questions than answers, like how both old Bear and the elderly Laura perished at the same time.

Pelting the cabin with raindrops, the deck gathered dots of pea-sized hail, while a glance upriver displayed a momentary clearing, after which another round of thunderstorms was apparent. Soon, clouds parted into a beautifully colored rainbow while droplets of rain continued to drip onto the flowing river, causing the wonderful illusion of dancing water. Rather than leave him breathless from fear or paranoia, the brief downpour and its aftermath of breathtaking scenery had emblazoned his mind with a collage of nature's exquisiteness. Apparently, the only obvious consequence of the brief storm was the churning white-capped water. With one last peek at the nearby cliff where the late Reggie was accompanied by his wife Laura's remains. Atticus could see well enough that the couple's grave site appeared undisturbed from the heavy rains.

Below that quiet, elevated area, Bear's resting place seemed well-off also, albeit a tad close to the marginally raging river. Atticus was quite satisfied with his job as a grave digger. Without the cover from departing black clouds, brilliant late-day sunlight arrived briefly as another line of storms approached. Further rain from heavy clouds would enrich the river and its lush surroundings.

> *"My night on the cabin's deck brought a supernatural treat from an electric sky. I had spent much time in the dark on this journey, especially in Belize, such a poor country that, in many places there was limited electricity. I also had more than my share of darkness growing up in an immaculate house in an affluent area, which one would think would be full of light. A large mansion-like house is tough enough on a misophonic kid who is subject to abuse. When it was dark, strange creaking sounds teemed from across the expansive wood floors and the 70-step winding staircase."*

Like a nocturnal animal, Atticus was adept at maneuvering in the darkness about the 6,300 square feet of his childhood home. Now, lying in a rustic bed, he was content to relive some unnatural moments of his life. All that was normal in his childhood changed when his mother, Vivien, and his father, Hank, separated. Vivien made no attempt to hide the desire to make her son the fall guy for her marital demise.

Her delusional personality would not allow for any blame on her part; in fact, this breakup proceeded when she declared that there was an absolute case of emotional abuse by Hank Carlisle. When it was otherwise obvious that any fault in this broken marriage lay at the hands of Vivien MacDonald-Carlisle, it mattered none.

Even Vivien's father, a respected attorney, was on record as saying his daughter had psychological issues, while his unfortunate son-in-law was a person he came to know as a man of high character. Though even he chose to abandon his grandson rather than affront his estranged daughter. Atticus's wrongdoing was that he was his father's son, and suffered from a yet undiagnosed developmental complication.

Part of the repercussions for these circumstances, though no fault of his own, were personal isolation and mental abuse. His development was stifled, for no other reason than it was Vivien's will. He suffered for no other reason than his mother's unprovoked need for vengeance.

Despite having a high aptitude in most areas of intellectual function, including being a savant when it came to numbers, Atticus had trouble interpreting social cues and facial expressions

Atticus found comfort in darkness; it did not bother him, at least not as many other things did in his difficult life. Courtesy of tonight's full moon, fully visible after the torrential rains departed as abruptly as they had arrived. Laying with exhaustive calm, he watched the moonlight glisten on the rapidly flowing river, with a crescendo of noisy cicadas providing a mesmerizing accompaniment. A spectacular ending to an extraordinary day.

> *"I am going home! I woke up to a day the way it was supposed to be: a beautiful day to travel. Rather than take time to have a morning run, I decided to make myself some pancakes on Laura's old wood stove. I would leave early, in plenty of time to be the first passenger on the bus. I cannot wait to get back to civilization, flushing toilets, gas cooking, electricity, and running water. This will be my last writing until I get on the bus with the new backpack, pencils, and a writing pad. What was most important was*

> *that I would have enough money to buy lunch along the way. I still hope I can get my old bookbag back. I know that I wrote some good stuff. My writings were my pictures of what I saw on this crazy trip."*

Atticus made certain he would not fall asleep on the bus home. He need not worry about the dubious meds and the threat of taking any; they would not jeopardize his journey home. Still, he did one last search for the drugs and located a note written by Laura taped to the pancake box.

"My dear friend," she had roughly scrawled, "just a big thank you for everything. Here is all the money I have left; it should be enough for your bus ticket and some lunch - get yourself some pancakes.

Thank you for your company. I wish you peace and a great life; you deserve it. Have a safe return home to your loving family."

Atticus stared at the letter for some time, wondering if perhaps that was where the pills had gone. It was, he still thought, weird that her death had occurred at an opportune time for him to bury her along with Bear.

Atticus peered sheepishly across the choppy Ocoee River one more time before departing the cabin. He slipped on his new backpack and turned to leave his home of four days.

"Mother of God! That's a huge fish," Atticus exclaimed, using one of Gramp's favorite expressions, his voice louder than its usual whisper. His firm words were loud enough to echo throughout the mostly empty cabin, void of any other living being.

Back at the river, the fish turned out to be a boy, and nearby, turning in a tight circle, was an overturned canoe! This was not a good sign for an aghast Atticus Carlisle, who was convinced this was a movie or a strange flashback. In an all-out panic, Atticus involuntarily swung around the kitchen a couple of dizzying times. Nothing changed; a fateful second look at the fast-moving objects now passing along the shore nearest to the cabin reinforced Atticus's initial glance.

With his forehead now fixed against the sliding glass door for a closer look, Atticus gasped loudly, astonishing himself at the sound of his startled voice.

Two boys, about 12 years of age, were in serious trouble; this was real-time, not a dream; this was a life-or-death matter.

Frantically trying to make it to shore, they seemed to be losing the battle against the cold current. Meanwhile, farther upstream, adults could barely be seen and heard with distant cries for help as they futilely tried to reach the boys along the shoreline lined with heavy, tangled vegetation.

> *"My mind was an outbreak of thoughts whirling around in and about my head. Turn around and get on that bus in town. Do not go down into the water; it is too cold; it is too deep. It's DANGEROUS. But I must do something. Why? Because Laura would want me to...I (maybe) can do it."*

Atticus tried reassuring himself to believe that he could perform a miracle. He recalled Laura's words: "I believe in you." Now was the moment! The hesitation may have already proved costly, as evidenced by the sight of a head going under the unforgiving current. A pair of floatation devices, one orange, one white, rode the waves of the gushing, splashing, cold water.

Atticus waded quickly and carefully along the river's edge, searching where he last saw the pair go under. Although the water was clear in these parts, the white rapids were churning up rocky sediment, making seeing and walking difficult.

Suddenly, another glimpse of a dark-haired head boosted Atticus's resolve; frantically taking an unnecessary deep breath, he reached below the water, gave a grasp of hair a serious tug, and lifted. When the heavy body floated up painfully slowly, a look of terror grew across Atticus's face. He glared fearfully at the head he held, hoping it wasn't too late. It was too late, not for a boy but for the head, which was corpse-less.

Atticus's own body shivered uncontrollably from the cold water he stood in and from the terror at hand. Fortunately, the body did not belong to anything human or alive; it was Bear, Laura's beloved dog! Much to Atticus's shaken spirit, the old dog's gravesite had obviously not withstood the recent heavy rains and was obviously not a large predator either.

Atticus pulled back, disgustingly alarmed by a quarter of a canine carcass, and quickly continued his frantic search for a missing adolescent whose frozen eyes he had stared into a moment ago.

Stradling a rock, Atticus's feet bumped against an obvious body. With determination, Atticus pulled the boy up and across the river onto the opposite bank, where family members were hysterically beginning to arrive at the scene.

Atticus recalled he had spotted two youths in the water, which felt colder by the minute, borderline hyperthermal cold.

With his mind working overtime, Atticus was bothered by an unwelcome childhood flashback. When his sister Lizzy and her boyfriend, Pecker Head, forced Atticus to bathe in an ice-cold bathtub. His penalty for not complying earlier with some whimsical command of theirs, any defiance by a young Atticus, the approximate age of these two lads, would bring more severe mistreatment.

Through the chaos of onlookers, rescuers working on the boy's body, and the river, Atticus could hear nothing else. There was only silence until he heard the hawk overhead, which inexplicably diverted his attention downstream where the other boy, in obvious distress and a dreadful grey in color was wedged, partially submerged, between a couple of fallen limbs. Utilizing the strong legs of a distance runner,

Atticus sprinted along the narrow river bank towards the other boy, who was clinging precariously to his flotation device. After running out of shoreline, Atticus re-entered the cold water and tiredly slipped, causing him to attempt exhausted dog paddling, the same stroke that Nina, his Ukrainian co-worker, had tried to teach him on the ship, to no avail. With the boy in danger of being swept off his perch into the rapids feeding the hundred-foot falls, Atticus snagged the boy and immediately used a death grip on the sinking youth. With an apparent last gasp of any semblance of life, the youth opened shut eyes to a squint. Reactionary, the boy's eyes widened to a panicked look of terror; he watched as a weird-looking, long-haired young man struggled with him.

Rushing water and the thin man with a wild look created an abundance of splashing water, adding to the anxiety for the kid in danger and the fading would-be rescuer.

Exhausted, Atticus made one final push. Looking like a runner giving one final effort at the finish line, Atticus lunged. Instead of breaking the proverbial tape, and with barely enough strength left, Atticus had the force to unhitch the boy from the branch he was precariously dangling from. Managing to drag him to the bank, this part of the river appeared to be picking up force. With the suffering boy barely, but hopefully, safely on shore and with help rushing to his aide, Atticus weakly collapsed back into the chilly water.

Too weak to stand, Atticus Carlisle tried one last attempt to hold on to a slick rock but quickly lost that battle, and tranquility gave way to the deeper part of the river. He surrendered his soul to his destiny as he floated downstream on his back, eyes wide-open, in the direction of the unforgiving waterfall.

Ceremoniously, a pair of hawks silently did a merited flyover.

CHAPTER 37
LOST

Recently released from an overnight stay at a local hospital, two boys, one twelve and one thirteen had received a clean bill of health. They had been close to hypothermia and drowning. Both boys were now eager to resume normal activities, avoiding being reluctant celebrities. On this day, they were being interviewed along with others present at the church outing which went horribly wrong. One of four local TV stations in Chattanooga had grabbed the scoop and was expecting about four witnesses to be present for the feature. By the crowd of people present, it was apparent that the number of witnesses had swelled since the accident. As part of a church outing on the Ocoee River, the boys, and particularly the adults in the group, were uplifted by the events of that memorable day. Since the rescue by a strange-looking individual, the boy's families had gone public with heartfelt appreciation for the rescuer. They pleaded for the person, who was wearing some kind of hiking apparatus on his back, to contact authorities so they could thank him personally. Without the quick action of the stranger, things would have gone horribly wrong: two boys could have been lost to the churning river. When the young man emerged from his on-land position, some in the church would say it was divine intervention. Without the quick action of the individual, the boys most surely would have perished. One witness described the scene as Biblical, likening it to the depiction of Jesus walking across the water with his long, wet hair matted down as if he had just baptized a disciple. Others said he had the look of an escaped prisoner. Another witness would ridiculously bet his life on the person being Native American, one who probably was a renegade, living in the bush, whose faith was tested as he noticed the two white boys struggling in the river. Once he had saved the boy's lives, he went about his business of creating revenge for his people. This testimony was one of the most preposterous of theories. More plausible, but still out there, was the one describing the event as supernatural, with the individual's post-rescue disappearance as spiritual or ghost-like; perhaps he was a roaming Profit?

"I was fishing along the river bank when I saw him." The bearded fisherman talked slowly and calmly into four microphones in his face. This exposé occurred the following morning and was now being shown live by all four television stations. Predictably, the growing story was gaining national interest. This latest *"Breaking News"* report was 'program interrupting' worthy for all local TV stations. National syndications were casually en route, satisfied just to be a few hours behind their affiliated stations.

"At first, I thought I had spotted him; ahh, what's his name? Oh yeah, 'Big Foot,' that's who I thought it was at first. It looked like he had a backpack on, so I figured maybe he was a lost hiker. I only had a couple of brewskis, so I was hardly intoxicated or anything like that.

"Moments later, the same guy comes out of the woods and seems to be searching for something; he spots me and then he backs slowly into the woods. It wasn't Big Foot, but he sure looked like a bushman, skinny with a wild look about him.

"So, I go up to the bait shop, I call the sheriff's office, you never know, there might be a reward for this guy, there's always people hiding out around here. That is when I found out about that young dude who rescued a couple of kids but was washed away himself. If this is the area where he ended up, he sure is one lucky SOB; another few feet, and he would have gone over the falls."

Officials with the National Parks search and rescue team were familiar with the area's terrain and the dam's waterfall history. If this was the rescuer, he, indeed, was lucky to be alive. They knew all too well the fall's history of not readily surrendering intruders, either mortal or ghostly, from its grasp. In fact, they were preparing to call off the search for the unknown rescuer further down river when came the fisherman's alert.

Uncertainty existed as to the identity of the fellow seen in the woods. Of utmost concern was he the rescuer? Was he alright? Was he an escapee?

In the following hours, the search intensified for the mysterious young man; now that there was a location, the search centered on the area where the fisherman reported his sighting in the woods. It would just be a matter of time for the purported hero, a person on the lam, or someone who just wanted to be left alone, to be found.

CHAPTER 38
AND FOUND

"My name is Atticus Carlisle; welcome to our humble home."

Disturbed by all the hoopla surrounding the rescue was the National Park Service Ranger who was unlucky enough to be nearest to the location being reported by the fisherman. Feeling bothered, he was scheduled to begin his long weekend in a few minutes; but now he trudged toward the reported area. An area rich in invasive thorn bushes, probably ticks, and probably a transient. Included in the Ranger's disgust, he would be working overtime because some yahoo said he found the rescuer.

"A likely story," grumbled the officer, "Probably someone fabricating a report in hopes of gaining useless notoriety. These nuts always come out of the woodwork during events like this."

He had read the crazy report from those in the church outing a few days ago that resulted in the rescue of two boys upstream. Supposedly, a strange-looking young man appeared out of nowhere and saved the lives of two boys after their canoe had tipped over in the churning rapids. While their life jackets hopelessly floated away unworn; the boys were in grave danger. In miraculous fashion, a lanky individual, appearing to be a drifter, quickly took charge and rescued two youths, one twelve years of age, the other thirteen, who were with the church outing and separated from their group.

Rather than take delight in the feel-good story of the rescue of two kids, the conservation officer had inner bad feelings about the whole incident. First, why were the kids in a canoe so far from the park area? Where was the adult supervision? Why weren't the kids wearing their life jackets? These are all violations for which Officer Donavan would have gladly ticketed the violators. Topping off the officer's list of grievances, this calamity had caused witnesses to the rescue to have gone public with absurd versions and various tales of a 'spiritual existence' being the rescuer.

This had raised interest in the near-fatal incident, leading to a growing number of visitors near the site. This reaction hampered search details, disrupted the general park activities, and stretched park personnel thin. Plants were being trampled, and trash was on the rise. False reports of sightings were already coming in.

The latest news, which had just been reported, was that of a resident, an old lady who lived near the accident, was now missing. Adding to the growing uneasiness, was this turning into a possible crime scene. Officer Donavan remembered having dealings in the past with an elderly woman in that area. Cantankerous and rude was how the officer's report described her. Obviously, she possessed a dislike for the park service, which stood to gain her property upon her demise. She had even threatened to sic her dog on the officer, which was hilarious as the old dog could barely hold his head up. Having worked up a sour mood, Officer Donavan was alerted to a transient-looking boy. When the park ranger cautiously walked up to the young man, he did not know what to expect. Who was he? Was he the rescuer? Certainly not this vagrant who stood before him, probably wasting his time.

Appearing delirious and frail, he nevertheless appeared relieved to see the officer, not at all fearful or disturbed by the intrusion into his makeshift campsite.

What is your name? Officer Donavan sternly demanded. With the question hanging in the air for a few seconds, the young, long-haired man seemed to perk up as he quickly smiled wide and deliberately announced - *"My name is Atticus. Atticus Carlisle; now that I'm twenty-one, I'm going to change my name to Hawk. I am trying to find my way home."*

The next thing Atticus knew, handcuffs were placed on his wrists behind his back. Instinctively, Atticus pulled back and was sternly admonished by the Ranger. "Do not resist; this is just for our protection," admonished Officer Donavan before calling in the young man's alias to the station.

"What is going on here? Atticus thought, puzzled by the sudden turn of events. *Am I going to jail for another false murder? Are they going to send me to another head doctor? I need my meds, not another psychiatrist."*

His elation at being found quickly turned to painful depression. By the time Atticus was asked what he was doing there, he frightenedly clammed up.

When the over-aggressive ranger returned to the County Sheriff's Office, he was brimming with pride over his capturing the suspicious vagrant. But things were soon to blow up in a big way.

Officer Donavan was constantly chided for his overzealous demeanor. His wacky nature was legendary around the sheriff's office, eliciting derogatory names like 'Officer un-Friendly' and 'Barney Fife.' Almost as soon as he arrived at the sheriff's office, he was sternly ordered to "remove those handcuffs, officer, and make a report. You are excused. They need you down by the Rawling's cabin. It seems Mrs. Rawlings has gone missing. This here is Mr. Carlisle. He has been missing for a month."

"39 days and 8 hours, to be exact," mumbled the sullen Atticus.

No sooner had news of the missing twenty-one-year-old man from Lexington, Kentucky being found gone public, it set off a rampant sea of rumors and misinformation. Before long, a squadron of authorities crowded into Jackson Falls, the closest municipality to where Atticus Carlisle was found, a few miles south of the Smoky Mountains. Besides FBI agents eager for details concerning a major case they were working on, there were state and local authorities who had interest in the case as well. All with questions to be answered, such as where had Atticus disappeared to? And with whom? Privately, they wondered about his mental competency to answer possibly incriminating questions. His family and their new attorney were almost a four-hour drive away, and when contacted, the grandparents joyfully cried at the news.

"Your grandson, Atticus, has been found, and though in a bit of a jumbled state of mind, he seems to be doing well and is unharmed. There are some bumps and scratches, which could be attributed to his hiding out in the heavy bush bordering the nearby national forest." At this point of the phone conversation, Harold and Madge Carlisle happily embraced while trembling uncontrollably. When they were finally able to, they called their new attorney, whom they had only once previously met.

Larry Baines was freshly hired as the Carlisle's pro bono lawyer, a no-brainer since he came free and with sterling credentials. He explained to the elderly couple he came courtesy of an anonymous donor because of his specialization in children and young adult cases.

With federal implications, discretion was of utmost importance for both Attorney Baines and the secret benefactor, a former protege, Samantha "Sam" Cross, who just happened to be the lawyer for the person accused of perhaps kidnapping his client's grandson.

Sam knew of the work that Larry Baines did, having worked with him on earlier projects when she was a young court attorney. He had toiled in the underfunded Children's Services Department before stepping down, disillusioned by cases involving child abuse and the lack of accountability. Mr. Baines also resorted to advocating against rampant child abuse through his writings and lectures.

Now, he needed only to study Atticus Carlisle's case, along with a roughed-up book bag provided clandestinely by the former magistrate turned defense lawyer, Samantha Cross. As a colleague of Larry Baines, the two of them stuck their necks out by bucking the inadequate Children Services. Not only that, but they were also risking their professional lives as well as personal legacies.

Mr. Baines was sold instantly, and pledged his support for Atticus specifically, because of the significant time he spent in a troublesome juvenile facility under dubious conditions. This case paralleled other cases that Mr. Baines rallied for to end the prosecution of children under 12. Despite exceptional careers working on behalf of justice for children and families, both attorneys understood they were treading on thin ice. Sam was Ezequiel's defense lawyer on federal charges, and along with Attorney Baines, had privately exchanged information relevant to subsequent proceedings. With a personal joint decision, the two lawyers agreed, based on the bookbag's writings, that Atticus was the true victim. All decisions were to be made with his interests solely. It would be the family's decision how to proceed, specifically with the bookbag's contents. Both veteran attorneys understood they could face severe reprimands for these infractions and conflicts of interests, in a federal case no-less.

Despite disregarding his legal oath, sixty-six-year-old Larry Baines felt good about aiding young Atticus. He would soon come to realize his new client was a hero, not a felon. Because of their unique heritages, Mr. Baines also found Atticus's grandparents to be of great interest. Hard-working people, toilers of the land with the proud work ethics of Irish emigrants and early Native American dwellers.

Once Attorney Baines was notified by the Carlisle's of Atticus being found safely, he immediately contacted the authorities in Tennessee. Attorney Baines made it clear after a contentious back and forth with stoic FBI agents and state police that his client would be picked up as soon as arrangements could be made and the four-hour drive completed. Atticus would not make a statement, nor would he answer any questions. He could not be kept in any holding cell. Utilizing a local National Guard armory, he would be kept comfortable and fed until he and the elder Carlisle's picked up their grandson. There was major disappointment among the FBI, the State Police, and the local agencies, all prohibited from questioning Atticus Carlisle about anything, so said an emergency ruling by a federal judge. Attorney Baines was successful in having Atticus Carlisle released to his grandparents on his own recognizance. They could not even ask the young man if he indeed was the rescuer.

With Attorney Baines behind the wheel of the large SUV, the Carlisle's let out a sigh of relief and held Atticus as closely as he would allow. Each was grateful for their own reasons during the four-hour trip back to the Lexington area. Attorney Baines was relieved to have secured Atticus's release without him being interrogated by multiple jurisdictions. Harold and Madge were relieved their grandson with them after all this time, but could not help but wonder where he had been. Atticus wished he would soon be able to take his meds. They collectively and silently hoped to not hear police sirens or see synchronized emergency lights illuminate the dim interior.

"Grams, did you bring my meds with you? I have had a long and stressful trip," Atticus whispered, clutching his new backpack with its smattering of his most recent writings.

Grams agonizingly replied, "No, Dear, we were in such a hurry to come get you that I didn't think of it. I'm sorry." Holding her grandson's hand tightly, she hummed a childlike tune, hoping to try and calm Atticus, who stared blankly out the highly-tinted window at silhouettes of mountains racing by. His mind recalled the contentious discussion back at the sheriff's office and how it fed his anxiety.

In lieu of meds for Atticus, pancakes seemed to be the answer to quell any anxiety. A couple of secretive calls up in the front seat by Attorney Baines went unnoticed by the family in the rear seat. When the vehicle pulled into a remote truck stop, care was taken to ensure that they had not been followed, before the night turned into a hopeful day.

Back out on the final leg of the trip, well before daybreak, Atticus would soon be returned to the wonderful farm, his horseshoe job, and running. Atticus wished he could run back from this location; instead, he scribbled in the dark vehicle as he had as a child in his dark room and, most recently, in the stolen car in which Lucifer had held him.

On the move as well, was as an almost thirty-year-old investigative reporter from a Lexington television station, Natalie Simms. She had been following the recent events in a town not far from Chattanooga, Tenn. It started innocently enough and heartwarmingly; two boys had been saved from drowning near a national forest. The hero? He has not been located; in fact, he may have been swept away himself and could now be dead.

Feeling something potentially big brewing, Natalie sped to her TV studios to proceed to do what she does best: investigate. Her features on TV were popular with the station's audience. Mostly, her reports were about community events, along with some human-interest stories. However, she was always seeking a bigger story, something she would have the scoop on, something perhaps with national implications. At least something of more substance than her recent feature on a memorial balloon release. She loathed this type of memorial, as the balloons could cause death to many wild species who tried to ingest the waste. The discarded balloons also added to the problem of manmade pollution. However, her private opinion aside, Natalie had covered the story as assigned.

It was time to check resources, the station's archives, talk to people, and, of course, there was always social media. This could prove to be newsworthy.

"This is turning into a bona fide front-page story," exclaimed Natalie to her station's producer.

Maintaining a close relationship with one's studio producer is always important, as she, without hesitation, agreed to give Natalie free rein to work on this story.

Natalie was soon driving with resolve toward the Carlisle farm. Her latest alert disclosed that the young Mr. Carlisle had been a sports page headliner three years ago for his running prowess in high school as an individual with autism.

In the meantime, stories by a bevy of individuals flooded social media with theories and alleged scoops on this mystery man; it wouldn't be long before the shadowy veil would be removed for all to see.

As rumors and speculations spread, they even hit the little mountainside café where Atticus had been seen with Laura Rawlings. She was a longtime local to the Mountain Springs area. She was described as a recluse, an eccentric who owned a cabin about a mile out of town. Her land was annexed years ago, while her husband was still alive, by the Park Service on a deed technicality. Mrs. Rawlings always blamed that legal meandering by the NPS, lead to her husband's deteriorating health.

On the other hand, the wanderer was a stranger who had been spotted suspiciously roaming the business area and the nearby trail area one day last week. Alarmingly, now the octogenarian was missing, as was her trusty old dog.

By the hour, the local buzz was surging in a place usually free of such disturbances. Where was Laura? Oddly enough, the old lady seemed to be in good health the last time she was seen, which happened to be with the weird-looking young man.

The latest report indicated the rescuer may not be dead after all, as it was reported that a young man was in custody and being questioned about the disappearance of a local, an elderly woman last seen with a young man fitting the rescuer's description. Fear was growing among area residents that there might be a killer among them. Accordingly, doors were locked, and guns were loaded.

Presto! Natalie's next alert was from a reliable source, allegedly with information (a disgruntled park ranger?) as to the suspect's name: *Atticus Carlisle*, from Newtown, Kentucky, a suburb of Lexington, incredibly minutes from where Natalie worked. From there, information swiftly flowed into her phone. Using various sources, she uncovered the name of the high school he had attended and the location of his grandparent's farm where he now lived. Most disturbing was a recent report that he had been reported as missing, a possible kidnapping victim.

In the event this slipped through the cracks, Natalie emphatically underlined this point of interest. Often, 'story-teases' like this fail to pan out, and follow-ups end up in a passing snippet. This fact should give her an inside track to a story, if there truly is one.

Atticus Carlisle's age was listed as a juvenile-like twenty-one-years of age, much younger than her dreaded thirty years. "Damn," she exclaimed sadly, "it sucks that I think of someone who is twenty-one years old as a kid. Soon, I will be one of those greying on-air TV personalities looking over her shoulder for some young chick to come along and take my job." One worry always led to another, that of a single female with a common scare; it seemed that all her friends her age were married.

She, in turn, had become the resident bridesmaid proving the adage "Always a bridesmaid, never a bride."

Still in soiled clothing from his experience in the river and his time spent in the rugged brush near the dangerous waterfall, Atticus waited for the tub to fill with hot water. His task at hand was, with sudden urgency, to transcribe as many of the events that he could recall from the moment Lucifer rolled up in a stolen vehicle and led him on this despairingly forgetful journey of blood, sweat, and fears. Feds and local authorities were adamant that Atticus make a statement and answer questions, most crucial, was he kidnapped or did he leave with Ezequiel Callahan willingly?

Reliving this immense trip covering over 14,000 miles via land, air, and sea was a difficult chore, but he would be steadfast now that he had his old backpack in his possession, this after letting Lucifer deceive him yet again.

Still, there were some things that he struggled with or cared not to remember. Little did Mr. and Mrs. Carlisle know of the extent of their grandson's ordeal, especially his recent act of heroism, which was yet to be confirmed by any law enforcement personnel involved in this complicated case.

Atticus watched as the dirty bath water swirled slowly down the tub drain. His hour-long battle to awake some memories-in-hiding, to store some recollections that he wasn't ready to release, and snuff out some loathsome thoughts like a bad-tasting cigarette butt; this pretty much covered the unlikely happenings of the past forty days.

With worries over her biological clock set aside, Natalie, ever the consummate Staff Reporter for WOWO channel 14, returned to her immediate concern: that of another clock ticking. She needed to act quickly if she was to secure a story before anyone else did.

Never one to fear a cold call, Natalie decided it was time to make a house call. Being fearless, she freely accepted, was a prerequisite for her line of work. Adept at seeking out interviews, Natalie's mantra was, "All they can do is say no, or they can shoot me." She would resort to a more proactive approach. She would go straight to the source; it was time to pay the Carlisle's a visit.

Urgency was key now, as after word spread that a stranger had rescued two boys near the national forest, it wouldn't be long before other reporters put two and two together that the unsettled farm boy, Atticus Carlisle, and the silent rescuer were one in the same.

Atticus had already come up with the idea that he could never divulge what had happened. It would not be hard, he felt, because he could easily make himself not remember everything. His writings of the last night would be hidden so well that even he would probably never locate this recent history ever again.

After inhaling a healthy stack of Gram's memorable blueberry pancakes, Atticus quickly headed for the door. It was time for a long-awaited run on the farm's homemade track. Staying behind in the dining room were three relieved adults. Mr. and Mrs. Carlisle and attorney Baines. With Atticus's safe return, it seemed that a weight had been lifted off the group's collective shoulders; his appetite obviously had not taken a hit. Worrying about his well-being would be an ongoing concern; his month-long absence would be something to be patient with, the hope being that Atticus would feel comfortable enough to divulge what had transpired in his time away from home. How and why had he left? There had been sleepless nights struggling for answers; now, it was imperative that, as concerned, loving grandparents, they learn the truth. It had already been emphatically stated by Atticus that he might never share with anyone what transpired the past month, more correct, 47 days and 12 hours. How would they deal with the media? Atticus left the three people to their thoughts as to what the strategy would be for any therapy that might help the reluctant young man.

Atticus stopped cold in his tracks at an unexpected sight: a well-dressed young lady was confidently approaching the front steps. At first glance, she had the look of official business. His return to the dining room showed how delicate his mindset was. His face exposed fright, leading Attorney Baines to rise quickly from his chair. *"There is a lady coming up the porch; I think she came to arrest me."*

CHAPTER 39
TRUST

"The best way to find out if you can trust somebody is to trust them"

– Ernest Hemingway

"We've only been back a couple of hours, and this boy has been through hell. Having been away from home for weeks now, he just wants to go for a refreshing run on his property now here we go." Mr. Baines mumbled angrily on his way to the front door, expecting a nosy, fast-talking newspaper reporter. After stepping out onto the porch, he came met a young woman with a familiar look about her. Her reaction indicated a familiar meeting between the two. "Most likely," he mused. "It had to have been a courtroom encounter, maybe a seminar, or an informational meeting."

Natalie immediately recognized the distinguished-looking man from a feature she had done four or five years ago as a younger beat reporter. Good memory was another prerequisite in the business, and Natalie's was excellent. In fact, she quickly detailed to Mr. Baines the shared feature dealing with a child abuse organization he was championing back then. When Mr. Baines heard her account of their previous meeting, he managed a smile, recalling the fine service she had provided the organization through her feature. After a short cordial exchange between the two, it was Natalie's turn to justify her purpose for being at the Carlisle's door.

"Mr. Baines, when I met you years ago, I found you to be a person of high integrity; you were involved with a very important social cause, so I won't mince words," Natalie felt she was starting out her presentation with good momentum for her spiel; she understood that time was of the essence.

"I know a little bit about your client, and I feel I can help your predicament. Soon, that road outside this place will be lined with cars carrying the worst of the worst in the media. Just like ambulance chasers give good lawyers like yourself a bad name, so do these vultures seeking a story give us reputable reporters a bad name. I am here to provide you and your client an opportunity to present your side of the story. From what my sources tell me, there are many unknowns to this story, from the bizarre to the ridiculous, full of suspicion and intrigue. It sounds like a story that needs to be told by this young man with, of course, the grandparent's approval and with you setting the ground rules. This will be an opportunity to set the record straight; I realize there are probably criminal implications that cannot be discussed that I would, of course, honor. If we do not provide a statement, preferably in the form of an interview, the underground press will have a field day."

After listening to Natalie Simms's proposal, Attorney Baines invited the news reporter into the house and sat her down in the living room before peering out at the still-empty road. "He indicated that he does not want to talk about what happened during his absence," Baines pointed towards the next room. That said, I am going to walk into the dining room and suggest that my client, Atticus, come here and talk to you, Ms. Simms. I will draw up some ground rules, but in the end, it is up to them in there. That may be a difficult sell to a private older couple who already tragically lost a son and are trying hard to save his son."

"I will talk to her," Atticus announced with newfound force, surprising himself as well as the others at the table. Mr. Baines had presented Natalie Simms's proposal to the elder Carlisle's, as Atticus sat, appearing not to hear. After a short bit of silence, *"She looks like somebody I know."*

Natalie Simms listened intently to this fascinating young man, or man-child as she would describe him in her report. When he first walked into the room with his lawyer, Natalie was so stunned she didn't even think of standing to greet her subject. Atticus's dark, longish hair had been cropped a good deal since she spotted him on television, a quick shot of him as he was being led into a county sheriff's office near Chattanooga, Tennessee. His walk was long but quiet, his boyish face showing the slightest signs of a mustache. Mainly, he appeared so fresh and clean that he looked as if he had been run through a car wash.

Saving two human beings from devastating drownings, the heroic deed was front-page worthy. When it is two pre-teen boys during Labor Day weekend that were rescued, now that is All-American, a huge piece of apple pie. Add to that the rescuer, a handsome twenty-one-year-old with features of his reported Cherokee heritage; you have a story. Add to all that this young man is reportedly on the autism spectrum, you have a headline.

When it was reported that he also happened to be autistic, that became national news, with the media clamoring for his story. This story had all the prerequisites of being documentary worthy, a *Netflix* series, perhaps *Sixty Minutes* may come-a-calling. While Natalie set up her mobile recorder camera, Atticus sat in Gram's favorite stuffed chair surrounded by old pictures of strange family members. Of particular interest to him was a portrait of a couple whose hair and features appeared to be Native American. Atticus was correct to presume the couple to be relatives of Grams, perhaps her parents, who would make them his great-grandparents. Frequent glances toward his interviewer, Natalie Simms, softened Atticus. He was getting antsy, his mind urging him to just head out the door and run over his favorite ground on the back twenty.

Suddenly, Ms. Simms was ready, but Atticus was not. He rose quickly from the stuffed chair, leaving Natalie in puzzlement. Taking a couple of minutes to compose himself and making a quick hair adjustment, he ran back to his seat, feeling more at ease, with his grandparents off in the dining room, where they fretted about allowing a newspaper reporter in their house. Bringing unwanted attention to their grandson or even opening him up to any legal scrutiny was the last thing the grandparents wanted for his sake. Thus far, the Carlisle's had been able to shield Atticus from any scrutiny despite the authority's veiled threats. An interview with an experienced TV news reporter was a coming out of sorts for their publicity-shy grandson.

"I was on my way home from Mountain Springs, Tennessee; I heard some screaming outside and saw something going on in the river. It looked scary, with much hollering, and the river sounded like a boiling pot of water magnified to extreme levels. I still don't understand why I reacted like I did; I don't know how to swim, so it made no sense for me to try to help, but there I went. Lucky for me, I was able to stay on my feet throughout my time in the water, or there might have been three drownings. Still, the water was very cold, and the rocks were slippery. Being a cross-country runner helped me, I guess."

Atticus reminded himself he had to be careful and not talk about anything other than the rescue so as not to open any sore memories. It would be acceptable to talk of the ending to his troublesome cross-country senior season in high school, but he cared not to revisit that period in his life. There would be more enduring events from his young life that he was determined to keep entombed in his congested mind.

"I am sure my story about saving these two boys is hard to fathom; I am even blown away by the accounts of this moment. The truth is that it happened; I am probably the most unlikely person to have done something like this, but I did it.

"After the boys were safely dragged ashore, I exhaustedly rolled onto my back and floated away.

"Yes, I said f-l-o-a-t-e-d, me, who could not float an inch – well, I could, and I finally did. I floated, even though I was aware that I was headed for the falls; I was helpless, like that constant sound seemed to be beckoning me.

"Such an eerie feeling came over me, and with my eyes remaining wide open, I could not even blink. I also remember watching clouds go by faster and faster.

"I remained at ease as I rode downstream atop the cold water as if levitating, but for how long? I could not calculate distance or time right then, something I have always been able to do.

"This happened for what seemed like an hour when, in fact, it was a few minutes. I ended up in some brush along the river's edge right before the hundred-foot dam.

"When I came around, I thought right away that I might be dead; I was tangled up in some sort of wild vine. My body ached, and I was dangerously cold; I knew that was bad. A brutal event was briefly awakened as I saw flashes of a horrible experience with cold water as a kid; I have always hated cold water. Somehow, before hypothermia overran my declining body temperature, I was able to free myself from the brush I was tangled in. From there, I was able to stumble to land, and through shivering teeth, I created some shelter and tried to ascertain what had just happened.

"It is funny I recall hobbling deeper into the woods and quickly resorted to survival tips that I picked up earlier in B-e." Atticus nearly slipped and almost divulged a huge piece of his mysterious journey. *"Lessons of survival from the antiquated Laura, whose words of wisdom resonated from her weakened soul. I was able to navigate my way from the jaws of death to today's freedom."*

When Natalie Simms submitted her interview with Atticus Carlisle, her reluctant subject, she was not the least bit apologetic to staff editors who desired more. There was a great appreciation that the Carlisle family had selected her for the only public interview of the hero who dramatically saved two boys from drowning. What was really hoped for was a touching bio of the farm boy with autism who was raised by local small farmers. His background was sketchy, with growing theories of who he was and where he came from. Was he as squeaky clean as previously reported?

Those who had memories of him from high school, where his father had made a name for himself, had positive things to say of the boy who was a heralded runner on the school's cross-country team, but little was known of him personally. Whispers surfaced that there always seemed to be more secrecies to his life than what was known. More sensationalism was needed if the paper was to penetrate national publications.

There were assurances from Natalie of a follow-up session with the secretive Atticus, where she would try to garner more information. The reality was that her real desire was not to elicit more stories from the twenty-one-year-old Mr. Carlisle but to continue her exploration of the mind of the fascinating young man.

Atticus, too, came away from the interview with Natalie Simms with a feeling of awe. When she interviewed him, she left a huge impression on him that she was interested in him as a person, not a novelty. Then, there was the closing goodbye that was accented by the most remarkable of handshakes. No pretenses were shown by Natalie, just a touch that left a mark on Atticus's spirit. A feeling that still stayed with him for days on end, as well as sleepless nights until the call he waited for arrived, much to his delight. A call that led to a lengthy discussion. Their conversation was just that: an exchange of words between two people that was respectful and revealing of each other's intimate thoughts. Atticus told her of the constant harassing of news-seekers that seemed to have, thankfully, waned. He wanted to tell her of his relief that his lawyer, Mr. Baines, was successful thus far in delaying any action on Atticus's behalf, to testify against Ezequiel "Zeke" Callahan in his potential federal kidnapping case and interstate car theft, as well as other offenses purported to have been committed by Lucifer.

Further, Attorney Baines argued that young Atticus was afflicted with a developmental disability that renders him effected by memory disassociation with unpleasant events. In fact, Atticus Carlisle had no bona fide memory of many things in his troubling life. Unfortunately, there were upcoming distasteful tests of his mental capacity, amounting to multiple tests from doctors chosen by both sides.

Atticus used the analogy of his experience as a long-distance runner.

> *"I am tired with the finish line not yet in sight. My head is drooping down, not the customary erect posture of a high-level runner. Sweat is burning my eyes, so I squint on. I am fighting the urge to just pull up; then I see the finish line. Yes, I am going to make it Get out of my frickin' mind once and for all."*

THE AFTERMATH

VIVIEN MACDONALD CARLISLE

Despite a life of controversy and deception, often fueled by hatred for anyone guilty of the unthinkable offense of crossing her, or the slightest semblance of having disparaged the self-proclaimed *Diva*, Vivien seemed to have reached the pinnacle of film making. Last heard was she had taken her riches and her hair-brain ideas to the South Pacific, where her vast wealth bought a grand following in a remote indigenous village on one of the thousands of islands that dot the South Pacific.

Vivien thought she could coerce the local tribe into becoming the cast of an elaborate film on the tiny, sultry island near her preferred destinations of Tahiti or Fiji. She attempted to re-create an old Hollywood classic from the '50s, *Tarzan*. Bankrolled by her bounty of money from various legal settlements and other dubious disbursements, Vivien threw cash at prospective movie extras and island tribal natives. In fact, Vivien's order of business for a profitable motion picture was to buy loyalty at a bargain price, leaving more profit for her.

Vivien obviously overplayed her hand. She failed to consider that the indigenous tribe she was dealing with had a shrewd governing council. Underestimating the local people of a hundred-strong village would prove to be Vivien's undoing when the extras demanded money up-front. Collectively, the native population was united in teaching the foreign, egotistical American woman a lesson in humility.

No evidence was discovered of any movie ever being filmed. Or what happened to the actress/movie director in waiting. Legend has it that she encountered extreme despondency after the island's local natives walked out of early productions. This came after she had already paid the movie crew in its entirety. It was reported that severe depression steered the once beautiful and charming co-ed to casually walk across the white-sand beach directly into the warm crystalline water, disappearing into one of the planet's most beautiful of sunsets, in a place of such daily marvels known as *"just another day in paradise."* Whether this was mythical or not, it could have been the plot for a real-life story. Or it could have been the epic film with enormous scope and sweeping panorama she had always thrived on.

JIMMIE LEE WALKER

While his one-time girlfriend's mother was reportedly sleeping with the fishes in the South Pacific, Jimmie Lee Walker, Lizzy's former boyfriend, had also yielded to hard times. He is currently serving a justifiably harsh 70-year sentence for child abuse in a brutal case of shaken baby syndrome. A toddler suffered a permanent brain injury at the hands of her mother's live-in boyfriend, Jimmie Lee, Pecker Head, Walker.

While serving his time in a state penitentiary, Jimmie Lee Walker, former bully, and child abuser, was assaulted and bullied so violently and so frequently that he was ordered to spend the rest of his time in solitary confinement.

ELIZABETH "LIZZY" CARLISLE

Her grave marker is the kind usually reserved for paupers. The grave site remains a compost of grass clippings, overgrown weeds, and musty leaves. Capped with groundhog mounds, the cemetery sits in an unincorporated area far from the girl's home where she grew up in a dysfunctional household or mansion as her eccentric mother referred to the property. Vivien had never visited her daughter's grave site – evermore.

MRS. MATHEWS

A tormented Mrs. Mathews, Vivien MacDonald Carlisle's long-time housekeeper, lives an undesirable life in a gloomy nursing home. She continues to be haunted by what she saw and heard at the mansion. Those moments were what she was privy to during her time on the job. What happened when she was off was left to imagination.

Her torment was fed by the fact she never reported the horrible conditions to anyone. Then she was overwhelmed when she saw young Lizzy take her last breath after being shot by her dear Atticus. To make matters worse, she never attended Atticus's trial. Surely a battered eleven-year-old would not be convicted of murder! When no lawyer ever contacted her to testify for either side, she chose to clam up and finish out her life journey in solitude and guilt-ridden silence.

HAROLD AND MADGE CARLISLE

The couple who had fought so gallantly to have their grandson released from his unjust incarceration. enjoyed many more years on their beloved near two-hundred-year-old family farm. Madge's health condition stabilized, and Harold began to relax more. With the upheaval of their lives behind them, the family farm came to life with a new direction: from a working farm to a co-op of sorts. Small animal pens yielded the grunting and squealing of pot belly pigs, the cluck of cage-free chickens and the bleat of friendly goats looking for a hand to feed them. Abandoned gardens were given new life with raised wooden boxes. These agricultural-sized planters, which were filled with garden crops and flowers for pollinators, bore impressive yields. With time came a widespread interest in the old farm. They established a farmstand to sell the bounty and encouraged the differently abled to mind the store and tend the planters. Drive-by visitors became walk-up tourists interested in viewing the new operation. Programs geared to eager special needs farmers were a hit.

Of course, it didn't hurt that the hero resident was becoming a celebrity to picture seekers. With the newfound transformation came other changes to the Carlisle household, new challenges to be sure, overdue joy, and magical moments were coming to fruition.

NEAR DROWNING VICTIMS

Although the parents of the two boys that Atticus Carlisle rescued were readily available for interviews with the media, their boys were shielded from celebrity status. One boy, the thirteen-year-old, relished the notoriety that came with his rescue. He even visited with Hawk at his honoring, where he was given an award for bravery from the city. In fact, upon learning that his rescuer had changed his name, the youth soon adopted the name "Hawk" as his preferred nickname. "Hawk soars in leading his high school to victory." This was an example of hype in a local newspaper headline after becoming a prominent basketball player and an adequate swimmer.

Whether because of the trauma of that fateful day or because he wanted no publicity for an incident he did not wish to relive, Boy #2 became that kid who just wanted to play his video games with a couple of friends, sit with them at lunch, remain unassuming, and avoid water at all costs.

SONYA LEE TURNER

When Hank Carlisle passed away from injuries suffered in an industrial fall, Sonya, the Chinese interpreter, felt betrayed. Her dismay was directed at her faith, which offered everlasting peace and eternal love if one fulfilled daily rituals. All plans and promises dissolved that fateful day. All hopes and dreams vanished; she would not return to the U.S. to be near her parents. Sonya's calling was now to remain in China as an educator and continue to help her school kids find peace and happiness.

EVA AND FERNANDO MARTINEZ

The Martinez's proved to be invaluable to the getaway back in Belize. Fate, it seemed, had brought Zeke and the old couple together that auspicious night in the forest, altering everything that lay ahead. From Eva's feeding the three young men who appeared near death from starvation, to her last-minute fete of miraculously starting the engine of the getaway vehicle, this amazing woman gave the trio, at the very least, a fighting chance to escape the menacing threats in the Belize City region.

Fernando, whose claim to fame was being the proprietor of the most fertile chickens in the area, was also a master in bartering. The locals referred to the *Viejo* as the 'egg man.' He also secretively traded in illegal liquor, aka moonshine. With the latter product came a useful entity for the three young men to utilize in their venture. After running into the haggard-looking American, Zeke, some impromptu business negotiations took place after some homebrew tasting, of course. Most valuable, as it turned out, was the amassing of, always valuable in this region, property. With the shack and land came the old cast iron wood-burning stove. In fact, the windfall from the sale of the stove was more than the shack was worth. Rehabbing the clapboard house was inexpensive, a beam here, a beam there, and before long, a new dwelling was fabricated. Recently serving as a wall that was opened up as an entry for a Volkswagen Beetle, it now was an oversized door that served as a dual-purpose drive-through door for quick sales. Despite all that the couple of many decades had done and seen, the mission executed by the two Americans and the sole local was something they had never seen. People, in fact, still come to the old shack to hear the story of the slug bug that could. As the story grew to legendary proportions, the old couple prospered handsomely.

SUNSET BAR AND GRILL

In Belize City, the crusty old building that housed the tarnished *Sunset Bar and Grill* met the deserved fate of the bulldozer. Previously heralded by one travel publication as a hidden gem in Belize City, tourists were urged to try their superb Cajun chicken sandwich.

Chickens and the bar were synonymous with Mutha. Seldom seen outside of his lair in the rear of the bar, the notorious "Chicken Plucker" was also known as the human guillotine, having taken the heads of thousands of chickens in his storied time at the *Sunset Bar and Grill.*

The local health department shut down the shady bar for a growing list of infractions, many of them related to the extermination of chickens and the unhealthy method of openly disposing of their remains.

Boss Man, the tyrant owner of the bar, was arrested for fraud and served three years in the state prison.

"MUTHA" THE CHICKEN PLUCKER

Mutha was sent packing as well, back to the States to face eighteen-year-old charges for manslaughter, for which there is no statute of limitations. Soon after his surrender, the charges against Ernest "Mutha" Morrison were dismissed when the two key witnesses in the case were listed as deceased, thus unable to testify.

After his legal problems were resolved, Mutha pursued the legitimate route and sought a patent for his chicken plucking machine. Without a single modification required by the government, a patent was granted to Mr. Morrison. It wasn't long after obtaining the patent, Mutha sold it for $50,000. With his windfall, Ernest Morrison returned to Belize, found property in a resort area to the south, and proceeded to live a very comfortable, if lackluster lifestyle.

MAXIMILLIAN "MAX" DUVALIER

Befriending two Americans and eventually helping both escape his country and their torments, Max had his own grueling cross to bear. Upon returning to the home near Belize City where he lived as a child, he immediately began to sense potential run-ins with the dangerous local gang members. Then there were his recently inherited possessions: a clapboard shack in a slum village and an iguana-infested VW Beetle, both seemingly worthless.

After his own escape to his Mayan community roots, Max re-connected with his childhood sweetheart, and the two joyfully married. Further complications with his kidney disease led Max to seek conventional treatment in a more populated city, much to the chagrin of the community doctor who prescribed a more spiritual solution; prominent among his healing solutions were herbalism and shamanism.

When these spiritual methods failed to provide beneficial results, Max, with resignation, decided to heed his American friend Zeke's advice "Don't listen to no fucking witch doctor, get your ass to the U.S, and get yourself a new fucking kidney." In a country where indigenous people have a life expectancy 13 years lower than the country's non-indigenous population, Max chose an aggressive resolve. With his failing kidneys not responding to the ethnomedicine system of the indigent Mayan village in the southern Belize mountains, Maximillian was forced to seek alternative, more conventional methods, with dialysis being a last-ditch effort.

Through the efforts of an International Kidney Foundation, Max eventually realized the answer to many of his supporter's prayers. His return to his birthplace and childhood home had to be the sign of a healthy resolve, he convinced himself. He was lonely though, as his wife was unable to join him for the treatments.

With a match eventually obtained, the emergency transplant took place in Belize City, the place where he had met the two unique Americans who helped make his move back to the South possible. He wished that they could be there with him for this sudden solo and scary endeavor. Surely, they would bring him luck, even make him laugh. He could hear Zeke remind him to "man up, dude." 100-99-98 Max went under with a smile. Though he made it through the surgery, rejection of the cadaver kidney was followed by his demise. A spiritual person, Max did not die abandoned.

OSCAR HERRERA

Oscar Herrara was the former conservation officer who spotted the defunct VW Beetle in the jungle. Thinking, at first, he had encountered a wayward spacecraft that may have crashed after burning upon entering Earth's atmosphere, Oscar Herrera was astounded to instead find something more out-of-this-world than any being from outer space. After a search for drugs or weapons, nothing, not even a secret space weapon, was found. Before Oscar could inspect the three apparent earthlings, who up close looked like a roaming troupe of clowns, Max took the officer aside. Ever the affable one and using his bond as a local, especially his distinct shared Mayan heritage, Max began his attempt to win over Oscar Herrera. Max was kind enough to give Zeke some credit for teaching him some tricks for negotiating, for before long, things turned amazingly brighter. Abandoning the once classic slug bug, the trio of transients were driven the remaining hour and one-half to Max's village to the south.

Oscar Herrera recounted some of that fascinating day when he first met Max in his emotional eulogy at Max's funeral. Oscar left the government parks job for a more meaningful calling, an advocate for indigenous Mayan rights. Towards the end, Max volunteered to work with Oscar, accomplishing much together in a short time.

1972 VOLKWAGEN BEETLE

Yes, it was a German car. At one time, it was considered a cool ride, especially this convertible style. In later years, the car became a source of entertainment on the nation's roadways as people would try to be the first to identify one, or sometimes painfully, many.

This particular slug bug was mercifully dragged out of the jungle to its final resting place. Back at the junkyard, a search of the vehicle's remains found little of value. In fact, the only value was that of a prop, what with its welded doors, an extended hand brake, and the *coup de grace*, cured animal skin for tires. If there was a MacGyver Museum, this vehicle could have been a star attraction instead, it met the *Crusher*.

ROSETTA AND JAQUES "BLACK JACK" DUVALIER

When Rosetta received word of her son's untimely death, she collapsed, crying uncontrollably. She quietly entered an extended period of mourning, grieving for her sweet little boy, a gentle soul, so kind, so beautiful. She felt ashamed for not being there for Max, for having left him in the first place. For what? She regretted ever having left it all behind: her family, her home, and, of course, her son. For what, she kept asking? Unfortunately, for the empty promises of a worthless vagabond. Jaques Duvalier was away again, working on some other scam, fooling only himself. His last great scheme had been to walk partway, hook up with someone with connections through Mexico and on to the American border. That jaunt came to a quick end as they only made it to Southern Mexico, to Chiapas, where they now reside with others in mostly indigenous villages of Mayans. The last report was that Black Jack Duvalier had left Rosetta to fend for herself in unfamiliar surroundings with his promise of coming back for her as soon as he made some money working for a cartel. Rosetta was facing a life of poverty and isolation, a harsh lesson learned about trust and deceit.

SAMANTHA "SAM" CROSS

Sam thought she had done all she could for her son as she slowly rose to hear the federal Magistrate read his decision. With much back and forth between the feds and Samantha, a plea deal was struck. Only the Judge's approval was needed for an end to this interminable ordeal. Rarely does it happen that a judge rejects a plea deal, except when he or she feels the prosecution is being too lenient. In that case, the two sides will be remanded to re-negotiate a more satisfactory agreement. If that were to happen here, the government prosecutors would happily drag out the proceedings further. Already, the length of this trial had stretched out for months beyond normal. Meanwhile, Ezequiel sat in his cell, supposedly finding God there. Samantha gave a quick thought to that scenario. "If God was truly awaiting him in a jail cell, I wouldn't have worked so hard to keep Ezequiel out of prison all these years." His trial's delay was the constant appeals and continuations brought on by the reluctance of the government's star witness to testify. No matter how many psychiatrists, psychologists, or doctors examined Zeke, their findings were always inconclusive or their testimony agreed with the defense. Atticus, the only witness who could clear up all pertinent questions, was steadfast in his claim of not being able to remember particulars of traumatic events. Previous cases and rulings were unanimous in their decisions that there must be pronounced evidence; thus, no testimony, no evidence, no proof of guilt. This left the prosecution to go after the grand theft auto charge, which would carry some state prison time because of his previous record. Eliminating the kidnapping charge was huge as that offense carries a ten-year minimum sentence. Currently, the judge was set to rule on accepting a plea deal that would place a three-year prison term. Ezequiel would be awarded with time served (one year) and eligible for parole after two years. Sam thought the deal was another huge break for Ezquiel, provided the judge OK'd the deal presented to him.

With feet up and a glass of wine in hand, Sam petted her crotchety old cat, Nelly. "Well, girlfriend, we're all alone again. No more bringing work home and scattering papers all over the floor." Her retirement as a magistrate in the family court was now in effect, and she was confused by all the free time she was now facing. Still, she knew what was ahead: lots of calls seeking opinions. There would probably be offers of her being an expert witness on occasion. Most importantly, she would be able to see her son, Ezequiel, released in a timely fashion. Every minute spent in the joint was another twist of a knot around Sam's neck. Regardless of whether Zeke deserved the sentence or not, she thought he got off with a relatively mild sentence. Was his big break something he earned? Probably not. Was it good lawyering on Sam's part? It could be, but if you ask Sam, it was a bad strategy on the government's part, in addition to just dumb luck. Because Atticus refused to testify, the government had no case. Samantha's need now was to realize some sort of getaway. Perhaps a trip to Europe for a month would suffice.

REYANSH "REY" JINDAL

As Rey followed the court proceedings from his Miami Beach office. Old man Beaureguard, his relic of a lawyer, was sending daily accounts of Zeke's court proceedings. Young Callahan's lucky streak seemed to be continuing, but what happens when it runs out? He took a plea for his auto theft troubles rather than risk a trial for kidnapping, which, despite the weakness of the government's case, still came with huge risks of a lengthy prison term. What this meant to Rey was the worry that his former protégé might be tempted to offer up information that could be damaging to his own luxurious lifestyle and freedom.

Trying to be proactive, Rey decided to move his operations to Aruba in the Caribbean. In Aruba, Rey would hopefully be out of sight, out of target of any investigation geared toward his growing business. His fear was the trouble that Zeke had on the cruise ship would negatively effect him, and cause a loss of his grand arrangement with this new cruise line. After all, it was at Rey's urging that both Zeke and Atticus were hired. Rey was upset at himself for enabling Zeke to continue his foolish ways. Even though Zeke was privy to some damaging information on Rey's ascension to chancellor at J.T. Boe, it was time to finally cut ties with Ezequiel Callahan.

EZEQUIEL "ZEKE" CALLAHAN

The judge read the plea deal that was worked out between the federal attorneys and Zeke's lawyer, his mother. "It is in the court's opinion that this plea is fair and just. The ruling supports three years to be served in the state prison. One year served. When Zeke turned to look at his mother, he whispered to Sam, "Don't come and see me; I'll be alright tell him for what it's worth I'm sorry."

Zeke not only survived another year, but he earned a real parole that required a blemish-free year to qualify. Then comes the parole meeting before a prison board, where a review of the prisoner's record is conducted, as well as an interview with the petitioner. Finally, maybe the most impactful part of the appeals process is the victim and/or family's chance for their opinion on the matter under consideration. When no representative of the family itself opts to attend the parole meeting, then it's taken as a vote of confidence in the board's decision. That was the case when no one from the Carlisle side, not Harold and Madge, the grandparents of Atticus Carlisle, chose not to attend, nor did their lawyer, Attorney Baines, make a statement on their behalf. In fact, one year to the day after Atticus returned home, he had not made a statement or testified against Zeke. Upon his release, Zeke never made another attempt to contact Reyansh 'Rey' Jindal, nor did Belize ever seek any retribution for the escapee. Since his parole, Zeke took it as a challenge to resist any urge to steal a car or any other silly infraction. He lived a solitary life and, most importantly, took his meds. Zeke and his mother, Samantha Cross, remained estranged.

ATTICUS HAWK CARLISLE

Remaining steadfast, Atticus never testified about his disappearance with Ezequiel "Zeke" Callahan. He freely shared with anyone who would listen, his meeting Zeke and subsequent 'joy-riding' spree with illegally borrowed vehicles. His story at that point takes a rare upbeat flavor as he proudly divulges that Zeke taught him to drive. "I was a good driver; Zeke always complained that I drove too slow; I was just being careful." His other talent that was done in a methodical manner was his making of horseshoes, which he continued to churn out at a deliberate pace, as more of a commemorative or gift giving venture. Speaking freely of his adventure in Spring Mountain, Tennessee, Atticus was quick to detail how he had a 'chemical reaction' that caused him to miss his change of bus heading home and end up where he did. Consequently, he met the kindly old lady, Laura Rawlings, who befriended him and offered to help him get home. In return for her generosity, Atticus provided Laura and her dog with a proper burial. Atticus had rehearsed the blow-by-blow account of the rescue in the river that he performed to all's amazement. According to him, the truly remarkable part of the rescue was his floating away from the event; he had overcome his fear of water and his being incapable of floating at all.

Atticus claimed that when he regained consciousness, he was in the middle of nowhere, a dreamlike experience. He was led back to civilization and consequently returned to his grandparent's farm, where he wrongly and unjustly faced another bout of scrutiny, one more dreaded psychological examination. Atticus was more than eager to put the past behind him; he had no interest in being involved in any legal maneuvering to put one Ezequiel Callahan behind bars or whatever else the authorities cared to do.

With continued support from his grandparents and a newfound friend, Atticus persevered. His life was slowly turning to an idyllic lifestyle, to a spiritual situation that not that long or many miles ago seemed unattainable. Oh, after more legal haggling and hoops to jump through, Atticus-became Hawk Carlisle.

THE RESOLUTION

"Tears are words that need to be written."

– Paulo Coelho

"From the loft, an addition to the old barn, I am amazed by what I can see; it is simply real. I am the one in a globe, looking out at three-dimensional life. My producer at my newsroom would always tell me, keep it real. Well, this place is real, as real is. Now that I have finished writing this amazing story, I have begun my next book, a children's book – Ye Olde Farm. Writing from this place is great, even though there are wonderful distractions to deal with. Here, I am gently aware of the farm's subtle beauty and am absorbed by all its harried activities. There are nests being attended to by devoted parents. Common sparrows and clumsy mourning doves search for desirous feed. All very simple, very beautiful in their own right, all very real. Growing up in a college town, although Lexington was minutes away, this is living a different lifestyle.

"Brassy notes from a hidden cardinal interrupt my writing as I stop to seek out the source of the sharp whistling. Then there is my favorite, the shrieking cry of a mighty hawk. I have learned to admire this place where one minute it is alive with a symphony of singing and chirping birds to the various mesmerizing sounds of nighttime noise-making insects, ending with the dead silence of a deep night.

"Come sunrise, the new day starts all over; it never grows old. Of all the creatures, I became most enchanted with hawks because of the tales of my dear husband, Hawk Carlisle.

"Yes, my name is Natalie Simms-Carlisle. I, along with my husband's dedicated help, presented you with this story of wonderment. This is his story, his blood, sweat, and childhood tears. Hawk is eight years younger than me but light-years wiser. His vocabulary is vast, and as the story indicates, he is self-taught and, in his teens, refined by loyal teachers. He was taught craftsmanship by his devoted Gramps. He was shown the meaning of love by his Grams, who read to him and made him her famous blueberry pancakes.

"As a former TV news reporter, I first heard of this remarkable story as it unfolded before my eyes. To the skeptical public, it may have seemed to be another bit of sensational journalism concerning a person with autism spectrum disorder (ASD). How could he have rescued two boys from drowning in white water rapids? Well, he did, and his story did not begin there, and I am here to tell you it didn't end there. Believing in fate was not part of my upbringing; I was taught that things were earned by hard work. This philosophy carried me through journalism school and to my dream job as an on-air news reporter.

"Being the first and only member of the media to interview Atticus Carlisle, I figured I was the first one there sniffing out information. My initial interview with the cautious twenty-one-year-old was uneventful; he described the rescue and little more. Fortunately, his family and their lawyer were so taken by my compassion for the man and his story that I was invited back for subsequent discussions. They felt that with my local upbringing, I was most adept at making Atticus comfortable. I was allowed a couple of other interviews, and evidently, I earned Hawk's trust and, just as important, his people's trust. With a second informal invite to the Carlisle farm, a connection transpired between Hawk and me. Before long, invites to the farm were more frequent, and Atticus began to talk more freely. Starting with his childhood and then his incarceration, those shared stories were told to me, both personally and as a professional story. I sincerely appreciated my established connection with Atticus and how he more freely spoke of his past. For me, it had ceased to be about a scoop, a feature story on the 10 o'clock news; it was a personal story he obviously felt better about releasing to those of us present. Still, he felt the need to not divulge any more of his time away

"No, it was shattering that the time was upon us for final goodbyes. First was Attorney Baines, an honorable man who stood by this family through a difficult time. Mr. and Mrs. Carlisle would always be special for their hospitality and trust, and of course, I would miss Mrs. Carlisle's delicious pies. We all exchanged hugs and gratitude before my departure, but there was someone missing. Atticus was conspicuous for his absence. "It can't end like this; I had grown more than an attachment to this man." I admitted to myself at that point that I had grown to really care for him. His attraction to me was more than his rock star looks and intelligence; his mental disability now appeared to be minimal. We had become friends, and I wanted more.

'Suddenly, he appeared from a back room with a big grin on his gorgeous face. In his outstretched hand was a small metal object. Standing a bit unsteady, I must have looked silly with my mouth hanging open and eyes watering. The eyes were moist, not from anything in his hand but from the just-lived moment. Here I was on the verge of tears because I was saying goodbye to some wonderful people, and I was emotional about Hawk, who was nowhere to be found for his goodbye and hug.

'Whatever it was that he held had to be nice, but the fact that he re-entered the room to see me was the clincher. When I saw it was a silver ring, I gasped loudly.

"I want you to have this; I hope you will accept this as a token of my love. I want to marry you; I hope you feel the same. This is a ring made of real silver. It is an engagement ring."

"With the room now dead silent, I did something instinctively that I quickly thought I might regret. "Oh, dear! I love you too," I replied with some trouble as I took the ring and gently kissed him. Nearly as smooth as any leading man could be, how could I say no? How did this go over with the other three? I assumed right then that we would be having a discussion soon after everybody had time to dissect what had just occurred. I went home and, as any good reporter would do, I researched. What was I thinking? What had I got myself into? Please,

Google, tell me that this is doable. I think I was more concerned about the age difference than I was about marrying someone on the autism spectrum. During our time together, I quickly realized that Hawk had to have a mild case of a developmental condition. More time together had shown some hidden secrets, a willingness to talk of his past, and a high level of intelligence. I pledged never to push him to tell me something he cared not to discuss."

THE END

In Memoriam

Rare is it that two people can join hands and effect so many people in a positive way as did Vicky and Eli Perez. Whether it was for family, friends or strangers, the inseparable couple were quick to provide aide to those in need. Among the recipients of their kindness and the generosity of their time were the youth, whether with direct assistance, supporting the sports teams or as advocates for better education. Together, they served four decades with the Parent Teacher Association (PTA) for the East Chicago, Indiana school system, the state PTA board, and were awarded honorary life memberships by the national PTA. Their efforts continue to impact those whose lives they touched.

DISCLAIMER

How to recognize the signs of child abuse and neglect is adapted from **www.childabuse.com**

Criminal mistreatment of children takes many different forms:

Physical abuse is any injury from a beating, biting, burning or other harmful acts.

Sexual abuse is any act of molestation against a minor child.

Emotional abuse can be caused by cruelty, repeated rejection, exposure to domestic violence or threatening a child's safety.

Neglect is the failure of a parent or guardian to feed, clothe, supervise, educate, or provide medical care.

How to help a child suspected to be in an abusive situation?

Contact child protective services in your area.

Contact the national child abuse hotline by calling or texting:

1.800.4.A.CHILD (1-800-422-4453)

or visit **www.childhelphotline.org** for a live chat option. Professional crisis counselors are available 24 hours, 7 days a week in over 170 languages.

Call 9-1-1 if you are in, or if you are aware of a child in an emergency. If unsure, always err on the side of a child.

Additional resources can be found at:

https://preventchildabuse.org/resources/

A note by the author Sotero Navarro

This novel is a work of fiction but loosely based on real dastardly deeds happening on a regular basis in our so-called civilized society. It seems not a day goes by that another report of a child - defenseless infants to young adults - being verbally, mentally, physically, sexually abused or abandoned. Sadly, many of these criminal acts result in severe trust issues, maiming or death.

I am attempting to bring this serious issue to the forefront, to bring awareness, to remind us to pay attention to the subtle clues, to do more incident reporting, to see more done through education to stop this onslaught. If we can put the time, effort and resources into this problem, even a fraction of the effort expended onto things such as warring, political bickering and taking human rights away from those who may be different than us, we can save the lives of these vulnerable, innocent children. We can make strides in leaving a positive legacy for those who follow.

Through much research and interviews I hope to bring some understanding of these problems, and the most commonly diagnosed childhood mental disorders such as ADHD, anxiety, autism, and depression.

"Children are our most vulnerable members of society, of human society, captive and dependent on their adult carers who have complete control over their advancement."

Pam Schulz

"Children are not goods or services that the state can guarantee or provide. They are human beings with rights."

Maud de Boer-Buquicchio

"There is no trust more sacred than the one the world holds with children. There is no duty more important than ensuring that their rights are respected , that their welfare is protected, that their lives are free from fear and want and that they can grow up in peace."

- Kofi Annan